THE FIRST WALL

THE HORUS HERESY®
SIEGE OF TERRA

THE HORUS HERESY®

Other Novels and Novellas

*Many of these titles are also available as abridged and unabridged audiobooks.
Order the full range of Horus Heresy novels and audiobooks from*
blacklibrary.com

Download the full range of Horus Heresy audio dramas from
blacklibrary.com

THE FIRST WALL

Gav Thorpe

BLACK LIBRARY

A BLACK LIBRARY PUBLICATION

First published in 2019.
This edition published in Great Britain in 2022 by
Black Library, Games Workshop Ltd., Willow Road,
Nottingham, NG7 2WS, UK.

Represented by: Games Workshop Limited – Irish branch,
Unit 3, Lower Liffey Street, Dublin 1,
D01 K199, Ireland.

10 9 8 7 6 5 4

Produced by Games Workshop in Nottingham.
Cover illustration by Neil Roberts.

A CIP record for this book is available from the British Library.

ISBN 13: 978-1-80026-024-5

See Black Library on the internet at

blacklibrary.com

Find out more about Games Workshop
and the worlds of Warhammer at

games-workshop.com

Printed and bound by CPI Group (UK) Ltd, Croydon, CR0 4YY

This book is dedicated to Bill King, the First Remembrancer.

——THE HORUS HERESY——
SIEGE OF TERRA

It is a time of legend.

The galaxy is in flames. The Emperor's glorious vision for humanity is in ruins. His favoured son, Horus, has turned from his father's light and embraced Chaos.

His armies, the mighty and redoubtable Space Marines, are locked in a brutal civil war. Once, these ultimate warriors fought side by side as brothers, protecting the galaxy and bringing mankind back into the Emperor's light. Now they are divided.

Some remain loyal to the Emperor, whilst others have sided with the Warmaster. Pre-eminent amongst them, the leaders of their thousands-strong Legions, are the primarchs. Magnificent, superhuman beings, they are the crowning achievement of the Emperor's genetic science. Thrust into battle against one another, victory is uncertain for either side.

Worlds are burning. At Isstvan V, Horus dealt a vicious blow and three loyal Legions were all but destroyed. War was begun, a conflict that will engulf all mankind in fire. Treachery and betrayal have usurped honour and nobility. Assassins lurk in every shadow. Armies are gathering. All must choose a side or die.

Horus musters his armada, Terra itself the object of his wrath. Seated upon the Golden Throne, the Emperor waits for his wayward son to return. But his true enemy is Chaos, a primordial force that seeks to enslave mankind to its capricious whims.

The screams of the innocent, the pleas of the righteous resound to the cruel laughter of Dark Gods. Suffering and damnation await all should the Emperor fail and the war be lost.

The end is here. The skies darken, colossal armies gather. For the fate of the Throneworld, for the fate of mankind itself...
The Siege of Terra has begun.

'There are three weapons in the armoury of the victorious. Endurance, Belief and Loyalty.'

– Monito san Vastall, First General-Maximus
of the Lucifer Blacks

'There is no foe so powerful or so innumerable that we cannot overcome them with single-minded determination. Our weapons are simply an extension of our will, and it is our will that shall conquer the galaxy.'

– Warmaster Horus, address to the Ullanor Triumph

'Faith exists to be tested.'

– Lorgar Urizen, *Lectitio Divinitatus*

DRAMATIS PERSONAE

HORUS   Warmaster, Primarch of the
                 XVI Legion, Ascendant Vessel of Chaos

The Primarchs

PERTURABO   'The Lord of Iron', Primarch of the
                 IV Legion

ROGAL DORN   Praetorian of Terra, Primarch of the
                 VII Legion

ANGRON   'The Red Angel', Primarch of the
                 XII Legion

FULGRIM   'The Phoenician', Primarch of the
                 III Legion

MORTARION   'The Lord of Death', Primarch of the
                 XIV Legion

JAGHATAI KHAN   'The Warhawk', Primarch of the
                 V Legion

SANGUINIUS   Archangel of Baal, Primarch of the
                 IX Legion

The IV Legion 'Iron Warriors'

KYDOMOR FORRIX   'The Breaker', First Captain, Triarch

BARBAN FALK   'The Warsmith', Triarch

KROEGER   Triarch

VULL BRONN   'The Stonewrought',
                 45th Grand Battalion

VOLK-SA'RA'AM   'The Obliterator'

GHARAL   Captain

BEROSSUS   Captain, Dreadnought

The VII Legion 'Imperial Fists'

SIGISMUND   Lord Castellan, Marshal of the Templars

FAFNIR RANN   Lord Seneschal, Captain of the First Assault Cadre

HAEGER   Lieutenant-Commander, Castellan of the Lion's Gate space port

ORTOR   Sergeant, First Squad, First Assault Cadre

The XIV Legion 'Death Guard'

TYPHUS   First Captain, Host of the Destroyer Hive

The XVI Legion 'Sons of Horus'

EZEKYLE ABADDON   First Captain

The XVII Legion 'Word Bearers'

ZARDU LAYAK   'The Crimson Apostle', Master of the Unspeaking

KULNAR   Slave of the Anakatis Blade

HEBEK   Slave of the Anakatis Blade

The XII Legion 'World Eaters'

KHÂRN   Captain, Eighth Assault Company

The Dark Mechanicum

INAR SATARAEL   Archmagos

The Neverborn

COR'BAX UTTERBLIGHT   The Life Within Death

Imperial Army

COLONEL MAIGRAUT	Chief of Staff, Lion's Gate space port
ZENOBI ADEDEJI	Volunteer, Addaba 64th Defence Corps
MENBER ADEDEJI	Volunteer, Addaba 64th Defence Corps
KETTAI	Volunteer, Addaba 64th Defence Corps
YENNU EGWU	Captain, Addaba 64th Defence Corps
OKOYE	Lieutenant, Addaba 64th Defence Corps
ALEKZANDA	Sergeant, Addaba 64th Defence Corps
SELEEN	Volunteer, Addaba 64th Defence Corps
SWEETANA	Volunteer, Addaba 64th Defence Corps
TEWEDROS	Volunteer, Addaba 64th Defence Corps
JAWAAHIR ADUNAY HADINET	Integrity High Officer, Addaba 64th Defence Corps
KATSUHIRO	Trooper, Palatine Arc quarantine zone garrison
NASHA	Tank commander, *Breath of Wrath*, Bakk-Makkah First Regiment

Imperial Personae

MALCADOR	Regent of the Imperium
EUPHRATI KEELER	Former Remembrancer
KYRIL SINDERMANN	Former Iterator
VALDOR	Captain-General of the Legio Custodes
AMON TAUROMACHIAN	Custodian
OLIVIER MUIŽNIEKS	Head of the Lightbearers
MANISH DHAUBANJAR	Hauler operator
DAXA DHAUBANJAR	Hauler operator

PROLOGUE

Himalazia, undisclosed location, date unknown

The smog of hundreds of engines blackened the sky, adding to the gloom of the filth-choked heavens. The thunder of tanks and transports, some the size of city blocks, created a deafening wave of sound that reverberated from the mountainsides, an assault on ears already numbed by the winds of the high Himalazia.

The growl of machine voices all but drowned out human shouts, even those amplified by voxmitters. Electronic clarions howled into the whirl of noise, sounding the advance or stand-to, their modulated calls overlapping.

Everything was sudden movement, dust billowing from treads and boots alike.

'This is it.' General-Captain Egwu did not raise her voice, but her words were carried by the tongues of those under her command. 'Everyone stand ready.'

Beside her, Zenobi Adedeji fidgeted with the cover of the

banner she carried, eyes flicking between her company commander and the scene of organised bedlam being enacted around the troopers from Addaba Hive.

'Everything we have done, the oaths we have sworn, the hardships we have endured, has led to this moment.' Now Egwu shouted, not simply to be heard, but filled with passion. Her remaining eye stared wide amongst the burn scars that covered most of her face, fresh tissue pink against her dark skin. 'Now is the time we strike at the enemy! Our families laboured and died to deliver us to this place. Our courage and determination have carried us this far. We may not live beyond this day, but our deeds will!'

'Now?' asked Zenobi, her voice quavering with emotion, a shaking hand reaching towards the cover of the standard.

'Yes,' said the general-captain. 'Now.'

ONE

The Lord of Iron
Farewells
An honour bestowed

The Iron Blood, *Terran near orbit,*
seventy hours before assault

Patches of static in the holo-display vexed Perturabo, causing him pain in a way that a wound to his flesh could not. Every blur marring the projected image was a failure of surveyors, each a gap in his knowledge.

His only companions were the six automatons of his Iron Circle, stationed at regular intervals around the periphery of the octagonal chamber. They stood with their shields raised, mauls dormant, the only movement that of their ocular lenses, which whirred and clicked as they followed the pacing of their creator.

'I could extrapolate the defences hidden from me,' Perturabo thought aloud to his bodyguard. Their unquestioning silence was a welcome break from the ceaseless doubts and queries that spilled from his subordinates of late. 'I have perfect recollection of other works raised by Dorn, and by patterning those memories with what is shown here I can fill the gaps to a high degree of accuracy.'

He stared at a glimmering hololith that filled most of his planning chamber aboard the *Iron Blood*, as though force of will could make it offer up its secrets.

'Extrapolation is not fact,' he growled. 'There is too much at stake for assumption, no matter how well informed.'

His mind, his military genius, was the key Horus needed to unlock the palace of his father, but it needed data like an army needed supplies.

He stepped into the display, his massive suit of armour hissing and wheezing. Its shadow obliterated whole sectors of the Sanctum Imperialis as he strode to examine one area in particular. He crouched, coming eye to eye with a fictional defender standing on the Ultimate Wall.

The yellow of Dorn's Legion was spread everywhere, though it was concentrated around the north-east and south-west. The red of the Blood Angels was strongest to the south-east, where Mortarion's Death Guard had launched a damaging but ultimately unsuccessful assault near the Helios Gate.

The Khan's White Scars were harder to place. They had sallied forth against Mortarion in support of Sanguinius, but had since been seen in several other battles to the north and west of that attack. The precise whereabouts of the primarchs themselves was a factor to be considered, but impossible to ascertain with any degree of timeliness or certainty.

Raising the fingers of his left hand, he gestured and the display rotated around him, placing him behind the wall so that he was looking out across the Katabatic Plains surrounding the Palace.

The Warmaster's forces were rendered in a more abstract sense; series of runes, numbers and sigils denoting troop type, strength, current morale estimates, longevity of engagement, and half a dozen other factors.

And there were more features, sketched with a nomenclature he was still creating. These were the forces of the warp, whose powers he had only just started to investigate. Daemons. Possessed legionaries. Word Bearers and Thousand Sons sorcerers.

And his brothers. Swirls of arcane conjunctions between the real and the imaginary, with a foot in the world of the mortal and immortal alike. Angron, so determined to prove himself, unable to hold his wrath, was still trying the defences at Helios. Mortarion had not personally attempted to breach the Emperor's shield yet, and at the command of Horus was redirecting efforts to the south-west, attacking a twenty-kilometre stretch of wall near to the bastion of the Saturnine Gate. The Emperor's Children and Fulgrim, who Perturabo considered the least trustworthy of Horus' other lieutenants, had been engaging the defenders to the west and north, without any breakthrough.

Of Magnus there was no sign, but his Legion commanders had been content to take assignment from Perturabo and invested the south-west of the continent-city, supporting the efforts of the Death Guard.

All of his brothers were baulked at the walls still, held back by the last and most powerfully enigmatic variable in the whole war.

The Emperor.

So many questions Perturabo could scarcely think of them, much less attempt to provide answers. Queries that stretched back decades, strategies and decisions he had been picking apart since first he'd come into the presence of his creator.

But it was equally simple to dismiss most of the unease. Questions of why his father had acted in certain ways, why He had treated His sons the way He had, were now irrelevant. All that was left was the how of the matter. It was connected to the powers of the warp. If Perturabo could unpick that relationship, he could break apart the psychic wards that held back his brothers.

'Titans,' he reminded himself. 'The Warmaster needs our Titans to break the siege. He is right – the war engines of our foes' Legios are a force we cannot yet counter.'

The reinforced plates of his armour rippled with projected light as he stepped back, fingers clenching and unclenching as he surveyed the Palace again.

'There is only the one place,' he said, gesturing to zoom the display to the middle of the Palace, where the two great loops of the Eternity Wall and Ultimate Wall met. It was both the weakest and the strongest point of the entire complex. If it were to fall, the entire fortress-city would be vulnerable; protected from both sides by immense fortifications, it would be death to any enemy that dared entry.

'But you left a key in the lock, Rogal,' said Perturabo. The display cycled closer, flickering with more static as the required data for the level of detail was unavailable. Even so, the edifice that drew his eye was plain to see, so tall that it made the surrounding walls and Palace seem like models though they were each ten kilometres tall and more. The lord of the Iron Warriors grimaced at the lack of recent reconnaissance. 'The Lion's Gate space port. All but part of the wall itself, like a growth on an artery. One cut here and Horus can move whatever he desires into the Palace.'

Yet failure would be costly, and victory only a little less so. The Lion's Gate space port was an immense fortress in its own right, an orbit-piercing city protected by shields, cannons and hundreds of thousands of soldiers.

'Perhaps an attack against the wall, after all,' he said, panning the view to the north, drawing back to see more of the Imperial Palace.

No commander in their right mind would attempt a direct

assault… Except that he was Perturabo, the Hammer of Olympia, and there was no wall he could not topple, even the defences of the Emperor's Throneworld arranged by Rogal Dorn. He was tested on all sides, but the greatest challenge was the one written in stone and guns and force fields upon the mountains of Himalazia. There were only two outcomes possible. Dorn's will prevailed, or Perturabo's genius overcame it. This would be his legacy, the triumph that no other could take from him.

If it cost him every warrior in his Legion, that was a price worth paying.

Addaba Hive, Afrik, one hundred and seven days before assault

The shrill whistles of the officers set Zenobi's heart racing with a mixture of excitement and apprehension. Around her the crowd of recruits surged towards the opening gates of the transit station, but she resisted the pull and held her ground, not yet called to succumb to the tide and the journey that was about to begin.

The sun was bright, as always, gleaming from the hub-keep of Addaba Hive, the only home she had known in her seventeen years of life. The transport yard jutted from the flank of the huge city-mound about four hundred metres up from the surrounding plains. Above, dozens more landing pads and shuttleways played host to a steady stream of craft, coming and going from the near-cloudless skies and forming a double line to the east.

It was not so dissimilar to any other day, for Addaba had always been a desert-bound industrial city, incessantly hungry and thirsty for orbital drops and the product of distant hydrofarms. In return, the output of its dozens of immense manufactories had been taken to the space ports and beyond.

Until four days after Zenobi's tenth birthday, when orders had come to cease production of the colony tractors and grain haulers that had poured by the thousand from Addaba's production lines.

Tanks. The Emperor needed tanks, and Addaba would provide.

And along with that change of purpose had come the first rumours. The Great Crusade had stirred up an ancient enemy that was coming to Terra. An unknown xenos species had been discovered. Traitors within the Legiones Astartes had turned on the Emperor. Each tale had seemed more incredible than the last.

Then the first of the Imperial Fists watch teams had arrived to oversee the new production and the rumours were quashed, replaced with a simple statement. Warmaster Horus was a traitor. Terra had to prepare for invasion.

With that, the Standard Templates for Rhino armoured carriers and their variants were provided to the manufactories and Addaba became part of the war effort.

Seven years.

To some the war may have seemed a distant thing, but in Addaba it was a harsh, instant reality. For generations the factory-dynasties had served the Emperor, and their vassals had laboured for them on the production floors. Born to lowly labourers, Zenobi had nevertheless benefited from the scholasta, learning to read and write and conduct mathematics; skills that barely twenty years earlier had been restricted to the factory-dynasty members alone.

She had imagined herself as a shuttle pilot. She didn't want to leave Terra, or Addaba, but did want to spend time outside of its manufactories. 'Do well at maths, Zenobi,' they'd told her, and she'd tried really hard. So hard sometimes her head had ached from numbers and equations, her studies at least two years ahead of the rest of the tutor-group.

All of that had stopped when the order for tanks arrived. The Emperor required armoured fighting vehicles, not shuttle pilots. And to meet His demands every able pair of hands was needed.

Zenobi looked across to the great chimney stacks that soared from the lower levels of the hive. Dormant. Always Addaba had been a place wreathed in oily smog, the plains stained rainbow hues at its feet even as the air sparkled with gases and exhaust smoke.

'Strange, yes?' She recognised the voice of Menber but didn't turn towards her cousin. 'Quiet.'

'Dead.'

'Not yet. Let's say asleep.' Menber laid a hand on her shoulder but still she did not turn away from her home.

Fourteen-hour shifts had been too much for children – even the Emperor was not that demanding. Eight hours a day had sufficed for Zenobi until she had turned fourteen, when it had increased to ten. On her eighteenth birthday, nine months away, she would have taken on full adult duties. The imminent arrival of Horus had spared her that.

Addaba was no longer sending out the wares of its manufactories; now it sent out its people. Millions of them had left over the preceding days.

'Why didn't they train us to drive the tanks we made?' Zenobi asked, at last turning to her cousin, picking up her kitbag and lasgun. 'We could have driven them in battle.'

'That would have been too good,' said Menber, grinning. Though taller than Zenobi – almost any man was – he shared her slight build and round face. His skin was marked by lesion scars from a bout of rustpox he'd suffered as an infant, so that his cheeks in particular looked to be stippled with paler brown.

'Why bother?' They both turned their heads to find Captain Egwu standing close at hand, arms crossed, her baton tapping her shoulder. While they were dressed in their light brown factory coveralls – newly decorated with regimental, company and platoon badges for Epsilon Platoon, First Company of the Addaba 64th Defence Corps – Yennu Egwu wore a trim uniform suit of deep blue, her dark curls braided tightly to allow a cap with a gold peak to sit on her abundant hair.

'Overse– captain!' Menber saluted, bringing his heels together smartly as he did so. Zenobi brought her hand up a second later, eyes directed to the ferrocrete at her feet.

'Look at me, Trooper Adedeji.'

Zenobi met the captain's dark gaze.

'You asked a question. Do you want the answer?'

'Yes… captain.'

Egwu tapped the end of her plain baton against the side of Zenobi's lasgun.

'It takes time to learn to drive a tank, trooper. Rogal Dorn, in his wisdom, concluded that our hours were better spent building them than being taught how to operate them. Other folk, menials and clerks of distant hives, contributed nothing to the direct war effort and so their time was best spent learning to be tank drivers, pilots and gunners.'

'I understand, captain.'

'You have been given basic infantry training, a lasgun and sufficient power packs for three hundred shots. It will take us several days to reach our placement. We do not know when we will be called upon to engage the enemy. Until that time you will drill every day and hone your marksmanship, close-quarters combat skills and tactical knowledge.'

'I look forward to improving myself, captain, and fighting for the cause.'

'I know you do, Zenobi.' A rare smile curved the captain's full lips. 'The Adedeji were amongst the first to dedicate themselves to our endeavour. Your tireless work on the production line is appreciated, and I expect will be duplicated on the line of battle.'

She looked at both of them and then cast her gaze towards the mass of humanity advancing slowly through the gates of the transit station. The quad rotors of large heli-transports thudded louder than the din of ten thousand conversations, muted by the kilometre that stretched between the group and the main landing site. Bladed craft lifted up, their places on the embarkation apron taken seconds later by a constant stream of descending heli-transports.

'It defies belief, does it not?' said Egwu. 'Somewhere else, a hive like ours spent all its days making these transports. All over Terra, each part dedicated to the whole endeavour according to its capabilities and the designs of Rogal Dorn.'

'By the will of the Emperor,' added Menber.

'By His will indeed were we set to our tasks,' said Egwu. 'Dorn's was the hand, but His was the thought that moved it, and He has had mastery over us for our whole lives.'

'And those of our ancestors, captain,' said Zenobi. 'Long the forges of Addaba have burned for the glory of the Emperor and the conquest of His domains.'

'And now we fight to protect what is ours,' said the captain.

They stood in silence and Zenobi contemplated the meaning of the course she was about to embark upon. The mobilisation confirmed that Horus was coming. There were quiet rumours that forces of the Warmaster had already reached the outer defences of the Solar System and been repelled. That had been followed by an increase in recruitment through the cradlespur, as the moment of truth came closer and closer.

'Do you think we'll see Addaba again?' Menber asked the question that had been loitering at the back of Zenobi's thoughts.

'Unlikely,' Egwu replied bluntly, crossing her arms once more. 'Even if any of us survive this, what we are moving towards will change our lives and Terra forever. This is the end of an age but also the beginning of a new, brighter era.'

The thought cheered Zenobi and she nodded, taking a step forward, her renewed eagerness propelling her towards the transports.

'A moment, Trooper Adedeji,' said Egwu, holding out her baton. The captain turned and signalled to her staff, who were gathered a few metres away. Lieutenant Okoye broke away from the others, carrying a long pole swathed in a canvas tube. 'This is for you.'

Zenobi stared wide-eyed as the lieutenant presented her with the standard.

'The company colours,' Egwu told her. Menber laughed and clapped Zenobi on the shoulder.

'Congratulations, cousin, you're going to carry our colours!'

Zenobi looked at the standard and then back at her captain.

'Take it...' said Egwu.

The trooper shouldered her lasgun and took the proffered banner, feeling the smoothness of the lightweight pole in her grip and the weight of the cloth furled beneath the plain canvas. She reached a hand towards the cover, but Okoye grabbed her wrist with a warning look.

'Not yet,' he said, pulling her hand away.

'I am entrusting you with these colours, Zenobi, because I know that I can,' said Egwu, laying a hand on her arm. 'It is an honour and a responsibility. If you fall, another will take them up, but it is your privilege and duty never to lose this standard. Never.'

Her stare was intense and just for an instant Zenobi was afraid: afraid that she was not worthy, that she would not be equal to the task. The standard, like others that were being taken from the hive, had been made by the Sendafan tribes in their own workshops.

The rulers of the Imperium had not seen fit to provide colours for most of their newly raised regiments. What need did conscripted menials and drafted notaries have for martial pride? The meaning was obvious, despite the messages calling upon all citizens of Terra to be prepared to make the ultimate sacrifice: some sacrifices were more expected than others.

She stroked the concealing fabric, as if she could feel the stitches within, and from them the hours of care that had gone into the creation of the artefact. Days of work. Days rationed between the back-breaking stints on the line. Days huddled around smuggled lumen and naked flame, tired fingers working with thread and material scavenged from across the work shifts – not even yarn had been spared the all-consuming audit required by the Emperor's war effort.

Perhaps Egwu read something of her doubts in her gaze and the captain's grip on Zenobi's arm tightened.

'You more than any other know why we must fight. Our futures depend upon what we do next. Your family, your tribe, the people of Addaba and all of humanity will be led by our example. I trust you, Trooper Adedeji. Trust yourself too.'

'I will, captain.' Zenobi shifted her grip on the standard, holding it in the crook of her left arm with her lasgun so that she could pull up her hand in salute to the officer. 'Thank you. I swear that I will not fail you, or our people.'

TWO

A simple plan
Family
A new commander

The Iron Blood, *Terran near orbit,*
sixty-nine hours before assault

Arriving at the doors to Perturabo's chamber, Kydomor Forrix was surprised to find that he was not alone in seeking audience with the primarch. Clad in full battle-plate and helm, the warrior that had been Barban Falk waited in the antechamber. Kroeger was there also, a hunched, hulking figure in Terminator armour who seemed on the verge of hurling himself at the closed portal. Each tread of his boots on the bare deck rang around the small room, accompanied by bull-like exhalations of frustration.

They both turned at Forrix's approach. There was a glimmer of something through the lenses of Falk's helm, while Kroeger's gaze was a mixture of confusion and annoyance.

'Why are you here, Falk?' Forrix demanded, striding into the antechamber.

'I am the Warsmith,' the warrior replied. It sounded like Falk,

27

tinged with the metallic ring of the external address system. Except for the studied enunciation, of someone taking care with every word issued. 'Address me as such.'

'There are a dozen warsmiths on this ship and its attendant flotilla,' said Forrix with a curled lip. 'Why do you assume the singular title? And you didn't answer my question – what are you doing hanging at the Lord of Iron's door like a hound waiting to be whipped by its master? Were you summoned?'

'I heard word that you sought the primarch's attention alone,' Falk admitted.

'Alone being the operative word.'

'We are the Trident, we should speak as one with the primarch. Unless you are seeking singular audience in an effort to undermine our father's confidence in me.'

'It would be harder to undermine a child's wall of bricks.' Forrix turned his eye to Kroeger, who returned the attention with a belligerent stare. 'And you?'

'I followed him,' replied Kroeger with a flick of the head towards Falk.

Forrix rolled his eyes and turned back to the great double doors that barred entry to the chamber. He moved towards the ocular security device set above them and looked up.

'I am here to see the primarch,' he announced.

His demand was met with a flat horn denying entry.

'I have already tried entering,' said Falk. 'Do you think I would have waited here otherwise?'

Before Forrix could respond he was silenced by the grinding of bolts in the doorway. With a hydraulic hiss, the massive plasteel portals opened, a flickering stream of light bursting into the antechamber.

The hololith projector within was at full power, throwing the lord of the Legion into stark, shifting silhouette as he stepped slowly across a projected image of the Imperial Palace.

Forrix hurried forward, knowing no invitation would be issued. Kroeger and Falk followed on his heel. With a clank, the Iron Circle marched forward, shields and mauls raised. They turned in synchrony to form a line between their master and the Trident, each visitor targeted by the shoulder-mounted cannons of two automatons.

'Lord Perturabo,' said Falk. 'It is your Trident, come to seek your orders.'

'I haven't,' growled Forrix. 'I'm here with a way to break the siege.'

Perturabo straightened, taller even than the mindless body-guards he had created.

'Really?' Perturabo's voice rumbled around the chamber, heavy with menace.

The automatons parted to form a path towards the primarch. It looked like a guard of honour but Forrix knew better. Hes-itation would invite instant criticism so he strode forward, stopped a few paces from his lord and crashed a gauntleted fist against his chest plastron in salute.

'The space port, Lord of Iron. At the Lion's Gate.'

'I have studied it in some detail.' The primarch's dark stare settled upon Forrix in the manner of a predator that had found its prey. 'What have you seen that I have not?'

'A mistake, Lord of Iron. Dorn's overconfidence has left a flaw we can exploit.'

'A mistake?' Perturabo's voice dropped to a dangerous whisper.

'Leaving the space port intact so close to the wall is an error,' Forrix said. He was committed now, and plunged on for good or ill. 'If we can seize the port swiftly enough there will not be time to reinforce the defences separating it from the main wall.'

'That is your plan?' The primarch's scorn was like knives scoring wounds in Forrix's pride. 'You think that a mistake?

Dorn does not make mistakes! Seven years he has pondered every detail here. Nothing is in error. Nothing is where it is except by his design!'

The primarch stomped through the hololith like a metal giant attacking the city. His fists crashed into the projector, turning it into a cloud of shrapnel and sparks.

'It is only by my superior intellect that his plans will be broken, his conceit revealed to the universe!' he roared.

Forrix stood his ground, pushing against every instinct that told him to back down. The remains of the hololith projector stuttered, strobing red and purple light across the chamber, like a malfunctioning blind grenade.

'Perhaps his mistake is in underestimating you, Lord of Iron,' he said quickly. 'And maybe your doubters' lies have blinded you to your power also. Dorn would not think you daring enough to strike so boldly and decisively at a place that seems impregnable.'

'No,' said Perturabo, but his rage was dissipating as his mind engaged with the issue presented. 'No, he taunts me with this flaw. It is too perfect... A trap. Dorn would see me commit to this attack and then reveal some secondary ploy in order to ensnare me and see me executed.'

Perturabo's eyes roved across the Trident, not really seeing them.

'But I see you, Rogal. I will turn the trap against you.' The primarch's gaze finally settled on his subordinates and a grim smile twisted his face. 'I will not be lured into the maw of the beast, but that does not mean I cannot ram my fist down its throat and rip out its innards.'

Falk stepped up quickly, fist banging in salute.

'I would be honoured to lead the attack,' said the Warsmith.

'I am sure you would,' Perturabo replied with a dismissive sneer. 'No, not you.'

'I–' began Forrix but the primarch cut him off.

'Kroeger shall have battle command,' announced Perturabo.

Practice allowed Forrix to internalise the bellow of rage that stirred in his gut – to have given the slightest hint of dissent was to risk immediate and fatal censure. He remained passive, showing not the least reaction that Perturabo's inhuman senses and paranoia might detect.

'I am honoured, my primarch.' Kroeger's brow was as furrowed with peaks and troughs as the Himalazia. 'Surprised.'

'It is time that you had opportunity to prove your full worth.'

'The Lion's Gate will fall to us, I give my bond,' Kroeger continued, somewhat unnecessarily. There was no need to iterate the price of failure, for the blame would not fall solely at the feet of Perturabo if the Iron Warriors were baulked.

'This is not a time for subtlety.' The Iron Circle drew back as Perturabo stalked through the strobing hololith, his cable-pierced scalp shining with glimmering beads of sweat. With unspoken intent, Forrix and Falk both retreated a few steps to leave Kroeger standing alone against the primarch. 'You are the most bloody-minded of my Trident, Kroeger. I know that you will not relent for a moment. I see the desire in you for brutal war, and the Lion's Gate will supply you with more brutality than any conflict you have seen before.'

'Forrix, remain with me.'

Perturabo's command stopped the warsmith in mid-stride as he headed out of the primarch's chamber with the other two members of the Trident. The Lord of Iron seemed placid enough, his tone even, but Forrix knew well that the churning passion beneath the veneer could break forth in destructive rage. He spun on his heel and returned to stand to attention before his master.

Perturabo said nothing more until the reverberation of the doors' closing clanged through the hall.

'Hololith off. Lights on.' The lumen strips above flickered into a wan yellow gleam, banishing the shadows that had wreathed the primarch. For a few seconds Forrix remembered his commander as he had been at the height of his power and insight; before the Warmaster had corrupted him, turned ambition into arrogance, curiosity into obsession.

The moment passed as Perturabo's features twisted into a scornful grimace. He lifted armour-sheathed hands, fingers flexing in agitation. The warsmith wondered if his misgivings had been obvious, or perhaps some other act or inaction had slighted the lord of his Legion. Forrix kept calm and tried not to let Perturabo's paranoia infect him as it had so many that surrounded the primarch.

'You think it wrong of me to appoint Kroeger to command this attack?'

The question was a gaping chasm opening in front of Forrix, but a lie could drag him into its depths as easily as the truth. Better he be damned in courage rather than cowardice.

'He is inexperienced and lacking much strategic expertise,' said Forrix, keeping his criticism focused on Kroeger rather than his primarch. A little flattery would not hurt either. 'Only you have the breadth of knowledge and depth of concentration to unpick the lock set by Dorn.'

'Though you were going to volunteer to command the Legion, were you not? Is that the role you see for yourself, Forrix? My heir?' Perturabo tilted his head, eyes narrowing. 'My successor?'

'I am happy to rest in your long shadow, Lord of Iron.'

'Indeed, you are.' Perturabo turned away and Forrix let his breath escape through gritted teeth, trying to relax every muscle that had bunched tight under the primarch's scrutiny. He almost flinched as Perturabo rounded on him again, but his lord's gaze passed over him swiftly and settled on the doorway, as though looking at the departed warsmiths.

'Kroeger knows himself and his place well. He will fight this battle for victory, not as some stepping stone to further glory at my expense.'

Forrix clenched his jaw against the instinct to protest innocence. His pride was pierced by the implicit allegation, but better a wound to his ego than a greater injury to the body. Perturabo stroked an armoured finger across his chin, like a file rasping on metal. His silence loomed over Forrix, demanding he say something.

'Kroeger is single-minded, that much I can say with certainty.'

'Single-minded. Not easily distracted.' Perturabo smiled but there was little about his humour that Forrix could share. 'Trustworthy. Uncomplicated.'

'All of those things,' Forrix agreed, wondering why Perturabo had bid him to remain. Evidently the primarch also realised he had not addressed his point.

'Dorn has set a trap for me, and I intend to use Kroeger to spring it. The Emperor's Praetoria-n has laid his plans with guile and patience, doubtless trying to anticipate my every move, countering in advance every stratagem, ploy and tactic he has gleaned from my previous work. Be sure, Forrix, that every stone laid in this palace was done so in consideration of *my* arrival. As certain as our foes have been that Horus would one day reach Terra, my brother has been equally sure that it is my wit, my siegecraft, that would be the test of his defences.'

Perturabo placed his palms together, fingers splayed against each other, his eyes wide with manic thought. His lips twisted in a terrible smile.

'But he never contemplated one eventuality. It is beyond Dorn's ego to comprehend that I might step aside and allow another to fight in my place. Kroeger is unsophisticated, a dull tactician and an uncharismatic commander.'

The primarch left his evaluation hanging in the air just long enough for Forrix to play his appointed part in the dialogue.

'Everything you are not, Lord of Iron,' he replied dutifully. He was rewarded by a nod and a smile that had all the benevolence of a hunting cat's stare. 'Dorn protects the Palace with the most complex lock ever devised, so you have given life to a sledgehammer to break it to pieces.'

'Very good, Forrix. A sledgehammer to pick a lock.' There was a moment of genuine humour in the primarch's expression. 'Kroeger will blunder and bustle and hurl my warriors at the enemy without relent, and Dorn... My brother will try to pick out my will from the anarchy, try to dissect intent from Kroeger's pitiful strategies. He will be looking for every sign of me, and I will not be there.'

Forrix nodded, not trusting himself to speak any further in case his doubts betrayed him. Even so, he was sure of one thing, and finally found his voice.

'I will do everything I can to ensure we are victorious, my lord.'

'You will follow Kroeger's commands to the letter, even if they seem disastrous or nonsensical to you,' Perturabo insisted. 'I have schooled you myself in war, and though you can never approach me in generalship you have been an adept student. Even a fraction of my genius might show through if you interfere and I want to confound Dorn utterly. Am I understood?'

'Perfectly, Lord of Iron,' said Forrix, raising his fist to his chest.

Perturabo dismissed him with a gesture. As the doors creaked open to allow his exit, Forrix glanced back to see his master half-turned away, arms clenched about himself, fingers drumming on his armour while his lips moved wordlessly in thought. Forrix considered Perturabo's logic in appointing Kroeger to command.

It was a move of genius or madness, or quite likely both.

THREE

Dorn waits
In transit
Mortarion's gifts

Bhab Bastion, thirteen hours before assault

There was nowhere within or below the Imperial Palace that was peaceful. The din of war and the noise of its defenders permeated every stone. Yet if there was a place quieter than any other it was the Sanctuary of Satya, located on an offshoot of the Bhab Bastion that held the Grand Borealis Strategium. It was one of twelve identical chambers that ringed the buttress-tower, each a domed hall forty metres across reached by a single covered bridge. It was part of the oldest building, arranged according to the design of the Emperor before Dorn had been instructed to reshape the defences. It was also numbered among only half a dozen places that had been left intact on the specific command of the Emperor, along with such locations as the Hall of Victories and the Senatorum Imperialis.

The hall was open to the elements, the domed crystal roof that had once covered the circular chamber shattered by the shock wave of supersonic bombers flying too close. Pieces of it crunched underfoot as Dorn crossed the wooden floor. Behind him Rann followed, Sigismund at his side, while Malcador sat upon a bench ahead, staring out through the broken dome towards the south-east. The Sigillite held his staff across his lap, spine straight, his hood pulled back so that the distant flare of detonations shone from his forehead.

Dorn stopped a few paces from the bench but said nothing. Rann felt that to speak would be to intrude upon something pristine, despite the scream of jets overhead and the muted thunder of explosions. There was a stillness about the Sanctuary of Satya that demanded respect and peace.

'The enemy will make their next move soon,' said Malcador, still facing away. 'Their troops are at the wall and the aegis fails daily.'

'It is only one defence of many,' said Dorn, folding his arms. 'It was never intended to protect us indefinitely. Horus can bombard for as long as he likes, shells and rockets never captured a city.'

'That is the truth,' said Malcador. 'So Horus' warriors will come.'

'Perhaps if you came to the Grand Borealis, I could better share with you the preparations.'

'The clutter of all that information is not what I seek, Rogal.' Malcador half turned, one leg moving onto the bench, creasing his robe. Stern eyes regarded the primarch and his companions. 'You fill yourself with data, but this is a place of simplicity. A shrine to clarity.'

'I do not take your meaning.'

'No. A pity.' Malcador sighed. 'With as little of your military terminology as possible, what do you expect Horus to do next?'

'Is my strategy to be questioned again?' Dorn jutted out his chin.

Rann thought his genefather's behaviour strange but had not been party to such conferences before. Few spoke to a primarch in such casual tones, but Malcador was the hand of the Emperor and clearly used to such encounters. Rann glanced at Sigismund but the First Captain's eyes were fixed on Rogal Dorn.

'You have the confidence of the Emperor, Rogal, and I am not a strategist. I wish to keep the High Lords informed and would spare you the chore of addressing them yourself and being bombarded with petty concerns.'

The primarch relaxed a little and cast his eye towards Rann.

'You have the latest reports, captain? What would be your assessment?'

'Against all sense, the enemy appear to be mustering their strength for an attack against the Lion's Gate space port, my lord.'

'Why would that be against all sense?' asked Malcador, standing up to face the Imperial Fists. 'It is a worthwhile objective.'

'It is outside the wall itself, and is very secure, Lord Sigillite,' explained Rann. 'An attack there draws strength away from the main assault.'

Malcador looked at Dorn, who had a finger lifted to his chin in thought.

'Do you concur with Captain Rann's assessment?'

The primarch did not answer immediately. He strode past the bench to look out through the frame of the shattered dome. Rann followed his gaze, seeing the stretch of walls curving together at the massive edifice of the Lion's Gate, and as a towering adjunct to it, the space port beyond. Distance and the smog of war rendered it a vague stepped pyramid rising out of banks of multicoloured cloud, its summit lost in the lightning-fractured storm that roiled constantly across the upper atmosphere.

'It could be a feint,' said the primarch finally. 'Having lost all orbital surveyors, there are massed movements beyond our sensors that we only learn of from scattered reports of physical sightings. While our gaze turns one way, perhaps Perturabo seeks advantage elsewhere.'

'We should let him, my lords,' said Sigismund, speaking for the first time since he had answered Dorn's summons. 'Until the blow descends, any reaction benefits the foe more than us.'

'What do you mean?' said Malcador. 'If we must make adjustments for an attack, better to start now.'

'Our time is better spent deciding *our* next blow, rather than second-guessing the enemy's intent. We must press on with our chosen strategy, force the enemy to make hard choices rather than taking them ourselves.'

Rann saw Lord Dorn's jaw tighten at Sigismund's interjection and said nothing until the primarch's gaze turned to him. Lord Dorn nodded for Rann to continue.

'It's true that we could chase ourselves in circles responding to every threat,' the lord seneschal told Malcador. 'I think we've learned enough from the void war not to trust appearances. Time is our ally, not the Warmaster's. Whatever gains Perturabo thinks he can make will take him time to achieve at the space port. For all that effort, there are other goals he might achieve more swiftly.'

'It reminds me of something an ancient Terran general once said,' Malcador told them. 'Never interrupt the enemy while he is making a mistake.'

'That concerns me,' said Dorn, who had continued to stare across the Imperial Palace at the vague apparition of the Lion's Gate. 'I can lay many charges at the feet of my brother, but idiocy is not one of them. If he is set upon taking the space port it is because it suits him in the grander scheme. If he was somehow to succeed, the captured port would serve him well in an assault against the Lion's Gate itself.'

'Or suits Horus,' added Sigismund. 'We should not forget that it is the fallen Warmaster that commands the Lord of Iron. Perhaps it is Horus' folly, not Perturabo's mistake.'

'A good point.' Malcador leaned on his staff, gripping it with both hands. 'There is the matter of intent. What gains might be made by the capture of the port?'

'That's simple,' said Rann. 'The traitors could bring down larger ships close to the Palace. Bulk transports, even the *Vengeful Spirit* itself!'

'Could there be… ritual significance?' asked Dorn. He looked ill at ease with the subject, in a way Rann had not thought possible of his primarch. The implication sent a shudder of apprehension through the lord seneschal, who had been engulfed by the daemonic assault upon the *Phalanx* and dared not imagine what his genefather had witnessed. 'Much of the opening assault was not to make physical gains, but to weaken the Emperor's psychic grip on Terra. Is there a further agenda that I do not understand?'

Malcador looked away, uncomfortable with the question.

'It is possible, yet impossible to know for sure,' he answered without looking at the primarch. 'Such matters are even less exact than military science.'

'The defences at the Lion's Gate space port are considerable. I feel no need to reinforce them at this point,' Dorn said decisively. 'If Perturabo wishes to attack, we shall allow it and we shall stop it. To respond in any other way would be to risk weakening against a concerted effort elsewhere.'

'I will make sure everything is in order,' said Sigismund.

'No, you will remain with me for the time being,' countered Dorn. 'This matter requires a steady hand. Rann will take command of the forces in the space port.'

The implied admonishment shocked Rann, but if Sigismund thought to argue this judgement he gave no sign. Instead he acquiesced with a bowed head and bended knee. Rann followed suit, fist to his chest.

'I am honoured, my lord.' Rann raised his gaze to the primarch. 'I will do my utmost to hold the port but suggest that

I am no equal to the mind of the Lord of Iron. Would it not be better to personally lead the defence?'

'I shall spare it due thought when needed and pass on such guidance as is required,' Dorn said in a measured tone, 'but I cannot risk being drawn into operational decisions when the whole Palace requires my attention. Should I have to extricate myself from the battle to deal with broader concerns it could prove disastrous to the fate of the Lion's Gate, and likewise if I am hesitant in response to wider developments because of local issues. As observed, it is Horus that commands and Perturabo that obeys. It could be the Warmaster's intent to draw me out, so that I am unready for attack elsewhere.'

'The Legion will not fail you, my lord,' Rann said. His gaze moved past the primarch to Sigismund, who stared at the ground with jaw clenched, whatever emotions he was feeling only barely held in check. Rann stood up, still watching the First Captain. 'I will prepare my company to move to the Lion's Gate space port. I hope to see you soon enough, brother. Your sword would be a welcome addition if our lord permits it.'

Sigismund replied with only a flicker of a nod, eyes meeting Rann's gaze for a split second before returning to the floor.

'As Lord Dorn wills it,' he said tersely. 'Glad would be my sword to join you in this coming battle.'

Whatever vexed the First Captain, it was not Rann's doing and he departed feeling better for the knowledge.

Djibou transition station, Afrik,
one hundred and six days before assault

The heli-transports headed down into the dawn light, which seemed somehow significant to Zenobi. A new beginning, something like that. She had left Addaba behind but was not sure what came next.

Zenobi was fortunate enough to be within sight of one of the small windows that pierced the hundred-metre-long cabin. She'd seen nothing all flight, but daylight now brought a fresh view.

The coast of an ancient, dead sea ran in a jagged line from north to south, and upon the very lip of the shoreline sprawled a maze of roads, landing strips and railway lines. Excited muttering greeted the sight and those further inside the fuselage left their seats and crowded across the craft for a glimpse of their destination.

Zenobi remained silent as her eye tried to follow kilometre after kilometre of wide highway and looping tracks. Bridges and tunnels turned the criss-cross of incoming traffic into a bewildering maze, half-seen past the constant flights of heli-transports and stratocruisers.

'Why don't they just fly us all the way there?' someone behind her asked.

'Fuel.'

Zenobi turned to find Lieutenant Okoye standing to the end of the bench on her left. 'Need to save every drop.'

'And so why not build the railway all the way to Addaba?' asked Menber.

Okoye leaned on the back of the bench and shrugged dismissively.

'Because Dorn chose not to. Rail lines are permanent and might be used by the enemy. There's probably a dozen of these air fleets moving people all over Terra, and when the fighting starts, they'll still be useful, but idle tracks won't. Efficiency and redundancy. If you ever wonder why something is the way it is… that's your answer, right there. Efficiency.'

The timbre of the engine noise rose in pitch and out of the

corner of her eye she saw that they were only a few hundred metres up.

'Better sit down, sir,' a voice from the back warned the lieutenant.

All across the compartment troopers were dragging themselves back to their seats, their squad leaders and officers rapping out commands. Okoye swept a last warning look over his charges and returned to his place a little way ahead of Zenobi.

The craft started juddering as it hit the swell of heat coming up from the massive transportation hub, the pilot dipping the nose hard to compensate for the sudden lift. Clattering and shouts filled the cabin as poorly lodged weapons skittered from their places and troopers that had not secured themselves tumbled from their benches. Zenobi rammed her feet into the foot loops and pushed herself back against the bench, fingers moving to the haft of the banner that was wedged between her and Menber.

She felt his hand on hers and glanced aside, drawing reassurance from the gesture and his expression.

The heli-transport dropped the last few metres and landed heavily, massive suspension coils squealing in protest, the packed defence troopers calling out and swearing as they were once more thrown around the crowded compartment.

'Stay seated!' bawled a sergeant near the front, the call echoed by other squad leaders along the rows.

The address system crackled into life.

'Companies and platoons will leave in reverse order of embarkation.' Egwu's voice was tinny, almost unrecognisable. 'Form up when ordered. No pushing and no loitering. We clear the transport in ten minutes or the whole company will be on reduced rations as punishment. Other troopers are waiting for this ride.'

* * *

Palatine Arc quarantine zone, six hours before assault

It had once been known as the Palatine Arc, a crescent of pala-
tial dorm-blocks for high-ranking administrators that covered
nearly a hundred square kilometres inside the Europa Wall.
Before the erection of the defences, the kilometre-high towers
had enjoyed views of newly verdant mountain valleys to the
south of the Imperial Palace. Each had housed only a handful
of diplomats, arch-clerks and other privileged attendees of the
Terran Council, in hierarchy only second to the seated Senatorum members.

After concerted efforts by the Death Guard, the Palatine Arc
had been renamed by the refugees that inhabited it.

Poxville.

The attempted levity did nothing to alleviate the suffering of
those within. Supplies were dropped once a day by gyrocop-
ter, crates of protein powder and barrels of barely drinkable
water. Nothing else. A few brave medicae – some of them already marked by one of many virulent diseases – ran clinics
inside the quarantined zone. If they saved any it was only so
that they would endure longer in a pit of unremitting misery.
Hundreds every day were transported into Poxville, but not a
single man or woman was allowed out.

Stationed upon freshly raised walls that surrounded the
ruins of the Administratum buildings, Katsuhiro felt more
like a ghost than a man, even more wraithlike than when
he'd been in the depths of battle shock on the outer defences.
He had heard rumour of a creed that declared the Master of
Mankind a divinity, but if that was so then Katsuhiro was
forced to wonder why he would be punished by the God-
Emperor in such malicious fashion. To be delivered from
the battle without had seemed a blessing. He had thought to
stand at one of the great bastions, but instead, like thousands

that had faced the plague-ridden sons of Mortarion, he had been despatched to guard the quarantine zone erected around Poxville.

Day after day the Death Guard kept up their attacks. He had almost laughed when he had seen the engines of war lumbering up within range of the walls. Crude-looking catapults – trebuchets and onagers his new captain had called them. Powered by twisted rope or sinew, made of rotting wood and rusting metal, they looked too weak to break even a hovel, never mind the immensity of the Ultimate Wall.

But the wall had not been their target, and their payloads had not been explosives. Instead they hurled infected carcasses, skulls filled with noxious slime and sealed with wax, pots of biting flies and other ammunition suited to a war twenty-nine thousand years in the past. But the cruel genius was that these infectious bombs were not of sufficient speed nor mass to trigger the void shields. It was not worth the might of macro cannons and volcano cannons to pick off the engines one by one, and so they crept forward beneath the gaze of the mightiest guns. Day after day small-arms gunfire raked the approaching weapons, and day after day enough made it through the fusillade to bombard Poxville for a few minutes.

It was not lost on Katsuhiro that the buildings once inhabited by the lords of the Administratum, the highest notaries of tax, account and statistic, were now home to an unknown number of infected. A few days after internment had begun, the authorities had stopped counting. Ten thousand? Twenty? Katsuhiro thought it a low estimate.

Those with any cogency left stayed away from the encircling walls. Those without were met by las-fire if they approached within one hundred metres. Even this cordon was little comfort to Katsuhiro. Plague could carry far on the wrong wind. Sometimes it seemed as though strange eddies would stir up the fumes and guide them towards one part of the wall. Sirens would wail, reminding him of the gas attacks on the trenches. He had been lucky so far, never his stretch of wall. But to hear that distant alarm dragged him back to those sickening days and nights where painful death was only ever a moment away.

Shooting the infected did not cause him any grief. He was inured to the misery of others, concerned only with his own survival. At times he was jealous of them, driven mad so they no longer knew what would become of them. Death was a mercy – a mercy he craved on the long, cold night shifts when the moans of the dying were loud enough to be heard over the continual bombardment, and the silhouettes of staggering pox-carriers could be seen against the fires burning deep inside the quarantine zone.

There were stories that the plagues of the Death Guard were not merely mortal. Some said they had seen the dead walk again. A lifetime ago, before he had set foot on that train of conscripts, Katsuhiro might have scoffed at such claims. Now… Now, he was unconvinced, he had not seen it with his own eyes. But if he did, it would not surprise him.

Katsuhiro was sustained by a single purpose, one which he pursued in his down-watch when he could. Somewhere the traitor Ashul – or Doromek, or whatever he was called – was inside the Imperial Palace. Ashul lived only because Katsuhiro had been a coward. He still was, but his guilt gnawed at him even more than his fear. He made enquiries when he could. His first adamant questions had been met with suspicion, and he had calmed himself lest he be thought one of the raving infected that he now stood guard against. And, when his health had returned a little, he'd realised that if he made too much fuss over an officer named Doromek, the traitor might hear of it.

Katsuhiro knew that finding one man amongst the teeming

millions was near-impossible. It did not matter, because the search was the only thing that gave him any purpose. Without that quest to restore his pride and silence his unquiet conscience, Katsuhiro had nothing to live for.

FOUR

Lion's Gate space port
Chosen One
A long walk

*Lion's Gate space port, tropophex exterior,
seven hours before assault*

It belied Rann's credulity to think that he was atop something that had been built by humans. The Imperial Palace had vast towers and walls, and he'd spent as much time in drop pods and gunships as any legionary, but standing on an open observatory platform thirteen kilometres above sea level was a singular experience.

He turned and looked at the soaring edifice behind him, astounded that it continued another sixty kilometres up. He was glad of his helm and armour, able to stand in the clear air and look down upon the massed cloud banks that boiled across the Palace. Without his war-plate he'd be frozen in moments and dying of oxygen starvation. The only moisture was a gentle drift from the vaporators of the Space Marines' power plants, tiny snowflakes falling from the vents and drifting away. Were their suits not environmentally sealed their bodies would have been desiccated and preserved for centuries. It made Rann think of the mummified remains of the Old Kings his people's ancestors had entombed on the mountaintops of Inwit.

Rann fancied that he could see glimpses of stars between the aurora of the upper shields, and the flickering shadow of void-ships passing across them. A product of imagination, most likely, but symptomatic of the sense of wonder he felt standing beneath the uncaring gaze of the upper skies. He was far more certain about the plasma-plumes of dropcraft he watched to the east, rising and falling against the coming night. The flare of other suborbital aircraft criss-crossed the twilight, far above the squadrons that duelled below the cloud cover.

The space port's immensity was impossible to bring down to human scale, so he regarded it in purely strategic terms as he would a city or smaller fortification. The outer portions of each layer, up to about a kilometre deep, were called the skin; this gave way to the mantlezone around the innermost ten kilometres, which itself was known as the core-wards, or just the core.

It had three main vertical portions, each of which roughly equated to atmospheric layers. The broadest and most populous area was the base, rising to his position, known as the tropophex, though the workers that lived and laboured within its shell referred to it as Low District. It was about this lower region that the bulk of the air transport pads clustered, where both jet and rotary craft could land and take cargo.

Through the tropopause into the stratosphere were a thousand storeys of transit machinery, sealed habitation towers and intermediary orbital platforms, where craft capable of both void and atmospheric travel could join. Sky City, properly known as the stratophex, controlled progress between the uppermost level and the bulk of the space port. These jutting skyquays were linked by communication and power cables, as though some vast spider had spun its web haphazardly over the flanks of the mountain-port. The skin was uninhabited, at least by anything more sentient than a servitor. Port labourers used envirosuits and powered crane harnesses when outside their habs.

The remaining spire soared over six successively narrower towers, and then broadened to a twelve-kilometre-wide landing pad at the summit. Starspear, it was called by the locals, a far more poetic designation than its official title: the mesophex. At its height atmospheric pressure was almost non-existent, allowing void craft to touch down and load directly into the immense conveyor shafts that dropped down through the core. An orbital lift mechanism provided counterweight propulsion, so that when fully in operation a constant stream of immense carriages rose and lowered from the landing platform. They were dormant now, locked down in case of attack.

It left Rann feeling overwhelmed, a tiny figure in yellow armour, not even a speck on the flank of the tallest structure on Terra. He turned to the warrior on his left, a lieutenant-commander by the name of Sevastin Haeger, a Terra-born recruit.

'Did you know I was a Chosen One?' said Rann.

'Your pardon, captain?'

The lieutenant-commander was Rann's subordinate in charge of the eighteen thousand Imperial Fists currently assigned to the space port's defence. Rann had a further seven hundred and ninety thousand non-legionary personnel under his authority, as well as several wings of fighter craft and direct-attack bombers. The inhabitants of the port had worked until the last moments of defeat in orbit, bringing in materials and survivors. They had refused to leave since then, barricading their homes and arming themselves, so that the Lion's Gate militia probably numbered even more than the registered soldiery. They would fight to protect their homes but Rann considered his command of them to exist in title only.

'I was a Chosen One,' Rann explained. He turned and the hundred-strong honour guard turned with him, thirty warriors of his personal Huscarls leading the company with shields raised. For the moment an attendant servitor carried his shield, though his paired axes were hung on his belt. 'My people raised me in the belief that I was marked for greatness, destined to be a powerful leader of the tribe.'

'Why?' asked Haeger, confused. Rann's laugh made him realise the question was an importune one and softened his doubts. 'What caused your people to have such a belief?'

'There is a great underground river on Inwit. It flows along the boundary between light and dark for thousands of kilometres, almost a kilometre below the ice plains. It has hundreds of tributaries and many of the tribes follow its course from one ice hive to the next. My people, the Rann, were quite far downstream of this mighty flow. The River of Life, we called it, the Bringer of Fates. The Dorn, our noble lord's adopted people, controlled the headlands of the mightiest tributary. Anyway, I was found by my mother abandoned on the riverbank.

'There was a woman's body close at hand, starved and pierced by wounds, and the corpses of two men armoured in the style of the Dorn. It was reasoned that she had fled them, to protect the child. Some thought I should be given back, lest the Rann earned the wrath of the Dorn, but my mother said she would slit the throat of anyone that tried, and offered the explanation that the Dorn feared I would rise up against them one day and that was why they wanted me dead.'

'They believed her?'

'My mother was a formidable woman, and a deft hand with a knife.' Rann took one last look at the skies before the

Space Marines passed into the vaulted arch of the compression chamber. 'I was raised in this belief until puberty, learning from the greatest of the Rann. Blade, hunting, sewing, cooking.'

'Sewing?'

'You've seen nothing beautiful until you've seen Inwit stitchcraft, lieutenant-commander.' Rann stopped, his train of thought derailed by the interruption. 'What was I saying?'

'The Chosen One story,' prompted Sergeant Ortor, with the tone of a man who had heard it more than several times.

'Right. There I was, all ready to become leader of the Rann on my transition to adulthood, though I was a bit wary of waging war on the Dorn, when the Lord Praetorian arrived and everything changed. The first time he came downriver everybody of the Rann knew their Chosen One was a poor imitation of the real thing.'

'And how did you end up as one of the Legion?' asked Haeger. There was a chorus of groans from the Huscarls.

'Perhaps another time,' said Rann.

He turned as the armoured portal began to grind shut, and saw again the distant lights of hundreds of landing craft. Rann knew enough to conclude there was no other reason for their appearance other than as a prelude to an assault on the Lion's Gate space port. The reports had alluded to it, but he had wanted to see it with his own eyes.

'I need to speak with Lord Dorn. This isn't a feint, and we're going to need more guns.'

Djibou transition station, Afrik,
one hundred and six days before assault

There was a sense of solidity that came from a large body of people moving together with a united purpose. Though no order was given, Zenobi found herself falling into step with those around her, finding the natural rhythm that joined them. As on the factory lines, there was a harmony between the troopers, an instinctual togetherness derived from long acquaintance and practice. Just as the line had its own pace and routines, so the work groups that had become defence corps squads settled into a unified movement.

The transports had deposited them and many thousands of others on a raised apron, after a brief glimpse of the dizzying sprawl of roads and rails. Since landing, Zenobi had seen nothing but the others around her and the lightening sky above.

She had no idea where they were going next and the thought was oddly liberating. All she could do was move with the crowd, directed by the officers and the course of the wide rampways and bridges – she knew they were still high up by the cold bite in the wind, like when she used to steal a few moments on the upper hive-skin between shifts.

The drone of engines and clatter of rail carts created a backdrop to the tramping of booted feet. There was little chatter – after nearly a day in close confines with each other everyone was content with their own thoughts.

Over time the footfalls became even more regular, a rhythmic thudding that reminded her of pneumatic die cutters and pounding shell-hammers.

A few metres ahead of Zenobi a woman raised her voice, the words familiar to anyone that worked in the lower east cradlespur, and Zenobi had heard of similar work songs all across the manufactories.

'I been working the line, working the line, working it all day.'

'Just like my father before,' someone sang the refrain from behind.

'I been working the line, working the line, working it all night,' the woman continued.

'Just like my mother before,' sang more voices.

'I been working the line, working the line, working all shift.'

'Just like my son will after,' sang Zenobi, her wavering voice joining dozens more.

Others took up the lead line, a mix of bass and lower notes from the men, higher-pitched and strident harmonies from the women.

'I been working the line, working the line, working all my life.'

'Just like my daughter after.'

The sound swelled around Zenobi, helping her forget the endless sky above, reminding her that she was with her people. With that thought came the comfort that she was where she was meant to be. The factory workers of Addaba were a fatalistic people, but not without contentment. Within their allotted lives there was room to rise a rank or two, to get a little more living space, an extra ration of fresh water and – if one reached the heady heights of overseer like Egwu and the others that had become officers in the defence corps – real fruit once a month. Having been raised on recycled water and air and having tasted nothing but synthetic protein slabs and nutri-mush, the idea of an apple or orange bordered on the mythical.

So they sang songs as they marched, of labour and love, of family and cherished moments, of building a world for their descendants and honouring the lives of their ancestors. Songs that carried them through long shifts of dangerous manual labour swept them along the seemingly unending march to their next stop.

It was almost two hours before the monotony of walking was interrupted. Zenobi reckoned they had covered more than ten kilometres since being put down by the transports. They came to a slow stop and Zenobi took the moment to crouch and rub her calves, her hamstrings just as stiff. The singing died away and was replaced by sighs and grumbles. It was just a couple of minutes' break before they were moving again, and a few hundred metres later Zenobi could see the reason for the delay.

The huge rampway dropped and split into three, dividing the defence troopers into contingents. The left and right paths curved gently away from the central road, the descent steepening sharply. Their destination was still out of sight.

She found herself being ushered left with the rest of Company Epsilon and as the body of troopers moved, she caught sight of the low wall that bordered the ramp. From this new vantage point she could see down into the mass of the transit hub, though at first vertigo threatened to topple her as she gazed at the bewildering maze of rail lines and roadways.

She turned her attention ahead and saw five massive roofed structures. They were not buildings as such, for they had no walls, and beneath each of them stretched eight straight tracks that continued underneath the walkway she was on.

The sound of rotors and engines had faded with distance but as they descended it was replaced by a background noise of a different kind – shouts, moans and cries. A disturbed muttering rippled through the Addaba companies as they encountered its source.

Beneath the bridge, on a platform many kilometres long, tens of thousands of conscripts were being herded towards the open-topped carts of a train that stretched out of view. Goad sticks crackled and the bellows of provosts with voxmitters cut through the audible misery of the massed people.

The anarchy sickened Zenobi, as much as the obvious suffering of those unfortunates being loaded for transport to their zone of deployment. It was such a stark contrast to the orderly manner of the Addaba Defence Corps.

'I wonder where they're from,' she said to Seleen, the woman between her and the retaining wall to their left.

'I don't know, yeye, but they don't look happy to be here.'

'Khertoumi wasters,' said Menber. 'Look at their tattoos.'

He was right: amongst the press of bodies it was possible to see the distinctive white facial tattoos of the nomads that lived in the Khertoum rad deserts.

'Grit-eaters?' laughed a trooper just in front of Zenobi. She recognised him from Gamma Platoon but did not know his name. 'Dorn will hurt his back bending to scrape so low for his armies!'

'They'll fire a lasgun just the same as you or I, Kettai,' snapped Menber. 'And their blood will water the ground all the same too. You think the war cares what station we each come from?'

'I'm just glad we're not sharing space with them, is all I'm saying, yeye. Don't be taking hurt for their feelings, they don't have none.'

'That would be us, if it were not for the cause,' said Zenobi, fingers tightening around the haft of the standard over her shoulder. 'Swept together and thrown into wagons like animals. Only because we work together are we marching like this, so you keep your mean words in your heart and not let them come to your lips.'

'She is right,' called out someone outside Zenobi's eyeline. 'We have bonds, we are all family, but when we fight we'll be doing it for all Terrans, yeah? All humanity! For Addaba!'

'For Addaba!' came the reflex cry in response, even from the mouth of Kettai. He fell silent but shook his head as he continued to glance down at the awful scene playing out below, the stink and sobs of the indentured troopers growing stronger as the rampway took the defence corps down to ground level.

FIVE

A monumental task
The assault begins
The locomotive

*Lion's Gate space port, eastern approach,
six hours before assault*

'Remind you of anywhere?' Forrix said to his companions.

'Cadmean Citadel.' Kroeger grunted the name of the place where Perturabo had elevated him to the Trident. To Forrix it seemed that journey had now been completed by Kroeger's appointment to general command of the assault on the Lion's Gate space port but Kroeger made no mention of it.

'As though drawn on a far larger canvas,' said Falk.

'Far, far larger,' agreed Forrix.

Cadmean Citadel had also been a space port, a mountain of a tower raised and defended by the sons of Dorn. Forrix recalled it as something of an arduous campaign, among many such labours of war in which he had taken part. Yet it seemed a mere anthill in comparison to the structure that rose out of the Imperial Palace, dwarfing even the mountains from which most of the Emperor's grand city had been hewn.

He was a considerable distance away and yet had to crane his neck to see its summit, lost against the haze of the upper atmosphere now fogged by bombardment debris and energy discharge. It was a ziggurat, in rough outline at least, half as broad at its base as it was high, large enough to be considered a hive city in its own right. One of the largest, in fact, though its purpose was not residential but logistical. From this angle he could just about make out the highest connecting transitways between the space port and the Imperial Palace – highways and monorails and viaducts, each half a kilometre across, big enough to carry the bulk transport of the immense cargos that passed to and from the ships docking at its summit.

Cadmean Citadel had been large enough for traders and carriers to land, but the very largest vessels – vessels like the Arks Mechanicum and the Legio Titanicus transports that had sworn for the Warmaster – could not enter so far into a gravity well nor withstand re-entry to any significant degree. They were giants born in the void and destined to die in the void. But the Lion's Gate space port was so tall that such considerations were no longer valid. Starships were not forced to shuttle down their loads in smaller landers but could disgorge the contents of their kilometres-long bodies directly to the massive elevators and carriages.

'Do you think we've brought enough guns?' said Forrix, turning his attention to the infamous siege train of the IV Legion. The landing had begun three days ago while Mortarion and Angron had occupied the attention of the defenders. Still the dark blur of shuttling craft could be seen linking the distant drop field with a succession of starships in orbit. The column of armoured vehicles stretched all the way back to that landing site, nearly forty kilometres of undulating metal serpent intent upon the Lion's Gate.

Like the Trident and the twenty-five thousand legionaries that accompanied them, the wall-breaker companies of the

Iron Warriors had been landed within range of only the largest defence cannons of the space port – and they were directed upwards to fend off any direct approach from orbit. Lead formations had encountered little resistance, the bulk of Dorn's forces having been withdrawn to the final defences within a few kilometres of the space port.

A mountaintop had been flattened by orbital scouring to create a level a kilometre across. Tiny compared to the vast expanse of the Katabatic Plains that had been flattened for the Imperial Palace but enough to allow heavier landers to bring down squadrons of tanks and assault guns.

'Two thousand, three hundred and eight Basilisk assault guns,' said Kroeger, reeling off the list as though pleased with the feat of memory. To Forrix it was the least requirement of command to have the complete logistics of one's force ready for immediate recall. 'Fifteen hundred and twenty-two Manticore assault rocket carriers. Thirteen modified Sicaran bombards. Four hundred and seventy-six Deathstrike platforms. Four hundred and ninety-five Medusa howitzers. Thirteen hundred and six Siege Dreadnoughts. Eighty-four Typhon siege guns. Seven thousand, one hundred and eighteen Thunderburst towed guns.'

Forrix allowed Kroeger's voice to become a drone as he continued to list the tens of thousands of support tanks, Land Raiders and other armoured beasts committed to the attack. It was nearly eighty per cent of the Legion's armoured might in the Solar System, the rest being kept in orbit or the outer reaches, or already deployed in support of the efforts being made by the other Legions and primarchs, particularly Mortarion's attempts to break the wall to the western side of the Palace.

Their efforts would be rendered obsolete if the Iron Warriors could break through at the Lion's Gate.

To the north and south stretched the support echelons – Imperial Army forces sworn to the Warmaster and appointed to

Perturabo, as well as various vassal hosts that had come under the sway of the Iron Warriors. One and a half million men and women, as well as countless beasts, mutants and freaks of the warp. Forrix didn't care much for such grist in the war mill, but viewed them more as a lubricant. Their blood would make the machine of battle turn more smoothly for the warriors of Perturabo.

For perhaps the first time in decades, Forrix felt that the IV Legion would be given credit for its victories. He thought back to when he had left Terra, just a line legionary, embarking on the Great Crusade for the Emperor. He had harboured no illusions regarding the glory of war – the brutal truth of battle had been revealed to him during Unification – but they had all felt something of a greater promise to the war they would unleash. Reclaiming Terra and Luna had been a stepping stone; the Great Crusade was the endeavour for which history would laud the Space Marines.

'I left from here, you know?' he said to his companions.

Kroeger grunted, annoyed at the interruption to his logistical liturgy. Falk turned a helmed head, cocked slightly to the right.

'Really?' said the Warsmith. 'I knew you were from Terra. I did not realise you were native to the Himalazia.'

'I wasn't,' Forrix corrected him. 'But before the Fourth Legion were despatched, we were granted honours by the Emperor. A parade to receive His salute. We went straight from there onto our first crusade campaign.'

He looked again at the sky-piercing stalagmite of ferrocrete and plasteel.

'It was smaller then, of course.'

Watching the seething mass of humanity and inhumanity spilling like a stain across the Katabatic Plains, Forrix realised that the non-Legion elements of the army were driving straight towards the space port. By the early morning they would be in range of the space port's main batteries and the heavy weapons of the trench lines around it.

'You're launching the attack without any preparatory bombardment?' he said, unable to hide his incredulity from Kroeger.

'Perturabo was quite clear in his orders,' the other triarch replied. 'Speed. It was your plan, wasn't it? Take the port-city before Dorn can respond? There's no point wasting shells on a city where the defenders are hiding behind the walls. The scum will bring them to their gun positions and then the heavy metal will fly.'

Forrix bit back any reply. He could think of half a dozen flaws in this approach but remembered the injunction of his primarch not to interfere. It was this brutish simplicity that Perturabo desired.

'I recall Cadmean Citadel again,' said Falk. 'The Lord of Iron's coming went very poorly for some. It would be wise not to draw the primarch's personal intervention, especially as he has been most specific in his desire not to become embroiled in Dorn's trap.'

Forrix was not convinced that there was any trap, but he was not about to argue the matter with Falk, whom he had once considered a close ally but now viewed with deep suspicion. The Warsmith would not hesitate in reporting any perceived misdemeanours to the primarch.

There was the added benefit that when Kroeger's lack of expertise led to failure, he would pay the price of the primarch's wrath. His replacement might be more amenable to Forrix's desires, or at the least more wary of ignoring him.

Djibou transition station, Afrik,
one hundred and six days before assault

Under the shade of the station Zenobi felt the chill, her bare arms sheened in sweat from the morning sun and the long walk. It was not just the sudden drop in temperature that set her skin prickling. As they passed into the shadows, she saw the gun towers. They were built into the great pylons that held up the roof, dozens of them stretching along the narrow platforms between the tracks.

Her fingers sought the arm of Menber next to her, gripping it tight just below the elbow. He glanced at her and saw where her gaze was directed.

'You've seen guns before,' he said with a shrug, his lasgun almost falling off his shoulder. He hiked it back into place.

'Look where they're pointed, cousin.' Quad-barrelled heavy stubbers tracked back and forth between the scores of companies filing into the station. On walkways between the pillars visored guards patrolled, heavy carbines at the ready. 'They're not here to protect the station against attack.'

'It doesn't mean anything,' insisted Menber. He cocked his head back towards the loading platforms where the waster conscripts were still being corralled into their wagons. 'Maybe there was some trouble before.'

'Why would they suspect us?'

'They don't. It's... It's like the dynastic security teams. They don't expect any trouble, it's just for show.'

Their pace had slowed to a few metres a minute as the companies pushed together on the raised rockcrete. There was nowhere to go, no way of avoiding a lethal fusillade if the guards decided to open fire. Her heart pounded harder and faster as she imagined the muzzle flare and screams. She remembered the stories Auntie Hermayla had told her of the old food riots, how the corridors would be filled with bodies, the stairwells red cascades of blood.

'I can't even lift my arms,' Zenobi muttered, 'much less fire my lasgun. What are they afraid of?'

'Nothing,' growled Menber. 'It's procedure. It's not for us. Why would it be for us?'

In the press of bodies the banner pole was pushed tight against Zenobi's chest. She ran a hand along it, seeking reassurance from the touch.

'Dorn put out the call, and we answered.' Menber leaned towards her, face earnest, voice quiet. 'There is nothing to worry about.'

Zenobi tried to look around to take her mind off the matter, but there was little to see. She was one of the shortest in the company and even on tiptoe she could barely see past the shoulders of her companions.

It was not long before the ground started to vibrate. It was almost undetectable at first but quickly grew in vigour. Through the soles of her boots, Zenobi could feel it thrumming, a slow pulsing sensation.

'I think the trains are coming,' she said, as excited muttering and whispers spread through the assembled platoons. 'It's nearly time.'

She saw Kettai was right in front of her. He was rangy for a factory-hiver, almost a metre and seventy-five tall. She heard Kettai gasp and there were other expressions of surprise and shock rippling through the troopers. Zenobi tugged at Kettai's collar.

'What is it? What is it?' She thrust a hand at Menber and then Kettai. 'Let me see! Help me up.'

The two glanced at each other and then sighed, turning towards one another and crouching so that their knees formed steps. It was common practice in the work crews, to help reach a fouled gear or belt, and more illicit destinations among the factory levels such as the crawlspaces used for a quick *mozo* smoke break or to share a flask of *tei*.

Zenobi's lack of height meant she was used to such improvised ladders and she quickly scaled the two men, coming to rest on their shoulders. From her elevated position she could see across the mass of troopers to the far end of the station, several hundred metres away. In the sunlight beyond the shadow of the vast roof something dark was approaching along the tracks, though it was hard to tell what it was amongst the dust kicked up from the old seabed.

At first she thought it was eight trains approaching in unison, for the dark patch within the dust cloud straddled all of the lines that came into the station. Another half-minute revealed the error of her assumption. It was not multiple trains but one vast engine, running along the parallel tracks, which meant that it had to be more than a hundred metres wide. She glanced up at the roof, understanding now why the station required such titanic proportions, to accommodate a vehicle that was easily thirty metres high.

Her upbringing in the confines of Addaba had not given her much of a sense of distance, and the train's massive size made a mockery of normal perspective, so it was only after watching for several minutes that Zenobi realised it was still some way off, at least half a kilometre. It was approaching slowly, probably no faster than walking pace, its slate-grey armoured prow forcing its way through the bank of grit and sand kicked up by its passage.

The rails between the platforms were humming now, their vibrations coursing into the rockcrete with increasing volume. A hushed sense of awe settled on the Addaba troopers as they watched the marvel of engineering bearing down upon them like the great elfants of Old Earth myth that could lay waste to armies with their curving tusks and fearsome bellows.

The hum became a rattle, while from the distant train came a grumbling of metal wheels accompanied by a higher-pitched whine. Zenobi could make out more of its prow as it neared the far end of the station. There was an offset cab at the upper left side – probably large enough to house a crew of dozens but seemingly small against the flat angle of the train's impossibly broad nose. On the other side was a multi-gunned turret, one of several that blistered around the engine car, each holding two large-bore cannons and a variety of small anti-personnel armaments, much like those of the gun nests beneath the station roof.

A fog billowed from exhaust vents along the sides, tinged by pale blue light from within the immense locomotive.

'Plasma reactor…' whispered Kettai.

Though it was still slowing, moving at barely a crawl as it passed into the gloom, massive air displacement sent a sandstorm roiling along the rails and platforms. Warning shouts greeted the cloud of swirling dust as troopers covered their faces and turned their backs in a ripple that passed back through the crowd.

'Watch yourself!' Menber cried out, pulling Zenobi down from her perch, one bulky arm crooked around her shoulder to pull her into the protection of his chest.

She scrunched her eyes shut, the rattle of grit and sand and the curses of the Addaba hivers heralding the arrival of the dust cloud. It scoured across the back of her neck and prickled at her exposed shoulders, swirling between her and Menber, who had his chin buried in his chest, a calloused hand like a visor on his brow.

The light disappeared as the dust wave passed over them, but the gloom was nothing compared to the darkness beneath the train as it snarled over their heads, the clatter of wheels like the deafening pound of a hundred forge hammers. The wheeze of venting coolant vapour, long shriek of braking plates and tremor of throbbing power lines churned in Zenobi's gut. She gripped the front of Menber's coverall with her free hand, fingers making a tight fist in the material as the monstrous engine continued to rumble over them, the absence of light combining with the noise to overwhelm her senses.

Only another minute or two passed, but it felt like an age until quiet suddenly descended. It was broken by the coughs and muttering of her companions and the slow tick-tick-tick of cooling metal.

Bright orange lumens flared into life along the length of the train, bathing the platforms with harsh light. Zenobi blinked tears away, teeth gritted against this fresh assault. As her eyes adjusted, she saw that the underside of the train was barely two metres above her head. Slender metal ladders rattled down from hatches to either side of the platforms, the interior of the train lit by a more ambient yellow gleam.

'Boarding begins now!' The command rolled along the station from the front, passed from officer to sub-officer to squad leaders. 'Ascend to the third level. Stow your kit beneath the cots. Sit on your cot and await further instruction.'

Again and again these orders rang through the companies, as the troopers recovered and started to move towards the ladders.

'This way, this way,' called Lieutenant Okoye, pushing his way towards a ladder on Zenobi's left, the sealed underside of the train blazoned with a numeral beside it – '143'. 'First squad, climb the ladder and take the stairwell to the top. Move it!'

The platoon shuffled forward as one, directed by their common destination. Zenobi waited until she had space to manoeuvre the banner into the opening, pushing it up the ladder towards Sergeant Alekzanda, who waited at the top. Her lasgun swung down between her legs as she climbed, threatening to trip her, until she wrestled it back onto her shoulder.

Shouts from below urged her to hurry and she almost lost her footing, swinging by one hand, just a toe on a rung.

'Here, here, your hand!' Someone reached down and she grabbed the proffered wrist, feeling iron-strong fingers curling around her own. She was almost bodily lifted into the opening and deposited on the decking. Zenobi looked up to see who had helped her and saw that it was Xirsi, the sergeant from third squad. He was short like most hivers, but so broad she wondered how he had fitted through the hatch.

'Come on, yeye, up you go,' he said, pointing to a metal spiral stair a few metres along the narrow passageway.

Zenobi took a couple of steps and then returned to claim the banner from Alekzanda. Her sergeant raised an eyebrow.

'Keep it safe, Zenobi.'

Face flushing with humiliation, not just regarding the banner but her whole undignified entry into the train, she hurried to the stairwell and ascended, not daring to look at anyone else until she had reached the top level.

The stair brought her out into a chamber that ran half the width of the train, filled with cots. There were no windows, but every few metres a ladder pierced the ceiling.

'Not that way,' called Kettai as she took a step away from the stairwell. He waved her closer and pointed to the bunks that lined the metal wall. 'First squad over there.'

She nodded her thanks and hurried over, joining the increasing throng of troopers spreading out into their strange accommodation. The cots were plain metal frames with thin mattresses, built atop a low locker box. She realised that each bunk had a serial etched into a small brass plate on the headboard and swiftly decoded it as company, platoon and squad followed by two initials. She found hers quickly enough, just as Menber and the others arrived, Alekzanda bringing up the rear.

'Welcome to your new home, brave troopers of Addaba,' the sergeant announced, tossing his bag onto the bunk next to Zenobi's. 'Next stop, Himalazia.'

'Oh, Throne-heart, we coming to you,' said Seleen, her grin flashing uneven teeth yellowed from too much mozo. She winked at Zenobi. 'Hope you packed clean baggies, yeye, we're off to see the Emperor.'

SIX

The first wave
Allies in blood
Integrity officers

Lion Primus Strategium, Sky City, six hours before assault

'Dross.' Fafnir Rann handed the data-tablet back to Haeger.

'A lot of dross, commander.' Haeger passed the report to one of the logistaria attendants, who withdrew to his post. The strategium was designated Lion Primus, and Rann had set it up in the two hundred and ninety-eighth level of Sky City, replacing the civilian command hub that had once run the core-wards' transport network. Vox-murmur and the clicking of augur relays provided a constant backdrop to the conversation. 'Three hundred thousand strong and growing by the hour.'

'It doesn't matter if there are a million of them, lieutenant-commander. Logistics and physics are on our side. A force that size can't bring all of its strength to bear against a narrow front.'

'We cannot allow them to reach the defence lines,' argued Haeger.

'We can and we will, but I'm not throwing valuable soldiers

away to hold a line in the dirt. All forces will withdraw to the Lion's Gate space port.'

An adjutant in the uniform of the Terran Conscriptia hurried across the strategium, her brow furrowed.

'Withdraw, lord commander?'

'Drop the "lord", I'm not a primarch,' Rann told the young woman. He saw confusion in her eyes, shared by Haeger. 'Perturabo is like a vox-broadcast on repeat. This tactic of sending in the worthless masses has been tried over and over since the traitors landed.'

'And Lord Dorn has seen fit to match them with our…' Haeger glanced at the adjutant, unsure of how to phrase his words.

'Basic mass formation troops,' the adjutant replied quietly. 'That is the correct term in the Imperial Army.'

'…indeed,' Haeger continued. 'The enemy would have us expend our strength slaying mutants and beasts. Our orders from Lord Dorn are simple – to hold for as long as possible.'

'I'll not have brave women and men slaughtered just to save some bolter rounds,' Rann growled. Haeger looked as though he might object further but Rann silenced him with a raised hand. 'It's not sentimentality. We have to take the initiative now and then, otherwise Perturabo and his generals will think they can do as they please. I want them to feel uncomfortable.'

'Am I to send the withdrawal now, Lor– Commander Rann?'

'How long until all the outer defence regiments can be inside the port?'

'Two hours,' the adjutant replied promptly. 'Three if you want us to set demolitions beforehand.'

'Do that,' Rann said with a smile. 'The first enemy wave will be here in six hours. Do not begin the withdrawal for another two, I want our enemies to commit to a plan before we change things.'

'The grand batteries of the Iron Warriors will be within range,' said Haeger. 'If you wait that long the withdrawal will be made under fire.'

'We'll boost the base layer fields, extend them a kilometre for the final hour of withdrawal. Redirect power from the mesophex to compensate for the drain on the reactors. Leave enough for the upper defence cannons to dissuade any orbital approach, but drop the shielding. If Perturabo wants to capture the space port he's not going to start by bombarding the landing docks.'

The adjutant waited for a few seconds to see if any more commands were forthcoming, and then snapped off a sharp salute before moving to the closest communications station. Haeger remained.

'You're not happy, lieutenant-commander.'

'I would not dispute your orders,' replied Haeger stiffly. 'However, Lord Dorn has been exact in his preparations, both in the raising of the defences and their manning. Is it really wise to discard that on a whim?'

'A whim?' Rann kept his temper in check, though his fingers tapped on the haft of the axe at his left hip. 'Is that how this seems to you?'

Haeger was intelligent and chose not to answer. Rann gestured for Haeger to come closer. The lieutenant-commander took a step and, being a few centimetres taller, dipped his head slightly. Rann's voice was barely a whisper.

'I have commanded the First Assault Cadre for many years. I bear the title Lord Seneschal, though I don't insist others use it often.' Rann leaned closer still, teeth gritted. 'Most importantly, Lord Dorn put me in charge.'

He stepped back, voice rising a little, but not enough to carry further than Haeger.

'I know you will follow my orders, lieutenant-commander, and I am not going to make a habit of explaining myself. But this

time, just this once, because I need you to trust me, I will make
something clear.' Rann strode across the strategium towards the
main display, a square table five metres across that was currently
showing an orbital view of the space port and the surrounding
twenty square kilometres. It was a simulacrum generated from
records and augur data; there were no loyalist orbital assets left in
the vicinity. A servitor burbled into life at their approach: a torso,
head and arms wired into the side of the table, a nest of cables
springing from its spine to other cogitating engines arranged
around the chamber. The logistaria hurried over from his al-
cove and took his place at a control panel next to the servitor.

'Top view, Highway Four,' said Rann, leaning forward with
fists on the plasteel edge of the screen-table.

'Analysing. Compressing.' The servitor's head tilted left and
right as it processed the information from the strategium's data-
banks. The logistaria's fingers tapped a few commands into his
panel. 'Display adjustment in progress.'

The table went slate grey for several seconds and then flickered into life, showing a rendition of the broad road that led
almost straight from the Iron Warriors' landing site to the space
port, entering by means of a three-hundred-metre-wide barbican and gate.

'Highlight emplaced defences.'

'Highlighting static weapon positions.' The servitor's eyes
rolled towards Rann and then back to the display. Red smudges
blurred the walls and towers that flanked the road.

'It's a killing ground,' Rann said to Haeger.

'Yes, lord seneschal. I oversaw the construction.'

'Of course,' said Rann, allowing the gentle rebuke. 'High-
powered laser batteries, macro cannons and assorted plasma
platforms.'

'A combination of anti-vehicle and anti-legionary guns. The
mass waves employed by the enemy will have no chance.'

'But the whole point of their assault is to sap our resources. If we sit in the trenches and behind the walls, we'll be doing exactly what Perturabo wants us to do. There's a better way to hold off the attack and ensure we have the weaponry available to meet the full-scale legionary and armoured assault which is bound to follow.'

Rann moved around to the logistaria's position and took up a light wand, with which he started to make marks upon the display. As he did so, he explained his plan.

'I will lead the First Assault Cadre to meet the enemy attack, supported on the wings here by two columns of heavy tanks and a mobile attack reserve – bikes and speeders.' Rann drew in the lines, forming a V-shape against the line of the enemy advance, with a few swipes to indicate the counter-attack movements from a pair of lesser gateways that flanked the main barbican.

'What will that achieve that the gun emplacements cannot?' asked Haeger. 'Or the Imperial Army remaining in their bunkers and trenches?'

'It's about planning for defeat,' said Rann. 'Rearranging the layers so that they work for us, not the enemy. We save ammunition on the big guns until the armoured assault, and keep the volcano cannons and other high-energy weapons dormant so that maximum power flows to the shields. It's all about time and how much of it we make Perturabo use up. We can't stop the enemy getting in, not forever. Cannons on walls are no good then, but thirty thousand massed infantry holding the interior will be.'

'And the assault cadre is as good as any wall,' said Haeger, nodding to himself.

'A wall we can put where we like,' added Rann. 'I can assure you that whatever else our enemies have in mind, they have not considered the possibility that our first act in defence will be an attack…'

'I shall issue orders to gather the flanking forces and reserve. I assume you will lead the muster of the First Assault Cadre personally.'

'You assume correctly, lieutenant-commander.' Rann caught the warrior's eye just before he turned to leave. 'I hope I have made myself clear.'

'The doubts were mine to own, not yours, lord seneschal,' said Haeger, banging a fist to his plastron. 'I have prepared for this moment for seven years, but in the event have fallen victim to predictable orthodoxy.'

'I can't take all the credit,' said Rann. 'Lord Sigismund put the thought in my mind. I recall what the Khan and his White Scars accomplished when set free. To be honest I think the Imperial Fists can do even better.'

'We will, lord seneschal. Death to the traitors!'

'Death to the traitors,' growled Rann. 'Every last one of them.'

He returned his attention to the display as Haeger strode away. The lines and shapes he had drawn looked so simple on the schematic, but he saw them with the eye of a battlefield commander, as ranks of warriors and squadrons of engines, lit by the fury of fire and resounding with the crash of war. It was a bold move, and he was certain of success. Even so, Dorn had not taught him to be rash. He started to think about the many ways the tide of conflict might turn against him and what could be done to ensure they did not come to pass.

XII Legion vanguard, proximity of Daylight Wall, four hours before assault

The tracks of a solitary Rhino transport carved furrows through mud made slick with blood, scattering shards of half-buried bones. Beneath the gore-spatter it was a solid gunmetal, its hatches and cupolas painted in yellow-and-black stripes. A banner pole bent beneath a broad standard, depicting the metallic skull face of the IV Legion, blazoned against crossed lightning bolts on a field of black. Battle honours were stitched into dozens of scrolls around the main device and the top edge showed signs of wear, charred by some historic conflagration that the Iron Warriors had seen fit to commemorate by leaving this scar unrepaired.

It passed between broken tank hulls and shattered fortifications, wending a zigzag route through the devastation left in the wake of successive attacks. Even now magazines and arsenals still burned, pouring thick black smoke into air choked with fumes and toxins.

A cordon of large troop carriers in the bastardised colours of the World Eaters marked the boundary of their zone of operation, but there was no challenge or hail levelled at the incoming vehicle. Its passage went wholly unremarked.

Within the crude encampment Legion slaves hauled at great tarpaulins piled with bodies, forging between sagging marquees and makeshift flakboard bunkers. A great pile of corpses was being assembled within sight of the main wall, where a hundred weary axe-wielders laboured to behead those that had fallen to Angron's sons. Their blades rose and fell with the monotony of a factory line, turning the dead into righteous sacrifices, though without the least pomp or ritual. Half-human ghouls – creatures suckled on mutant blood and Khorne's power – stripped flesh from bone and polished the skulls, in turn passing them to box-laden beasts of burden driven by more slaves to the immense mountain being erected in the Blood God's honour.

These dreary tasks were left to menials, for there was none among the World Eaters that desired ought but to face the enemy and add to the body count of the war. It was industrialised sacrifice, at odds with the highly personal battle-lust of Khorne's chosen, who favoured only the slaying in their god's name.

And at this bloody task a greater part of the Legion still laboured. There was little semblance of Chapter and company command remaining, and even individual squads had started to break apart as champions rose from the ranks to create fief-doms of authority within the fragmenting Legion.

Angron cared nothing for this fracturing, for in his presence all were cowed to his will, and cohesion, of a sort, could be maintained. He was, for the present, absent the battleline, seeking his bloodthirsty pleasures elsewhere around the overrun defences, butchering whatever he came upon.

There were a handful of others that could command similar obedience, but they were not of any single mind, no more than the greatest of the warlords that were starting to hold sway where once all was dictated by the *Principia Bellicosa*. Of these the most admired was Khârn, whose lists of titles seemed to grow daily as his feats of death-dealing continued – the Axe of Khorne, the Death-gifted, the Walking Ruin and more.

He watched the approach of the Rhino from close to a pyre of blackened bones, which he had lit as a beacon for the transport to find him at the appointed hour. Of all the warriors of the XII he retained a modicum of strategic interest in the war and had agreed to the parley on behalf of his primarch. Now that his battle-brothers were intent upon the last survivors outside the wall it was safe for an outsider to enter, though he knew there was a substantial risk that his own self-control might slip, potentially bringing the World Eaters and Iron Warriors into conflict with each other.

The Rhino stopped a short distance away and a solitary figure disembarked. His armour was reinforced Terminator plate, with heavily riveted, banded strips like the oldest marks, a brutal throwback to the earliest days of the Legions. His oversized left fist gleamed with a power generator, a similarly blunt weapon, and Khârn felt himself drawn to the other warrior's simplicity.

'I expected to meet with your primarch, Angron of the Red Blade,' the Iron Warrior declared as he stopped a few metres away.

'I… Hnnh.' Khârn snorted hard, clearing the blood-fugue from his thoughts to focus on the burly Iron Warriors commander. He wanted to bury *Gorechild* into the mask of the warsmith's helm, just to see the spray of blood. He plucked the man's name from the whirl of gore-choked daydreams that swelled up from the implants in his brain.

Kroeger. Commander of the IV's attack on the space port.

'The primarch fights where he chooses. I am not… Hnnh. I am not his master. He bends to the will only of the Blood God.'

'So it doesn't matter that I am here for Perturabo?'

'No, Kroeger, it does not.' Khârn pointed his blood-flecked axe towards the companies of the World Eaters storming the last of the outer defences between him and the eastern stretch of the Eternity Wall. 'Angron demands that we breach the Palace.'

The warsmith stood silent for a few seconds, shoulders hunched.

'Fulgrim has already agreed to bring his Legion to the attack,' Kroeger said, his attempt at guile obvious. 'Would Angron be outdone by his brother?'

'You are fortunate… Hnnh. Fortunate that my lord is not here to respond to such taunts.'

Khârn gritted his teeth, biting back the urge to cleave the Iron Warrior's head from the torso as payment for his petty remark.

'I don't need Angron,' snarled the warsmith, fists rising. 'I need your legionaries. You'll all die before you set foot on the Eternity Wall, but I have a plan that will get you into the Lion's Gate space port.'

'You'll need... Hnnh. You'll need more inducement than that.'

'Dorn's sons.' The man's savage grin was audible in his tone. 'Never mind mopping up the scum of the Imperial Army, don't you want to cut down the brothers that betrayed us?'

'Hah! I understand where the betrayal lies.' Khârn stalked back and forth, wanting to end the conversation to join the assault. The crack of bolters and battle cries of his companions called to him, the urging of his implant like a hot barb dragging him to the wall.

'The World Eaters I knew would never seek the easy battle. Perhaps I don't need you, after all.'

Kroeger turned away and Khârn was about to let him go. Another force, the whisper voice that ran through his blood, sounded louder than the insistent bark of his Nails.

'Hnnh. Wait, Kroeger.'

Khârn could sense the mettle of this soldier and heard the thunder of Khorne in the Iron Warrior's hearts. This was one who could be kin to the World Eaters. The Blood God was willing to lay his hand upon Kroeger and that demanded special attention.

'Angron might listen... Hnnh. A call to arms from one dedicated to the Skull Throne might catch the primarch's ear.'

'What do you mean?' Kroeger stepped back, his fist rising. It took every effort of the XII Legion captain not to react to the implied threat. The hand clasping the haft of *Gorechild* almost moved of its own accord.

'You have the qualities of a great warrior,' said Khârn. 'The sort of warrior Khorne would bless with his blood-gifts. He demands nothing but what you want to give already. Hnnh. The deaths of your foes.'

'The Emperor has already made me stronger than any mortal man,' said Kroeger. 'What other gifts do I need?'

A wreck of a Rhino transport protruded from the blood-slicked earth a few metres away. Khârn turned to it, the teeth of *Gorechild* spinning faster until the weapon howled in his grip. The champion of Khorne took two long strides and launched himself into the air, leaping higher than any normal Space Marine was able, axe in both hands. He brought the weapon sweeping down as he landed next to the wreck, its shining teeth slashing through armoured hull and track housing with a single mighty blow. Shattered ceramite and scattered track links exploded around him. Khorne's power flowed through him, energising, setting his mind aflame through his Butcher's Nails so that the growl of his axe was a soothing purr.

Khârn balled a fist and drove it into the flank of the armoured transport. His gauntlet split under the impact but his bone did not, punching through the armoured plate to the elbow. He tore the panel away with a wordless shout, hurling it far out across the blasted wasteland.

'Nothing stands before the chosen of the Blood God and lives!' he roared, turning on Kroeger. 'No blade will pierce my skin. No bolt can scar my flesh. Swear yourself to Khorne and you will become his bloodied killer. Every life you take shall be offered up to his glory, and every moment you will know the joy of slaying.'

'All I need to do is kill in his name?' Kroeger laughed, long and deep. 'No oaths? No rituals? No sacrifices?'

'Hnnh.' Khârn staggered towards the Iron Warrior, letting *Gorechild* fall to his side, ignoring the smell of his own blood flowing from the ruin of his hand. 'As long as the blood flows, Khorne cares not for words.'

Kroeger lifted his combi-bolter, shining in the flash of artillery and the continued flare of orbital lance strikes.

'Then let Lord Angron know that a brother-in-blood calls on him to carry his holy slaughter to the Lion's Gate space port and we shall please the Blood God together.'

* * *

Djibou transition station, Afrik,
one hundred and six days before assault

The scale of the train defied belief. Zenobi and others inves-
tigated their new surroundings while the rest of the regiment
boarded; even the idea that a single vehicle could transport
the ten thousand-strong 64th Defence Corps seemed insanity.

On trying to ascend the ladders, they were rebuffed by armed
provosts and told that the upper deck was for the crew only.
These menacing sentinels bore red sashes over their uniforms,
marking them out as dynastic chosen, the direct servants of
the factory-dynasty overlords of the hive. Zenobi didn't know
when they had arrived; they certainly hadn't travelled with the
worker platoons over which they now stood watch.

A few scouts that dared glances past these impassive-faced
guards reported weapons storage and doorways that the gathered troopers deduced were for access to the gun turrets that
lined the roof. There was speculation as to what else might be
found, and within half an hour the upper level had attained a
semi-mythical status as a realm of plenty and comfort.

Conversations with wanderers from the decks below confirmed that each level was identical and windowless, save for
the bottom deck, which was home to huge cabling links that
connected the immense carriages together. There were basic
cooking facilities at one end of each carriage but no mess
area – they would be expected to eat at their cots it seemed.
At the opposite end were the ablution blocks, which seemed
woefully inadequate for the number of people that would be
using them. The prospect of extra latrine duties rapidly became one of the worst punishments the sergeants and officers
could threaten.

Two hours after boarding, the train still hadn't moved.
Zenobi broke open a slender ration bar she had smuggled

into her kitbag and sat down on Menber's cot to share it with her cousin.

'Everything else is all about "move, move, move", what's taking so long?' Zenobi asked but received only a silent shrug in reply as Menber chewed his portion of the ration bar. 'They must have everybody on board by now, what's the delay?'

'You're eager,' said Sweetana from where she lay with her hands behind her head, two bunks over. 'This isn't so bad. I think this bed is bigger than the one I had back at Addaba!'

It was odd to realise the truth of what she said. Zenobi had never realised how cramped life had been in the hive-factories but comparing it to the space on the train – a train! – it was clear that all things considered, there was more comfort in this mobile barracks than in the worker dorms of their home.

A sudden stir amongst those quartered near the foremost stairwell drew attention from across the barracks-deck. Zenobi stood on the cot to see what was happening. Just as she gained her elevated position, she caught a glimpse of swirling crimson and purple as a knot of officers gathered with equal suddenness in the vicinity of the new arrivals.

'Dynastic colours,' Zenobi told those around her, her voice hushed with respect. 'Maybe the ruby-born are coming with us.'

'Don't be such a *fala*, Obi,' said Menber, pulling at her arm to dismount the bunk. She snatched herself away from his grip so she could carry on watching. 'They're staying at Addaba to oversee the defences and keep things running.'

The scattered discussions were silenced by barks from sergeants and platoon officers, and a few moments later the officers parted to reveal half a dozen newcomers, three men and three women, whose blue officer uniforms were additionally adorned with silken sashes of red and mauve, as Zenobi had seen. They were all shaven-headed and clean-cheeked and bore the lean, muscular build of uphiver enforcement. Red ink marked their eyelids and lips, giving them a stark, other-worldly look.

'I guess that was who we were waiting for,' said Menber.

Captain Egwu stepped forward, eyes scanning back and forth across the assembled company.

'These are our company integrity officers, sent on behalf of the dynastic chiefs to ensure their reputation and intent is maintained by the defence corps assembled in their names.'

One of the integrity officers joined the captain, a woman with a sharp nose and cheeks, her forehead adorned with an additional red diamond tattoo.

'I am Jawaahir Adunay Hadinet, integrity high officer for your company. Some of you may know me by the name my inmates gave me as punitive overseer of the East Main Spur correctional complex – the Iron Warden.'

The name meant nothing to Zenobi, but judging by the scattered muttering from across the company the announcement meant something to others. It was certainly a title that bode poorly for any transgressor.

'We are not here to uphold Imperial Army regulations. We will not be judging the quality of your kit, nor monitoring your training drill. We will deal with disciplinary infractions that reduce the fighting effectiveness and discipline of this company. We will ensure that you adhere to a deeper truth of loyalty and dedication to the cause.'

This was met with silence. The assembled troopers were experienced enough in the work line to keep their lips sealed when a superior made such an announcement. Right from the outset the integrity officers would be watching for any with a loose tongue or showing signs of insubordination.

Zenobi suddenly felt quite exposed standing on the bed of her cousin but dared not climb down in case the movement drew further attention.

'There will be one integrity officer for each platoon,' said captain Egwu. 'They will make themselves known—'

She stopped as the train trembled. The growl of reactors being brought to full power could be heard through the walls. The floor trembled as motors were engaged. There was barely any feeling of movement, just the slightest tug of inertia giving way to acceleration.

'They will make themselves known to each of you in time,' Egwu continued, raising her voice as the throb of the locomotive continued to grow. It was joined by the first metallic clatter of the wheels, muted by the thick hull of the carriage. She glanced at Jawaahir. 'You will defer to the commands of the integrity officers at all times. Their word is law, their judgement absolute. I advise you now not to test their patience or resolve, but to comply with their wishes without hesitation or dispute.'

The integrity high officer cleared her throat and Egwu retreated a step, ceding even her authority to Jawaahir.

'The entire corps will be subjected to introductory interview in the coming days, to get to know each of you better.'

'Thank you—' began Egwu but she was cut off by a glance from the high officer. The look was passive enough, no scowl or other visual admonishment in her expression, but it silenced the captain immediately.

'I want you to bear no illusions, troopers of Addaba,' Jawaahir told them, folding her arms. A movement in the crowd between Zenobi and the integrity officer briefly afforded her a full view. A long maul hung at one hip and a pistol was holstered at the other. 'There are those that are looking to turn us from our purpose, seeking weakness in our hearts. The enemy will stop at nothing to strangle all liberty and resistance, and their agents are moving amongst you even now.'

Zenobi glanced around, expecting these spies to somehow reveal themselves immediately upon being accused. There were others darting suspicious glances at their companions and she started to ask herself just how well she knew the people in the other platoons and companies. She caught a look of annoyance on the face of Menber and she threw him an enquiring gaze. He subtly shook his head, motioning with his eyes towards the integrity officers.

'This is a war we will win with courage, determination and sacrifice,' Jawaahir continued. 'Your resolve will be tested. Your stamina will be pushed beyond anything you have ever endured. Your loyalty... Your loyalty to the cause will be called into question time and again. Against all of these threats, physical and mental, you must stand strong. We will be here to remind you of your duties and oaths.'

Her hand dropped to the pistol at her hip, whether unconsciously or not Zenobi could not tell, but the message was clear.

'Company!' snapped Egwu, bringing them all to attention. She paused for several long seconds, her gaze passing over every trooper under her command. 'Lunch rations will be issued in thirty minutes. Your platoon officers will detail those on catering duty. The rest of you will attend to maintenance. The forces of Horus are not far away and soon the battle for Terra will begin. You *will* be ready when called upon.'

With a flick of her head, she dismissed them and turned to her officers, pointedly ignoring the integrity officers, who moved as a group towards the nearest ladder leading up to the roof level.

A collective sigh escaped the mustered troopers when the last of them had disappeared through the hatch, and Zenobi dropped down on the bunk, a nervous laugh escaping from her as she landed.

She heard her name being called by Okoye as he made his way across the carriage, along with others being summoned to the kitchen.

'We've nothing to worry about,' said Menber, gripping her hand as he dragged her off the cot. 'Whatever these interviews are about, just tell the truth. Remember that you are of the Adedeji and our ancestors were kings.'

She gave him a half-smile and a pat on the arm before she moved to join the others assembling around the lieutenant. She gave a last glance back to the banner pole that she had stowed between her cot and the wall. It was her badge of pride, her talisman of loyalty.

Surely she didn't have anything to worry about from integrity officers?

SEVEN

Big guns never tire
Serration
News from the void

Katabatic Plains, assault hour

A lifetime of war had inured Forrix to the pound of heavy guns as much as it had the beating of his own hearts. Yet there was something majestic about the power unleashed onto the Imperial Palace by the Warmaster. The sky itself was blackened, a roiling storm of discharge and plasma, through which burning mass driver rounds crashed like meteors and beams of lance light strafed.

Perturabo had unlocked the secrets of the aegis that had warded the walls, exposing them to direct bombardment and assault, but the Sanctum Imperialis and surrounds were still swathed by energy screens. So too was the Lion's Gate space port. The air about it shimmered with barely contained energies.

Great guns about the circumference of the space port prevented warships from lying-to in orbit directly above for fear of counter-bombardment. The risk of a broken starship crashing upon the landing docks they were trying to capture was too great a risk, which had been pointed out to Kroeger when he had sent request to their primarch for orbital support. Smaller weapon arrays – still dwarfing those carried by anything smaller than a Titan – ringed the port in bastion outcrops.

They roared now, spitting defiance down into the packed regiments of turncoat Imperial Army and devolved creatures. Anti-air batteries awaited their turn to bark rebuke, for Kroeger had not yet committed his aerial assets to the attack.

If Forrix had assessed the situation on what he could see, without knowledge of what was to come, he would have laughed off the assault as a piecemeal, uncoordinated affair with no chance of success.

It would have been a mistake. Kroeger was a straightforward warrior, raised in the best and worst traditions of Iron Warriors stubbornness and dogma. He lacked finesse, or even any desire for finesse, but that did not make him an idiot. He had explained his plan at length to Forrix and Falk, ensuring they understood their parts well enough as well as his overall objectives. There was nothing to do but enact Kroeger's will or risk the ire of Perturabo, and so Forrix had accepted his allotted role without question. There was every chance that his directness was just the hammer needed to break open the lock of Dorn, as Perturabo believed.

Advancing with bolter in hand, a tide of soldiery and beasts around him, Forrix's auto-senses picked up the first distinctive cracks of the siege train loosing its wrath. A dozen kilometres behind him, battery after battery of cannons coughed forth a cloud of shells. The muzzle flare of their anger lit the skies, silhouetting their deadly rounds. A rolling thunder of noise followed, a shock wave that swept over the advancing legionaries and auxiliaries, bending banner poles, fluttering top knots on Crusader helms and washing over the unarmoured masses with a hot wind that brought cries of astonishment and dismay. They howled as eardrums split and sinuses burst, those foolish enough to look upon the moment of firing left reeling as a flare brighter than the sun burned out their sight.

The noise of the weapons loosing was as nothing to the detonation of the defensive shields. The bombardment could not reach the highest sections, but was targeted at the middle layers, so that the space port seemed girdled by a ring of fire five kilometres high, arcs of power forking ten kilometres to the ground below. The release of so much energy created a counter-blast that flowed down the uneven flanks of the port like an avalanche, gathering roiling vapour and debris as it descended to smash into the first companies of auxiliaries daring the lesser guns at the base. Bodies by the hundred were picked up and dragged through the crushing cloud of shell shrapnel and fire, cutting a swathe through those that followed.

It was the single most powerful explosion Forrix had ever witnessed, and was yet the overture for the fusillade that was to follow.

As the last after-shimmer of the void shields dissipated, the cannons spoke again, this time accompanied by the hiss of fifty thousand rockets and twenty thousand missiles. This fresh wave of brutality smashed into the labouring shields just half a minute after the first. Purple and blue coruscated through the air a few hundred metres from the armoured skin of the space port. Explosions wracked its surface, hurling chunks of plate and showering burning rubble down its mountainous slopes – not from impacts but void shield generators that had torn themselves apart under the strain of resisting the gigatons of rage unleashed upon them.

And again the great guns of the Iron Warriors fired.

* * *

Lion's Gate space port, surface approach, Highway Four,
one hour before assault

It was almost impossible to think, much less hear, under the
force of the bombardment. The ground shook constantly, while
dirt rattled down from the rafters of the gun pit. Trooper Alijah
Goldberg cupped a hand to his ear to listen to what Sergeant
Kazhni was shouting to the squad. He was standing at the vox
hard-line from the headquarters fortification and had been silently nodding for the last sixty seconds.

'It's our time!' The sergeant hung up the vox-receiver and
gestured towards the two support guns mounted in the firing
slits. 'There's no tractor, we'll pull the lascannons ourselves.'

'This is ridiculous!' Goldberg shook his head and pointed
to the intermittent flashing of shell bursts outside. He cupped
his hands so that he could be heard. 'They want us to give up
a nice, safe bunker and go out in this?'

'You can stay here and wait for half a million mutants, traitors and beastmen if you want,' the sergeant replied.

Goldberg considered his options and sighed and pushed
himself to his feet.

'Do we have to take them?' asked Trooper Kawar. 'They'll
slow us down and the space port has got plenty of big guns.'

'We take them,' Kazhni said decisively. 'I don't want to be
shot by my own guns tomorrow.'

The squad busied themselves making the lascannons ready
for moving, locking them onto the metal trails, securing the
energy cells and detaching the breaking pins so that the rubberised wheels touched the floor. They had started with three,
but a third of their small battery had been taken out by a rogue
piece of shrapnel through the firing slit three weeks earlier,
along with Trooper Sabbagh.

Goldberg and Kosta lifted the trails of the closest lascannon and hauled it towards the ramp out of the gun pit. Closer to the opening the bombardment was even more shocking. Blast waves washed hot wind over his face and he blinked against the fire and detonations.

'Where are we going?' he yelled to the sergeant.

Kazhni waved a hand directly through the doorway.

'Just head for the space port and keep going.' The sergeant looked around as the second lascannon trundled up behind him, Kawar and Adon at the lifting bar. He pulled out a las-pistol, though Goldberg had no idea what it would be used for. 'Everyone ready?'

They all nodded and set their backs to the task, a slow pull becoming a steady walk as they mounted the crest of the ramp. Goldberg glanced up to see the heavens dancing with blue and orange fire, coruscating over the screen of the void shields. Despite the energy fields, stray rockets and shells fell to the ground, cratering the broad ferrocrete strip of the highway and its muddied surrounds, tearing bloody holes into the tide of soldiery pouring back to the sanctuary of the Lion's Gate space port.

The heavy weapons squad picked up pace as they hit the flatter surface of the road, joining thousands more Imperial Army troopers. Alongside, halftracks and flatbed trucks bobbed and swayed as they picked their way over the shell-rucked earth, carrying the wounded and those that deemed themselves too important to walk. Above one mud-spattered transport Goldberg saw the huge banner of Colonel Maigraut, bright scarlet and edged with gold braiding. It seemed incongruously colourful among the mud and drab uniforms.

Everyone looked as tired as Goldberg felt. Some trudged with a half-vacant look he had come to know well, uniforms of grey and green splashed with blood – their own or others' – and dirty from the long siege. Faces smeared with grime, bandaged, arms in slings or showing other wounds, they became a river of humanity flowing together along Highway Four.

Goldberg barely flinched when a shell detonated a few hundred metres to his right, turning an armoured carrier into a flaming wreck that pitched down a slope away from the roadway. His back burned with effort as they broke into a slow jog, feeling the crowd around them moving faster.

Nobody was counting exactly, but everyone knew that the enemy would be at the defence line in minutes, if not there already. At any moment las-fire and bullets might start chasing them up the highway, far deadlier than the rage of the artillery being expended on the void shields above.

A deeper, longer rumble sent a tremor along the road. Some troopers cried out, living their waking nightmares; others called warnings and broke into a run, ignoring the shouts of sergeants and officers.

'That's not a bomb,' said Goldberg, looking back. The others stopped with him and turned.

In the distance, a couple of kilometres back, a wall of fire spread behind the line of retreat, following the arc of the last defence line. More detonations stretched the flames further and further, every trench, gun pit, bunker and foxhole turned into an inferno.

Adon laughed and patted the barrel of the lascannon.

'We'll be waiting for the survivors.'

Goldberg spat in the dirt.

'Burn, traitor scum!' he shouted. 'You can all burn!'

Lion's Gate space port, surface approach,
Highway Four, assault hour

Traitor corpses were piled so high they formed a bloody rampart in front of the Imperial Fists shield wall. The enemy continued to press on regardless, scrambling over their own dead, to be picked off by heavy weapons and marksmen as they crested the ridge of cadavers about twenty metres ahead of Rann, silhouetted against the fires that continued to rage along the former Imperial Army positions.

A line of yellow-armoured warriors stretched almost from one promontory of the outer defence to the next, half a kilometre wide, a solid bank of power armour and boarding shields as inflexible as a plascrete rampart.

The line was unmoving, a last obstacle to be overcome should any foe survive the storm of fire that roared over their heads from support squads and Dreadnoughts, as well as the bastions of the space port itself.

Here and there a mutant creature or turncoat army trooper staggered almost impossibly through the cannonade, only to meet the solid wall of Imperial Fists. The smallest partition allowed a bolter to fire with deadly accuracy, taking off the traitor's head or ripping apart their chest with a single bolt. The line would close again, as though nothing had happened.

Rann watched through the visor of his shield for any threat, as alert two hours into the battle as he had been the moment he had led the counter-attack from the armoured bastion. So far the Iron Warriors continued to direct their fire against the space port, mostly ignoring the force of Space Marines that had sallied forth. The shorter-ranged artillery that supported the attack had so far been kept at bay by the extended defence screen. Rann glanced up to see an aurora of gold and green above, rippling beneath the impacts of rockets and airbursts.

Should any enemy gunner feel like encroaching within the dome of the fields, a whole flank of lascannons and multi-launchers were poised to greet them with counter-battery fire. Similar precautions had been prepared for aerial attack. Even so, Rann expected to hear the telltale whistle of a descending

shell, ready to abort the armoured attack and withdraw his force
the instant the murderous barrage of the IV Legion started to
fall upon his warriors.

'*Commander, this is Verdas, on the left flank,*' his vox crackled,
the message from one of the Dreadnoughts assigned to support the First Assault Cadre. '*Lines of fire are getting very narrow.
The dead are blocking our sight beyond thirty metres. Suggest an
advance to establish a new base of fire.*'

The phrasing was so respectful, it made Rann smile, coming
as it did from a Terran veteran of the Chapter who had served
longer than he had.

'Understood, Verdas. I'll give you more room.' Rann switched
the vox-channel to contact Lion Primus. 'Status report on armoured attack.'

'*Preliminary bombardment underway. Gates opening now, commander. Estimate contact with the enemy in three minutes.*'

'Inform the lieutenant-commander that I am moving forward our battlezone by fifty metres.'

'*Affirmative, recalculating safe zone for air and artillery strikes,
commander.*'

A mutant ogryn shouldered its way through a narrowed part
of the carcass mound. It was clad in pieces of angular armour,
a bladed helm strapped across its misshapen head. In its hands
it carried a length of metal topped with a lump of ferrocrete: a
broken lumen pole from the highway partition. Bolts exploded
off its makeshift war-plate, and those that found flesh did not
hinder its advance in the least.

Five more seconds and it would be on the line. The risk of
even a single breach was unacceptable and Rann responded
instantly.

'By threes, target front, converging fire,' he told his Huscarls, finger slipping into the trigger guard of his bolter. 'Single
round. Fire!'

Every third warrior hinged his shield to the left, allowing the Space Marine on their right to fire through the gap. Fifty bolters, Rann's included, barked as one, engulfing the monstrous aberration in a storm of detonations. Shards of metal and hunks of flesh flew from the welter of bolts, leaving a ragged mess to flop to the floor, the lumen pole crashing down beside it. As swiftly as the line opened, it closed again, shields crashing back into place alongside each other.

Rann didn't believe in the concept of 'overkill'. Whatever it took to ensure the target went down he considered proportionate. Even fifty bolt-rounds for a solitary ogryn.

He checked the chronometer. Ninety seconds until the armour columns hit. That too might be considered more force than necessary, but he was determined to send a message to the Iron Warriors that Dorn's sons were not at this battle just to take punishment.

The IV Legion would be following on the heels of their expendable horde and the last reports had detected both Fulgrim's and Angron's warriors moving in support of this offensive. It was nearly time to withdraw to counter the approaching Traitor legionaries coming at the Lion's Gate from the north and south. Rann forced himself to wait a further thirty seconds, ensuring they drew in as many of the traitor scum as possible for the armoured attack.

'Cadre to attend,' he voxed his entire command, hearts beating faster in anticipation of action. 'Huscarls prepare for serration and advance. Echelon squads to give support fire.'

He took a deep breath, holding himself for just another two thunderous heartbeats.

'Three, two, one. Serrate!'

Starting with the warriors either side of Rann, every other Imperial Fist in the front line lifted his shield and advanced five strides. Two warriors from the rear ranks followed on the heel of each, one firing left, the other to the right, sweeping the ground before them with a welter of bolt-rounds. No sooner had the first serration planted their shields than the remaining front-line legionaries lifted theirs and advanced ten paces, each also joined by two support warriors. Rann advanced with them, measuring his stride, and then drove his shield down into the filth of mud and gore that soaked the ground.

Again and again the line advanced, pushing with fusillade and shields into the charging enemy, the Huscarls like a saw cutting into the heart of the attack while any foes that tried to circle behind them were mown down by fire from the flank squads and supporting Dreadnoughts. Twenty metres at a time, through ten times their own number, they pushed onwards.

'Echelon squads advance, hourglass attack. Huscarls, link for breach.'

Flank squads withdrew behind the shield walls to allow the enemy to flow to the left and right of the line. Rann judged the moment, waiting twenty seconds, then gave the command for the advance by spear point. Like a wedge through dirt the Imperial Fists forced their way onwards, using their shields as a bulldozer's blade, pivoting outwards to trap the flanking foes against the spur walls, treading over the slain as they did so. The support squads held the centre with rapid bolter volleys and heavy weapons, until the line hinged together again. Dead eyes stared at Rann from the ridge of bolt-cratered bodies and broken bones.

Rann felt a swell of pride at the discipline of the manoeuvre. It had been simple enough to sketch it on the tactical display, but the precision of his lieutenants and sergeants was a thing of beauty to him. He wished Lord Dorn had been present to appreciate it.

With the full line advanced as far as it could, the Huscarls clamped their bolters and took up their close-combat weapons – chainswords, for the most part, a few with axes like Rann. As they had with the serration manoeuvre, they alternated hewing at the dead and living alike, while their companions pushed forward with their shields, pressing into the mounds of tattered flesh. Rann heaved, angling his shield slightly so he could chop at limbs and bodies as though cutting through tree branches across a jungle track. Pieces of corpses were trodden into the muck as he moved forward.

Push, step, hack. Push, step, hack. Push, step, hack.

The dead were heaped deeper than he had realised, nearly fifteen metres of flesh to hew through before his warriors broke clear, forming up once more on the far side of the charnel mound. Still the enemy did not give in, rushing at the Imperial Fists with hoarse yells and shrieked invocations to their dark masters. Volleys of bolter fire cut down scores of traitors at a time. The Huscarls battered with shield and slashed with blade, dismembering and decapitating any enemy that reached the line.

Through the smog and gas, past the heaving mass of foes, Rann saw yellow plunging into the horde half a kilometre ahead from the left and right. As the armoured columns came around the defence spurs like ancient ships of the line rounding headlands into a harbour, flares of las-fire and muzzle flash lit the sickly cloud, the strobing of multi-lasers flashing like red navigation lights.

Caught between the tanks and the shield wall, the traitor horde finally slowed, unsure whether to press on against the infantry or turn to swamp this new threat with their numbers. The armoured columns linked up on the highway and turned inwards together, spaced so that they could shoot past each other, heading back towards the shield wall, weapons firing non-stop to both sides, turrets spewing lascannon blasts and autocannon rounds. The fusillade cut lines through the

unarmoured enemy, their dead falling in waves like the spreading ripples of stones tossed into a pool.

'Huscarls, gate formation!' Rann bellowed when the lead
vehicles were just a hundred metres away, approaching fast.
Like a double door opening, the shield line divided, Rann at
the right-hand end of one 'gate', Sergeant Ortor securing the
other. They marched outwards, so that the line shifted but still
faced directly towards the enemy. Rann could see mutants and
traitors crushed against lowered dozer blades or speared by
assault spikes as the column came on without slowing, punching through the horde like an armoured fist.

They roared past the line, guns falling silent at the last moment, tank after tank grinding through the gap between the
two gates of the shield wall. They split again, peeling to the
left and the right to form a support line behind the infantry
companies, taking up positions beside the Dreadnoughts.

There were barely a few hundred foes left to target, many
of them running one way or another in terrified confusion,
some huddling among their dead to hide from the Imperial
Fists' wrath.

'Permission to seek and destroy, commander?' came the call from
Lieutenant Leucid, leading the fast reserve.

'Granted. Ten minutes only, then withdraw to the port.'

'Understood.'

'First Assault, withdraw by squads. Armour to provide cover
fire and then withdraw by squadron.'

The last of the vehicles passed through the line, a Spartan
assault tank that slewed around to come to a stop a few metres
behind Rann, guns tracking back and forth over his head. The
lord seneschal strode up to it and rested his shield against
the side. Using the sponson for handholds, much to the audible amusement of the gunner within, he hauled himself up
to the roof. The tank commander was standing in one of the

forward hatches, the grips of a pintle-mounted combi-bolter in his hands. He slid the weapon aside and pulled himself up to join Rann, fist clashing on his chest in salute.

'Welcome aboard, commander. That's quite a view, isn't it?'

The whine of anti-grav engines and scream of propulsor jets filled the air as six squadrons of Land Speeders swept overhead, just a few metres above the defensive line. Rann grinned as he watched them pass, a fist raised to salute them to victory.

'Good hunting!' he called over the vox.

The chatter of heavy bolters and hiss of missiles faded with distance as Leucid's fast reserve chased after targets of opportunity. Rann looked back to the Lion's Gate space port and then out along the highway. Multi-spectral filters flickered across his view, picking out the body heat of the cooling dead. It was as though the ground were carpeted with undulations of fading orange and dark red, as far as his enhanced senses could penetrate the smog banks.

With the Emperor's Children and World Eaters inbound, it was just the beginning. However, he thought, three hundred thousand enemy dead in two hours was not a bad morning's work.

Arabindian massif, ninety-seven days before assault

As far as anyone could tell, the train was moving at a conservative ten kilometres an hour, which surprised nobody given its immense size and weight, even with two plasma reactors driving its motors. Its purpose was to convey large volumes of people, but it was certainly not doing so swiftly.

Routine had been the cornerstone of life on the factory line and it quickly became the bedrock of Zenobi's existence as a member of the defence corps. Each day was carefully scheduled

and regulated, assigned duties moving through the platoons of
the company as the roster and occasional punishment dictated.
They drilled with their weapons – power packs removed – and
turned spare mattresses into dummies for bayonet practice. The
food was pretty much indistinguishable from day to day but
given that they had all lived in the downhive spurs for their
whole lives, such culinary tedium was of no remark.

The integrity officers were a constant, low-key presence. As
warned, they started conducting interviews from the very first
day. Names were called and troopers were escorted up to the
top deck. They returned either within minutes or after more
than an hour – there never seemed to be any absence between
these two extremes. They were loath to discuss what they had
seen, but persistence pried a few details from hesitant lips –
though there was little enough to tell, as they had all been
taken up the central ladder and down a narrow passage to a
bare interview room. They had glimpsed the gunnery rondels
and other doorways, which they assumed were the quarters of
the crew, but little else.

A few of those that had been summoned had spied a little
of the train's surroundings through open turret doors and the
firing slots beyond. Even so, there was nothing in their reports
to excite, for they all returned with descriptions of endless
grey sky and, if they saw the ground, an undulating expanse
of dried seabed.

Of what occurred within the interview chamber even less
was said, other than that there was nothing to worry about
if everybody told the truth. Zenobi had expected to be inter-
viewed early, being part of the command squad of the platoon
and the company standard bearer, but days passed without her
name being called. She had started keeping note of who had
been in an effort to predict when it would be her turn, but
after three days she was forced to conclude that either she had

no idea what the criteria were for the order of selection, or the troopers were being taken upstairs at random.

About a week after leaving Djibou, the captain and lieutenants disappeared shortly after the midday inspection, ascending en masse to the mystery world of the upper deck. Like many others, Zenobi wanted to follow, to try to sneak a look at what delights and secrets were housed above. However, the dynastic enforcers were around in number, visible at the top of every ladder.

It was not just Zenobi's company. Officers from the lower decks went past until it was clear that the whole carriage had been emptied of every rank above sergeant.

'I hear there gonna be some big news, yeye,' said Seleen. 'Everyone gonna be told at the same time. No rumours, just one truth.'

'No rumours?' laughed Menber. 'Then what are you saying? That's a rumour!'

'You know what I mean, fala,' said Seleen with a shake of her head.

'It's got to be Horus,' said Kettai.

'Keep it down,' shushed Menber, glancing towards the closest ladder to the top deck.

'What?' The trooper shrugged. 'Saying his name a crime now, is it?'

'It could be,' growled Menber.

'Nah, I been in with the integrity officers,' said Seleen. 'Our platoon is good. We're all true to the cause and they know it. Volunteers, yeah? We were doing the recruiting.'

'I don't care if you've got a signed letter from the dynastic chiefs themselves,' said Menber. 'I don't think those integrity officers need much to take offence.'

'Even if the news is about Horus, it might not be bad news,' said Zenobi.

'It could be anything,' agreed Menber. 'But I don't think everyone would be so subdued if they'd just heard Horus was dead.'

'True, very true,' said Seleen. 'My bet? Horus' ships are here, in the system.'

'I'd not bet against that,' said Kettai. 'If the stories are right, that there was void war in the last few months, testing the defences, the main attack had to be coming...'

He trailed away as they heard footsteps above, lots of them. They watched the officers coming down again. Fewer than went up.

'Where are the others?' Zenobi asked, when the last of the officers from the lowest deck had gone – those that were now coming down wore the badges of Beta Company, quartered in the deck directly below. 'Twenty went up, only fifteen came down.'

'Special duties?' suggested Menber, though even he didn't look convinced by his answer.

Those officers that were returning were tight-lipped, glancing at each other with pointed expressions whose meaning was lost on the watching troopers.

'Do they look worried?' said Kettai.

'They don't look worried,' said Zenobi. 'Not scared for themselves, worried. More like guilty. I–'

She stopped as Captain Egwu descended the rungs of the ladder at the centre of the carriage. Okoye followed, as did most of the others from the company.

'Three?' whispered Seleen. 'Who's missing?'

'Gbadamosi, Adeoyo, Onobanjo,' said Kettai quickly. 'All lieutenants.'

'Adeoyo was a platoon commander!' said Zenobi. 'What does it mean?'

'We're about to find out,' said Menber, directing their attention back to the newly returned officers.

Captain Egwu stood in the middle of the deck while most of the lieutenants made their way back to their respective platoons and squads. Okoye stopped a short distance away, eyes flicking from one subordinate to the next, agitated.

'Eyes and ears on the captain,' he said quietly, turning on his heel to face their company commander.

Egwu stood with her hands behind her back, pacing a slow circle to look at the whole deck. She kept glancing at the ladder to the top deck and the hatchway to which it ascended. It was impossible not to be drawn to the object of her attention, so that Zenobi found herself staring at the iron rungs with growing unease, transmitted from the captain though Egwu said nothing and kept any telltale expression from her face.

A succession of sharp reports followed by loud thumps on the deck above caused Zenobi to flinch – not alone amongst the gathered troopers. Around her, troopers were looking up, murmurs of disquiet rippling around the room.

There was no mistaking the noise, even muffled by the deck: gunshots.

Zenobi's first reaction was to turn, wide-eyed, and look for Menber. He glanced at her, shook his head a fraction and returned his gaze to the ladder. Booted feet appeared a few seconds later, soon revealed to be those of an integrity enforcer. A score of them descended, followed by Jawaahir and her cohort of officers. Six assigned to the company remained and the rest descended with enforcer escort to the decks below.

The integrity high officer gave a nod to Egwu, who cleared her throat before addressing the company.

'The forces of Warmaster Horus have reached the Solar System. Naval and Legion fleets are engaged in void warfare against these flotillas at the gates near Pluto and Neptune.' The captain paced as she continued. 'We have no further intelligence regarding the ongoing status of that battle and we do not plan to provide a running commentary. We will try to keep you informed of any major strategic developments, but the assumption from this moment forward is that Horus will, sooner or later, reach orbit over Terra and commence invasion.'

Whether it was discipline or shock that held their tongues, the troopers of the defence corps greeted this news in stoic silence. Though Zenobi had agreed with Seleen's prediction and had been expecting something like this to be announced, to hear the actual words set her heart racing. For a great part of her life she had been prepared for the coming battles, and to think that they were weeks, possibly even days from combat was exciting and terrifying.

Mostly terrifying, the more she considered it, but it was tempered by the knot of duty she felt hard in her gut. She was no warrior-born. Not a legionary or even a proper soldier of the Imperial Army. But when the recruiters had come and spoken to her and the rest of her family they had all been in agreement. For Addaba, for future generations, they had to fight, and give their lives if needed.

She remembered not quite understanding what was happening, but feeling her mother's grip on her shoulder, reassuring and proud. And every day since then, whether on the line or with the company, she had turned her thoughts to the time when the promise would become reality.

She was brought back to the present by the raised voice of Jawaahir.

'The Warmaster's forces are closing upon Terra.' Her words were calm and assured, bearing no threatening undertone as they had on her first introduction. She might as easily have been telling them the latrine rota had been changed. 'Nothing but the utmost dedication to the task ahead will be tolerated. We have completed our inspection of your officers in light of this news. Those that fell short of our expectations have been executed.'

Again, there was little reaction from the Addaba troopers. The noises they had heard had left little doubt as to the missing officers' fate. There were, however, voices of consternation rising up from the lower decks. Zenobi realised that they could not have been forewarned and were hearing this news first from the mouths of their integrity officers.

'Such action may seem harsh, and in a time of peace you would be correct,' Jawaahir continued. She turned her gaze as she spoke, addressing them all, her eyes seeming to fall upon everyone present for a second each. Not long enough to register a reaction, but a feeling of constant scrutiny all the same. 'The decision was not made lightly, nor arbitrarily. Do not grieve for them. Had they been left in their positions, their lack of commitment would have eroded your own, and jeopardised the integrity and courage of this fighting force.

'Just as we will not allow any of you to waver from the course that must be followed, so we hold those that lead you to the highest standards. Hesitation in the face of the enemy will cost lives. Doubts that we serve a cause greater than ourselves will undermine discipline.'

Her expression softened, becoming almost matriarchal as she pivoted slowly once more.

'We do not wish to terrify you into obedience. It is natural that you look upon the decisions you have made and wonder if you have done the right thing. Such lapses are understandable, but they have no place in battle. You must act without thought, without question, without regret. To do otherwise is to risk the victory towards which we all strive, for which we should all be prepared to give our lives.'

Silence followed, broken only by the background clatter of wheels on rails and the hum of energy cables. Zenobi felt herself swaying, thinking it the motion of the carriage at first, but increasingly so as a sense of unreality descended on her. She was reminded of the time she had been told of the Warmaster and what had occurred during the Great Crusade, of being subjected to ideas so much larger than she was that it was almost overwhelming to think about them.

A hand on her elbow steadied her.

'Breathe, cousin,' Menber told her with a concerned look. 'Breathe…'

'I will be working with the integrity officers to select suitable replacements for those…' Egwu paused, glanced at Jawaahir and then continued. 'Gaps in the command structure will be filled from the ranks. Just like on the factory line. That is all.'

Zenobi sagged, realising that she had been holding herself as taut as a wire for several minutes. The babble that erupted across the deck was immediate, divided between the two topics of conversation: Horus' imminent arrival and the executions.

Before she could say anything, Zenobi felt a tap on her shoulder and turned to find Sergeant Alekzanda looking at her. He took a step back and tilted his head towards the integrity officers. Zenobi looked past him, her gaze meeting the stare of Jawaahir.

'Interview time, Zenobi,' said Alekzanda. 'You're up next.'

EIGHT

Charge of the berzerker
Loyalty scrutinised
The telaethesic ward

Lion's Gate space port, surface approach,
Highway Two, assault hour

The barrage of the Iron Warriors lit the peak of the Lion's Gate like a candle. Red flames crawled across its hab-units and docks, long licks of scarlet that danced with a strange life. In the south-east, on the far side of the artificial mountain, purple flames silhouetted high shipyards and kilometre-long boarding quays – the twin beacon to Fulgrim and his Emperor's Children.

'That's… hnnh. That's the signal!' barked Khârn, slamming his fist onto the roof of the Land Raider to alert the driver. All around him others were responding in similar kind, raising war shouts and cries to Khorne that rolled down the highway along with the sudden growl of engines coming to life.

It had taken all of Khârn's willpower to linger with his brothers, fighting back the urge to charge headlong at the enemy. To do so would have meant throwing themselves into the teeth of the defence without any support from Perturabo's Legion.

He lifted *Gorechild* in his other hand as the engines of five hundred transports and tanks grew to a roar, their tracks snarling over pitted ferrocrete – Rhinos, Land Raiders and Spartan transports flanked by an echelon of Predators and Vindicators. This support element was much diminished, for many of Khârn's brothers were incapable of controlling themselves sufficiently to steer or guide a heavy gun. Slaves were chained into their positions, or servitors installed to take the place of the truly living. Freed from other concerns, the legionaries would be able to storm forth and slaughter without distraction once they reached their target.

Khârn was thrown back in the cupola as the driver rammed the assault transport forward, the Land Raider heeling and swaying as it picked up speed, thundering across ground cratered by thousands of shell bursts. Around him others vied to take the lead, their shouted urging crackling across the vox, mixed with boasts of the souls they would send to Khorne's realm that day.

The roar and smoke of the assault column surrounded Khârn, a battle-din that started his hearts thumping their own percussion, the implant in his skull adding an insistent, rapid pulse to the symphony.

But it was inside that the music swelled. He felt the Blood God reaching into him, lighting a fire in his gut to ignite a rage that no mortal shell could contain. He revved *Gorechild*, delighting in the glitter of the signal flame on the whirr of the mica-dragon teeth that served as its blade. He let out a roar that became a howl, and then from deep within he gave voice to the demands of Khorne, slamming his fist upon the armour plate in time with his chant.

'Kill! Maim! Burn!'

* * *

Arabindian massif,
ninety-seven days before assault

The thrill of finally being allowed to tread upon the hallowed
upper deck momentarily quelled the sickness roiling through
Zenobi's gut. She held her breath as her eyeline cleared the
hatch and she was granted her first proper look at the domain of the officers.

It was disappointing. Bare metal bulkheads created a small,
square space directly around the ladder. A bench was bolted to
the wall, and though it was currently unoccupied the scuffing in
front of it was evidence of the sentries that had been using it.
Beside it a few steps led up to an armoured hatch with a small
round window, though all she could see beyond was a sky
smeared with dark clouds underlit by the early morning sun.

To the left and right stretched narrow corridors lined with
more doors, leading to another ladder landing about ten metres
away, and so on and on for the length of the carriage.

She turned about, away from the bench, to find another corridor, broader than the others, that ran across the width of the
train. There were ladder rungs cut into the wall here, leading
up to roof entrances, armoured like the other gun turrets. A
few metres away a dynastic enforcer waited, maul held across
the front of her thighs in both hands, feet shoulder-width apart
in regulation pose.

'This way,' she told Zenobi, stepping to one side and pointing
to an open door a few metres further along the passageway.

The sound of footsteps on the rungs behind her prompted
Zenobi to move, aware that Jawaahir was following. She hurried past the enforcer and into the waiting chamber. Inside was
more metal, and at first she took it to be a cell. There were
holes in the walls where shelf brackets had been bolted, revealing the chamber's original purpose as a storeroom. In place of

whatever crates and sacks it had contained it now played host to a small metal table and two chairs set opposite each other.

There was a triangular banner hanging on the wall – real cloth from a pole of real wood. The design incorporated the six symbols of the dynastic chiefs, gold against a red background, the whole trimmed with coiled purple thread.

'One of the old standards, from Unification.' Zenobi turned to find Jawaahir at the doorway. The integrity high officer glanced at the chair with its back to them and Zenobi moved next to it immediately. 'A reminder to us that Hive Addaba has a history with the Emperor that stretches back generations.'

Zenobi opened her mouth to reply but was silenced by a raised hand. Jawaahir stepped into the interview cell and closed the door behind her. She placed a hand on Zenobi's shoulder as she walked past, firmly pushing her into the metal chair, before taking the seat opposite. She knitted her fingers together on the table and Zenobi noticed the bright scarlet of her fingernails – implants she guessed, not painted. Like the tattoos, they were permanent modifications to declare her position and allegiance.

'You are Zenobi Adedeji, line worker and now trooper. Captain Egwu vouches for you and has even entrusted the company banner to your care. That is quite remarkable, a serious responsibility for a seventeen-year-old.'

Zenobi kept her nerve, and her silence. There had been no question asked and it seemed unwise to volunteer information.

'I think she is right.' Jawaahir leaned back and her hands moved to her lap. 'I'm sure you know all about the history of the Adedeji.'

'I share the name of a ruby dynasty. Their blood is in me even if my family have fallen low in status in recent decades.'

'Former ruby dynasty. Shamed by the Emperor, for resisting Unification.'

Zenobi fought the temptation to defend the honour of her

ancestors. Many a squabble, and a few outright brawls, had proven that whatever the facts, the accepted story of the Adedeji was that they had betrayed the Emperor.

'The Adedeji are no longer among the Gifted Six. I'm a line worker, I don't know much about the top-hive politics or what happened to my distant relatives.'

'And you are loyal to Addaba.'

Zenobi nodded. There seemed nothing further to add to the assertion. A ghost of a smile passed across Jawaahir's lips.

'Do I frighten you?'

The truth, Zenobi remembered. Everyone that had come out of the interviews had a single message to pass on: just tell the truth.

'I find you and your officers intimidating,' she said. 'I know that my loyalty to the cause is as strong as the foundations of Addaba. Even so, I worry that you might not see that.'

Jawaahir pursed her lips, eyes never straying from Zenobi's. The trooper met her stare for as long as she could, out of pride more than defiance, but eventually her gaze dropped to her hands. She was gripping the edge of the table tight and hadn't realised it.

'You've not said a single word to convince me of your dedication,' said Jawaahir. 'You're very calm.'

This time Zenobi could not hold back the urge to speak.

'I haven't anything to fear, if what you say is true. I am loyal. I swore the oaths. Oversee– Captain Egwu herself recruited me, and my family. If I didn't trust you, I'd still trust her. And since she came back down after… Since she is still commander of the company, I guess that you must trust her too.'

'Do you find that logic reassuring?' Still Jawaahir's eyes bored into Zenobi. She wasn't sure if the integrity high officer had even blinked. 'Is that how you see the world, a place of reasons and rules?'

'I lived on the factory line, bana-madam,' Zenobi said. 'Every-thing works a certain way or it doesn't work at all. People die if it goes wrong.'

Jawaahir smiled again, though now the expression was dry, devoid of any humour.

'I meant no offence,' Zenobi added quickly.

'People die in battle too, if people do not follow the system. You are a follower, aren't you, Trooper Adedeji?'

'I will obey the orders of my officers, bana-madam,' Zenobi assured her interrogator. 'I would never bring disgrace to the name of Adedeji.'

'No, I'm sure you wouldn't. That you have retained the name, when most of your distant relations threw it away like an old jerkin, tells me it means a lot to you.'

Zenobi had to clamp her teeth shut to stop the words that wanted to burst from her. For more than a week she had hard-ened herself to the idea of being shouted at, accused, insulted and threatened but she hadn't expected this nagging, bait-ing line of conversation. It was like her grandmother's silent stare when they'd been assembled as youngsters to uncover the perpetrators of some infantile misdemeanour. The guilty were always the first to spring to their own defence. It wasn't until she was fourteen that Zenobi had realised this. Unfor-tunately, too late to make use of it, her grandmother having been passed to the endforges two years earlier.

'What are you thinking about?' Jawaahir sat forward again, clasped hands back on the tabletop. 'Answer me now!'

'Abay Su-su,' Zenobi replied without thought. She flushed, embarrassed at the childish nickname. 'My father's mother. She was the law keeper in the family when I was little.'

'I am older than your grandmother was, Zenobi. Can you believe that?'

'No, bana-madam. You... Your skin, your hair... Maybe,

for top-hivers. No work smog in your lungs, no forge heat on your skin.' Zenobi frowned, her eyes flicking to the tattoos and fingernails. 'Maybe the dynastic chiefs give you a pick-me-up, right? I heard that top-hivers can live seventy, eighty years or more.'

'That is right, and also wrong. I am a little over ninety years old. I will live a few more years but I cannot have another treatment. This journey, this battle that we travel to, will be my last effort for the dynastic chiefs. No endfires for me, I expect. Nor you, Zenobi. How does that make you feel, to know that your body will likely end up on a pile, rotting under the sun in some place you have never heard of?'

'I'll be dead, I'll not care either way. What matters is how I die.'

'And how will that be?'

'Fighting for freedom and the lives of my companions, bana-madam.' Zenobi stood up, feeling a wave of assertion pushing her to her feet. Her knees wobbled slightly but she held her place, and a look with the integrity high officer. 'If my words don't convince you, then I hope I live long enough that my actions do. If you doubt me, then pull your gun and shoot me like those officers.'

'Really?' Jawaahir stood and flipped the top of her holster. She slid out a long-barrelled autopistol, the crest of the Ellada dynasty engraved into a plate on its side. The muzzle swung towards Zenobi, the small black hole swallowing all of her attention. 'Is this how you would die for Addaba?'

Zenobi tried to speak, cowed by the muzzle, regretting her rashness and the hint of pride that had led her to dare the anger of this woman. It had been a foolish, selfish act. Insolent.

She closed her eyes and bowed her head, accepting her punishment.

'If I have done wrong, chastise me, bana-madam. But ask

yourself a question first.' Zenobi straightened and looked the officer in the eye again. 'Would you rather not have one more bullet for your real enemies?'

Lion's Gate space port, surface approach,
Highway Two, assault hour

Ahead of the assault, thousands of slave-beasts and the serfs of the Iron Warriors continued to throw themselves at the defensive line that had been drawn across the highway leading into the south-eastern gate of the space port. Gun towers and pill boxes spewed fire into the numberless mass, prevented from targeting the incoming transports by blocked lines of fire and the fear of being overrun by the much closer foe. Gun captains further up the Lion's Gate port's flanks had no such concerns and it was not long before shells began to fall among the blur of red transports carving furrows through the ash, dust and smoke that blanketed the Katabatic Plains.

The tanks leading the charge opened fire, their accuracy severely diminished by the rate of advance and inexperience of their crews. Even so, a welter of siege cannon shells, las-blasts and plasma punched through the swirl of smog and debris, flaring against the local power fields and smashing into ferrocrete walls.

The support echelon slewed aside, guns still firing, allowing the transports to race past, their own weapons flaring and roaring.

'Into the heart of battle!' snarled Khârn. 'Drive your blades down their throats!'

The road was littered with the corpses of earlier attacks, crushed beneath the tracks of the Land Raider, sending splashes of blood up its blue-and-white flanks. Khârn's enhanced sense of smell was awash with the scents of death and battle. His eyes rolled back in his head as he took a deep draught, intoxicated by the thought of imminent bloodshed.

The Land Raider slowed and Khârn forced himself to focus. Ahead, a throng of turncoat soldiers and Legion slaves pressed along the highway, blocking the way.

'Drive on,' he yelled down through the hatch. 'Go through!'

The driver laughed and accelerated again, bringing the Land Raider back up to full combat speed. Some of those unfortunates at the back of the crowd heard the approach of engines above the din of the barrage and turned in time to flee. Others did not and were slammed aside, or crushed under the tracks, or pinned upon the razor-sharp blades that had been affixed to the front of the tank.

Their screams bypassed Khârn's ears and flared through his brain like bolts of electricity, causing him to howl again. Drool fell from teeth bared inside his helm as animal hunting urges overwhelmed any higher human sense.

Like a blade parting flesh, the assault column carved through the press of lesser warriors, coating the highway with a slick of pulverised organs and bone. The spray from the tracks coated the following vehicles in gore. The warriors within wrestled with each other to push themselves to the open hatches so that they might be anointed in blood for their new god, armour already much crimson-stained getting fresh slicks of life fluid.

Several vehicles slewed aside, falling by the wayside as their running gear became clogged with viscera. Their passengers poured out of the assault ramps and through roof hatches, leaping down onto the road to continue the assault on foot.

As though a curtain peeled back, the throng of serfs and soldiers parted and Khârn heard a great rumbling over and above that of the flying column and the big guns of the Iron Warriors. Detonations blossomed amongst the lead wave, incendiary shells and airbursts scything down hundreds of mortal troopers and mutants pressed into the breach. Beyond them loomed towering armoured vehicles clad in the ochre yellow of Dorn's Legion. Mighty Leviathans and Capitol Imperialis, three of each, emerged from the vast gateway, guns laying down a carpet of fire that ripped whole companies to bloody shreds in seconds. With them came other super-heavy vehicles – Baneblades, Shadowswords and other variants in colours of the Imperial Army, and VII Legion Malcador heavy tanks with plasma cannons and rapid-firing laser blasters.

The first wave slowed, baulked by this sudden wall of armoured might and the beams of deadly energy that lanced from their batteries. Some of the rearmost horde regiments turned to flee the counter-attack, only to find themselves in the path of the onrushing chosen of Khorne. Guns roared retribution for their cowardice, cutting them down even as they fell beneath the armoured vehicles.

Even through the frothing madness of his Butcher's Nails and the spirit of Khorne rushing through his body, Khârn vaguely recognised the danger. He tried to order the column to slow, so that guns might be brought to bear. The words would not come. He thought to signal the Iron Warriors to redirect their strikes or bring in attack runs from gunships that circled overhead, but all he could manage was an animal panting.

So it was that instead of fear he embraced the nature of his master and admitted in that moment what he had known in his soul for many years. He would die in battle, broken and bloodied, but his spirit not quenched. Now he gave his death to a cause far worthier than the Emperor, for his blood would spill for the God of Battle and one day his skull would be raised up and placed in honour on the throne of Khorne.

But it would not be this day.

The beacon-barrage had called not only to the legionaries

of the World Eaters. Khârn felt a shimmer of anticipation run through him and looked up as he heard an unearthly bellow cutting through the tumult of war. Against the lightning-wreathed clouds that crowded above the Palace, a silhouette of a great winged beast appeared. It dived down, trailing godfire and shadow, the gleam of its magic blade like a thunderbolt in the darkness.

Angron, daemon primarch of the World Eaters, did not slow to land, but speared into the nearest of the Capitol Imperialis. Shields flared and failed, engulfing the titanic engine in brief layers of gold and purple. The tip of the sword sheared through armour like that of a castle's bastion, and a shower of molten plasteel and shards of ceramite fountained from the gaping wound. Though the vehicle was the size of a hab-block Angron's impact was enough to rock it on its huge tracks. With a sound of tortured metal it fell sideways as the primarch beat his wings and howled his anger.

Khârn's last sight of his lord was amid sparks and flames, as Angron leapt into the exposed innards of the fallen war machine. He grinned as he imagined the carnage being wrought within, the slaughter of a company of soldiers in tight confines, the walls and floor and ceiling decorated with their blood and body parts, their skulls offered up in praise of the Blood God.

The remains of the super-heavy command vehicle exploded, engulfed by a plasma fireball two hundred metres across, overloading the shields of its neighbour and incinerating several smaller tanks in the gap between the behemoths.

Khârn recovered his sight from the blinding flash to see Angron striding from the molten ruin, pieces of burning wreckage jutting from his armour and unnatural flesh, trailing black flames.

A Leviathan turned its main cannon upon the primarch, belching forth a shell that could break open Battle Titans.

Angron cleaved the air with his curse-edged blade, cutting the shell in flight so that its detonation rolled harmlessly around him.

The mobile command bastion blazed away with full batteries, slamming shell after shell and laser volleys into the unfeeling form of Angron. There was nothing that could stop him: a blood miasma surrounded the primarch, warding away attacks like a power field, drawing energy from the continuing slaughter.

The counter-attack faltered in the face of the unstoppable beast, and the super-heavy tanks withdrew, leaving a Capitol Imperialis as rear-guard. Platoons of soldiers alighted from its ramps, not to challenge the primarch but to flee for the safety of the space port. Angron bellowed after them, thwarted in his pursuit by a fresh cannonade from a slab-sided Leviathan.

The column had almost drawn level with their lord, their sponson weapons and pintle mounts chasing the fleeing troopers into the shadow of the Lion's Gate space port. Khârn dragged himself from the cupola and leapt to the ground as the Land Raider slid to a halt, surrounded by a surge of power-armoured berzerkers chanting for blood and calling upon Khorne for battle-favours.

The primarch hacked apart the Imperial command vehicle as Khârn and the assault column neared. Angron broke open the ammunition stores and the shells within detonated, surrounding his immortal form like celebration fireworks. Blade aloft, his sons a red tide around him, the daemon primarch led the advance. Ahead, the great gates started to close.

Angron snarled and leapt to the wing, soaring past the ruin of the Capitol Imperialis, becoming a scarlet blur as he gained speed.

He was perhaps three hundred metres from the still-open gate when a flare of silver light pulsed around him, hurling him from the sky. The primarch crashed, breaking stone, furled wings trailing silvery sparks, eyes aflame with pale light. Roaring defiance, he came to his feet and launched himself again at the fortifications but was repulsed a second time, the silver energy coiling about his limbs like chains as he tumbled to the ground once more.

On foot he approached, sword and fist pounding at the insubstantial barrier, but every blow was reflected back at him, so that he recoiled from his own fury, armour rent in a dozen places as though his mystic blade had carved it open.

Khârn's vigour left him as he witnessed the impotency of his lord, flailing mindlessly at the psychic barrier that kept his daemon form at bay. The defence guns that had fallen silent during the counter-attack came to destructive voice again. Transports exploded under the renewed barrage and legionaries died by the hundred, forced to take shelter in the defences they had overrun, while still-laden transports drew back, seeking sanctuary.

Angron lifted away, thwarted by the shield, and soared north. Lightning crackled from his wingtips as he tested the extent of the barrier. He disappeared with altitude, and then returned, before winging southwards seeking easier prey.

Clarity burned through Khârn's battle rage. His World Eaters would be trapped against the closed gate, super-heavy tanks ready to strike from within, guns pounding them from above. Without their Khorne-blessed primarch the Legion would break uselessly upon the space port's walls.

To die in close battle, eye to eye with the foe was one fate, but he would not let Khorne's favoured be blasted apart from afar, raging at an enemy out of reach.

Reluctantly, sickened by the notion as his Butcher's Nails threaded chastising agony through his brain, Khârn voxed the order to withdraw.

* * *

Lion's Gate space port, surface approach,
Highway Three, assault hour

Heaving up a bucket of water, Aggerson doused the breech of
the gun again, steam filling the ferrocrete bunker as it hissed
from the overheated cannon.

'Give it two minutes,' said Olexa, the gun captain. She pulled
a lho-stick from her pocket and lit it. Aggerson frowned and
looked at the three shells lined up next to the ammunition
elevator from the magazine below. Olexa shrugged. 'What?
There's a full-scale attack. Nobody's doing gun inspections…'

Aggerson didn't bother arguing, but exchanged a glance with
Maxxis, the third and final member of their gun crew. He came
to an unspoken agreement with her and they both moved to
the slit in the wall that served as their only window.

Battery 65-B was situated overlooking Highway Three, which
ran north from the Lion's Gate space port. The other four guns
of the battery still fired, sending their shells down into the
swathe of purple-armoured figures a kilometre below. Around
them larger guns thundered their deadly payloads even further along the road, targeting the command vehicles and
super-heavies that had moved up in support of the Emper-
or's Children attack. Smaller anti-personnel weapons rattled
and barked from emplacements in the lower levels, though
much was wreathed in smoke and choked with rubble from
the enemy's attacks.

Distance gave the scene an unreal quality. Target coordinates
would come through on the command feed and they fired at
that spot, never really seeing what they were aiming at. Even
with the naked eye the procession of Traitor Space Marines
and swarms of lesser warriors seemed like something from a
vid-projection.

Aggerson saw a swathe of purples and gold, swirled about

with multicoloured fog that reminded him more of his mother's incense burners than the smog of battle. Pennants and banners flew from vehicles and company standards, their aquilas and honours replaced with stylised runes that he had never seen before, but which made him feel queasy to look at all the same. Vehicles were festooned with new decoration, like baroque railing spikes with body parts impaled upon them.

And among the din of engines and crash of weapons he thought he heard music: disharmonies of strident orchestral works alongside nerve-shredding electronic screeches and inhuman wailing.

'They're pulling back!' gasped Maxxis, pointing out of the slit.

Aggerson realised it was true. Under cover of a renewed bombardment, squads of the Emperor's Children were moving away from the space port, while squads of power-armoured warriors pulled back from the breaches in the lowest batteries. They filed onto their transports, kaleidoscopic smoke belching from engines as the troop carriers picked up speed, heading northwards. Others followed on foot covered by fire from squads positioned along the sides of the highway.

'And don't come back!' Maxxis laughed, shaking a fist.

Aggerson didn't share her good humour. Something was off.

'Cap, pass me the magnox,' he said, stepping back from the slit to hold a hand out to Olexa.

'They're mine,' she said.

'Please.'

'Fine.' Olexa tossed him the spotter's magnox, which he only just caught.

Turning back to the slit he leaned out as far as he dared, magnox raised to his eyes. Autofocus lenses clicked until he sighted on the ground below. He swept towards the main highway and saw hundreds of purple-armoured Space Marines marching back to the road. They were not alone. Each carried or dragged two or three prisoners, some unconscious, others flailing futilely at their superhuman captors. Rhinos, Land Raiders and other tanks crawled out of range of the guns, captives piled on their roofs and strapped to their flanks like bundles of baggage. Most wore Imperial Army uniforms, seized from the lower batteries and the regiments that had been defending the highway approaches.

'They're taking people,' he whispered. Scanning along the road, he saw hundreds, maybe thousands being hauled back to the waiting transports. He pulled himself back in and looked at his companions, mouth dry with fear. 'Why are they taking people?'

NINE

A war song
Fresh assault
Flawed iron

Karachee Flats, seventy days before assault

'Two minutes!' the call went around, stilling all sound and motion as it moved from one part of the carriage to the next, hopping from squad to platoon to the whole company like an auditory epidemic.

Two minutes.

Two minutes was the call on the line to prepare for the shift change. Two minutes to set the safeties on the machinery. Two minutes to rack the tools. Two minutes to clear the pipes, secure the cables, stow the lock-bolts and perform the hundreds of other small but essential duties that led to a smooth and safe handover.

Zenobi looked around, chest swelling with suppressed emotion as she saw the company coming to a halt as one. Across the divide she caught the eye of Sweetana, waiting with a few others by the stairwell.

'I been working the line, working the line, working it all day,' Zenobi began, her voice wavering a little.

'Just like my father before,' Sweetana sang back in reply, joined by more voices from the company.

'I been working the line, working the line, working it all night,' Zenobi continued, growing in confidence. She could see Lieutenant Okoye hiding a smile behind his hand, other officers showing a mixture of amusement, pride or contempt. The enforcers stopped their prowling as the chorus grew, swelling to fill the carriage with voices.

An even louder, defiant burst of song erupted from the deck below, pulsing through the stairwells like a physical thing.

'All my days, working in the dark, all my days, carrying my own light!'

Zenobi remembered that Second Company came from the lowest part of the cradlespur, mostly hivecore miners that clawed raw materials back from the city's ancient substrate.

'I been working the line, working the line, working all shift!' she cried, her voice almost cracking with effort as she competed with the song from below, the two forming a harmony. The muted words of a third from the lowest deck drifted in and out of rhythm. All three songs rose and fell in competition.

Zenobi almost choked, her throat tightening with emotion, stalling her words. It didn't matter, the carriage was almost rocking from the combined voices of all three decks, which segued together into the unofficial anthem of Addaba: *Onwards, Lords and Ladies of Industry.*

She heard the first faltering notes disturbing the song a few moments before movement drew her eyes to the ladders from the upper deck. The singing fractured as one after another the troopers caught sight of Integrity High Officer Jawaahir. Disconcerted by the disharmony creeping in from the upper deck, perhaps wondering what was amiss, the companies below stuttered and quietened in the following minute.

Other integrity officers filed past their leader, heading to the lower decks, silencing the last voices raised in song.

'You need not silence yourselves on my account,' said Jawaahir, her voice raised to carry across the hall-sized compartment. 'But perhaps it is time to stop singing about the past. You are not on the line any longer. Now perhaps turn hearts and tongues to the future. A new song for Addaba. A war song.'

This declaration was met with speculative muttering, soon silenced by whispered threats from the lieutenants and sergeants.

'It is time,' the chief of the integrity officers declared, rubbing her hands together with relish. Quite what she was so animated about, Zenobi didn't know. As the order was passed round to prepare for disembarkation, she remembered a piece of advice from Menber and tried not to think about it too much.

Katabatic Plains, four hours since assault

Forrix found himself viewing the continuing attack from the roof of a burnt-out way station, about seven kilometres from the Lion's Gate space port. The highway that ran alongside had been churned to ferrocrete grit by the passage of so many tanks and mobile fortresses.

The IV Legion had created circumvallation works in a twenty-kilometre arc around their objective, formed of armoured vehicles and self-creating fortifications based on ancient Standard Template Construct systems. The Khan had led his White Scars against the engines of the Pneumachina and Mortarion's warped legionaries and caused great damage and delays, and the surprise sally by the Imperial Fists against the opening assault had caused Kroeger to reflect a little on his impatience. If Dorn or any of his allies thought to launch another counter-attack against Perturabo's Legion they would find far stiffer opposition.

Thoughts of what had happened to the Death Guard gave Forrix pause. There had been no formal report about their delayed arrival, but it was clear their transit through the warp had met with complications. Those he had once known as Dusk Raiders were no more. Their primarch had become an embodiment of nightmare, like Angron and Fulgrim, and their bodies had been changed by exposure to something beyond Forrix's knowledge. He was not naive about the forces to which the Warmaster had pledged himself, but he was no expert either. He had seen daemon-altered Word Bearers and mutated sorcerers, as well as the results of the Pneumachina's experiments with previously forbidden warp tech. Watching the sea of once-human and pseudo-human creatures hurling itself at the outer defences left a sour taste in his mouth. The thought that the Iron Warriors might one day succumb to that kind of degradation made him feel sick.

He turned to his companion, Soltarn Vull Bronn, who was known as the Stonewrought. Overall commander of the barrage, he was observing the effectiveness of his cannons and rockets. A cluster of Cataphractii Terminators loitered behind him, their presence more a badge of the Stonewrought's rank than a military precaution.

'I'm glad at least one true Iron Warrior stands alongside me still,' said Forrix.

'What do you mean?' The Stonewrought did not turn his head, gaze fixed upon the conflagration engulfing the Lion's Gate space port.

'I'd have you in the Trident, you know? You have a talent for destruction.'

'I am content with my allotted role,' Soltarn Vull Bronn replied. 'The Trident is not missing a member.'

'It would be an outrageous stretch of fortune if all three of us survived this battle, you know that. I would rather have someone steadier at my shoulder.'

Now the Stonewrought turned, his burnished helm catching the light of a thousand fires, sparkling as volcano cannons spat back their fury in counter-battery fire against his siege machines.

'You assume that you will survive while the others might fall. That borders on a threat.'

'None was intended, to you or them.' Forrix stepped closer, dropping his voice. 'However, the loss of one or both of my fellow triarchs would cause me no grief. Personally, and as a commander of the Fourth, I have grave reservations.'

'Both have the favour of Perturabo.' The Stonewrought paused as hundreds of rockets flared overhead, lighting the sky as if it were a celebration day. His head turned as he followed their progress, and gave a nod of satisfaction as they dipped and fell onto the lower levels of the port, not far from the foremost lines of attacking infantry. He returned his attention to Forrix. 'To speak against them is to speak against the primarch.'

'Favour is fleeting, you know that as well as I do. Just ask Berossus. Kroeger is fast becoming unstable. I saw him with the World Eaters and even in a span of hours he has become even more irrational, as though tainted by their bloodthirst.'

'It is no secret that you desired Toramino to replace Harkon, but Kroeger was raised in his place. Your disdain for Falk I find more surprising. His recommendation spilled easily from your lips when Harkon was dishonoured, but now you speak against him.'

'That was the Barban Falk we knew.' Forrix stepped beside the Stonewrought and gripped the remains of the wall that edged the flat rooftop. Ferrocrete crumbled beneath his fingers, weakened by anti-fortification viruses that had been released into the air by the Pneumachina. 'The thing that insists on being called the Warsmith is not the same Barban Falk.'

'And you have a common complaint against both of your companions?'

'Their loyalty is questionable,' said Forrix. 'I sense that Kroeger has set foot on the road that leads him to the same mania as our allies in the World Eaters – the whisper of a bloody power now speaks in his ear. As for the allegiance of the Warsmith, I do not believe it is for mortal concerns any longer.

'This malaise, this power that grips our once-proud cousins and strips away all honour and humanity... It comes from the Warmaster himself, and hungers for us all.'

'We have already turned traitor on the Emperor, would you have us turn once more, on the Warmaster? Or even against our genefather?'

'No!' The thought that such an accusation might reach the ears of Perturabo made Forrix shudder. The primarch's hands were bloodied already by subordinates that had wronged him, for crimes both real and imaginary, and Forrix had no desire to dare such wrath. 'That is not what I said. But Horus is not our genefather, and he is using us just as the others have used the Fourth since we left Terra.'

'I wish for no part in your conspiracies, Forrix.' The Stonewrought gestured towards the Lion's Gate space port. 'I have a task at hand and it is all the occupation I need. Since the battle with the eldar... Since we saw what became of Fulgrim and his sons... I prefer to focus on immediate, physical problems these days. I have no desire to venture into the less tangible realm, and that is what your plotting would entail.'

'I cannot force you to share my doubts, but I would give further warning. These powers at play are courted by some of our brothers, knowingly or not. They desire us, and ignoring them will not rid us of their threat. When we are done with the Emperor's lackeys there will be reckonings within the Legion.'

'I hear nothing,' said the Stonewrought, and turned away.

TEN

The Lord of Iron baulked
A sorcerer's aid
Piercing the Starspear

The Vengeful Spirit, *Terran near orbit,*
ten hours since assault

Abaddon despised Horus' court chamber aboard the *Vengeful Spirit*. Each time he returned it seemed more a mockery of what it had once been, what it had once meant to him. His master spent ever more time behind the portal of the empyrean, supposedly to do psychic battle with the Emperor Himself, though Abaddon wondered if there might be darker reasons why the Warmaster retreated so regularly to his unreal sanctuary.

Word had reached the *Vengeful Spirit* of the failure of Angron and Fulgrim to enter the Lion's Gate space port. Like the Palace proper it was under the Emperor's protection. No being of daemonic origin could cross the threshold. Was there a similar price for Horus to pay when he was not awash in the energies of the empyrean?

The leader of the Mournival was surprised to find himself the only member of that honoured group present, and dismayed to see that the Crimson Apostle shadowed him as usual. Zardu Layak and his silent blade slaves slipped through the shadows around the periphery, perhaps choosing to observe rather than intervene for a change. The Word Bearers sorcerer's mask-eyes shone, six flashes of yellow in the gloom.

Horus was present, his bald head sheened with thick sweat, his eyes sunken, ringed with darkness as one suffering heavy fatigue. Abaddon thought it impossible for a primarch to show such weariness, much less his master, but Layak had told him of how the Ruinous Powers' presence in his mortal form taxed the Warmaster's strength to its limits.

Horus' expression was grim as he raised his gaze to meet the stare of Abaddon.

'The war progresses too slowly, Ezekyle,' the Warmaster pronounced. There was no accusation, simply a statement of fact. Horus gritted his teeth and sucked in a breath, odd lights dancing across his eyes for a few seconds. He blinked them away and seemed restored, his face not so lined as moments before, his shoulders straighter.

'I did not think Perturabo would fail you,' said Abaddon. 'If he cannot devise a means to enter the Palace, I do not think his brothers will do so. Perhaps it is time that the greatest of our leaders takes his rightful place at the forefront of the battle.'

'You think I shirk my duties as general?' Horus seemed amused by the idea.

'Not at all, Warmaster. I think your Legions and countless other servants would fight harder to see you at their head. Your vision has brought us to the door of the Emperor's throne room, but at the moment of your victory you stand aside and let others break it down.'

'It cannot yet be done,' Horus said with a slow shake of the head, his expression turning sombre.

'Because of this psychic shield that bars the daemons?'

'In part. But also, the powers that work through me gather yet more strength. When I strike, I must annihilate my father entirely, body and soul, physically and psychically. Not a shred of him can survive lest it grow again in some future century.' Gauntlet-claws tapped on the arm of the throne for several seconds. 'Perturabo is the sanest of my brothers. His agenda is solely to serve me, to prove himself as strong as he believes he can be. You have already seen how the others work at cross purposes except under firm hand. The Lord of Iron must be allowed his time of glory or he will lose faith. And if I lose my reliable commander, what can I achieve with unreliable ones?'

'What is to be done?'

'We shall see.' Horus turned his head and nodded to one of the army of lesser creatures that attended the court. Incense billowed from burners and the hololithic comms array flickered into life, bringing with it the images of the Warmaster's primarch allies. Angron licked gore from a clawed hand, twitching with the taste of it, his bestial features broad and large in the column of light that projected from the ceiling. Fulgrim seemed to be lounging on a couch made of corpses, tail languidly flicking back and forth, while attended by creatures with eyes and mouths stitched shut, offering flagons and platters of treats to the primarch. Mortarion seemed the most attentive, though his features were obscured by billows of vapour erupting from his mask with each stentorian breath. He was clad in darkness and what Abaddon first took to be vox static soon resolved itself into the buzzing of thousands of flies.

It was several more seconds before Perturabo answered the council. He paced, appearing and disappearing from view as he passed in and out of the comm-capture unit aboard the *Iron Blood*. His fingers flexed murderously and Abaddon caught glimpses of wreckage in the primarch's hall.

Of Magnus there was no sign.

Perturabo stopped his pacing and glared through the projection at his brothers.

'The space port should be invested by now! We wasted many lives and much time in pointless attack, when my cursed brothers cannot cross the boundary into the Emperor's domain.'

'Cursed?' drawled Fulgrim. **'Says one that has not experienced the delights an immaterial existence has to offer.'**

'Cursed,' Perturabo snapped. *'You are less than I, for you cannot even set foot upon the Palace grounds.'*

'Then take Forgebreaker and knock upon the Emperor's doors yourself,' replied Mortarion, gaseous puffs accompanying his words.

'I did not think the Lord of Iron was so cautious of spending his warriors' lives,' said Abaddon. 'The Fourth rightly earned themselves a reputation for forcing battle even in the face of costly resistance and tremendous casualties.'

'I would spend them for good cause, not dash them against the walls while my brothers amuse themselves with inhuman delights.' The image of Perturabo turned towards Horus and lowered to one knee. *'I know that I promised you the walls, Warmaster, but I have not the tools to dismantle this shield. It not only spurns the presence of the Neverborn, I am sure it steels the hearts of the Emperor's servants. I could spend a century taking the space port apart piece by piece and yet my brothers would never lead their Legions upon the ground hallowed by our father.'*

'My faith in you is not misplaced, Perturabo,' said Horus, standing up. He gestured for the Lord of Iron to do likewise. 'One setback is not defeat, as you know well. It was wrong of me to send you forth unarmed against the foe you would face.'

Horus twisted, a clawed gauntlet stretching to point towards Layak.

'In the absence of Magnus, who aids the soul-battle in his own way, the greatest proponents of these arts are the Word

Bearers. I send to you my Crimson Apostle, the oracle of the
Neverborn.'

'I am honoured,' said Layak, stooping from the shadows in
a bow. 'I have some theories regarding the telaethesic ward
of the Emperor. I shall summon the most powerful of our
brethren, and if the Lord Mortarion permits, discuss matters
with Lord Typhus. Our efforts combined will find a means to
break this shield.'

'*You will share all that your art can tell me,*' insisted Perturabo.
'*If I am to deliver the Palace to our Warmaster I must have proper
understanding of all the elements.*'

'Of course. It will be necessary for me to be on Terra, if you
are willing to hold council there with me.'

'*I will,*' agreed Perturabo.

'And you will have Abaddon to accompany you,' added Horus.

'There are better aims to which I might be employed,' argued
the First Captain. 'The Sons of Horus can draw defenders away
from the Lion's Gate by presenting threat elsewhere.'

'You will go where I command,' Horus said heavily, eyes
flashing with anger. 'Layak is to my soul as you are to my body.
Where the one goes, so too does the other.'

Abaddon restrained any argument. He looked at Layak but it
was impossible to read any reaction from the Crimson Apostle's masked, inhuman face.

'By your will I am commanded,' said Abaddon, bowing his
head to his primarch.

'*I will have Typhus ready for your instruction,*' said Mortarion. His image wavered and then vanished.

'*Then I will prepare for my descent,*' said Perturabo. '*Transmit
your coordinates, Layak, and the time of meeting.*'

The Lord of Iron's feed blinked out of existence.

Fulgrim muttered a distracted farewell and faded also, leaving
Angron's immense face floating in the midst of the chamber.

'Be ready, Angron, when Perturabo calls upon you,' said Horus, returning to his throne. He gestured and the link was severed, plunging the chamber into gloom once more.

Lion's Gate space port, mesophex core,
eighteen hours since assault

Manish Dhaubanjar did not like the quiet at all. For all of his forty-eight years he had lived and served the Emperor within the great tower of the Lion's Gate space port. Starspear by birth, and hauler operator by labour, he rarely ventured below the thirty-kilometre level. His world had always been one of clanking machinery, shouting overseers and the rumble of starship plasma engines.

Now all he could hear was the distant tremor of the Palace bombardment. The orbital attack had moved on from the space port. Through announcements and hall briefings, Colonel Maigraut had warned the people that this cessation of the artillery attack was likely a forewarning of a renewed assault. The upper gun batteries had fallen silent for the time being, denied targets for their wrath while the enemy regathered their strength.

'We've still got to be ready,' he told his wife, Daxa. She nodded, fingering the autogun in her lap as she sat in a rocking chair made from spare hauler parts.

'We'll be ready, flower of my heart,' she replied. 'When the alarms sound, we'll wait in the hall with the others.'

'When the alarms sound,' said Manish.

He pushed himself out of his low chair, limbs stiff with arthritis protesting at the sudden movement. Leaning his gun against the cupboard of their small kitchen unit, he picked up a pan and filled it from the water urn – the mains supply had been cut off in case it was poisoned by the enemy. Plague was rampant in the main Palace, but the space port had so far been isolated from the flux and poxes that were killing hundreds of thousands beyond the wall. The electric cook ring was also disconnected but the Imperial Army had issued tens of thousands of camp stoves. One sat on the countertop, smelling faintly of refined alcohol fuel.

'Tea?' He looked over his shoulder. Daxa was rubbing a smudge of gun lubricant from the cuff of her dress.

'What's the special occasion?' she replied with a smile. 'We won't be getting any more for a while.'

'Might as well drink it,' he told her.

Just as he reached for the caddy, fifteen thousand kilometres away in low orbit the Iron Warriors cruiser *Rebuke* prepared to fire its main lance array. As did the seven ships of its battle group, plus scores of others. Simultaneously, a hundred gunships entered targeting range, loosing a storm of missiles and shells.

The combined weight of this gunship fire overloaded a patch of the Starspear's protective fields roughly three hundred metres across. Into this relative eye of the needle the *Rebuke* and its fellow warships fired beams of energised particles powerful enough to punch holes through starship armour and level ground fortifications.

The upper atmosphere caused almost no diffraction at all, so that the combined beams hit the weakened patch of shielding at almost one hundred per cent strength. In microseconds scores of laser blasts punched through the skin of the space port, sheared through ten kilometres of bulkheads and supports but avoided damaging the core shafts of the transport network.

The first Manish and Daxa knew of the attack was when their bedroom vaporised, leaving a glowing hole in the wall between it and the living space. Decompression lifted them both from their feet along with chairs, pots, burner, guns and other detritus.

Manish's scream ripped from his mouth as a wisp of vapour, a moment before his lungs emptied, their fabric disrupted by the sudden loss of pressure. The roar of winds disappeared as his eardrums burst. Manish spun through the air alongside his wife, moisture icing on his skin, the bodies of thousands of other workers flying alongside them until the onrushing winds dragged them into the atmosphere, forty kilometres above the ground.

Despite the freezing cold, his body temperature was warm enough to boil his blood at that altitude, though thankfully he was unconscious from hypoxia before his eyes leaked blood and his tongue swelled up to choke him.

He was already dead before he started falling and the silhouettes of hundreds of gunships appeared against the rising dawn.

Back in Starspear, alarms started to howl.

ELEVEN

The archmagos
Obliteration
A concealed blade

Lion's Gate space port, mesophex core,
eighteen hours since assault

Olfactory sensors translated the stench of death into a series of quantifiable molecular components while audio interceptors turned the snap of volkite blasters and thrum of rad beamers into wavelength data. To Archmagos Inar Satarael these added to the beauty of battle rather than detracted from it, just as the annotation for an orchestral symphony contained all the potential for drama that was then expended during a performance.

For the insertion into the heart of the Lion's Gate space port he had built himself a warform smaller than the cybernetic monstrosities he had favoured of late – it would be shameful to be denied entry to the control halls because the doorways were not large enough for such a body. Instead he had focused on anti-personnel weaponry and maximum shield efficiency, as well as the mobility afforded by a heximal limb layout. Even so, his bulk was twice that of a legionary, though composite

materials meant he was no heavier than a normal man. Of
these augmentations, the shield boosters were proving the most
valuable, deflecting las-blasts and autogun rounds by the score
every minute as he pressed forward along the arterial passage
to the main dockwork controls.

Speed was vital. The Iron Warrior, Kroeger, had devised a
simple plan, and a greater part of it relied upon the systems
of the defenders being blind to the true nature of the attack
being launched. Should the archmagos and the ally he was
due to meet suffer undue delays the entire endeavour was at
risk. With this in mind, Satarael ploughed into enemy fire with
little concern, knowing that the clave of battle servitors that
followed would cut down anything that evaded the attention
of his maxim bolters and graviton imploder.

Via noospheric pulse he could also feel the converging
approach of his allies in the Iron Warriors. Arriving at an angle
of seventy-two degrees to his own attack, the IV Legion assault
force was equally small but specialised. Their combined firepower would swiftly overwhelm any defenders still alive to
hold the central command hall.

The archmagos swept through the outer chambers without
pause, slave routines directing the fire of his weapons while his
conscious mind applied itself to the matter of the armoured
portal sealing the inner sanctum.

It was substantial, reinforced with thick bars and heavy gauge
locking wheels. Sparks emanating from the control panel at
its side betrayed a desperate ploy by the defenders – the electrical locks had been blown from the inside, impossible to
override. They were sealed inside, but it was an effective barrier
to Satarael's entry. The continued buzz of overloaded circuits
highlighted that the measure had been taken perhaps only
a minute earlier, in response to the rapidity of his advance.

Melta-burners seemed the best option, but there were none

in his vanguard. His graviton imploder would eventually twist the door locks into scrap metal, but that would be costly in terms of time and energy output, during which his part in War-smith Kroeger's plan would be unfulfilled, risking the success of the entire enterprise.

Though he had every confidence in his own abilities, Satarael considered that it was somewhat foolhardy of Kroeger to place so much necessity into a single operation, especially one carried out by a relatively small military force. Whatever the merits of the plan, if the New Mechanicum was to thrive, the overthrow of the False Omnissiah was essential and Satarael was deter-mined to play whatever part he could in that revolution. The future would be written by visionaries such as himself.

As he flashed active surveyor beams across the armoured door to assess its internal structural qualities, Satarael picked up an energy surge close at hand. Two pinpricks of white light resolved into bright patches around the central lock gears. The energy build-up continued until sparks erupted from the near side of the door, moments before the wash of high-intensity radiation burst through the two neat holes.

Something powerful slammed against the portal from inside the command terminal chamber, rupturing the remains of the lock's gears. Molten droplets and slivers of metal showered out-wards as the door cracked in half, the shriek of tortured metal filling the antechamber as it twisted on its immense hinges.

A figure the size of a Legion Dreadnought loomed through the smoke of vaporised metal and ceramite, the telltale gleam of two melta-cutters where eyes should have been.

'*You are late, archmagos.*' The creature's voice warbled with artificial modulation, but there was also a strange after-effect that did not register with Satarael's sensors: the daemon-voice of the creature's cohabitant.

'Volk-Sa'ra'am, I am grateful for your intervention,' said the archmagos. 'It is a privilege to finally be in your physical vicinity. It is an honour to find alliance with the one who will usher in a new age for the Mechanicum and Legions alike.'

Volk-Sa'ra'am looked like a legionary in the same way that a battleship might look like an orbital shuttle if one mistook size for perspective. Everything about it was larger in scale, bloated with the power of the daemonic coupled with the technophagic enhancements it had been given by noted members of the New Mechanicum. It was impossible to tell where ancient battleplate ended and iron-hard skin began, but the gunmetal of its old armour gave way to patches of dark flesh in places, while horns and spines both of bone and metal protruded from breaks in the glistening carapace that had once been the Space Marine's power plant backpack.

Its form was not static but an ever-shifting mass, more than simple mutation. The melta-cutters – or the analogue the daemon-machine hybrid had created – receded into the face and something approximating human features returned, a flat face with a bulbous nose. The eyes still gleamed with circuitry, devoid of any human feeling.

'Are you ready for the transference?' Volk-Sa'ra'am asked, turning away. Bone gears whirred and pistons shuddered with each step it took into the chamber, heading for a hexagonal console bank at the centre. A clawed hand as large as a service hoist lifted towards the cogitators. 'There is still a connection here we can exploit.'

'You understand what will be required of you?'

'I will… divide and conquer,' said the hulking creature, a sketch of a smile twisting its assumed face. 'I will obliterate all opposition.'

'Obliterate? Yes, that is certainly the word. All trace of the previous incarna machina will be replaced by your anaethemix.'

'Blood is required, I was told.' Volk-Sa'ra'am turned its arm as though offering a wrist. Metal plates peeled back like the petals of a mechanical flower, exposing blood vessels ribbed with cabling. Thin pipelines carrying other fluids ran alongside, pulsing with red and green and blots of purple.

At an urge from the archmagos a servitor advanced, a length of sanguinaxial cable coiled in its hands. One end was tipped by a standard Imperial five-pin interface, the other fitted to a device that looked like the unholy offspring of an intravenous cannula and an ornamental dagger. Satarael snaked out a mechandenrite from beneath his battleform, gently lifting the jagged end of the sanguinaxial cable while the servitor connected the other to the main console.

'You need to appease me, first,' said the hybrid-machine, drawing the arm away from Satarael's approach. *'This is the power of Chaos, there are forms and rituals to be observed.'*

'I understand,' said the archmagos, though in truth his comprehension was limited.

There had been nothing like Volk-Sa'ra'am before, and Satarael's studies in the esoteric area of warp manipulation were shallow. It was only his self-recreating experience that gave him any insight at all – having rebuilt his consciousness from scattered parts he was best placed to convey a partial daemon consciousness into the systems of the Lion's Gate space port.

'I offer up fealty to the Powers that Wax and Wane,' intoned Satarael, recalling the words imprinted to him via the Iron Warriors from the Word Bearers' Neverborn experts. Truly this was an effort of the great new alliance that would shape the future galaxy beneath the rule of Horus. 'Of the mortal we take, and of the immortal we give. Threshed to the soul of the warp, I steer the ship of will through the storm of need. Glory to the powers!'

The mechadendrite speared out, plunging the sanguinaxial blade into the exposed arm of Volk-Sa'ra'am. Light flared at the contact, like sparks leaping from a broken wire, and travelled along the length of the cable. Blood seeped from the wound, quickly congealing around the entry point like coral accretion on a shipwreck, bubbled and blistered.

'I feel the connection.'

The voice came from a communications grille situated above a display screen cracked by bolter impacts. The monitoring station flickered into life, showing a horned face among swirls of static, teeth of lightning flashing in a grin.

'I shall obliterate all.'

Lion's Gate space port, surface approach,
eighteen hours since assault

It had been twenty years since Bious, and Forrix had not previously thought of that world since its eventual compliance. But there was something about the unreality of this battle that took him back to that campaign. His auto-senses had overloaded within three minutes of the main assault beginning, reducing his hearing to that of his own enhanced ears, though muffled by his helm. Roving banks of smoke and gas swathed his view, so that his lenses constantly flickered between different spectrum images depending on where he looked, one moment bright with infrared radiation then sliding through the visible light and back again, before switching to dampened night vision and cycling back into ultraviolet. All was cut through by streaks of tracer rounds, continuous muzzle flare and the after-glow of plasma detonations.

He couldn't remove his helm: even his enhanced physiology would start to succumb to the mixture of toxins billowing among the ash and debris – toxins his own side had unleashed in the bombardment that now choked the Warmaster's allies

as much as they had devoured the lungs of the Emperor's
servants in previous weeks. The warsmiths cared little, driving
hundreds of thousands of mortal chattels into the deadly mists
and scything cannonade.

Like an autoharvester's spinning blades, battery after battery
of anti-personnel and heavier weapons ripped hundred-
metre-wide swathes through the snarling, wailing morass of
troops. Staccato heavy stubber bursts rippled through the
slower, deeper beat of macro cannons, whose every shell ripped
open craters fifty metres across. Airbursts rained a razor-edged
hail of shrapnel, leaving hillocks of rent flesh for following
companies to toil across.

Forrix heaved himself up one such mound, boots sinking into
the bloodied meat of a beastman's chest, bolter mag-locked to
his armour so that he could use both hands to aid his ascent
of the hill of the dead. Around him were mortal troopers – he
had paid little attention when their commander had introduced herself and named their world of origin – nearly three
thousand of them, armed with crude solid-shot pistols and
axes. They seemed inordinately proud of the fact they had been
chosen to deliver him to the Lion's Gate, not understanding
that their purpose was as a literal meat shield. Five hundred
had already been cut down by long-range artillery, the others
would be lucky to come within sight of the broken armoured
portals in the southern slopes of the space port – gates that
had been painfully wrested open by the proceeding five hundred thousand soldiers.

Bious had been what the adepts of Terra would later desig-
nate a death world. A single brood organism, utterly inimical
to other life but for the sole advanced human society that had
made their home there. A whole world and populace bent
upon destroying those it deemed interlopers. An advanced
people and an eco-system coupled together in shared purpose.

Now he faced similar opposition, but there was a single mind directing that enmity, a figure whose intent was written in the strewn bodies and scouring cannonades – the Emperor. And as with Bious there would be no surrender, no chance of compromise. Only total extermination would see the IV Legion to victory.

Cresting the mound of the dead, booted foot snapping the curling horn of a mutant slave, Forrix paused for half a second to gaze left and right, before continuing down into the ragged crater on the far side. Ahead of him, about three hundred metres away, a rapid series of explosions tore the ground apart, hurling body parts high into the air. How the minefield had not been triggered by previous waves was a mystery – or perhaps the mines had been deliberately left dormant until now – but as body parts fell in a grisly shower Forrix veered left, the troopers around him turning as well like shoaling fish, angling towards ground chewed over by thousands of earlier footfalls.

The drone of jets drew his eye to the heavens but he could see nothing through the smog of battle. His chronometer told him that the aerial attack had begun, the second front in Kroeger's simple plan. As he watched, it started to rain, but on magnification the rain turned out to be tumbling bodies. Tens of thousands of them, falling through the cloud cover, glittering with ice and trailing shards like human comets.

He watched the first hit the side of the space port about four kilometres up, a strange combination of shattering and splattering as frozen heads, limbs and torsos scattered like broken glass while their warm interiors smeared down the ferrocrete flanks. Bodies descended like hail, smashing into gun batteries and ricocheting from cannon barrels. Corpse after corpse, until the flank of the space port was carpeted in a compacted mass of flesh and congealed blood. Even Forrix was taken aback by the sight of tens of thousands of the IV Legion's victims tumbling, splitting and bouncing off the metal skin of the Lion's Gate facility.

The Iron Warriors' auxiliary horde was about half a kilometre from the armoured barbican that had protected the southern approaches, the structure now a smoking ruin of metal and blasted ferrocrete. Ahead, protected by directional power field generators, siege tanks with dozer blades carved paths through the ruin of masonry and flesh, while pioneer teams with flamers and phospex missiles cleared the remaining bunkers of the outer ring.

Funnelled by natural ridges and the projecting walls of the space port, the assault wave slowed as it reached the defences, a sea of living creatures pressed closer and closer while fire raked down from above and mortar shells dropped in constant bombardment. With enemies to the front and sides, and the guns of their masters threatening equal ruin behind them, the vassal regiments poured on, each warrior trusting that some form of providence – or perhaps warp-spawned patronage – would see them survive when millions of others had fallen.

If the Iron Warriors had been able to call upon such unquestioning, endless hordes at Bious, the campaign would have lasted weeks, not months. It was the crudest use of raw power, typical of Kroeger's thinking. But in the midst of the incalculable carnage there was a kernel of brilliance. Kroeger was not a master strategist, not in the mould of Forrix or Perturabo, but he was a brawler, a street fighter that cared nothing for honour or the forms of combat. As Kroeger had put it, reflecting perhaps a youth that Forrix did not want to know more about, sometimes a shiv was more effective than a broadsword if it was pushed into the right place.

He'd continued by explaining some tradition of his people on Olympia, something about eating the grubs found near their city. Most were harmless males but the females had hidden stings, indistinguishable from the males except during one mating season. It was a time-honoured assassination method to hide a few females in the meal of an enemy. Via this drawn-out analogy, Kroeger had told them of his plan to get a thousand Iron Warriors into the space port, hidden amongst the living debris of the vassal troops.

It seemed to be working.

Forrix was one of only a thousand Iron Warriors hidden in the tide of the attack, his armour on minimal systems and coated in gore, vox-silent to reduce the chances of detection. Only close manual inspection would pick him out from the churning wave of mortals, and only the indiscriminate barrage that assailed the horde might take him by chance.

Las-fire joined the projectiles of the larger weapons as they came within a hundred metres of the broken rampart of the barbican. The lower levels of the space port yawned beyond, full of smoke lit by an inferno raging within, as though they stormed the mouth of some ancient hellscape.

The ground shuddered with impacts and recoil, causing those around him to lose their footing. He scrambled and crouched and staggered his way forward among them, trying not to reveal himself amidst their struggles.

Mouth dry, hearts beating like an Olympian forge hammer, he came into the shadow of the broken gates, towering forty metres above him. Grenades flashed and the screams of the dying added to the din, but he paid them no heed. Troglodyte mutant ogryns, larger even than a legionary, smashed at side doors with gleaming mauls and hammers, while hundreds of lesser mortals streamed into the firelit innards, only to be scythed down by volleys from platoons of ochre-uniformed defenders.

The siege-breaker mutants crashed through their objective, ripping open the emergency access doors adjacent to the courtyard within the barbican. The troopers flowed on, bearing down the lines of defenders with sheer numbers, while Forrix and scores of others turned towards the new avenue of attack.

A shiv indeed, he thought, pounding down a side corridor into the dark of the space port's maintenance labyrinth.

TWELVE

Update from the front
Apostle of Chaos
The Utterblight

Karachee Flats, sixty-nine days before assault

Stepping out from under the huge train, Zenobi had been expecting it to be night-time and so was surprised to discover a strange twilight greeted the disembarking troops. Her immediate surrounds were devoid of illumination except for the gleam of the train's reactor vents and a few hooded lumens stretched out on cables strung between high poles that led away from the tracks. Others were shuffling slowly forward, eyes cast upwards, and she looked up with them, mouth dropping open at what she saw.

The night sky was alight with colour – bursts of red and purple, searing arcs of green and blue. Shooting stars were a constant flicker of movement across the vault of the heavens, beyond which a shifting miasma of glittering dust blotted out the stars.

'Debris,' said Menber, and Zenobi knew he was referring to the falling sparks.

'Void war.' She uttered the two words in an awed whisper, scarce believing that she was witnessing such a thing.

'Keep moving,' Lieutenant Okoye bellowed from behind. 'Others have to get off the platform!'

Still looking up, Zenobi joined the shambling horde of troopers that made their way down the dimly lit track, just one of a crowd of distracted onlookers moving more by mass consensus than individual volition.

'Look!' Someone ahead thrust a finger towards the smudge of orange dusk light. A flare of bright white burned across it as a crippled starship plunged into the atmosphere, trailing more sparks as its hull disintegrated. A chorus of gasps greeted the sight, like a crowd watching the celebrations on Unification Day.

'Horus is in orbit...' This came from Sergeant Alekzanda, betraying his normal stoicism. 'The Warmaster is nearly here.'

'If he's winning,' replied Kettai. 'There's a lot of ships and guns between him and Terra.'

'Remember what Jawaahir said – we have to assume the Warmaster's armies will land,' said Zenobi.

'Not here,' replied Kettai. He pointed north-east. The sky beyond the horizon was a constant fluctuation of colours, the intensity of the space battle like an artificial aurora. 'Himalazia. The Imperial Palace.'

'It might be over before we get there,' said someone behind Zenobi.

Zenobi's head turned one way and then another as she tried to see everything, almost falling as her toe caught in a rut on the unpaved path. The near-fall brought her mind back to the present and their surroundings.

'Where are we going?' Other than the faint lumens overhead and the bulk of the train behind them, there was nothing to see. She thought about the platforms, simple raised slabs of rockcrete, seemingly in the middle of nowhere. 'I thought this was Karachee?'

'I don't know,' answered Menber, shaking his head. He looked around and shook his head again. 'I don't see anything.'

'Did you see what happened to the others? The ones that left the company?'

'Nothing, they were long gone by the time we got off the train.'

Zenobi lapsed into agitated silence and followed the huge herd of troopers. Tens of thousands of them were tramping across this featureless wilderness; perhaps even those at the front didn't know their destination. After a few minutes the light poles stopped and the only illumination came from the orbital pyrotechnics that continued to shine down in rainbow sprays of laser and plasma.

As the minutes became half an hour and then an hour, the sense of unease grew. The cold was starting to bite and the troopers struggled to get heavier coats out of their kitbags whilst still pressed together and moving. Lieutenant Okoye cut his way through the mass to help them, organising them into trios that would assist each other in turn, two holding bags and equipment while the third pulled on their coat. Zenobi had the additional burden of the standard, which she briefly relinquished to the care of Seleen and Sergeant Alekzanda but retrieved the moment she had buttoned up her coat.

'I thought this was just a transfer, bana-lieutenant,' said Zenobi. 'We've walked kilometres by now.'

'Just keep walking, trooper,' the lieutenant replied, but it was clear from his manner that he had no more idea of what was happening than any of them.

They walked on, dispersing slightly more as the group spread from the main line of advance. Zenobi heard shouts as dynastic enforcers barked at those they judged to be wandering too far from their invisible course. There was no sign of Captain Egwu nor the integrity officers, but now and then Zenobi thought she heard the grumble of motor engines and assumed that some form of transportation had been secured for the upper ranks. She certainly couldn't picture Jawaahir trudging through the seemingly endless dust bowl.

'Lights!'

The call echoed along the column from the companies at the front, but Zenobi couldn't see anything at all and her enquiries with her taller companions yielded nothing. It was only after a few more minutes' advance that Menber spoke up.

'Lights. They look like… Vehicles. Searchlights?'

The column slowed and then stopped, though for those any distance from the front the reason for the halt was unseen. Slowly, platoon by platoon, they started to shift again, edging forward only a few paces every minute, until finally First Company of the 64th could see another railhead a few hundred metres in front. It was far less imposing than the great station where they'd been deposited by the heli-transports. Just a maze of connecting tracks and dozens of multi-chimneyed locomotives – far smaller than the one that had brought them here, though each still pulled a snake of carriages several hundred metres long. Interspersed between transport compartments were armoured wagons with gun turrets on their roofs and smaller firing ports along their lengths. All was illuminated by the headlights and mounted lumens of a score of halftracks. When a train was filled it groaned away beneath plumes of exhaust smoke, each a machine serpent near three hundred metres long. Company by company the troopers from Addaba were funnelled into the waiting transports and shipped east, towards the brightness of the orbital battle.

A cabal of company officers waited by the trackside. Zenobi was relieved to see Captain Egwu among them.

'The orbital blockade has collapsed,' the company commander announced. Zenobi heard the collective intake of breath around her, her own gasp lost among the reaction of her companions. 'Forces of the Warmaster broke into the atmosphere four hours ago. Karachee has already been subjected to sporadic orbital bombardment and so we are avoiding the transfer stations. Landings are expected across Terra, but our destination and purpose remain the same.'

An integrity officer – a lean-faced man named Oyenuzi assigned to Alpha Platoon – held out a handful of paper sheets as Egwu continued.

'Squad leaders will each take one of these and disseminate the information to their squad. They detail specific orders and behaviour to minimise detection by orbital scan and aircraft overflight. There are far larger and more important targets than half a dozen trains crossing the Arabadlands. Even so, we have several days' travel ahead of us and the less attention we draw, the better.'

She stopped as a junior officer appeared out of the gloom, the coils and box of a long-range vox hanging from a shoulder harness. Zenobi wasn't close enough to hear what was said, but the urgency in the young man's expression and the reaction from the captain were enough to communicate that the news was not welcome. Zenobi's throat tightened sympathetically as Egwu started a hectic, hushed consultation with the integrity officer and the handful of nearby lieutenants.

Those behind were unconsciously but inexorably pushing forward to see or hear, creating a building pressure wave against those nearer the front. Someone stepped on Zenobi's heel as they shifted position, one hand steadying on her shoulder. There were snarled complaints ringing around her, and she saw elbows and even fists being flung around as the troopers started pushing into one another.

'We have to get moving!' Kettai shouted, waving his hand at one of the enforcers lining the side of the train. A group of troopers from the platoon, Zenobi included, shuffled forward several steps, trying to allow more space, but this vacuum simply drew in those behind, causing a ripple to flow back through the growing crowd of waiting soldiers.

Then the lights went out.

The sudden darkness sucked at Zenobi, leeching the last of her nerve from her body. A squeak of a cry escaped her lips before she clamped down on the fear. Mixed shouts of panic and anger broke the stillness of the night.

Zenobi took another step, twisting her ankle on a buried rock. She threw out a hand and grabbed an arm to stop herself falling, heart hammering as she imagined the company surging forward, trampling over her in the moments of her fall.

'Steady.' It was Sergeant Alekzanda that grabbed her coat, keeping her upright. He turned, teeth bared as he berated the troopers directly behind them. Her eyes were getting accustomed to the dim illuminations of the orbital battle, the outline of the train and people resolving into focus in front of her.

A small lantern appeared from the left, illuminating the enforcer that carried it. The knot of officers broke apart, the lieutenants hurrying into the twilight.

'Everybody, onto the train now!' barked Okoye, slapping a hand on Menber's shoulder, almost shoving the trooper towards the locomotive. 'By squads and platoon. Now, now, now!'

It was the worst possible decision.

Like water through a broken dam, the defence corps soldiers burst forward, spooked by the darkness and then panicked by the sudden command. Gripping the banner pole tight, her lasgun and kitbag slapping against her side, Zenobi started forward, got caught with her neighbour and fell. Hands grabbed her shoulders, wrenching her up, and she was propelled towards the nearest train door, a set of metal steps folded down for access. She regained her feet before she had to be bodily thrown aboard, wrestling her burdens sideways through the door even as Kettai pushed in beside her.

By the same miracle by which he always seemed to be ahead of his squad, Sergeant Alekzanda was in the companionway just inside the door, marshalling the new arrivals.

'Across to the other side, all the way to the far end. Across to the other side, all the way to the far end.'

The troopers piled on, into the darkness of the compartment. It was about thirty metres long, six wide, and the only light glimmered through a row of small windows that ran the length of the join between the wall and roof. There were hammock nets bundled to the ceiling and the benches that ran crosswise along the carriage had cloth pockets for those seated behind to stow small possessions. The carriage was split along its length by a thin latticework, through which Zenobi could see others herding onto the train. Curses followed the troopers as they negotiated their way around wooden benches with foot lockers beneath, navigating by bruised shins and clattered knees until they found space.

With the soldiers came the froth of muttered speculation.

'Enemy on their way, I heard.'

'Something's spotted us.'

'Gotta be a ship in orbit.'

'Airstrike, she said. Definitely airstrike.'

'I heard the captain say we had to get moving in five minutes.'

'There's no way we'll all be aboard by then,' said Menber in reply to this last claim.

Zenobi climbed onto a bench to look out the window and saw figures flowing between the wagons, heading to other trains on parallel sidings. A grumble announced the motors starting, and with a jolt a few seconds later the train began to move, almost spilling Zenobi from the bench.

'No! Stop!' she shouted, as though the driver would hear her, two hundred metres further up the track. 'There's people cutting past!'

She pressed her face back against the window so she could peer through the reflections into the darkness, others around her ascending the benches to look as well. The train was moving at a crawl, and still some of the troopers were daring to dart between the carriages. She couldn't see but heard screams as some of them weren't quick enough, disappearing beneath the grinding metal of the wheels.

Turning around, she looked over the packed troops to see that the doors were still open. Alekzanda and some others were there, hauling latecomers through the opening as they ran up alongside the moving vehicle. A little closer amidst the mass were the uniforms of the officers, Egwu among them.

People were coming on board from both sides now, but the rate of their boarding had slowed to a person every few seconds, not the constant rush that had greeted the original command. The train was picking up speed, moving from a walk to a jog, enough that those that had been chasing it started to fall behind, legs unaccustomed to running giving way to tiredness after a few hundred metres.

The track was curving to the left. Through the window Zenobi could see groups of abandoned troopers silhouetted against the glimmer of lights on the horizon. Brighter flares flashed across the night. A chorus of distant cracks cut across the clanking of the train.

'Bolters!' someone yelled. More small flares of red crisscrossed the gloom, converging in the patches of darker shadow that were the troopers left behind. A sudden, stark flash of muzzle fire lit the distance and a rapid-fire thunder drifted after the departing trains.

A few seconds later an explosion lit the middle distance, briefly highlighting ramshackle buildings that lined the track – a makeshift way station that the night had hidden. Zenobi flinched from the brightness, the sudden light searing her vision. But in the instant before momentary blindness she thought she had seen armoured figures against the billow of flames.

She stepped down from the bench and dragged her kitbag and lasgun to her lap, flopping back onto the seat in stunned silence.

'Did you see them?' whispered Menber, bending over the back of the bench from behind.

Zenobi stared ahead, not really looking at anything, her vision fogged by shock.

'I'm not sure what I saw.'

She raised a shaking hand to wipe her brow. Her coat was now hot in the throng of troopers and her short curls of hair matted with sweat from the brief but sudden exertions that had got her to the train. Her gut was spinning and her pulse was unfeasibly loud in her ears, drumming incessantly like a forge hammer. Everything else was muted, a hundred conversations taking place in a neighbouring room.

In that moment she knew that the war was real. It wasn't some distant battle beyond the stars. It wasn't even a future conflict at the end of a train line, to be fought around the walls of the Imperial Palace. Folk of Addaba were dead now, slain by the violence of the struggle between the Emperor and Horus. Thousands had probably died on the production lines, worked beyond their limit, injured by machines that should have been maintained better, their bodies aged by the greater toil of the war effort. But that was different. That was at home, where they would be remembered, their bodies taken to the endfires. What would happen to those they had left in the Arabadlands? Did she know any of them? Would they be missed?

It was suddenly so large and impersonal.

Would anyone remember her?

Drops of water fell on her hands and for several seconds she was confused, unable to recognise her own tears.

Katabatic Plains, eighteen hours since assault

Descending the gunship's ramp, Abaddon paused for a second before stepping onto the bloodied dirt of Terra. He halted a few metres on and looked around, for the first time seeing the siege from below rather than above. Behind him came a bodyguard of Sons of Horus, but a raised hand stopped them as they disembarked.

'Await me here,' he told them, turning to the broken remnants of a defence keep that Layak had chosen to be the site of his ritual. The ground about it was littered with the corpses of Imperial Army troopers, skin blotched, tongues lolling, slain by some deadly disease or poison.

Passing into the ruin Abaddon came upon Layak in a central hall. In the hours before departing the *Vengeful Spirit* he had been absent from Abaddon's presence, unusually so, and the Sons of Horus commander had found the experience partly a relief and partly filled with suspicion. On the premise that one should keep one's enemies close, he was sure that he shouldn't let Layak out of his sight, for all that the Word Bearer enjoyed almost unparalleled support from the Warmaster.

Now he found himself in close proximity to the Crimson Apostle and was of the firm opinion that absence was always preferable. The sorcerer had selected one of the overrun defence

positions, a bastion of the outer defences directly north of the
Lion's Gate space port. Through the broken roof Abaddon
could see the spear of the port reaching into the storm clouds.

Evidently the bastion had changed hands several times and
nobody had bothered with the expense of energy required to
remove the dead. Halls and corridors were choked with casualties from both sides: mostly human but a few abhumans,
mutants. There were two power-armoured bodies, in the livery of Mortarion's Legion. The bastion was located close to
the central axis of the Death Guard's first assault, more than
a thousand kilometres from the Lion's Gate.

'Why here?' growled Abaddon. 'How will this get Perturabo
into the space port?'

Layak gestured to the ground. Carrion-eaters crawled across
the bodies, giant millipedes, mutant rats and black-backed bee-
tles, impervious to the toxic fumes that lay like an ankle-deep
cloud across much of the Katabatic Plains. Fungal growths
wavered with strange life, puffing clouds of spores into the
polluted air.

'The God of Decay has already passed his eye across this
place and found it pleasing. The barrier to the Neverborn
comes not from the Lion's Gate port but the Emperor. It is from
within the heart of the Palace that we shall erode the shield.'

Typhon of the Death Guard was there also, crouched next to
a distended corpse, allowing a segmented arthropod to crawl
around his hand like some obscene pet. Since Abaddon had
last met him, Calas Typhon was as much changed as his genefather. Abaddon recalled that Mortarion had named him
Typhus, as though the morphing of his body necessitated a
new identity. Though he still wore his heavy Terminator plate,
as did Abaddon, it was pitted with odd corrosion, the ceramite
covered in lesions like diseased bone. Organic-looking fun-
nels splayed from the carapace across the power plant upon

his back, a fume of buzzing insects constantly leaking forth. A horn protruded from the brow of Typhus' helm, reminiscent of the emissaries of the God of Decay that Abaddon sometimes witnessed in the Warmaster's warp chamber. The Death Guard bore a long scythe, a smaller replica of Mortarion's signature weapon. Its pitted blade shone with unearthly light, a pale gleam in the death-fog.

Perturabo arrived soon after, his sour demeanour filling the bastion as much as his bulk. His presence was more oppressive than Horus', his glare a challenge to any that dare meet it as it swept across the chamber at the heart of the bastion.

'Your mechanical companions must wait outside,' said Layak, gesturing towards the Iron Circle advancing through the door behind the primarch.

'Send away my guards so that I remain alone amongst some of the Legions' most powerful warriors?' Perturabo turned his head towards the blade slaves, who stood a little back from Layak. 'We all know how deceit is the handmaid of sorcery. I have not forgotten how Fulgrim earned his transformation at my expense.'

Layak's blade slaves turned as one and departed by an archway. The Crimson Apostle kept his inhuman gaze upon the primarch, his voice tempered by patience.

'Your presence is not necessary, Lord of Iron, if you wish to leave. You were invited so that you might observe, as you requested. Their soulless minds disturb the etheric qualities of the ritual.'

With his own command reflected back at him, Perturabo had little choice but to comply, and the Iron Circle withdrew, clanking into an antechamber. When they were gone, Layak stepped into the centre of the room. His gaze moved from one to the next, then stopped, his words intended for the primarch.

'Were you to question Magnus or one of his Thousand Sons about the nature of the warp, you would come to a very different understanding to what I will demonstrate to you. The mystics of Prospero analyse the warp as analogy, thinking they might discern patterns and laws and equations from its movements. While it has moods and phases and textures, the warp is a law unto itself, and so that is how Magnus' hubris led him into folly. You must abandon any sense that there is a science to be learnt, and instead focus on the concept of ritual and faith.'

Perturabo grunted, listening intently to every word. Abaddon was not sure whether it was wise to impart too much detail to the Lord of Iron. Perturabo excelled at perfecting what others started and creating marvel from nothing. Armed with deeper knowledge of the powers there might be no limit to what his imagination and craft could conjure.

'Think of our place within the warp as a relationship, emotional rather than physical. Just as you and I have a context with each other that is separate from our bodies – our past, our attitudes to one another, our shared experiences. These cannot be catalogued. They defy calculation. They might even be misremembered or imagined. Yet to the warp, all of that is real, while the physical is unreal.'

'I am not sure I fully grasp your meaning, but continue,' said the primarch.

'The ritual we used to allow your brothers to land upon Terra had a physical component and a spiritual one. Slaughter played its part.' Layak waved a hand to the corpses that surrounded them. 'Slaughter is meaningless without emotion. If I chopped down a forest of trees I would end as much life, but nobody would call it slaughter and I could not use it to summon the smallest manifestation of the powers. Death is intangible, as is fear, hatred, anger. These are the energies of the warp, the sustenance of the gods. The physical creates the spiritual. When the two are moulded and directed appropriately, a bond is made and passage between the realms can occur.'

'I see your meaning more clearly,' said Perturabo. 'And how is the bond connected?'

'That is the art, not the science,' purred Layak. 'It is the be-lief that shapes all things, and the dedication in heart to the powers. Words, symbols and actions are still physical properties of the ritual, to help shape the faith that stems from within. I have studied these mysteries for years, to smooth the passage, but it is my faith that creates the bond between me and the gods. For their boons, you must give yourselves over to them.'

Abaddon saw Perturabo's eyes narrow.

'Like my brothers?'

'That is but one way. They have taken to themselves a pa-tron and have become shaped by their inner desires. The gods are collectively happy to receive your worship.'

'Worship? Gods?' Perturabo clearly struggled with the con-cepts, though whether intellectually or dogmatically it was impossible to know.

'You once followed a god, though He would not let you call Him such.' Layak glanced now at Abaddon. 'Why not serve powers that grant favour in return, rather than spurn your love and dedication?'

'We are here for a more specific purpose,' grunted Abaddon, uncomfortable beneath the gaze of the Crimson Apostle. 'To break the barrier that protects the space port.'

Layak crouched, dipping his fingers towards the exposed vis-cera of a body at his feet. Bugs scuttled away, clustering around the feet of Typhus like chicks seeking protection from their hen. The Word Bearers sorcerer stood, pulling out a rope of intestine. It was clearly diseased, marked by pale blisters and dark scabs.

'The gods will feast upon the light of the Emperor and in doing so will extinguish it. We must empower them with our prayers and sacrifices, lending them strength with our faith, gi-ving of ourselves unto them that they may provide for us. In our commitment we grant them energy. We come upon this world at an auspicious time, when the warp waxes strong and the physical power of the Emperor wanes. The same thinning of the veil between realms that allowed our ships to penetrate the star system also brings close the breath of the gods.'

Talk of extinguishing the Emperor's light, and what the Chaos Gods intended for humanity, sat uneasily with Abaddon, but he said nothing. Perturabo was ill at ease for a different reason.

'You speak in metaphor, clouding the truth with esoteric nonsense.' The primarch flexed his fingers in agitation. 'Do not hide your knowledge with these riddles. Speak in plain terms.'

'I return to my initial point,' said Layak, looking at the organ in his hand. 'The physical and the immaterial. The telaethesic ward is generated by the Emperor Himself. He is the physical. There is none except perhaps Magnus that could break it in direct opposition, and it would slay your brother in the doing. The only way to remove the barrier is to pile upon such pressure of the immaterial that its creator cannot sustain it. And, as you would know, master of sieges, the greatest way to seize a wall is from inside as well as out.'

'We need to be inside the ward?' Perturabo snarled. 'But it is to gain entry to the port that we need to bring down the barrier!'

'Not so, Lord of Iron,' said Abaddon. 'Perhaps we need the presence of your brothers for the victory, but a breach can be made beforehand. Your plan surely does not rely on having Angron leading the charge all the way to the bridges?'

'No.' Perturabo glared daggers at the First Captain. 'I can break open the gates by conventional means.'

'That is good,' said Layak. 'We can begin the binding of the immaterial before we need to create the physical. Something to start the process, you could say. Do you remember Samus?'

'The daemon that almost destroyed the *Phalanx*?' said Perturabo. 'That was a masterful plan, though Dorn thwarted it eventually.'

'We were able to insert Samus into such a vulnerable position by implanting a connection into the form of Mersadie Oliton, who was already bound to the entity by shared experience. In order to breach barriers of the nature we face here, to create a gateway across the telaethesic ward, one can use a physical vessel to mask the Neverborn presence or anchor it. No pure daemon can set foot on Terra yet, but our daemon primarch allies can do so because of their once physical nature. Though made of the immaterium now, they yet leave an imprint on the real universe that gives their presence… solidity. Similarly, my possessed brethren and certain Neverborn-powered artefacts have been brought to the surface because of their physicality.'

'*And what will you use?*' Typhus stepped closer, a fume of tiny flies issuing from the grille of his helm as he spoke. '*Why am I here?*'

'You have become the host of the Destroyer Hive, and that gives you considerable power,' said Layak. 'Your voice echoes far in the warp and there is one you must help me call.'

'*What will you summon?*'

'Samus is of an order of Neverborn the Word Bearers call the Heralds of the Ruinstorm. There is one for each of the powers, strong in the favour of their patrons. Your grandfather, the Lord of Decay, can send to us a creature that is named Cor'bax Utterblight.'

'I thought you said no daemon can be summoned to the surface of Terra,' said Abaddon.

'And we stand outside the ward,' added Perturabo. 'What use is a creature barred entry as much as my distorted brothers?'

'No daemon can *manifest*,' Layak said sharply. 'Samus was a Neverborn of the soul, working through the minds of those it sought. All of the Heralds of the Ruinstorm are such, their greatest power being the corruption of thought, not body. The Utterblight does not need to take form to begin its work. The Life Within Death. The Breath on Your Lips. It is the Spirit of Hope, seeded in the hearts of all humans.'

As he spoke, the intestine started to move in his grasp, a slow pulse rippling along its length. The pulsing grew more vigorous, becoming writhing, and then curving up out of the corpse like a viscera serpent. With a wet tear, the organ pulled from the body, its ragged end growing maw-like, rows of fangs erupting from the pallid flesh.

'Behold the cosmic worm, the cruach-maggot that feeds upon the universe,' declared Layak. He held out the coiling mass towards Typhus, who held out an arm for it to crawl onto, looping about the wrist and forearm.

'A marvel,' said the Death Guard, turning his hand one way and the other to examine the entity. '*A tendril from the worms that burrow through Nurgle's garden itself.*'

'Indeed, that chew their way through all of existence – the worms of entropy.' Layak crouched and punched his fist through the chest of another corpse. He prised open the shattered breastbone and then reached in to pluck free the heart within. It seemed a shrivelled, small thing in his palm. 'The source of life. The seat of love. The vault of hope and courage and defiance.'

The Word Bearer held up the heart and began to chant in a strange tongue, witch-light playing around his hand. Abaddon felt something tugging at him, an insubstantial grip that teased at his own hearts, seeming to pluck at the arteries in his chest. He tried to catch a breath but found himself unable, as though he were drowning.

His gaze flicked to Perturabo, who watched the proceedings intensely, his eyes moving from one component of the ritual to the next, never stopping long on Layak or Typhus or their grisly accoutrements. Layak's chanting grew louder and the warp glow intensified, the heart in his grip like a weak yellow lumen.

Abaddon's hearts had almost stopped, so slow was their beat, but he could not take the breath to utter an injunction and his body seemed paralysed. He stared at the heart in the sorcerer's hand and saw it beat, in time to the thud in his chest. Only his human heart functioned; his secondary organ was like a useless weight behind his chest bone. His heart pulsed again and the thing in Layak's fingers twitched in sympathy. The sorcerer turned to him then, proffering the heart like a prize.

Abaddon raised his hand to take it, almost drawing his fingers back as the heart pumped once more in time to his own, gaining rhythm and speed. Layak's six eyes bored into him, yellow will-o'-the-wisps in the fog and flies, moving in and out of focus as oxygen starvation started to affect Abaddon's vision.

As the offering plopped down into his palm Abaddon felt a moment of release and took in a long, shuddering breath. Now he felt a triple-pulse, of his own hearts and the organ in his hand, thudding in unison with each other.

From Typhus the gut-snake lifted up as though scenting prey, its toothy mouth gaping, sweeping left and right in an eyeless search. Abaddon took a step closer, holding out the beating, glowing heart. The intestinal serpent stood out straight from Typhus' arm, like a rearing cobra, a gurgle issuing from its rippling throat.

It descended with purpose, not striking swiftly, but almost delicately plucking the heart from the palm of Abaddon's gauntlet. Leaving a rope of thick drool, it pulled back, the passage of the heart into its innards visible by the bulge that travelled its length.

Layak's chanting resumed, become more strident, almost a screeching. The gut-serpent started to weave back and forth, and leapt from Typhus to judder across the floor, spasming as if in pain. It coiled about itself, teeth sinking into its own flesh where the glow of the heart shone through. Razor-sharp teeth opened up its meat with ease, and it swallowed the heart again, chewing it from its own insides. It started to swell as it ate, spines and scales breaking from the surface, rows of paired wings splitting in the manner of a moth emerging from its cocoon.

Lifting from the ground with a buzz of dozens of wings, the scaled serpentine creature weaved around the legs of Layak, moving in time to the tempo of his voice. It moved to his icon staff, and then around his head, forming an obscene halo. Then it ascended, flitting across the chamber, coiling and uncoiling as though at play, growing larger still until its girth was as wide as Abaddon's waist.

With a shriek that was echoed from the mask of Layak, it plunged down, spearing into the corpse pile in front of the sorcerer. Like a las-drill it burrowed swiftly into the charnel heap. It was several metres long, far greater than the depth of the bodies, but continued downwards, disappearing into the ground. As its tail vanished into the exposed viscera Abaddon caught a momentary sight of a flowering bloom made of gristle and veins, a swirling hole at its centre, before the disgusting petals closed and the wound erupted into a pile of festering meat laced with hundreds of maggots.

With a gasp Layak stumbled backwards, eyes dimming. Abaddon made no move to assist him, but watched as the Word Bearer straightened, leaning a little on his staff for support.

'*Beautiful*,' whispered Typhus.

'It is done,' croaked Layak. He turned three pairs of eyes upon Perturabo. 'The Utterblight will begin its burrowing into the souls of the defenders, now it is time for you to launch your attack.'

The primarch surveyed the chamber, examining Layak and

Typhus, the corpses where the worm-daemon had disappeared. He nodded, once, and then left without a word. The clank of the Iron Circle joining him reverberated through the bastion.

'Now we return to Horus,' said Abaddon.

'No, not yet,' replied Layak. 'The ritual must be completed within the ward, when the Utterblight has thinned the barrier sufficiently. Typhus, return to your primarch and continue your assaults. Know that every disease-ridden corpse feeds the cruach-worm and makes it stronger.'

'We shall make a banquet for the Utterblight,' promised the plague sorcerer, lifting his scythe in salute.

Abaddon watched him go and then approached Layak. He stopped, two paces short of weapons' reach, aware of the blade slaves that had silently re-entered the chamber behind the Word Bearer.

'What did you do to me, sorcerer?' he growled, holding back the urge to seize Layak and pound the answer from him.

'I gave you a taste of what will come. The slightest inkling of what your genefather has endured to gain his power. When you come before the gods and demand their support, you must give of yourself for their favour.'

'And am I... The ritual, it bound me to that creature somehow?'

'No, you are free from any bargain or influence. It is to Typhus' fate that the star-maggot is drawn, not yours. This will not be the last time Typhus seeks out the worm of entropy for his designs.'

'You speak of matters beyond the end of the siege.'

'Horus' victory, or defeat, is not the end – it is the beginning.' Layak turned away, took a step and looked back at Abaddon. 'In time you will embrace that destiny.'

Abaddon watched the Word Bearer depart, his mood sour. He thought about the Warmaster and his brothers, the changes wrought upon Typhus and his companions, and of the

Neverborn and possessed that he had seen in Horus' court – Tormageddon and others. He could see clearly what price the powers demanded, beyond simple allegiance. Layak seemed convinced that Abaddon would one day voluntarily pay it. What was he willing to give to serve his father and brothers?

THIRTEEN

The ghost
Dangerous beliefs
Short supplies

Palatine Arc quarantine zone, Barracks-C, two days since assault

Several different nightmares had tormented Katsuhiro since he had arrived at the defence line. Coming within the walls, he had hoped perhaps his night-time tortures would end. Like all hopes he had nurtured since arriving, that was another to be crushed by reality.

He murmured in his bunk, trapped in a vision in which his skin and flesh fell away piece by piece. He felt no pain, but was left a bare skeleton, green-and-grey moss growing from his bones as he lay in a shallow grave. The moss thickened into fresh muscle, giving him a new form, and flowers blossomed on his verdant not-corpse. All the while he heard singing, wordless but the notes like a waterfall, sometimes light and refreshing, other times booming and powerful.

It was not the dream that was the nightmare, but the waking.

This night he was ripped from the embrace of the plant-death by Chastain barging into the dorm he shared with fifty other guards. All of them were veterans from Outside. Nobody ever called it the first line or the outer defences any more. The Outside was all they had to say. 'I was on the Outside, were you?' Even through the farts and snores, every man and woman woke at the loud footfalls of the new arrival, their senses keyed to any potential danger, a paranoia that even kilometres of high walls and gun towers would never set at ease for the rest of their lives.

'What's the racket?' demanded Sergeant Ongoco.

'Something's in the mess hall!' Chastain told them. 'Get your guns!'

'Where's the officer of the watch?' Ongoco asked as Katsuhiro and the others rolled from their bunks. Katsuhiro dodged aside as Corporal Lennox in the bunk above him dropped straight to the floor.

'Quick, forget your shirts!' Chastain hovered at the doors ashen-faced and wide-eyed, and then disappeared back into the corridor.

Bare feet padding on the varnished ferrocrete floor of the barracks, East Wall Second Guard Company followed, snatching lasguns from the wall racks as they flowed towards the passageway.

Katsuhiro was about five from the front of the line, Lennox beside him.

'Why didn't he sound the alarm?' asked Katsuhiro. Lennox just shrugged in reply.

It was only fifty metres to the mess – probably the reason Chastain had headed to the dorm rather than the watch station on the floor above. Lasgun in hand, Katsuhiro followed the others through the double doors into a broad hall filled with tables and benches, enough for five hundred troopers to be seated at one time. The only light was from dull orange night-lumens set in the walls, barely enough to see the vague shapes of the furniture.

The serving hatches in the far wall were all closed with pla-steel shutters but a paler light shone through the gaps from the kitchens beyond, swaying and dipping as though the source were moving back and forth.

'First and third squad with me,' called Ongoco, not both-ering to wait to see if any officers were going to turn up. He pointed to the doors to the right of the shutters. 'Second and fourth, that way. Fifth hold the rear.'

Part of second squad, Katsuhiro hurried towards the right-hand doors. The light played out through the cracks between and below, ripples of white tinged with green. His hairs prickled across his arms and the back of his neck as he caught a strange scent. It brought to mind a forest canopy and mouldering leaves beneath, though he had never seen such a thing. While Lennox reached for the door, Katsuhiro had a flash of the dream, the earthy scent of mulch soft beneath his rebirthing form.

'Weapons ready,' croaked the corporal, voice breaking as trembling fingers curled around the door handle.

Katsuhiro brought up his lasgun, Spilk and Kalama to either side of him with weapons readied too.

Lennox dragged open the door and the trio stepped forward, Spilk turning to the left, Kalama to the right while Katsuhiro was focused ahead.

The light came from everywhere, flashing from the reflec-tive surfaces of the massive ovens and stove tops, dancing around the dormant lumen fittings, gleaming from rows of pans hanging on wall hooks. The thud of the opening doors at the far end drew their attention, guns swinging towards Ser-geant Ongoco and his squad.

Katsuhiro advanced, allowing the rest of second squad into the kitchen, gun barrel swinging towards the shadows cast by the erratic light. The tiles were cold underfoot, the sensation helping to keep him grounded amid the otherworldly shimmer.

The smell of nature grew stronger and Katsuhiro thought he heard the sound of wind in trees, the rustle of leaves and creak of arboreal giants.

'There!' Kalama jabbed her lasgun towards a patch of wall between the chimneys of two bread ovens. Light rippled over bare brick, seeping along the lines of mortar. Dust crumbled where it touched, each speck falling slowly, glinting like a tiny particle of light.

Blinking, Katsuhiro thought he saw an outline in the gathering motes. Instantly he thought of a man, beautiful and strong, an arm reached out towards the troopers.

He heard Spilk snarl in disgust and the hum of an energy cell charging.

'No!' Katsuhiro knocked his companion's lasgun upwards as he pulled the trigger, the beam of red light blasting into the ceiling. Panicked shouts came from others and a flurry of shots erupted along the kitchen from both ends, hiding the wall in a cloud of exploding brick dust.

For a heartbeat longer Katsuhiro saw a face amidst the billowing specks, frown creased in disappointment, full lips pursed.

Then it was gone.

'By the Forefathers, that was disgusting,' muttered Kalama. Katsuhiro turned to see her lip ripple in disgust, eyes fixed on where the apparition had appeared.

He was confused. The entity he had seen in the ghost-light had been anything but disgusting. The memory of it left an ache in his chest, longing for its return.

'Everyone stay where you are!' barked Sergeant Ongoco. 'Nobody's going nowhere until this is reported.'

Katsuhiro caught a last flurry of leaf-whisper and the forest scent.

'What are you happy about?' demanded Lennox, eyes narrowed.

'Nothing, corporal,' Katsuhiro said quickly, pushing the smile from his lips.

Karachee Flats, sixty-eight days before assault

A strange light brought Zenobi from a fitful slumber. She awoke huddled on a bench, the company banner clutched to her like a child, her pack and lasgun sticking out of a half-open locker underneath. Her head rested on Seleen's shoulder, a folded coat for a pillow, who in turn was butted against Menber, who sat wedged against the wall.

The light came through the windows in a wavering, golden haze. It was sunlight, itself a rarity to the downhivers, but unlike anything Zenobi had seen before. She had managed the occasional trip to the hive-skin to watch a sunrise – it was virtually a rite of passage for those working on the line – and recognised that there was something sickly about the light that crept into the carriage to cast thin, long shadows.

There were far more people inside the compartment than intended, so that the benches were filled with half-asleep troopers, nearly as many curled on the floor between. She rose quietly, mumbles and groans sounding from those around her as their weight shifted, though she tried to ease herself free without disturbing them. She almost tripped over her kitbag and took a couple of seconds to shift it around and force it fully into the wooden locker.

'What are you doing?' murmured Achebe, slumping sideways into the space created by her departure. His eyelids fluttered open, a yawn splitting his face to reveal a dark tongue and stained teeth. 'Is it breakfast?'

Others were stirring or had already awoken, either just sitting quietly where they had found themselves or, like Zenobi, picking their way carefully through the maze of bodies to see what was going on.

She saw nothing of the officers – integrity or regular – and assumed that they had found alternative accommodation more suited to their rank. Sergeants Alekzanda and Asari-dokubo were crouched in the vestibule by the doors, sharing a knife to pare away slices of something from a rations packet. Alekzanda looked up as her movement caught his attention. His eyes were bloodshot, dark rims around them, but his expression was as determined as ever.

'I need some fresh air.' Zenobi said the words and a moment later realised how ridiculous the request must sound, coming from a downhiver who had lived in a family hab-chamber only a little less crowded than the train car. 'I feel…'

Alekzanda handed the knife to the other sergeant and stood up, hand moving to the handle of a door behind him.

'There's a sort of gantry on the roof.' He opened the door and the noise of the train's passage intensified. 'There's a few folks up there already.'

She thanked him with a nod and stepped past. A gnarled hand barred her, the fingers moving to the haft of the banner that Zenobi had brought with her.

'Don't want that going over the side, do we?' Alekzanda said sternly.

Zenobi reconsidered going outside, but her head was spinning and she really did need to get away from the smell and the heat of everybody. Reluctantly, she relinquished her grip on the banner and watched Alekzanda stow it in the corner.

Through the door was a short walkway that connected to the next carriage, made of wooden slats and canvas. Guide ropes lined the sides at waist and shoulder height, but it didn't look at all inviting as it swung with the motion of the locomotive. Thankfully the ladder to the carriage roof was a set of metal rungs bolted to the end of the car itself. Zenobi pulled herself up, taking deep breaths as she did so. The air was cool, not cold, tainted by the oil fume of the engine that passed along from the smokestacks, but it didn't taste of sweat and fear so that made it the most refreshing draught she had ever taken.

Another smell lingered on the breeze. Mozo. It reminded her of her aunts and uncles – her mother and father were both against smoking, a rarity among their family – and her thoughts strayed thousands of kilometres back across the world to Addaba.

There were three others on the gantry, which was little more than a metre-wide strip of metal with a short lip that ran the full length of the roof. There was nothing to stop anyone falling off, but the train wasn't going fast so if the fall didn't cause a serious injury it wouldn't be too much trouble to run and jump back on.

She didn't recognise the three that were there, two men and a woman. Their eyes flicked to her chest and hers to theirs, checking out their identity badges.

'Epsilon. Command squad?' said the woman, raising an eyebrow and affecting an air of being impressed. Her eyes were lined with wrinkles, a touch of grey at her temples. Her hands had calluses from manual work, a few burn scars on her cheeks that spoke of labour near the forges. If she'd been an uphiver she might well have been forty or fifty, but life aged one fast on the line and Zenobi guessed the other woman was ten years older than her, perhaps fifteen at the most.

'Zenobi,' she introduced herself, choosing to drop her second name for the time being. 'You're all from Beta Platoon?'

'Better Beta than nothing,' one of the men joked, flashing a gap-toothed grin. He extended a hand. 'Name's Wrench. Well, not my name, obviously, but what folks call me.'

'Wrench? You good at fixing things, I guess.'

He nodded and drew a slender hand-rolled paper tube from inside his coat, and offered it. Zenobi shook her head with a polite smile and pulled herself up the last couple of rungs. They all shuffled as best they could to allow her to step by, venturing further along the top of the carriage. Zenobi picked her way carefully past. She'd ridden moving crane booms when she had been no older than ten but the manufactories were definitely lacking in crosswind, unlike the roof of the train.

She looked back along the length of the vehicle, saw the track beyond it stretching into nothing. The ground was hillier here than where they'd embarked, a line of low mountains visible along the horizon to the right. There was a smudge against the sky, perhaps smoke where they'd transferred. It was dwarfed by vast columns of black fumes billowing into the sky from beyond the horizon. Every now and then she thought she saw a flash or heard the distant thunder of a detonation. It could have been a trick of sunlight and the rattling of the car.

Turning around, she looked where they were heading. An indistinct haze in the furthest distance might have been more mountains but it was impossible to tell. The sky above them danced with constant colour, reds and oranges of fire mostly, sometimes struck through with flares of blue and purple or a stark beam of yellow blinking down from orbit.

She watched for several minutes, thinking the display would stop. It didn't. She swallowed hard, confronted by the impossibility of imagining the power that was being unleashed upon the Imperial Palace. It stretched reality to consider the forces raging through the atmosphere, and the titanic energy holding it at bay. How long could such defences last against such unruly might?

Zenobi turned quickly as she felt someone standing behind her. It was the third of the Beta Platoon members, the one that had not introduced himself. The other two were deep in quiet conversation, arguing over something Wrench was holding, a book or pamphlet of some kind.

'When we find ourselves powerless, we understand what it is to look for the power beyond our knowing,' said the man. He smiled warmly and thrust his hands into the pockets of his coveralls, swaying gently with the motion of the train. He had the easy balance of one that had lived as an ore-rigger, riding the monorail cars from the foundry to the production line.

'I know where this power comes from,' Zenobi replied, eyes turning heavenwards. 'The wrath of Horus visited upon the city of the Emperor.'

'And He resists, doesn't He?' The man took in a deep breath, nostrils flaring. 'I'm Natto. Zenobi, right?'

She nodded confirmation.

'What if I told you that this wasn't about the Warmaster, but something vaster and more majestic?'

'I'd say you have a knack for stories,' Zenobi replied cautiously. 'Or perhaps fancy yourself a line philosopher.'

'We all wonder about life, don't we? What's it about? Why do we do what we do? Who makes us what we are?' He stepped closer, so Zenobi moved aside. Natto sauntered past, still talking, not looking at her. 'Most of the time it doesn't amount to a bucket of bolts, am I right?'

Zenobi said nothing, not sure what he was talking about. This didn't deter him.

'We're standing on top of a recommissioned mining train – that's what this is, I've seen them – heading towards the most destructive force ever to visit Terra. Wouldn't you like to know what that's really about? Why this war had to happen?'

'It's about Terra,' replied Zenobi. 'We all know it. Control Terra, you can control the Imperium. Slavery on one side, freedom on the other. For Addaba, for Terra and for all of humanity.'

'The recruiters' words, so well crafted, aren't they?'

'Are they false?'

Natto turned, still casual, a half-smile on his lips.

'I'm not trying to trick you, Zenobi. I'm not going to tell you what to think, what to believe.' He put his hand inside his coverall and pulled a small book from within. It seemed to be the same as the one Wrench was holding. Zenobi glanced back to see that the other Beta Platoon troopers were watching her and Natto, glancing up from their discussion frequently.

'I don't know why you think I'm here…'

'This book doesn't claim to have the answers,' continued Natto, oblivious to her suspicion. 'It does ask some interesting questions. It's called the *Lectitio Divinitatus.*'

'The lecto-what?' said Zenobi.

'*Lectitio Divinitatus.* That means Book of the Powers, something like that, in the language of the Palace. There's a whole sphere of understanding that's been kept from us. The Emperor, Horus, is all part of a universe that was hidden away.'

He held out the booklet but Zenobi folded her arms, determined not to be dragged into the man's lunacy.

'What sort of thing do you mean?' she found herself asking. Almost immediately she regretted opening her mouth, but Natto gave her no time to revoke her interest.

'The warp. It's not just another part of our universe that lets ships travel fast.' His hand still held out the book and he thumbed open some pages, trying to show her the lines of small print within. 'And the Emperor. The Emperor isn't a man, Zenobi. He's a–'

'I don't need to hear this,' she snapped. She advanced, but there wasn't room to push past. For a moment they both teetered around each other, almost falling from the roof, but he spun away with an easy movement, letting her regain her balance. Natto said something else but she was deaf to his words.

The other two stood up but didn't try to stop her passing.

With an effort to still her trembling hands, Zenobi swung down onto the ladder and descended to the carriage at a slide.

She barrelled through the door and almost straight into someone on the other side. She saw the flash of crimson and looked up into the unforgiving features of an integrity officer. His name was Abioye, assigned to Gamma Platoon.

'Is something amiss, Trooper Adedeji?'

She backed away, heart thumping. He stepped after, eyes intent on her face, trying to read her like a book.

'You seem out of sorts.'

Zenobi steadied herself, feeling squeezed between the integrity officer and the end bulkhead of the carriage. It was difficult to see past him, to the press of soldiery that filled the rest of the compartment, where her platoon companions and friends were.

There was nobody to help her.

She swallowed hard, but her fear subsided, replaced by a sudden anger. She hadn't done anything wrong, why was she feeling so guilty?

The lie of omission. That's what it was called, when you knew something but didn't tell someone.

'On the roof,' she said, flicking her eyes towards the ceiling. 'Beta Platoon. They tried... They had a book they wanted to show me.'

It took a moment for Abioye to understand her meaning. When he did there was just a flicker of recognition in his eyes.

'I see.' He stepped back, allowing her past. 'Return to your platoon. Tell nobody of this.'

'Yessir,' she snapped, her hand rising in automatic salute.

She stumbled past into the main part of the carriage. There was more of a semblance of order than when she'd awoken. Sergeants were gathering their squads and proper billeting arrangements were being made with weapons and kitbags.

Zenobi glanced back and saw that Abioye was gone. She felt pleased at her honesty, and not just because it assuaged the guilt by association that had tarnished her conscience the moment she had seen the prohibited book. As company standard bearer she had to hold herself to the highest standards of loyalty and, yes, integrity.

Rejoining her squad, she was soon swept into the daily life of the defence corps trooper, coming to terms with the same routine but in different circumstances. About half an hour later they were called to attend to the captain, who had reappeared in the carriage from whatever quarters had been secured away from the bulk of the company. She stepped up onto a bench near the door so that she could be seen by the whole compartment, several hundred pairs of eyes all turned towards her as one.

'The transfer station where we boarded has been destroyed,' she told them, each word enunciated carefully, her expression a study in sober impassivity. 'There were no survivors.'

Zenobi took this news with a sigh of resignation, and there was no particular reaction from the rest of the company.

'The trains we boarded are following different lines to the battlefront. It is unlikely that we will see the others again. Certainly not this side of victory for us. Elements of the 64th, 65th and 70th Defence Corps have come together on this train. Nearly six thousand troopers and three hundred officers and other ranks. Colonel Tadessa is not among them. The corps are combining higher officer staff functions and we will come together as a single operating unit. Old squad, platoon and company designations will remain for the sake of simplicity. However, we are no longer the 64th Defence Corps. All troopers, officers and other ranks aboard this train are now proud soldiers of the Addaba Free Corps.'

There were smiles and shouts of approval to greet this news.

Zenobi grinned, catching a look from Menber past the bodies of her companions.

'The Free Corps!' someone shouted.

'The Free Corps!' Zenobi called back, along with a deafening chorus of other voices.

Egwu smiled, nodding her acknowledgement of their enthusiasm.

'Yes,' she laughed. 'We thought that would be popular.'

The shout of 'Free Corps' went up again, and once more, until the captain raised her hands for quiet. The troopers settled as her expression became serious.

'The truth is, the hurried transfer has left us in bad shape. We have the same manpower as before, but heavier weaponry and specialist equipment was still being loaded at the time of our quick departure. The same is true of rations, water sanitation packs, ammunition and other supplies.'

The captain paused to allow the importance of this to sink in. Her stare roamed across her command.

'In addition, the crew that were trained to operate the defensive systems of this locomotive were mostly on the ground.' Disquieted mutters greeted this news, and Zenobi sagged with the thought of going almost defenceless into the attack on the Palace. 'A few that were servicing their weapons remained behind. You will each be shown how to man the guns over the next few hours and defence shifts will be drawn up by your platoon officers.'

Once more she waited for this information to seep into the minds of the troopers, hands clasping and relaxing round the baton she held at her waist. Zenobi could only imagine the strain the past twelve hours had placed on her commander and the other officers. She had no illusions that the rest of her life was likely to be brutal and short, but at least she didn't have to weigh up decisions that would alter the life chances of hundreds, perhaps thousands of others.

'Alpha Platoon, you will be first to report for gunnery training.' Egwu lifted her baton in dismissal and received the salute of her company in return. A burst of chatter filled the carriage as she stepped down from the bench and disappeared back through the door.

'Was never going to be a long fight anyway,' said Lieutenant Okoye.

FOURTEEN

The shiv cuts deeper
Evidence of daemons
Punishment

Lion's Gate space port, tropophex core, twenty hours since assault

A hundred and twenty strong, the Iron Warriors insertion force pushed up into the Lion's Gate space port like a splinter worming its way towards a person's heart. One by one they had gathered, the small force coming together over the course of several hours, while similar formations did likewise in other parts of the port-city.

Forrix had expected more resistance but having passed through the outer skin of the space port the warriors of the IV Legion had encountered little in the way of opposition. Most of the defenders were occupied with the tumult of beastmen and rogue troopers rampaging through the lower levels, or defending against the aerial attacks and landings that had begun in the uppermost reaches. As yet it seemed that the Imperial Fists and their allies thought the middle levels of the port unthreatened.

'Auspex shows nothing within seven hundred metres of our

position,' reported Allax, sweeping the scanning device left and right as the company waited at the junction of a dormant travelator and an arterial corridor.

The innards of the space port betrayed its purpose as a place of labour rather than a domestic hive. While the outer regions had been packed with defended hab-blocks, communal areas and transit plazas, the core of the Lion's Gate space port was filled with immense machinery for the transportation of materials to and from the landing docks at the summit and arranged in a spiral down the flanks. They had passed loading bays vast enough for Emperor-class Titans to pass through, accessed by lifters capable of carrying a company of battle tanks. Monorail stations abutted these cavernous spaces, their locomotives missing but their sidings filled with carriages, each a hundred metres long and forty high.

With vox contact too much of a detection risk, the IV Legion infiltrators were reduced to picking up the energy signatures of power armour, coupled with transponder beacons with a range of only two hundred metres – signals too faint for the standard monitoring stations to pick up. The click-click-click of the auspex on passive scan was audible above the creaking of the port's ancient metal skeleton, the clatter of chains swinging and the rumble of the ongoing barrages.

'We'll move up,' said Forrix, pointing his bolter towards the stationary travelator. They swept suit lamps into the dark tunnel, the light swallowed after forty metres. 'Nobody to find here.'

Captain Gharal led the way, a ten-strong squad with him. The others followed a hundred metres behind, close enough to give support if needed, far enough to slip away if that proved the more prudent course. Each of the thousand Space Marines had been chosen by the Trident, based on the reports of the field commanders regarding temperament and patience. No

glory-hound heroes, no warriors that would put personal honour above the mission.

An army of pragmatists, Falk had called it.

Forrix was in command, but his objective was nebulous. Kroeger's cunning plan was good enough to get them inside the
space port but ran short of details on what to do once they
were inside. To follow the shiv analogy, Forrix had promised
to find a vital organ to pierce.

Lacking any detailed intelligence regarding the interior of the
space port – their allies in the Alpha Legion had been disappointing on that account – Forrix was left with finding a target
of opportunity. In lieu of any defined objective, he had chosen a
geographic rendezvous, appointing a grid coordinate as the final
meeting point for the force. Smaller formations within the army
had been given waypoints so that they approached from different
routes, their full strength concealed until it had come together.

Falk had laughed at the plan, accusing Forrix of confusing
the IV Legion with the Raven Guard. The Warsmith's taunts
were easy to ignore: he would likely soon be dead, his body,
such as it remained, lost in the upper reaches of the space port.

Forrix checked his positional relay via a blinking dot and
rangefinder in his visor display. They were two kilometres
below and four hundred metres south-east of the final meeting
point. It was too much to expect that all one thousand warriors assigned to the mission would evade detection, but Forrix
hoped that he could gather a sizeable enough force before the
defenders realised what the scattered Iron Warriors signified.

After that it would simply be a question of holding out for
reinforcement. Would the dual attacks above and below re-
connect with Forrix's force in time, or would they be crushed
by the sons of Dorn and their allies, trapped in the depths of
the space port far from assistance?

* * *

Palatine Arc quarantine zone, Barracks-C, two days since assault

The quarters of the Imperial Army personnel had become the
abode of giants. Three Custodians stood watch at the entrances
to the main garrison block, barring all passage within. Those
stationed at that section of the quarantine perimeter had
been moved to a holding location deeper inside the Imperial
Palace – to the relief of many of them.

Inside, at the mess hall where the apparition had been witnessed, the only figure that did not look out of place was
Malcador, garbed in his robes of office, staff in hand. With him
were Constantin Valdor, the commander of the Legio Custodes,
and the primarch of the VII Legion, Rogal Dorn. They made
their surroundings look like some strange undersized play-stage
for children. Other elements of the Palace defences were of a
ratio suitable for demigods so that Space Marines, primarchs
and war engines could pass at will, but these hastily erected
barracks were meant for mortal humans alone.

Dorn crouched inside the kitchen rather than stand with his
head awkwardly cocked to one side, while Valdor had removed
his high-plumed helm before ducking through the doors.

'The Silent Sisterhood have been over every part of the
barracks,' said Valdor. 'There is nothing psychic here.'

'Yet four dozen men and women saw something in this
place,' replied Dorn. He glared at the spot of bare brick where
the vision had appeared, thinking back to recent events on the
Phalanx. He could barely countenance the threat of daemonic
attack here, within the perimeter of the Palace walls.

'Saw what?' said Valdor. 'Some reported a woman clad in
robes of green leaves. Another confessed to seeing fist-sized
flies bursting from the wall. Some claim the bricks turned to
putrefying flesh, others a one-eyed monster with broken claws
and the stench of faeces.'

'Some kind of hallucinogenic toxin?' suggested Dorn.

'Possibly.' Valdor looked around the rest of the chamber. 'There is no central environmental system through which it could be introduced. Something in the food perhaps.'

'Why here? Why now? Mortarion's Death Guard have been bombarding this sector for a month without relent, but there is nothing worth attacking here except lunatics and plague victims.'

'Perhaps this is the point,' said Valdor. 'Sooner or later something has reached the quarantine zone. That gave rise to this… apparition?'

Malcador coughed, one hand raised to his mouth.

'The both of you seem intent on dancing around the real subject at hand.' The Regent stared at them, eyes regarding each equally for several seconds. 'It was a daemon.'

'Daemon?' Dorn growled. 'Impossible.'

'Daemon. Neverborn. Nosferatus. Diabolarum. Nephilla.' Malcador sat on one of the stools beside a preparation worktop. 'Many names. All the same thing. A warp incursion.'

'How?' Valdor stepped towards the bare wall, a hand raised towards it. 'The Emperor's might shields us from attack of that kind.'

'We have seen that the telaethesic ward is imperfect.' Malcador looked at Rogal Dorn. 'Your tainted brothers setting foot upon Terra being the most troublesome example. We must assume that the bombardment by the Death Guard and this arrival are connected. Perhaps it was unwise to gather all of the plague victims in restricted spaces. Such confinement concentrates their misery. It provides a… Think of it as a power source.'

'Power source? A warp ritual, you mean?' said Valdor. 'Like the great slaughter that allowed the twisted primarchs to make planetfall?'

'That would suggest assistance from within,' Dorn said

heavily. He turned his attention to Valdor. 'I have every warrior I can muster stationed on the walls. I cannot spare any for patrols inside the Palace as well.'

'I have few enough Custodians remaining after our withdrawal from the webway. However, I agree with you, this is a matter for my people.'

'A proportionate response, Lord Valdor,' said the Regent.

'We should not let ourselves be too drawn on this issue, Malcador,' added Dorn. 'The Emperor will protect us against any dangerous assault from the netherworld.'

The Regent looked away at that moment, hand moving to his mouth as though to hide his reaction.

'What do you know, Malcador? Are you holding back?'

The Sigillite scratched the side of his nose, his glance moving from Dorn to Valdor and then back again.

'There was a time before when the telaethesic ward was broken.'

'When?' demanded the Imperial Fists primarch. 'Why was I not told of this?'

'You know of it,' said Valdor, catching Malcador's meaning. 'When Magnus came before the Emperor, he broke through the psychic wards.'

'I see.' Dorn set his gaze on Malcador. 'Do you think this is the work of Magnus?'

'Doubtful.' Malcador rubbed a thumb and finger together as he thought. 'His last, uh, arrival was done by sheer force of will. It would require a similarly unsubtle concentration of effort.'

'Yet you look concerned,' said Valdor. 'Is Magnus orchestrating a more insidious attack?'

'I do not know,' confessed Malcador.

'It should be obvious enough,' said Dorn. 'I know little about the realm of the psychic but I do understand that a being as potent as the Crimson King would leave traces for one of your ability to detect.'

'I...' Malcador sighed heavily. 'I do not know where Magnus is. I have felt his brothers, the ones touched by the enemy powers, but of the Lord of the Thousand Sons I sense nothing. He may not be on Terra.'

'His legionaries are,' said Dorn. 'It seems unlikely he would release them to the command of Horus unaccompanied.'

'I cannot give you an answer!' Malcador stood, staff thudding on the tiles. 'As I said, I do not know where Magnus is.'

Dorn took a moment to absorb this and decided there was nothing to be gained by pressing the Sigillite further. If news of Magnus surfaced, Malcador would be certain to share it.

'In the absence of any obvious cause, what are we to do?' the primarch asked his two companions.

'I will have a Custodian investigate to see if any further action is required.' Constantin Valdor regarded the Regent with a faint smile. 'Is one Custodian proportionate enough?'

'A perfect amount,' Malcador replied. 'Who do you have in mind?'

Karachee Flats, sixty-six days before assault

There was a bulky analogue chronometer mounted above each door of the carriage, though somewhat predictably their filigree-decorated hands told slightly different times. Zenobi found her attention drawn to them again and again, checking the passage of time. It was something she'd never been able to do before. Personal chronometers were expensive, only uphivers would have such things. Everyone else was ruled by the shift sirens, their personal observances and the routine of daily life. Zenobi had always known when it was ten minutes before the shift change warning siren because her neighbour, an older lady named Babette, was a habitual singer and broke into a tune at the same time every day when she was washing her clothes in the 'tweenshift. That she could now break down her day by the minute was incredible and she found herself timing various activities to see how long they took. Three minutes to unpack and repack her basic combat kit; five minutes for a self-heating ration can to bring itself to full temperature; less than two minutes to devour the warm contents afterwards.

Several times Sergeant Alekzanda admonished her for being distracted, but her new fascination meant that she knew it was sometime around two thirty in the afternoon when the squeal of brakes brought the train to a long, slow halt. The lieutenants and sergeants barked chastisements as the troopers started to move towards the windows to investigate if anything could be seen outside.

'Form ranks!' came the call from the doorway as Captain Egwu entered.

The squads fell hastily into place by their benches, arms by their sides, eyes fixed on their commander. Egwu entered flanked by Jawaahir and another integrity officer. Two other officers loitered behind her in the door vestibule.

'As of this time, I am assuming command of the Addaba Free Corps,' Egwu announced. 'My rank will be general-captain and I will have joint authority with Integrity High Officer Jawaahir. It is an honour to have been chosen for this position by my fellow officers.'

'The vote was unanimous,' Jawaahir interrupted with a smile.

'Indeed, an honour,' continued Egwu.

Before she could say anything else, a cheer erupted from the survivors of her company, a roll of congratulations and compliments. Egwu waited patiently for the ovation to subside, her expression oddly grim. When the last voices of celebration died away, she looked across the company, eyes moving from one officer to the next.

'The corps will assemble to witness punishment,' she said gravely. 'Alternate squads will ascend to the roof. Others will disembark to view from the ground. Punishment will be enacted in twenty minutes.'

This pierced the mood instantly. Egwu and her escort advanced along the carriage, the ranks parting as she approached, until they had moved on to the next compartment. Lieutenant Okoye rounded on his platoon.

'You heard our general-captain. First squad to the roof.' The troopers bustled towards the gangway but were stopped by the lieutenant, who plucked a lasgun from beneath the bench and thrust it into the arms of the closest solder. 'Armed. We are at war.'

They retrieved their lasguns, checked their power packs as they had been trained to do and then followed their sergeants in orderly fashion out of the doors and onto the roof.

Now that the train had stopped the ascent was less precarious. They led Epsilon Platoon up, meeting the first squad of Alpha Platoon halfway along the carriage. Zenobi found herself between Seleen and Menber. The crackle of the orbital attack to the north-east had not changed one bit in the hours since she had last been up there and her squad-companions marvelled at the display as she had done.

'It's been going like that for half a day now,' said Menber. 'How long can the Palace shields last?'

'I heard the lieutenant say we should be in the Himalazia within two days,' said Kettai from further along the roof. 'Do you think they'll last that long?'

'Doesn't matter.' This came from the Alpha sergeant. Zenobi didn't know his name. 'Bombardment might level the Palace but you need soldiers on foot to clear the ruins. The Emperor isn't going to stand on top of the Sanctum Imperialis and let Horus drop bombs and plasma on His head, is He? There will be plenty of fighting before this is over.'

'You sound eager,' said Menber.

'In the years from now, when my son and daughters have grown up, I want to look them in the eye and say I fought for them,' the sergeant replied, his eyes drifting to the distant, unseen Palace. A half-smile danced on his lips. 'I will tell them I was with the Addaba Free Corps, and I fought at the Imperial Palace to ensure they would never be the slaves of tyrants.'

'The Free Corps!' Zenobi shouted, swelling with pride, her fist punching the sky. A few others echoed her shout, but Menber gave her a quizzical look.

'Remember what we were saying earlier? What the lieutenant told us?' He dropped his voice and leaned closer. 'Nobody's going to make it back to Addaba. Nobody's telling their kids or grandkids nothing.'

'Maybe not,' conceded Zenobi, 'but our names, what we're going to do, will be remembered for a long time.'

'Careful, yeye,' said Seleen. 'Glory is an empty plate to feed from.'

'I don't want glory, I want to inspire,' said Zenobi. It was the first time she had been able to articulate that particular ambition, but the words seemed to capture her feelings well enough. 'Maybe someday a child in Addaba will read about Zenobi Adedeji and how she carried the banner of the company at the Imperial Palace, and maybe they'll think that was worth something and maybe want to do something brave and strong too. I'll be dead, I know that, but at least my life and death would mean something.'

'Not many heroes on the line,' said Kettai.

'No, everyone that works the line is a hero,' said Menber. 'You don't have to fight and kill to be a hero. Everyone still back at Addaba, manning the guns, heaving energy packs, pumping the water filters is a hero.'

'Said like a true believer,' said Kettai. 'The recruiters really did their work on your family.'

Any retort was cut short by activity further down the train. One of the storage wagon doors opened, wheezing down on hydraulics to make a ramp to the grey soil. A procession of integrity officers appeared, several dozen of them. They descended in pairs, each carrying a body. Zenobi sucked in her breath as she saw them, dressed in Free Corps coveralls, their collars and fronts stained dark. The bodies were unceremoniously dumped in a pile about thirty metres from the train and the integrity officers returned but emerged minutes later with a fresh cargo of the dead.

Speculation whispered back and forth along the roofs, and from those squads closer to the action came the rumour that they could see the badges on the bodies – most seemed to be from Beta Platoon in Zenobi's company, some from other platoons and two other companies. There had to be more than four hundred dead heaped together in the dust by the time the integrity officers were finished.

'Throats cut,' came the murmur along the line.

'Not wasting ammunition,' followed soon after.

Voxmitters crackled into life along the length of the train. The distortion in the voice that followed was so bad it took several seconds for Zenobi to decipher it as belonging to Jawaahir.

'These are the dishonoured dead. They have been found harbouring intent that is against the cause to which we have all pledged ourselves. The rot of false belief had taken root in their hearts and was deep, but fortunately had not yet spread far amongst us.

'In better times we might forgive such transgressions with milder punishment, but we are at war. Spare no sorrow for these traitors, for they would have doomed us and the cause for which we will fight. It is not for their beliefs that they have been punished, though they are at odds with our ideals. It is the disobedience and clandestine conspiracy that surrounds their actions that has taken them from the path of integrity. By allowing these forbidden ideas to foster, to

indulge in the conceit of speculation, they have shown themselves to be untrustworthy in all matters. They have allowed themselves to give ear to false promises, to consider fantasies that would erode their dedication and courage.'

A score of integrity officers marched into view, two columns of ten; between them shambled half a dozen other figures. They were naked and even at this distance Zenobi could see they were bruised and bloody, eyes swollen shut, some limping, others holding broken arms awkwardly.

'Their leaders. Had they been ignorant then punishment for negligence would be due. Worse, they were orchestrators of this dishonesty. Harbour no illusions, warriors of Addaba. The enemy has spies amongst us still. You were warned that elements dangerous to our cause were among you and yet these criminals not only protected lawbreakers, they encouraged them, sponsored their lies in an effort to further pollute our resolve.'

Feedback whined through the speakers. Zenobi winced, teeth gritted against the hideous noise. Jawaahir's voice was replaced by a deeper tone – General-Captain Egwu's.

'Free Corps, attend for punishment,' she ordered through the crackles of the voxmitters. Zenobi, like the thousands of others lining the roof, came to attention, lasgun at her side, the banner pole gripped tight in her right hand. *'For the wilful spreading of enemy propaganda and other actions at odds with the cause of the Addaba Free Corps, these officers before you are condemned to summary execution.'*

The naked men and women were compliant, spirits broken, as they were forced to their knees next to the mound of those they had led into deceit and death. The integrity officers stepped back and drew their pistols. One of the captives suddenly rose to his feet, fists balled. The report of pistol fire snapped through the air and he fell, half twisting from bullet impacts. Another volley rang out, felling those on their knees, puffs of blood exploding from their foreheads before they slumped into the dirt.

'In forty-nine hours, we will reach the terminus of our journey,' Jawaahir announced over the voxmitters. 'You must remain vigilant for all deviancy. Failure to disclose transgressions is itself a crime against our integrity.'

These last words made Zenobi shudder. Menber must have felt her unease, for when they were dismissed, he turned to her.

'What's the matter, cousin?'

'They spoke to me,' she said quietly. The words came as a stammer as the magnitude of what had occurred hit her. 'The conspirators. Tried to recruit me. I could have... What if I hadn't...?'

She tailed off, gaze dragged back to the corpses left beneath the careless sun. Already a cloud of flies was gathering. There would be maggots and other insects. No cleansing farewell in the endfires. Perhaps the integrity officers had already known about their secret. It seemed unlikely. Zenobi knew in her heart that the pile of dead was a direct consequence of her actions. She had never raised her lasgun, had not pulled her knife. With just a few words she had killed several hundred people.

The thought numbed her.

'You didn't, and you wouldn't,' Menber said, grasping her arm to pull her along the roof with the rest of the squad. 'You would never betray us.'

The train jolted into movement, the snarl of immense engines throbbing along its length. It brought Zenobi's thoughts back into focus. Those that had been snared by the lies of the Lectitio Divinitatus had been targeted for a reason. It was a virus, claiming the Emperor was a god. It eroded everything they fought for. And someone had been the first to whisper its untruths in the ears of Beta Platoon. The rot had been introduced, perhaps not even maliciously, but it was not her that had killed those men and women.

Someone had corrupted their companions, knowingly risking them for their own ideals. It took just one traitor to taint everything around them. Zenobi steadied herself and looked at the other squad members, eyes resting on her cousin, and then past him, catching a glimpse of Kettai as he swung himself down to the ladder.

It wasn't her loyalty that she was worried about.

FIFTEEN

A Custodian investigates
Stand by your guns
Berossus

Palatine Arc quarantine zone, Barracks-C, two days since assault

For three hours Amon Tauromachian had walked the halls
and corridors of the quarantine force barracks to acclimatise
himself to its layout and atmosphere. It was cramped for the
Custodian, who had disrobed of his armour after an hour so
that he could inspect some of the smaller spaces. Clad in an
anti-ballistic tunic and nothing else, he returned once more
to the kitchen where the manifestation had been encountered.

He crouched before it, eyes closed, picturing the scene as it
had been when the Imperial Army troopers had clustered into
the tiled chamber. He had read their accounts and spoken to
each of them in person, and could locate almost all of them
within a metre or two of where they had likely been standing.

He stood, head brushing the ceiling, eyes still closed, using
his mind's eye rather than any physical sense. Two forces,
converging from each set of doors. Afraid, some of them had
opened fire.

Amon moved to the wall, fingers gently moving across the rough bricks and lines of mortar. The indentations where las-strikes had hit. Some from the left, most from the right. No grouping that he could discern.

He backed away half a step, adding the strike pattern to his mental picture. Why here?

He retreated a few more paces and opened his eyes, glaring at the silent brickwork. What was important about the kitchen?

The first witness, Trooper Chastain, had confessed to sneaking into the mess facilities to procure an illicit off-shift meal. Cross-interrogation had revealed nothing amiss in his character or record. An opportunistic pilferer, but not an enemy of the Emperor.

So why had the apparition appeared in the kitchen? Had Chastain's guilty presence triggered something? Would any of them have been the wiser had not the hungry trooper entered at that time to encounter the manifestation?

He let his mental gaze widen again, encompassing the whole garrison block and the kitchen's place within it. It was a squat, unappealing building butting against the low quarantine wall around the Palatine Arc, now the plague slum nicknamed Poxville. The kitchen, one of three, was located in the south-west corner, closer to the outer wall than the others. Was that significant?

As though controlling a pict-drone he cast his mind back to the corridors, retracing the steps of the troopers as they had come to the kitchen. A short journey, nothing of importance there.

That was the moment Amon realised there was a blind spot. He'd paced out every passageway and room. There was a void of about four metres square next to the kitchens, right behind the wall.

With quick strides he circumnavigated the mess area and

came upon the officers' quarters that were set behind it. A large, tattered banner hung on the far wall of the main hallway, which led to four individual officer dorms. The hallway was about four metres short.

Amon carefully lifted the banner from its hook and set it aside. The wall was plasterboard, painted light grey like the rest of the barracks.

He set his hand to the right side of the centreline and pushed. There was a tiny amount of give but nothing else happened. Moving to the left-hand side he did the same. This time there was a faint click and the wall section spun about on a central spindle, revealing a chamber beyond.

His eyes pierced the darkness and took in the surrounds immediately. As soon as he saw what lay beyond the wall Amon activated his vox.

'Signal Regent Malcador. Tell him that I need him to come to the quarantine barracks immediately.'

It was an exceptionally humble shrine.

Two crates had been covered with a rough canvas for an altar cloth. Upon this had been set two metal cups, battered from much use, the regimental inscriptions still clear on the sides – Mercio XXIV and Gallilus XXXI. A ewer of red liquid – cheap wine, Amon's nose told him – sat between them. In front was neatly set a small cushion upon which had been placed a book.

The book was little more than a sheaf of mismatched paper held together with thin wire. Two words were written on the front, in plain handwriting.

'*Lectitio Divinitatus*,' said Amon.

'A fane of the Emperor,' said Malcador, eyes passing over the rest of the room's contents. Amon's gaze followed his, taking in a few chairs in a circle, and some tall candlesticks likely looted from a senior officer's belongings.

'And this?' Amon pointed to a stain upon the bare wall, directly behind where the apparition had been witnessed in the kitchen beyond. The rime had almost fully melted, leaving streaks down the brickwork. The floor beneath was also damp, bare ferrocrete darkened by the liquid.

'That…' Malcador cleared his throat and peered at the phenomenon more closely. 'That is not good news.'

Amon sniffed the air, detecting old sweat, gun oil and boot polish, as well as the musky scent of the unlit candles and the sharp, ozone-like tang he always associated with the Emperor's Regent.

'It's just water ice, nothing else.'

'Yes, just ice,' said Malcador, scratching his chin. 'Created by a massive localised drop in temperature.'

'But it's between two large ovens on the other side,' said Amon. He could picture them precisely, without even recourse to his helm's special suite of visual systems.

'Very localised.' Malcador flipped open the small book, eyes scanning the pages.

'We have known the cult of the Emperor has been active in the Imperial Army for some time – this is not a revelation,' said Amon. 'The Lectitio Divinitatus is even more widespread in the civilian population. Efforts to curb its influence were suspended when the siege began.'

'Yes, resources better spent elsewhere. I recall being at the senate when such decisions were made.'

'You disagree?'

'I am unsure. The Lectitio Divinitatus could end up being an enormous distraction from the real problem.'

'But…?'

Malcador gestured towards the ice-soiled wall.

'This is residue of psychic activity.'

'Does not the Emperor's shield suppress such energies?'

'Hence my concern,' said Malcador as he met the Custodian's gaze. 'The fane and this are connected, but it is not clear how.'

'What does it mean?'

'That's a rather complicated question, isn't it, Amon?' Malcador chuckled for a moment and then grew serious again. 'It means a crack, a tiny crack in the telaethesic ward. Forced from the inside.'

'There may be other instances that have gone undocumented. Perhaps even taken as signs of the Emperor's divinity.' Amon stepped outside the shrine room, his memories of the webway battles trying to surface at the thought of daemonic activity. 'The captain-general must be informed.'

'Valdor has many concerns, as does Lord Dorn. This will be brought to his attention during the hourly briefing as usual. And he will say that you must continue to investigate, because you only have evidence of one minor incident so far. Is this an isolated phenomenon or cause for wider concern?'

'This worship of the Emperor is forbidden. Monarchia was destroyed and a whole Legion of Space Marines chastised for misplaced piety. The Emperor has made His thoughts on the matter very clear.'

'I was at Monarchia too, I need no reminder of what the Emperor thinks about divinity,' snapped Malcador. 'And yet we cannot fight our own people at the same time as we combat Horus. Practicality necessitates some leeway.'

'Leeway is just a euphemism for a weakness that can be exploited,' said Amon.

'Our war cares little for absolutes. The matter at hand requires careful examination. You cannot hope to find and prosecute every gathering of the Lectitio Divinitatus. Find out what is particular about this group. Why did the manifestation occur here?'

'I think it obvious that the proximity to the assault of the Death Guard gives us some answer.'

'But how widespread is the effect? Not every plague victim is found. Is there some other connection we can chase down?'

'The cult is secretive. It will take a long time to make progress into its workings.'

The Regent joined him in the hallway, staff tapping on the hard floor as he stepped past. The Lord of Terra stopped a few paces ahead of Amon and turned back to him.

'There I may be of further assistance to you, Amon,' said Malcador. 'Someone with an… inside knowledge of such things.'

Nagapor Territories, sixty days before assault

A series of staccato machine bleeps over the voxmitters roused Zenobi from a half-slumber. She opened her eyes, still slumped against the back of the bench, and looked first towards the windows – still daytime, moving to evening. She sat up as her gaze passed over the others around her. All were looking at the speakers with some confusion, a loud hiss emanating from them.

Brakes squealed into life, suddenly slowing the train. As a human wave, those standing tottered and swayed from the sudden loss of momentum, several troopers tripping over each other or benches, their swearing lost amid the laughter of their companions.

The lights flickered and went out as the train came to a stop. The yellow light of late afternoon did little to illuminate the interior through the grimy windows.

The voxmitters crackled again, and then came the voice of General-Captain Egwu.

'There is a high risk of detection by orbital scan. All systems are being reduced to standby to dull our energy signature. Remain inside the carriages until further instruction.'

A worried silence followed this pronouncement until Lieutenant Folami broke the stillness.

'You can talk,' she said with a shake of her head. 'They won't be able to hear us in space…'

'This is all just a precaution,' added Okoye, making his way between the benches. 'Command have received word that a starship is passing over this sector. It is unlikely we will attract any attention, not when there are far more important targets to attack.'

The mention of targets and attack did nothing to ease Zenobi's concerns. She stood on the bench to look out the window, hoping to see something that might take her mind off the sudden stillness. The ancient dry seabed stretched for kilometres around them, nothing else in sight. It felt a blessing and a curse to be so isolated. It seemed unlikely that they would be discovered amongst the expanse of wilderness, but on the other hand any energy signature or vox signal detected would stand out like a guide flare at night.

A flurry of movement drew her eye to the door at the far end of the cabin. The slash of scarlet announced the presence of an integrity officer. Another was prowling between the benches on the far side of the lattice that divided the length of the cabin.

'Remember, be vigilant at all times,' he told them as he started a slow patrol of the compartment, his hands clasped behind his back. 'Be aware of your companions, watch for any oddity in their mood. It takes only a moment for security to lapse and betrayal would see us destroyed.

'As you are watchful, know also that you are being watched. Not by your brothers and sisters in arms, but by enemies masquerading as troopers loyal to Addaba. They will see your laxity and exploit it. They will appeal to your compassion and empathy and turn those virtues into weaknesses to be exploited.

'It is not just our guns that will carry us to victory over those that would make slaves of our future generations –. it is our resolve that will prove the greatest of weapons. If one of us flinches now, before we have even been tested, what will be their actions under fire?'

The integrity officer stopped about two-thirds of the way along the carriage, almost level with Zenobi. His eyes were a startling blue, unusual amongst the folk of Addaba, and they were like daggers of ice as they passed momentarily over her. She held her nerve, reminding herself that she had no shame to bear, that she feared nothing from the scrutiny of that piercing gaze. The officer moved on.

'Just sitting here, waiting for it to happen.'

Zenobi turned her head to find Babak climbing up next to her. He was almost as short, his delicate, callus-free fingers fidgeting with the belt of his coveralls. She knew him as a spindle-wright, one of those who maintained the machines that made the parts for the production line.

'I know what you mean,' she said. 'I think I'm ready for battle, but this isn't that. No chance to fight back. Just waiting for a beam of light to come down and obliterate us.'

'Don't be silly,' said Kettai from across the gap between benches. He looked relaxed, hands behind his head. 'A ship's not going to waste a lance strike on a train. Even if they spot us, it'll just be catalogued among all the other data.'

'Starship surveyor expert, are you?' said Babak.

'It's just sense, isn't it?' Kettai sat forward, hands moving to a pocket from which he produced a slender plastek flask. He pulled the stopper and offered the drink to them.

Zenobi caught the smell of spirits. She had never drunk before and was curious, but now was not the time to give in to that temptation. She shook her head.

'Isn't that contraband?' said Babak, his gaze flicking

nervously around the carriage. 'What if the integrity officers find out?'

'It's like the train and the starship,' said Kettai with a shrug. 'This isn't important enough to bother them. Maybe Lieutenant Okoye will put me on latrine duties, but nobody is taking me out and putting a las-bolt in my head over some tei.'

'Throat cut,' said Babak. 'Like those others. You're not worth the las-bolt.'

Kettai laughed and stoppered the flask before slipping it away. Zenobi noticed that he hadn't actually taken a drink himself but said nothing.

A sudden blast from the voxmitters made Zenobi jump, almost sending her sprawling from the bench. The engines grumbled into life and motors whined through the floor as the train started to get underway.

'See, nothing to–' started Kettai, but he was cut off by an announcement over the speakers.

'Defence quarters! All active squads to their guns. All inactive squads assume protective positions.'

A siren wail replaced the voice, its urgency setting Zenobi's heart hammering against her ribs.

'So much for not being spotted,' said Kettai, heaving himself up from the floor.

Zenobi's diminutive stature made her an ideal gunner and she crawled up into the cupola while the others got ready behind her. Squads from the carriage on the opposite end of the gunnery car were coming in and moving to their positions too.

She strapped herself into the gunnery chair, a single loop over her waist, and then pulled the lever that elevated her into the armourglass dome at the top of the car.

In front of her on a pintle was a quad-barrelled autocannon. It was far too heavy to aim manually; instead her hand came to a control stick between her legs, a firing pin projecting from the top.

'Engage traverse motors,' she called back. She was answered by a whine of power and the stick juddered in her grip. A few test movements set the autocannons rising and falling and adjusting slightly to the left and right. Her feet found the pedals that rotated the entire gun assembly. 'Engage rotary motors.'

A test of the pedals sent her in a circle first to the left and then the right. She reached forward and flicked a switch, activating a grainy greenscreen display just in front of her – the gun imager. There was nothing to see except clouds, almost indiscernible among the flashes of static and the darkening sky.

'Check ammo feeds disengaged.'

'Ammo disengaged,' came the reply from below, sounding oddly distant within the confines of the cupola. Zenobi depressed the firing stud. The autocannons clicked and clacked against their empty breeches.

'Firing test complete. Engage ammo feeds.'

There was a heavy crunch and scrape of metal as the four belt feeds were levered back into place within the turret mechanism. Zenobi's thumb hovered over the firing pin. If she pushed it down, a stream of high explosive shells would be sent searing into the sky.

She had live-fired her lasgun during their scarce training drills, but this was of a totally different magnitude of destruction. Added to that was the knowledge that she would likely be firing in genuine combat. The thought made her legs tremble and her head spin. It was not the idea of her death that set her nerves quivering but the knowledge that others were relying on her to protect them. If she failed, if she messed up in some way, it wouldn't just be her that died but Menber, Seleen.

Even Kettai…

Like a battle tank emerging pristine from the end of the line, Zenobi's experiences all came together in that heartbeat to bring another realisation. Everything the integrity officers said about vigilance was just as true and important as her stint as gunner. A single slip could bring calamity. If one enemy spy or sympathiser was allowed to infiltrate the Addaba Free Corps they could ruin the entire cause.

Her legs had stopped shaking. The speaker set into the bulkhead just above her head had quietly hissed into life. She could hear someone moving about in the command chamber set into the heart of the gunnery car; the squeak of a chair, the thud of something being dropped on the floor. A few breaths wheezed mechanically across the internal vox-link.

'This is Lieutenant Okoye, fourth gunnery car command officer.' Feedback whined. There was a pause punctuated by a few beeps and a hiss of static, which then faded, leaving the connection clear but for an occasional crackle. 'There are aircraft inbound to our position from orbit. It could be an overflight, they could be heading somewhere else, but we have to assume the worst. All weapons are now live. Anti-aircraft explosive rounds have been loaded.'

There was another pause and a sound that Zenobi didn't identify immediately but realised after a few seconds was the crinkling of plas-transparencies.

'The crew gunners have been spread across the train to provide experienced, accurate fire. Remember what they taught you earlier. Follow the line of your tracer rounds and lead your targets. Between the time something appears on your targeting imager and the time you open fire, a fast-moving craft will have covered a hundred metres and more. Weight of fire will keep them off us, do not conserve ammunition unnecessarily.'

* * *

Lion's Gate space port, mesophex exterior, one day since assault

Seventy kilometres above the ground assault, where the atmosphere became space, scores of drop-ship and attack craft squadrons descended towards the Starspear. They had been travelling for the better part of twenty hours, drifting tens of thousands of kilometres from ships beyond the range of the greatest defence lasers.

As they closed to near orbit, one by one their engines lit, a firmament of plasma jets springing into life against the blackness. Like shooting stars they fell, hundreds of craft each intent upon a different target, angling towards one of the Starspear's more than three hundred docking spars, platforms and quays.

Six strike cruisers powered through the void, dashing into the surveyor-wake created by the massed gunship assault. Drop cascades opened, disgorging payloads of assault pods, ejected from their bays by rocket boosters in the absence of sufficient gravity. As the laser beams of defence cannons speared out, the emptied starships broke away. The last was not quick enough, its void shields lit by the impact of a volatile blast. Like a pack of hounds the other defence positions converged their fire on the struggling vessel, swiftly overloading its remaining shields. One final slash of red energy tore through its engines, plasma detonations spilling like blue fire along its length.

Aboard one of the larger pods lit by the brief flash of azure was Berossus, once favoured of the Trident, fallen into disrepute after near-death at the hand of his primarch. The systems of his artificial body flashed with sensor data, highlighting the outcrop of ferrocrete to which he fell, as well as a spike of radiation from the detonating vessel above – the ship he had been aboard only minutes earlier. He cared nothing for the loss of the ship, and was long past any fleeting thoughts of mortality its destruction might have engendered, his thoughts wholly concerned with his immediate future.

It was quite rare for an objective to conveniently have three hundred square kilometres of dockspace for gunships and drop pods to land on. It was not a fact that amused Berossus as the metal capsule depositing him towards the Fourth Eastward quay-spur slammed through the thin atmosphere above the space port. It should have been his assault to lead, a glorious campaign for one of the IV Legion's most lauded warsmiths.

Instead he was encased in an artificial frame, scorned by the primarch and almost forgotten by his battle-brothers. The body of a demigod with the authority of an infant.

Retro-jets fired, slowing the pod's descent almost as harshly as an impact, but cocooned in the sarcophagus of his Dreadnought armour Berossus felt nothing. He was only dimly aware of pneumatically powered legs, his arms replaced with heavy weapons. Not for him the familiar pre-battle rush of hormones, a stacked atomic fuel cell for a heart. Crude kinaesthetic feedback gave him a rudimentary awareness of self, but to all purposes he was a mind trapped in a prison of ceramite, titanium and plasteel.

It was easy to regard his salvation as a punishment instead. Those that had kept him alive, had wired the broken remnants of his body into this machine, had thought they were preserving his legacy. All they had done was extend the life he would live knowing the shame of Perturabo's censure. More than the physical agony, the imagined pain of ghost limbs, the mental torment of that failure vexed Berossus. He had been ascending towards his prime as commander, a long service in the Trident assured.

And all because he had the misfortune to bear bad news.

The drop pod slammed into the ferrocrete apron amid a blast of jets and the scattered shrapnel of frag launchers – not that there was a living soul on the platform to oppose the landing. The access ramp whined down and explosive bolts detonated to release the crash-clamps that held his armoured form in place. Taking a heavy step, the thud of his footfall lost in the thin air, Berossus advanced onto the metaphorical ground of Terra.

With ocular contacts and inhuman sensors he observed his surroundings. Seven hundred Iron Warriors formed the landing force tasked with securing the uppermost ten kilometres of the space port. There was barely anything alive, the airless upper levels now a haunt only of those with power armour or vac suits. Pieces of debris from the destroyed starship fell around the Starspear. This far up they had little momentum, thousand-tonne chunks of metal and plascrete that drifted through the midnight blue as serene as snowflakes.

Berossus barely spared the descending meteors a thought. Even this mission was punishment, assigned a guard dog's role rather than spearheading the assault.

Not this time. He was a warsmith in his soul even if he was stripped of the prestige.

'My warriors, hearken to me!' His bellow leapt across the vox-links to his battle-brothers. 'Are we to stand upon this barren apron while lesser warriors steal our glory? Those with souls forged in battle do not stand sentry, they seek out the enemy and destroy them!'

Not caring whether any followed him or not, Berossus turned his massive frame towards the closest rampway leading into the body of the space port. He would reclaim his status as war-smith or be destroyed in the attempt.

SIXTEEN

Aerial attack
Khârn's gambit
On the trail of the faithful

Nagapor Territories, fifty-nine days before assault

Zenobi felt the vibration of the turret behind her moving. Looking up through the armourglass dome she saw the tips of twin lascannon barrels swing overhead towards the front of the train.

She depressed the left-hand pedal and swung in the same direction, attuning herself to the speed of the rotation. It seemed painfully slow and there was a second's delay between her foot pushing at the metal and the motors activating. The stick controller was more responsive, angling the guns towards the sky, but their range was limited to about ten degrees to either side of the centreline of the turret.

The voxmitter crackled into life.

'We have a confirmed contact. Aircraft descending from orbit to the north-east.'

'Which way is that?' Zenobi then remembered she needed to push the transmit stud in the control panel in front of her. Her left hand found the switch. 'Which way is north-east?'

'*Check your bearing sphere,*' came an unfamiliar voice. The accent was from a more southern Afrik hive, perhaps the Cape City. After a moment she remembered it was DeVault, the gunner that had run them through the brief training earlier that day. '*It's up and to the right of the transmit switch, like a floating ball behind a plex-glass disc.*'

Zenobi scanned the cluster of controls, trying to recall the hasty tutorial from DeVault. She found the bearing dial, a grubby white sphere marked with compass points and an elevation level, which showed where the turret was pointing and at what angle to the train. She saw that she was aiming almost due north and used the right pedal to swing back east a few degrees.

'Thank you,' she said, remembering to activate the transmit.

She peered through the scratched dome, trying to find something against the blue of the sky. There were occasional flashes that might have been the sun reflected off incoming aircraft, or equally might have been the flashes of the last orbital defence stations being destroyed, or perhaps anti-surface fire from one of the ships in the void.

'*Aircraft heading our way, confirmed three larger bomber-class signals. No escort detected.*'

'You okay up there?' Menber's voice was distorted by the metal tube that linked the main gangway with the turret.

'Don't distract me,' Zenobi snapped back. 'Just make sure you're ready to change feed lines when the ammo runs out.'

'Don't worry, cousin. We're all here on the line with you.'

She flexed her fingers on the control stick, her knuckles pale from the intensity of her grip. Her other hand fidgeted with the seam that ran down the left thigh of her coveralls, picking at a loose grey thread.

There was no chronometer within the turret. It might have been two minutes or ten since she had first climbed in, she wasn't sure. Panning the gun down, she used the imager to look back along the long line of carriages. Fumes from the engines obscured the already murky view, but she could see there was a slight curve to the train, the track bending them left, towards the north. Circling around, she looked ahead again. The mountains were larger than when she had seen them from the roof, the skies above them a constant strobe of emerald light and darkness on the crude screen.

The siren blare from the main compartment caused her to jerk against the belt over her lap. Her head banged against the plain metal seat back, bringing her focus sharply back inside the turret.

'Targets detected at thirty kilometres.' Lieutenant Okoye spoke quickly, the first time she had heard him sound anything but controlled and calm.

It was easy to forget that despite being officers, those that commanded the platoon and company were as inexperienced with actual war as the troopers they led. Authority on the line was very different to the prospect of combat. They had been assigned their roles underneath the general staff of the 64th Defence Corps, but that entire officer cadre had been left behind or wiped out.

It was inevitable really, she decided. At some point the appointed hierarchy was going to have given way to the reality of war. In some ways it was better that it had already happened, rather than later when they were embroiled in battle.

'Still on an intercept approach. Targets will be in range in four minutes.'

Zenobi started to hum one of the work songs to keep her mind settled. She trained the gun imager back towards the north-east, panning left and right a few degrees in the hope that she would see something against the artificial storm that boiled above the distant mountains. Clouds scudded across the view, further obscuring the sky.

She thought she saw a brighter flash but it might have been

from the ongoing bombardment of the Imperial Palace beyond the horizon. A second later warning horns blared again, ringing through the metal bulkhead and up through the accessway.

The spark became a distinct flare, racing towards the train from beyond the clouds.

'Brace for–'

Okoye's warning was cut off as a thunderous detonation rocked the train. The scream of tortured metal and ripple of noise from carriage to carriage swept around Zenobi. Engine protests snarled below, wheels screeching along the rails.

'Missile hit, missile hit!' Okoye was breathless on the vox, voice loud in her ear, cutting through the after-noise of the explosion. 'More incoming!'

A faster, higher-pitched rattle replaced the noise of struggling motors. Two pounding heartbeats passed before Zenobi recognised it as the gatling turrets firing at the incoming missiles. Small streaks blurred across the gun imager view, lit by the brighter spark of tracer rounds every few seconds.

Something larger sped past the jade circle of her world, a split second before another blast rocked the train. Perhaps it was only a glancing hit, or perhaps she had become accustomed to the violence of the first detonation. Whichever it was, the second impact seemed less traumatic.

'Zenobi! Open fire!'

Okoye's yell across the voxmitter dragged her back to the view on the gun imager. To the top right of the screen three birdlike shapes blurred against the clouds. She nudged the control stick towards them, pressing the firing stud as she did so.

The thunder of the quad cannons smashed into her like physical blows, her head crashing against the chair back again as she flinched from their fury. On the imager screen streaks of darkness whirred uselessly into the sky below the murky dots of her targets.

Two flashes, almost simultaneous, announced the firing of

more missiles. It took barely three heart-wrenching seconds before they hit. As before, they struck somewhere towards the rear of the train, the dual detonations briefly eclipsing the cacophony of guns that raged around Zenobi.

She felt the entire train lurching, the drawn-out shriek of wheels far longer than before, accompanied by a hideous metallic scraping.

Zenobi gritted her teeth, ears ringing, and fired again, using a combination of control column and pedal to guide her long fusillade towards the larger blots on the viewing scope. Other streaks of shells converged from further down the train, along with airburst blossoms from the dedicated flak guns mounted on the locomotive cars.

The enemy craft parted, becoming three distinct shapes now. One seemed to come right towards Zenobi. Two others headed away to her right. She tried her best to track the strike craft coming in her direction, aiming low in the hope that the diving craft would descend into her line of fire.

She could see the distinct silhouette as it dropped below the cloud line, stark against the mountain peaks. Broad, flat-tipped wings carried a fuselage that bulged with gun positions. Bright red bursts stabbed from the battery, scoring hits somewhere just behind Zenobi's position.

Perhaps they hit the carriage of Epsilon Company.

Her mouth went dry and her gut curdled at the thought. She slammed her foot onto the right-hand pedal, turning the turret hard as the attack craft banked away, coming alongside with its flank guns roaring shells back at the transport train.

She thought her next burst hit but couldn't be sure. Glitters of shrapnel and torn metal fluttered away from the vortices cut by its wings and she heard a defiant shout from one of the other gun positions.

'Reloading!' came the cry from below. She realised she had

been holding down the trigger stud for several seconds, ripping through the last of the ammunition feed.

She took her thumb away so that she wouldn't jam the mechanism the moment the new belts were fed into the loader. Her ears were accustomed to the din of the guns and through their roar she heard the howl of plasma engines. The attacking aeroplane banked away, twin plumes of blue pushing it upwards again as it sought altitude, the ire of the train's guns following it back into the cloud.

'Reloaded!' Menber's shout came a heartbeat after the loud crunch of the loader being rammed back into position.

Her target was gone, either circling for another attack run or heading back to orbit. Zenobi breathed a sigh and lifted a shaking hand from the control stick.

Her relief lasted a few seconds, only until the growl and thunder of the other guns reminded her that there were two other aircraft in the attack. At the same moment she came to this recollection, the gunnery car bucked like a snapping cable. Flame washed over the top of the armourglass dome, carrying with it spinning pieces of jagged metal.

The boom of the impact consumed her as the car tipped, hurling her against the strap of the chair. She threw up her hands, but not quickly enough to stop her face smashing into the control console.

The world listed crazily and she tasted blood. The screech of twisting metal, screams of her companions and flicker of flames faded, replaced with the blackness and silence of unconsciousness.

Upper mesosphere, one day since assault

Boarding torpedoes had never been used outside of a void assault and Khârn was starting to understand why. Even in the thin air of the upper atmosphere, friction was starting to overheat the nose cone. His vision was filled with amber displays from the network-linked system of the torpedo. A slight warping caused the whole forty-metre-long missile to shudder erratically, while heat crept deeper and deeper into the circuitry within the nose.

It could set off the impact detonators, tearing away the nose cone and ejecting an intense melta-blast designed to cut through the metres-thick hulls of starships, thirty kilometres above sea level.

The alternative was perhaps even less enticing – the circuits would overload, turning off all the impact systems so the torpedo would hit the side of the Lion's Gate space port at four hundred kilometres an hour with no retro-thrust or breaching detonation…

'I am Khorne's blade,' he muttered to himself. 'There is no life without death. Hnnh. Kill or be killed, such is the law of battle.'

The readout flashed as they passed the five-kilometre mark. Less than a minute until impact.

As with the rest of the strike on the Starspear, vox-silence was absolute, to give the defenders no warning of what was about to hit them. Other World Eaters were following in gunships, three thousand of Khorne's chosen, but the point of the spear was Khârn and five hundred of his deadliest fighters.

'How thick are the walls?' The question came from Balcoth, who was strapped into his harness four seats down from Khârn, one of thirty in the boarding torpedo. 'Will the melta-blast cut through?'

'Hnnh. Too late to ask now,' the captain grunted back. 'Should have thought of that earlier.'

Laughter greeted the reply.

'My knife will feast on the entrails of Sigismund,' growled Khordal Arukka.

'If the Blade of Dorn is there, he is mine,' snarled Khârn. His fingers flexed around the haft of *Gorechild*. 'I'll kill any that challenge my claim.'

Cowed by his assertion, the rest of the warriors lapsed into silence.

'Ten seconds,' Khârn told them.

The restraints pressed tighter, hydraulic rams sliding into position along the sides of the torpedo to absorb some of the impact.

Lights blinked amber and then red. Khârn felt sudden deceleration with a surge of relief. Twenty metres from impact the meltas fired, turning the nose of the torpedo into a white-hot lance.

Armour squealed protests and the rams split, showering hydraulic fluid as the prow met ferrocrete. Khârn's neck twisted hard and he heard a curse from Galdira, who lost his grip on his chainsword, the weapon clattering past them along the deck. Khârn looked at the chains he had used to bind his axe to his vambrace. Yes, he had unfinished business with Sigismund, a lesson to complete.

The booming detonation throbbed along the length of the torpedo even as the remnants of the nose cone petalled outwards into an assault ramp. The restraint exploded upwards and Khârn was out of his seat, plasma pistol in one hand, *Gorechild* in the other.

The torpedo had struck a gunnery position, punching through the outer revetment of an anti-orbital laser. The remains of the crew were smeared amongst the debris, their environment suits turned to black tatters, their gun little more than twists of molten metal splashed against the walls.

Plunging through the vapour, sirens wailing around him, Khârn headed straight on, hearing the pounding of his hearts and the thuds of his companion's boots on broken ferrocrete.

Shapes loomed ahead, helmed and semi-armoured. *Gore-child* roared, taking the head of the first, sweeping the guts from the second. Khârn let his Nails take him to the bliss of destruction, knowing there was nothing but enemies in front.

Sanctum Imperialis, three days since assault

The sky over the Sanctum Imperialis was a sheet of flickering purple and black, and had been for months now. The unnatural twilight had cast its shadow over the Emperor's capital for so long that Amon barely paid it any heed. Now he looked at it with new insight, wondering if the storm above was more than just a physical symptom of the long bombardment. Was it indicative of that other, invisible war?

He enjoyed a good vantage point on a walkway that ran alongside an abandoned terrace overlooking the Via Principa – the main arterial route from the plaza of the Lion's Gate to the immensity of the Sanctum Imperialis itself. A city within a city that housed millions, large enough that in past times it would have been considered greater than most nation states. Its populace had been purged initially but as more and more of the outskirts by the Ultimate Wall were demolished in expectation of a traitor breakthrough, increasing numbers of their displaced inhabitants sought shelter in the sprawling shanties that had grown up among the colonnades and fora of the great and powerful.

It was to one of the tent slums that Amon travelled, eyes fixed upon a lone figure in the masses half a kilometre below.

Colonel Nhek Veasna. A decorated officer of the Angkorian Dragoons, itself one of the lauded Old Hundred regiments that had taken part in the Unification of Terra. It was her name that the lieutenant in charge of the quarantine garrison had finally confessed as his introduction to the Lectitio Divinitatus.

Finding her had been easy enough; she was attached to the Dragoons' Third Brigade as a command liaison. A position, Amon had noted, that allowed her to move freely between many different elements of the defence force without hindrance. In all likelihood she had a more senior patron in the general staff of one of the defence regiments, but for the time being Amon had focused on her as the most promising lead to follow.

He'd spent two days trailing her from one Imperial Army garrison to the next, and she had interspersed these duties with visits to several refugee encampments. Amon had decided not to attempt to infiltrate such gatherings, content to know that the only reason for her presence was the proselytising of her faith to the homeless and desperate. A Custodian was not such a rare sight that he drew unwelcome attention, but to get closer to such gatherings he would have to divest himself of his armour, which seemed unwise given that the Palace was under direct attack.

Earlier that day, Colonel Nhek had been summoned to a council of senior officers – arranged at the instigation of Valdor on request from Amon. He had left the request and then initiated blood games protocols on the assumption that the Lectitio Divinitatus could extend as high as the Imperial Senate members. He could not afford for anyone to influence his mission, nor risk any report of it passing beyond the Legio Custodes. Vox-silent, he had single-mindedly tracked Nhek without any further communication with his order, and would make no contact until he was ready to make his report.

Brought to the Sanctum Imperialis, Nhek Veasna had used the opportunity to make contact with several other heralds of the Lectitio Divinitatus. She had barely attempted secrecy, such was the growing confidence of the cult that they would not be prosecuted. It was not Amon's decision to make, but he was of a mind to argue for a very visible and memorable chastisement.

Amon could understand their weakness of spirit, but he could not forgive it.

Nhek had also been granted a leave of twelve hours before being posted back to her commander. The first six she had used for rest and sampling some black-market luxuries – nothing specifically contraband, just consumables that were becoming very rare like fresh water, menthol lho-sticks and some mild alcoholic beverages.

Amon had been on the verge of following up some of her contacts he had discovered when he realised that he had been party to a well-organised deception. It was not aimed at him specifically, but the more obvious meetings and exchanges had been intended as lures for anyone following the colonel. Six hours of low-grade indulgence provided the perfect opportunity for any move to arrest Colonel Nhek, and at the same time offered cover for a far more subtle communication. After all, what did a colonel have to exchange for rare goods? Currency had rapidly fallen out of favour except among the most optimistic dealers who thought it would have value after the siege was lifted. For most it was information or barter, but Nhek Veasna had not been misappropriating supplies. The same applied to sensitive data that her position afforded her. There was no evidence she was betraying the trust of her military rank.

That left only spiritual exchange.

If his suspicions were confirmed, he was following Nhek to a secret gathering of faithful inside the Sanctum Imperialis, consisting perhaps of a few high-ranking officials with dealings in the black market themselves. The illicit trade was a convenient mask for those wishing to communicate about an even more sensitive issue, and those that acted as vendors would be as likely to trade information about faith and the Emperor's divinity as they were powercells and rations packs purloined from front-line consignments.

She faded into the thousands-strong sprawl of humanity that swelled around the Processional 16 gate, where almoners from the Palace distributed medical and nutritional packages to the needy. Amon's research had shown that burgeoning religions frequently preyed upon the least fortunate for support, and he expected the Lectitio Divinitatus was no different.

Reaching the conveyor at the far side of the terrace, he lost sight of Nhek, but he was not concerned. Her particular scent – enhanced by illegal beer and pungent lho-sticks only an hour earlier – would make her easy to track even through the interior of the Palace.

Descending to almost ground level, Amon crossed to the outer districts of the Senatorum building about three hundred metres from where the Via Principa ended at the huge Bastion Argentus. Once inside he picked up Colonel Nhek's trail near the Concordia Central, and from there followed it until he had her within sight in the concourse leading to the Hall of Widows. He saw her enter by a side door, and ascended several floors to come upon a sentry balcony overlooking the main hall. As he approached, he found the sentry post unguarded, the guards doubtless relieved from duty while the conspiratorial gathering took place.

Slipping inside he picked up the babble of voices from below – far louder than he was expecting. Moving up to the curtained edge, he peered down into the amphitheatre and saw that there was at least a hundred people gathered. Others were still entering.

At the same time he observed this Amon's senses prickled, drawing his eye to one of the other sentry balconies on the opposite side of the hall, about three storeys lower down. A woman of middle years was standing there looking directly at him. She was blonde, pale-skinned, dressed in a long skirt of light blue and darker blue blouse. She picked up the closed-vox dialler on the wall and an instant later the device installed on his balcony purred into life.

He answered it.

'How are you here?' he asked.

He had recognised the woman the moment he had laid eyes on her. Like many of those detained by Dorn or Malcador, her image had been circulated amongst the Custodians in case she somehow escaped her confinement. Now she was looking at Amon with a wry smile, obviously expecting him.

Euphrati Keeler.

SEVENTEEN

Technophage
Unexpected assistance
Smoke and fire

Lion Primus Strategium, four days since assault

Rann disliked red lights and sirens. The Lion Primus Strategium was alive with both in strobing, screaming harmony. Though he was immune to panic, lesser soldiers were not and he felt that sudden clamour was a poor way to bring about quick, clear thinking. Despite his misgivings, the adjutants, logistaria and legionaries moved with brisk purpose from console to console, updating the primary and secondary displays in wake of the latest alert. Schematics of the Lion's Gate space port flashed up on every screen, covered with warning symbols and scrolling runes.

It was almost an hourly occurrence as fresh enemy attacks from above and below assailed the defenders. Surveyor malfunctions and system errors had made a mockery of trying to predict their landings and movements, and this time it appeared as though the entire port was on the verge of being overrun. It was impossible, the enemy were far from such a victory, but the sight of hostile signal returns throughout his command zone was a shocking reminder of what Rann was trying to prevent.

'Shut off that noise, and those lights too,' he snapped. Rann leaned over the main display table, trying to take in the sudden wealth of information. He rounded on the logistaria at the control panel. 'How is this happening?'

The tech-priest clicked and warbled for a few moments, brass eye-lenses dilating and narrowing several times within the folds of her red hood.

'There has been another noospheric intrusion, Commander Rann.'

'That's not an answer.' Rann waved a hand at the data still accumulating on the display. 'Is this real, or not?'

'There have been confirmed enemy landings on the meso-phex platforms, Commander Rann. There have been confirmed enemy contacts in the stratophex core, Commander Rann. There are ongoing engagements in the tropophex skin- and mantlezones, Commander Rann.'

'But many of these signals are… false? Errors?'

The logistaria worked the panel controls and a pulse of static rippled across the display, in places turning some of the red data sigils blue, and in others green. There was still a lot of red all across the space port. Much of the base was swathed in green, which Rann took as a good sign until the logistaria spoke.

'The green runes signify confirmed contacts with enemy weighted eighty or more on the threat-factoring scale employed by my data set, Commander Rann. The blue runes signify confirmed contacts with enemy weighted thirty or less on the threat-factoring scale employed by my data set, Commander Rann. The red runes signify unconfirmed contacts with enemy of unknown weighting on the threat-factoring scale employed by my data set, Commander Rann.'

'So, the red ones are fakes?'

'Unknown. The red runes may represent legitimate but unconfirmed enemy contacts of variable threat level, Commander Rann.'

'Do what you can to confirm the reports and scrub the rest,' he told the Martian.

He gave the screen one last inspection, trying to see if strategic experience could tease any truth from the clusters of flashing icons. If he looked at the patterns in a certain way, there appeared to be a general movement from the uppermost levels down. There were certainly enemy in the surrounding areas of the bridgeways and monorail connections to the main Lion's Gate. The connecting rails and roads were well defended, but if they were to fall into the hands of the enemy, the traitors would be within striking distance of the gatehouse itself.

Rann knew his strengths, and the limitations of his authority, and both were being tested by the impending crisis.

'Comms, I need an urgent connection to Lord Dorn. *Urgent.*'

'Yes, commander. Prioritising a command vox for you.'

He felt like he should be reeling off orders to deal with what was happening, but the truth was Haeger was already in place to make those decisions. The majority of his field commanders were experienced enough to assess for themselves the local situation; better than he could with unreliable battle-data.

He checked the display again, but it was no clearer than thirty seconds earlier.

'Commander, I have Lord Dorn's equerry in vox-contact.'

'Tell him I need the primarch. I need to speak with him immediately.'

There was a quiet exchange between the legionary and the equerry at the other end of the vox-link. For the first time in several years the commander heard several Inwit curse phrases, including a pointed comment that the listener would go into an ice storm without a coat, one of the gravest insults from Rann's home world.

'Shall I connect the channel to the briefing room, commander?' the vox-operator suggested, nodding his head towards the adjacent chamber.

'That seems sensible,' replied Rann, realising that some discretion might be needed in the circumstances.

Rann strode into the chamber and sat down at the broad oval desk within, punching the vox-connecting button set into a rune pad upon its surface. The speaker built into the ceiling hissed into life.

'I am conducting contra-siege operations against the Death Guard attack, and Lieutenant Takko is demanding an honour duel with your vox-officer. Explain quickly.'

The lord seneschal took a breath, figuring out where to begin. There was no point trying to be coy about the situation.

'The defence of the Lion's Gate port is compromised, Lord Dorn. The traitors have made ground through the base, established a presence in Sky City and in the last hour conducted massed landings in the docking spires. Our response is being hampered by an intervention through the noosphere and electronic systems, rendering augurs and comms erratic.'

'Give me an assessment of the threat. Can you recover the situation?'

'It depends on what you want me to do, Lord Dorn. If I concentrate defences around the gate connections I will have a static position that can hold for some time. If you want me to retake lost ground… The attack in the base can be contained but I think that if we do not press them in the Starspear, they'll have a steady reinforcement route. Of course that will leave the bridges vulnerable.'

'Do not allow the enemy to gain a foothold. It sounds as though you have a plan, what do you want from me?'

'Permission to destroy the bridges, Lord Dorn.'

'*Denied. Retaining possession and access to the space port is preferable. Time is of the essence and it may be the case that when Roboute Guilliman arrives we will need the Lion's Gate port to bring down his troops with sufficient speed to turn the battle. Every hour could be the difference between the Emperor's victory or defeat. The bridges also provide the means for a massed counter-attack should too much of the port be overrun.*'

Rann bit back the arguments that rose to his tongue, knowing that the primarch had made up his mind.

'Understood, my lord. In that case, I request the despatch of a second ranking commander to ensure redundancy of leadership. I intend to take to the field to combat the enemy gains.'

'*You have someone in mind?*'

'First Captain Sigismund's presence would be invaluable.'

Rann resisted the urge to drum his fingers on the table edge as he waited for Rogal Dorn's answer. That the request had not been turned down immediately was a good sign, he thought, but he started composing his arguments in favour of the decision just in case.

'*I can spare three thousand more legionaries. It will take some time to assemble them from across the Palace so that we are not weakened elsewhere. You will have to make do with that.*'

'They will be a great help, my lord. If possible, I would suggest a counter-aerial assault to coincide with a renewed offensive from my attack from Sky City.'

'*You want me to send Sigismund's force in by air?*'

'That would be the swiftest way into the battle, my lord.'

'*I agree. I will have Sigismund contact you directly to work out the details once the strike force is ready to leave.*'

'Thank–'

The vox hissed into dead static, the connection broken. Rann flicked the dial to his command channel.

'Lieutenant-Commander Haeger! Bring my strategic council to the briefing room. We have a counter-attack to plan.' He sat back in thought for a moment before activating the switch again. 'Have Magos Deveralax come as well. We need to discuss how to eliminate this new electronic threat. And have her bring her best demolitions experts.'

Sanctum Imperialis, central zone, three days since assault

Looking across the expanse of the Hall of Widows, Euphrati Keeler watched the Custodian carefully, the steady tempo of his breathing coming to her ear through the vox-receiver. He hadn't raised his weapon, which was encouraging only to a certain point. Her next words would frame the rest of their relationship. She wanted to tell him that the Emperor had guided her to this time and place, but a lesser truth would have to serve for now.

'Malcador sent me to help you.'

'I see. How did you know I would be here?'

'I'm sorry, but you've been led on something of a false trail.'

'Explain.'

'You went into shadow guise before Malcador could tell you that I would be assisting you. Your training meant you would ignore all vox contact. I tried to find you but had to give up, even though I knew you were following the colonel. You're very good at what you do.'

'How did you know I would follow Colonel Nhek to this place?'

'I wouldn't feel put out, Custodian Amon. It was Valdor himself that helped lay the bait once it was clear we could not contact you by conventional means. From your request he deduced you would follow the lead of the colonel and Sindermann received word that she would come to this meeting.

I thought I would have to wait a while longer but you were very prompt.'

'*Has this been some kind of trial? A reverse blood game to test my abilities?*'

She shook her head.

'No, Custodian Amon. This is all very real. The apparition, the confession, the gathering you are witnessing were not staged for your benefit.'

'*These are members of the Lectitio Divinitatus. Conspirators in the cult of the Emperor.*'

'High-ranking, as you can see. They are unaware of our presence. I agreed to help you navigate the labyrinth of the Lectitio Divinitatus. Conditional upon my aid was Malcador's promise that nobody within the cult will be prosecuted unless found guilty of some greater crime. You are here to uncover the source and scale of the daemonic intrusion, not to wage war upon the Lectitio Divinitatus.'

'*I do not take orders from political agitators, nor does Malcador's oath bind me.*'

Keeler sighed.

'Firstly, without my help you will find out nothing. The moment the Lectitio Divinitatus knows you are seeking them, they'll disappear. Secondly, perhaps you miss the meaning of Valdor's involvement. I am here with his full, ah, blessing.'

Amon stared at her silently for several seconds longer, not moving at all. His expression was impossible to read, a blank canvas of emotion. Eventually he gave a perfunctory nod.

'*Very well. We need to agree our objectives and approach. There is a disused common area on the fourth level of the adjacent quarters. Do you know it?*'

'I can find it. I'll meet you there in ten minutes, Custodian.'

He hung up the receiver without further acknowledgement, disappearing back through the curtains a heartbeat later. Keeler slid her vox-handset back into its sconce and turned to lean her back against the wall next to it, letting the tension flow from her body. The curtain twitched.

'Is it done?' a voice asked from the hallway beyond.

She pulled back the curtain to reveal a silver-haired man, face lined with age. Despite his wizened features he held himself straight, gaze firm, voice strong. He was every bit as imposing and charismatic as he had been at the height of his prowess as one of the iterators of the Imperial Truth. Kyril Sindermann, now her herald to the growing masses of the Lectitio Divinitatus.

'That went better than expected,' she told him. 'Malcador warned that he is a hardliner when it comes to matters of faith. He was at Monarchia.'

'Perhaps that was why Valdor chose him for the task.'

'If Valdor wanted the Lectitio Divinitatus eradicated, he would have ordered it so, long before now. I think Custodian Amon has a talent for rooting out hidden things. Nothing more.'

'Even so, you cannot trust him too much. You are a saint, a valuable hostage…'

Keeler stepped through the curtain and answered with a smile.

'Trust is a commodity that comes and goes, my dearest friend. Faith is eternal.'

Nagapor Territories, fifty-nine days before assault

An insistent banging and the stench of smoke woke Zenobi. She was still strapped to her gunnery chair, hanging over the control console. The armourglass of the dome was intact, heavily smeared and scratched, but through it she could see the bent barrels of the autocannons and the furrows they had scored through the dirt as the car had tipped off the track.

The metallic clang of a hammer dragged her senses back inside. Between each blow she heard the crackle of flames and through the ringing in her ears caught her name, very muffled from outside. She braced a foot against the side of the turret and unclasped the strap, falling sideways between the control console and the dome. From this new position she could see that a panel had torn away, blocking the access ladder into the cupola. Flames flickered from the cables that had been exposed. The fire didn't seem very big, but it was between her and the route out.

That was when she remembered the ammunition feed.

'Help!' She slid boots first along the hatchway and slammed her foot against the twisted metal sheet. 'I'm alive! I'm in here! Draw the ammo feed! There's a fire!'

She battered the metal several more times, shouting for her companions to remove the ammunition belt feeds. The fire was growing in brightness, sputtering and flaring as it reached the lubricated turntable of the quad cannons. She worried that an electrical discharge might make the whole metal turret live and scrambled back, trying to wedge herself into the non-conductive armourglass dome, one rubber-soled boot pressed against the chair.

A thump right behind her jolted her head back, banging it again. There were figures outside, scraping away at the grime that had accumulated on the dome. Menber peered through, eyes shielded by his hands, a cry of relief becoming a short laugh as their eyes met. He grinned and said something but the thick armourglass reduced it to meaningless mumbling.

'I can't hear you,' she mouthed deliberately, shrugging her shoulders. 'There's a fire. You need to disconnect the ammunition before it blows.'

He nodded and gave a thumbs up. Zenobi focused on his mouth as best she could, turning her body so that she was more or less parallel with him. Menber nodded but she couldn't tell if he had really understood. She raised her voice, shouting each word with careful intonation while pointing back to the hatchway.

'Fire! Get! Me! Out! Of! Here!'

A few others gathered, their lasguns turned in their hands. They started hammering at the armourglass with the butts of their weapons, but the only discernible result was deafening noise within the turret.

'Stop, stop!' Zenobi waved her hands and then shielded her ears. Menber noticed and called for the others to back away.

Zenobi's eyes were stinging and it was getting more difficult to breathe as smoke continued to fill the cupola. She swivelled around to look towards the ladderway. The fire was still burning within the exposed bulkhead. It wasn't large but the fumes were acrid, a mix of burning lubricant and melting plastek. Looking around the turret revealed nothing that could put out the flames.

The smoke was far more dangerous than the heat from the fire. Zenobi was almost unable to keep her eyes open, blinking hard all the time as tears streamed through the grime on her face. Every breath felt like inhaling razor blades.

That was when an idea struck. Zenobi turned her attention back to the dome and signalled for Menber and the others to move back. Almost blind, her fingers fumbling every delicate motion, she persisted. Every few seconds coughs wracked her, doubling her up. She eventually unlaced her boots and wedged them under the control pedals. A dizzy spell stopped her for several erratic heartbeats. She wanted to suck in air but knew that would only make it worse.

Next came the coverall, an even more awkward struggle in

the confines of the turret. First one arm then the other came free. A sudden crack and green flare from the entranceway marked the fire reaching some new source of fuel. The smoke became darker, leaving a black slick along the metal as it flowed up into the turret. She shifted to the rubberised seat, nearly lying down to pull the heavy uniform off her legs. Folding a rough rectangle, its arms and legs tucked inside, she put it to one side and drew her boots back on, still nervous about electrocution.

She moved along the ladderway at a crouch, trying not to touch anything. The curls of her hair stood up with static and the choking smoke was thick in her throat. With the folded coverall held out before her like a shield, she lunged forward, thrusting it into the exposed cable compartment.

The thick folds of material fitted almost exactly, cutting off the air. Cautiously, she drew it back to see if there were any flames left. A spark from a severed wire caused her to flinch, but as far as she could see, the fire was gone. Zenobi filled the hole with her uniform just in case, hoping it wouldn't catch alight from a stray discharge. She started to kick at the cover that had come away to block the entry hatch.

'Can you hear me?'

There were voices and movement below. Lieutenant Okoye's face appeared in the small gap between dislodged sheet and floor.

'We are improvising a cutter out of the laspacks. Step back.'

'What about a melta?' she replied.

'Too powerful, it might blast all the way up into the turret.'

She obeyed, scuttling back up to the dome. A hiss joined the symphony of other noises that creaked and rattled through the derailed car, and she saw a red glow appear on one corner of the lodged metal plate.

Hammering resumed, bending the metal where it had been

heated. Gloved hands grasped at the torn edge, twisting and pulling. Zenobi almost blacked out again, trying to breathe as little as possible – the fire was producing no more smoke but there wasn't enough ventilation to let the trapped fumes escape.

The sheet buckled. Almost unconscious, Zenobi threw herself towards it, slamming shoulder first into the metal. Corners screeched along the entranceway but it gave under the impact, sending her, the metal and several troopers sprawling into the main gangway. A shriek left her lips, coming from somewhere she hadn't known existed, quickly followed by a lungful of acrid but smoke-free air.

She lay on the metal, eyes closed, chest heaving for several seconds, the heat from where the lascutter had melted it warming the back of her legs.

It was this that reminded her she was dressed only in her undergarments. Slowly opening her eyes, she found herself with five troopers and Lieutenant Okoye looking down at her with a mixture of humour and amazement. Kettai was among them.

'I need a drink,' she croaked.

'I have some water here,' said one of the other rescuers, pulling a canteen from her belt.

Kettai met her gaze as she swigged down tepid water, a smile on his lips.

'Let's get you outside,' he said, draping an arm over her shoulder to lead her away, his other hand moving to the flask in his pocket.

EIGHTEEN

Abaddon joins the attack
Among the masses
A question of faith

Lion's Gate space port, mesophex core, two days since assault

There was a lot to be said for the simple pleasure of combat. Abaddon had always been a fighter, first and foremost. Born to be a king, he had chosen the road of battle rather than rulership, giving up that birthright to honour his blade-kin.

Wreathed in armour-shattering energy, his fist made short work of the VII Legion warrior that barred his passage into the upper sensoria of the Lion's Gate space port. Another fell to the sleeve-blades of Layak's bodyguards, while the sorcerer ended a third with a fork of black lightning from his staff.

This was purity. To be victorious and live, or to know defeat and death. A clear foe, a defined objective.

Abaddon's gun roared, a hail of bolts cracking open the plastron of an Imperial Fists legionary in the livery of a veteran sergeant. He followed up with long strides, smashing his gauntlet into the broken armour, pulverising bone and organs beneath, the blow hurling Dorn's fighter across the tiled floor.

Bolt and blade did not care for allegiance, nor the wiles of priests and sorcerers. They were loosed for many reasons, honourable and vile, but once set on their way they either hit their target or missed. Abaddon remembered a time of similar clarity, when he had been a legionary, newly recruited into the Luna Wolves.

Follow orders. Kill the enemy. Protect your brothers.

Now he could barely stand to be in the same room as those he had once thought close as kin. He raised his blade alongside an abomination that paid service to powers existing beyond mortal comprehension. And more than anything, he fought for a lord whose true ambitions were impossible to know.

Despite his doubts, perhaps because of them, the First Captain of the Sons of Horus was not content to be an observer during the battle for Terra. Behind him came three thousand Sons of Horus, their weapons raking fire through the warriors of Rogal Dorn. By Stormbird and Thunderhawk they had been summoned, another blade aimed at the heart of the Lion's Gate space port.

It had not been by the order of Abaddon that they had come; rather they had been despatched by the Warmaster on the word of Layak. Though he had received no order himself, Abaddon had assumed command.

Ezekyle Abaddon, First Captain of the Sons of Horus, the right hand of the Warmaster and victor of countless campaigns had not come to Terra to watch others overthrow the Emperor. He would sooner die in battle than see a Word Bearers sorcerer lead the first of his battle-brothers into the Imperial Palace.

The line of yellow that held the hallways around the upper sensoria buckled under the attack, unable to hold against the ferocity of their newly arrived foes. In the close confines of the interior Abaddon swapped his bolter for powered blade, so that with sword and gleaming fist he carved his path through to the objective.

With him came the Justaerin, their Terminator war-plate

proof against withering volleys of fire, their loyalty to Abaddon as certain as their armour. In a time when he trusted little but himself, he placed his life in the hands of his close guard without question and they followed him without hesitation.

A last knot of VII Legion warriors held the doors to the sensoria. At a conjuration from Layak a black cloud blinded them, flickers of warp energy in its heart. Abaddon charged into the gloom, ignoring the sporadic bolt-rounds that burst from his war-plate. His sword took the head from the first foe he encountered, his fist deflecting the gladius of the second. A blade slave pounced past, burying its dagger-like limbs into the Space Marine's neck, its momentum carrying them both into the murk.

Abaddon pivoted at the sound of heavy footfalls, driving the point of his sword forward to meet the onrushing Imperial Fist. He slowed too late, running onto the blade tip. Abaddon advanced, driving the sword on until it erupted from the Space Marine's back. Ripping his sword free, the gloom dissipating as Layak's spell faded, he stepped past the falling body into the broad chamber of the upper sensoria.

'We will blind their commanders too,' said Layak, hurrying past, head turning quickly as he surveyed the room.

'Secure the orbital augur channels,' Abaddon told the Terminator-armoured legionaries fanning out into the chamber. His sensor data carried the signals of the rest of the force dispersing to secure the area against counter-attack. Within thirty seconds the sensoria was ringed by Sons of Horus.

'Over here, First Captain,' one of his Justaerin replied, indicating a nearby console.

Layak strode over, staff leaving trails of sparks where it struck the bloodied floor.

'Yes, this is perfect,' crowed the Word Bearers sorcerer. 'I will guide Volk's essence to the auguries to mask the arrival.'

'And what of the barrier of the Emperor?' demanded Abaddon. 'I have seen little enough from you to prise open the shield that guards against the Neverborn.'

'That work is ongoing. All elements must come together, Ezekyle.' Layak turned to regard the First Captain with six gleaming eyes. 'The gods are with us and the Utterblight is growing in strength. Our work here aids the greater plan. Even as Dorn must commit more strength to the defence of the space port his grip on the Inner Palace is weakened, his eye drawn elsewhere. Progress is being made, though it is not visible to you.'

'We are on the brink of taking the port, regardless of your efforts.'

'The gods will decide when the space port falls, and we shall claim it not a moment earlier.' Layak returned his attention to the console. He drew a curved knife and started etching symbols into the plasteel of the terminal housing. The scratching of its point punctuated his words. 'When we move to the Ultimate Wall, would you have the elevated primarchs be baulked again, or shall they lead their Legions in the final battle?'

'Fulgrim has already wearied of the attack and withdrawn from the vicinity of the Lion's Gate,' Abaddon told him. 'Angron rampages without purpose outside the walls and Mortarion continues his bombardments. I see little to be gained from their participation.'

'Horus and his ascended brothers are the chosen of the gods – they are the will of Chaos given form,' the Word Bearer replied. He stepped back, looking at his handiwork. The runes glimmered, soft green and dark red. 'To be in their favour is to be favoured by the gods themselves. These are forces you will learn to balance when you come to accept your destiny.'

'If it is my destiny, then it will happen whether I accept it or not,' Abaddon growled. 'You seem keen to persuade me I must make a choice whilst telling me that I have none.'

Layak had no response to this and busied himself at the augur terminal for some time, daubing ritual marks on the console in the blood of the slain. With his staff he ignited the fluids, so that sigils danced in flames, strange intersections of the mystical and mechanical.

'None of this would have been possible without the patronage of the gods,' Layak told Abaddon when his ritual was complete. 'Victory is not certain except by their favour.'

'Victory is never certain.'

'Without the gods, your ambitions would have died in a flame-lit lodge on Davin.' A note of anger entered Layak's voice, the first time Abaddon had heard such a thing. 'Without the gods the Warmaster's star would have ascended and fallen, and even the shadow of his memory would have eclipsed anything you had achieved.'

This time it was Abaddon who was robbed of a retort. He was unsure where the cause and effect lay between Horus seeking the power of Chaos and the gods reaching out to him.

'Is it done?' he asked, pointing towards the augur terminal. 'The sensor array will fail completely?'

Layak examined the images that flickered across the screen. Abaddon saw spirals and jags, coming together like waves or overlapping flames. To his eye they were meaningless shapes.

'Volk has seen the beacon and is coming. Darkness will fall when we need it.'

'Then we will press on,' said Abaddon, clenching his fist. 'The Imperial Fists strengthen their grip on the skybridges – it is only a matter of time before we face a counter-attack from within the Palace. Kroeger has extended too far without consolidation, rushing the attack. If we fail to seize our objectives in the next thrust, we will never do it.'

'And you think you will seize victory by your strength alone?' Layak cackled. 'Such hubris.'

Abaddon held up a lightning-wreathed glove.

'Not by my strength alone, but in the close-fought war, a single blow can turn the course.'

Sanctum Imperialis, western zone, four days since assault

The environs of the Sanctum Imperialis were a sprawling refugee camp. Several thousand square kilometres of habs and dorms and other blocks inside the Eternity Wall had been cleared in preparation for fresh assault. Some, like the Palatine Arc, had been hit by the enemy, turned to rubble, scoured by flame and toxin. Tens of thousands, later hundreds of thousands, had been displaced, fleeing through the Lion's Gate into the city around the Sanctum Imperialis before that impenetrable barbican was closed against the coming of the enemy.

The streets throbbed with a different life. Firelight replaced lumens that had been turned off to conserve energy. Against the thundering backdrop of siege guns, the murmur of a thousand conversations echoed down regal boulevards. Fountains had become wells. Plazas had become markets. Every scrap of material was pressed into use as shelter, transport or both.

And into the mass of humanity, Amon followed Keeler.

'I wonder what a Custodian sees when he looks upon this,' she said, casting out a hand to encompass the mass of people making their homes in the streets, archways and abandoned buildings.

He did not answer straight away. Very little surprised Amon, but he took a small delight in seeing how places could change so dramatically. He had seen the Imperial Palace raised upon the ancient city of its foundations – a city that the Emperor had apparently built in a past age before Old Night. A monument to mankind – not its master, the Emperor had assured

His creations. It had been a place of beauty and awareness of humanity's strengths and frailties. Not just a museum, but a building block to the future. A template not a temple.

Function had started to subsume its form. It became a capital not just of Terra, but of a burgeoning empire beyond the stars. The Administratum had grown out of the need to officiate such an immense endeavour. Hab-blocks, arcologies and hives had appended the statue-flanked processionals and broad cloisters. Edifices dedicated to a different kind of deity, laying sacrifice at the idol of bureaucracy, hoping to tame a galaxy with numbers in vid-ledgers.

The Emperor had been concerned with the webway project and the Custodians had accompanied Him. They had surrendered the greater part of the Palace to humans, overseen by Malcador – though not wholly mortal in body, certainly in mindset. It amazed Amon even now to think of the sprawling otherworld a few kilometres beneath his feet, past the wards and gates and bastions of the Imperial Dungeon. It also gave him pause to recall the limitless horde of Neverborn that waited below, closed off from Terra by arcane machines and the will of the Emperor. The traitors did not need vile rituals to summon their unnatural allies: a legion of the warp tested the defences constantly, a whole dimension yet a paper's breadth away.

'I see the flotsam of a Warmaster's pride,' he told her. 'Seven years ago, the Imperium was turned upon its axis by the selfishness of Horus. That moment has led directly to this and every suffering felt here, every hurt upon the people of the Emperor that has followed, can be laid upon him.'

Keeler said nothing in reply.

Rogal Dorn had come to turn the Palace into a fortress. Immense walls, domineering towers and buttresses by the thousand had strengthened the Sanctum Imperialis, and about it the great curtain fortifications of the Eternity Wall and the Ultimate Wall had been raised and widened, each stretch a city-state in its own right. Administrators remained but labourers in their millions joined them. The latter were eventually given guns and became soldiers, ordered to defend the ramparts their hands had built.

Amon had changed with it all yet remained constant at his core. Through the blood games he had learned of the ever-shifting societies and ecosystems that existed both in the centre and at the fringes of the Imperial Palace. Some things never changed, like the demagogues and black marketeers and gangsters. Only the means of trade, threat and payment altered with the passing decades.

And in the last months the Palace had metamorphosed into something new again.

His presence caused some reaction, a stirring among the listless crowds, but this close to the Sanctum Imperialis the presence of a Custodian was not rare even if it was not commonplace. A few desperate souls called out petitions for aid, the more unhinged demanding audience with the Emperor Himself. Others approached with thanks for the Custodian's vigilance, mistaking his presence for one of the irregular patrols through the growing encampments.

'It is no surprise the dispossessed have a ready ear for the sermons of the Lectitio Divinitatus,' he said to the self-professed Holy Lady of Terra. 'When one has no power, one will seek hope from any source.'

'Indeed,' said Keeler with furrowed brow.

They passed across a square dominated by a wide bonfire. Among the flames Amon recognised the broken shapes of shelving and Administratum lecterns. The building on the far side was a counting house, the windows long since broken in, the contents looted. Makeshift lamps flickered inside.

'Have you considered the alternative?' Keeler continued. 'If these impoverished folk do not turn their thoughts to worship of the Emperor, where else might they seek succour?'

'You do not understand the extent of the folly.'

'I have witnessed first-hand the darkness of the warp that can consume a soul,' she replied quietly. 'You forget that I saw the Warmaster fall prey to that same delusion.'

'All the more reason that such knowledge should not be shared widely,' Amon told her. He stepped carefully over blanket-wrapped forms. Only the faintest of movements showed them to be alive not dead, in the grip of deep fatigue and oblivious to everything else.

'To accept His own divinity does not suggest any other exists,' countered Keeler.

'Where did you hear such a thing?' Amon asked sharply.

Keeler pulled out a book from a bag over her shoulder. Amon did not need to look at it closely to know that it was the *Lectitio Divinitatus*.

'It is the wisdom in these pages,' she told him.

'Yet it is a sentiment that fell from the lips of Lorgar, one who has long since passed from veneration of the Emperor to a far darker life.'

'Knowledge is power, ergo ignorance is weakness,' Keeler said. 'It is a battle into which the Emperor would have His servants go unprepared and unarmed. Is it any wonder that so many have fallen when it appears to them that the Emperor deceived them?'

'The Emperor is above judgement. I have walked beside Him many times and would not claim to know His mind in these matters.'

'Yet you are sure He would condemn my faith?'

'To accept any superstitious nonsense invites speculation and unreason. It is the path that leads to the end of everything the

Emperor has built. It is to combat those very powers that…'
Amon fell silent, aware that he should not share too much
with Keeler. She had a unique perspective on events around
Horus, but the secrecy of the webway and the Emperor's true
goals was inviolate. 'To know is to be tempted.'

'I know and I am not tempted.' She stopped at the steps
into the portico of the Administratum building and looked
up at Amon's face. 'The Emperor gives me the strength to resist their wiles. Did He not create you to be immune to such
desires also?'

'Each Custodian is a singular labour, imbued with individual strength and purpose,' Amon told her. 'When primarchs
can be led astray, there is little hope for the common human
to withstand the barbs and lures of the hidden foe.'

'I do not think we will agree, nor that this will be our last discussion on the matter. All I ask is that you approach what you
see,' she gestured to the building's interior, 'with an open mind.'

'And you think I will see something different today? This is
the fifth gathering you have brought me to, and all I see are
empty rituals and charlatans.'

'Perhaps that is for the best, from your point of view. What
if you were to witness a true miracle of the Emperor? Would
you accept it?'

Amon said nothing, but simply gestured for Keeler to proceed him into the counting house.

A man and a woman waited in the foyer but remained silent,
standing aside to allow them to pass the main stairwell and
head towards a hall beyond. Ducking through the arch, Amon
found himself in a circular chamber about thirty metres across,
the floor muddied from many footfalls, the original mosaic design lost beneath the grime. The ceiling was black with soot from
a handful of fires, a few broken skylights acting as chimneys.

The first thing that struck him was the singing. Those

gathered were mostly knelt in haphazard lines on an old carpet that had been salvaged from somewhere, hands in their laps. He picked out three dozen different voices from the assembled worshippers, some of them skilled, many of them not. The effort that went into the singing was not related to the quality of the outcome. He stopped at the threshold for a short while, listening to the words, decoding the euphemism and metaphor as best he could.

It was a song of praise, and of hope, and thanks.

'For what do they thank the Emperor?' he quietly asked Keeler, who waited beside him. 'Their homes are destroyed. They live in abject poverty. It is likely they will die of exposure or violence very soon.'

'But they are still alive today,' said Keeler, eyes glimmering with moisture. She held her hand to her breast, the lump of the book inside her coat beneath it. 'The Emperor has guarded them through the tribulation when so many others have perished.'

'Survivor bias is not blessing.'

Keeler ignored him and entered. Kyril Sindermann had come ahead of the pair to prepare the way and was leading the verses from in front of the group. There were several others with him, presumably the group leaders.

As their presence was noticed, the singing faltered and stopped. The congregation turned their attention to the newcomers, some with gasps, raising hands to mouths in surprise. At first Amon thought it a reaction to his presence, for he had come clad in full panoply, as Keeler had suggested. But he heard whispers – 'The blessed one is here!' 'She walks among us!' – and saw that though eyes strayed to him, they lingered on Keeler. It was the first time he had been in the presence of a human, except Malcador, that had commanded more attention than him.

Keeler responded, her face flushed in the firelight, eyes wide. He heard her heart racing.

'Come, come,' Sindermann called out, ushering them to the front of the group. He made introductions but Amon did not recognise any of the names as people of significance. The congregation were of a kind, much like those he had seen on his previous excursions with Keeler. Men and women, mostly older than average because the younger, healthier ones had all been drafted into the Imperial Army. There were a few he took to be adolescents, not quite old enough to be trained with a lasgun.

They looked at him with a mixture of suspicion and awe. The first was due to the illicit nature of the gathering, he had learned, and the second down to his existence as a creation of the Emperor's labours. He found himself uncomfortable under their gaze, but showed nothing of his feelings in his expression, a study in calm interest.

And the evening continued in predictable fashion, with a few more songs, some discussion of certain passages from their holy book and an exchange of goods in the form of food, drink, medicines and such that had been scavenged since the last gathering. These were taken by the group leaders for distribution to those most in need, or so they claimed. Whether they were true to their word was not Amon's concern.

Finally, prayers were offered to the Emperor in exchange for protection, guidance and forgiveness. The last of these confused Amon particularly, as though the Emperor cared anything for the supposed moral infractions of these people. At the conclusion of the ceremony, Amon approached Sindermann and the other cult leaders.

'It is such an honour to receive your visit, Custodian,' said a grey-haired woman called Coral. She looked at him oddly, hand half moving towards his armour and then withdrawing. 'To think that you have been in the presence of the God-Emperor.'

Amon stiffened on hearing that term, plucked as it was from the forbidden book written by the traitor Lorgar. That it had entered common parlance was testament to the price of laxity. Coral acted as though something of that supposedly divine connection might be passed off by simple proximity.

'Sindermann assured us that you are not here to condemn our practices,' said another, a dark-skinned man with a walking cane, dressed in the robe of a minor administrator.

Amon glanced at Keeler. She raised an eyebrow.

'I am seeking those that may have witnessed strange phenomena,' said the Custodian. 'A shared vision or dreams, perhaps. Voices, images, anything that cannot be explained by natural law.'

'Like signs from the Emperor?' asked the youngest of the trio, a mother with a babe in a sling no more than a few months old. Amon realised the child must have been born since the siege began. His surprise must have slipped through his guarded expression.

'His father fights on the walls,' the woman said proudly, stroking the babe's cheek. Her voice quavered a little. 'At least, he did when I last heard a month ago. I pray to the Emperor to see him safe through his travails. I don't suppose you could get word of him?'

She looked at Amon with a hope that was in stark contrast to her sunken features and dark-rimmed eyes. He could see that the child was malnourished also, as were most of the congregation. Their clothes were tatters, homes destroyed. Yet they gave thanks to a fiction of the Emperor and asked for news of loved ones rather than decrying the Master of Mankind who surely some might blame for their predicament.

The sheer scale of the battle for the Imperial Palace meant that any single soldier could not be accounted for. Whole companies died without remark. It did not seem productive to share this point with the desperate young woman.

'I do not think it possible,' he told her softly.

'Life goes on,' said the older woman. 'Horus cannot halt all of humanity.'

'Indeed, the great cycle continues,' said Keeler, joining them having finished a conversation with one of the congregation. She looked at the mother. 'What do you know of the group that meets in the Basilica Ventura?'

'A strange lot,' said the man, limping closer. 'Gave themselves a name. What was it, Chikwendu? The ones that follow Olivier?'

'Oh…' The older woman rubbed her chin for a moment. 'The Lampbearers? Lamplighters?'

'Lightbearers!' said the young mother. 'I saw one of their emissaries on the west arch road just this morning.'

'Yes, the Lightbearers,' said Chikwendu. 'You want strange happenings, the Lightbearers are the ones to watch, for sure. Olivier, he's claiming he can heal the sick, and that's just the start of it.'

Amon exchanged a look with Keeler. She smiled and held her hands out to the group leaders, embracing each in turn.

'Stay strong,' she whispered to each of them.

'My thanks for your assistance,' Amon said with a nod of acknowledgement. He was about to depart but felt he could not do so without some further comment. It was not his place to fuel false worship, but nor was it his duty to quash all sense of hope. 'This time shall pass. The Emperor will prevail.'

NINETEEN

Pick a target
Vox-silence
The Lightbearers

*Lion's Gate space port, stratophex core,
two days since assault*

Slowly accreting more warriors on the advance, Forrix's hidden force had pushed far from the hordes pouring into the base of the space port, cutting through several Imperial Army cordons to reach the heart of the stratophex. It transpired that the rendezvous point Forrix had selected was located in a nest of hab-dorms clustered about one of the main drop-shafts. Civilians with autoguns and kitchen knives had proved less of an obstacle than the distance to cover, their bodies left cooling in the passageways and rooms they had called home.

The advance had not gone unnoticed – indeed was not meant to be wholly clandestine. With the defenders unsure of the threat posed by the Iron Warriors, several scouting forces had been sent after them, each greeted by a sudden and overwhelming counter-attack. To Forrix it seemed that the Imperial Army colonel or whoever was in charge of the sector had finally decided enough was enough and despatched a company-level force to deal with the interlopers.

As soon as the augur pickets had detected the incoming soldiers Forrix had responded, setting ambushes and a mobile reserve. Twenty minutes had passed since the first shot had been fired and more army personnel were being thrown into the fight. A few mortars and support guns had been brought to bear, frag bombs and armour-piercing shells forcing the Iron Warriors into a more defensive mode around the central hab-cluster. The warsmith was keenly aware that his mission to draw the enemy away from the coming offensive above and below was starting to have an effect.

It was hard to pick out what Gharal was saying over the sound of bolters and thud of shells landing not far above Forrix's position, though his second-in-command was only a few metres away.

'It's safe to break vox-silence now,' Forrix transmitted to the captain. A red las-blast slashed across his left pauldron, leaving a grey mark through his insignia. 'I think they know where we are.'

'*Counter-offensive is still sporadic, triarch,*' the captain told him. '*I can confirm eight hundred and eleven warriors have reached the rendezvous.*'

'We've been inside more than twenty-four hours, I don't expect anyone else to make it to us.'

'*No, triarch. What are your orders?*'

'No contact from either the aerial attack wave or the surface reinforcements?' As soon as he asked the question Forrix realised it was redundant. 'Forget that, you'd have told me if there was.'

'*All squads are currently on perimeter guard or mobile reserve assignments, triarch. This is a defensible position. Ingress and exit is only via four corridors. Should we dig in?*'

'Easy to defend, but if we get stuck here, very hard to break out. The longer we stay, the more chance we'll get bogged down by an insignificant defence force. To draw their attention we need to pose more of a threat. I'm not going to wait for any more stragglers – it's time to identify a target and push this shiv a bit deeper.'

Another enemy thrust along the passage to the east drew Forrix's eye. Scores of troopers in plated carapace armour led the fresh offensive, daring the bolter fusillade as they dashed from one doorway to the next. They'd lost half their number in the first fifteen metres. He could not decide if they were brave or stupid to try a forced attack against his Space Marines.

'I have some schematics, triarch.' Gharal pushed through the squad protecting Forrix and proffered a slate-projector, its surface criss-crossed with a wireframe rendition of their surroundings. 'There are a number of potential targets within three kilometres of our position.'

'The point of our attack is to open up a front inside the space port to allow the upper and lower forces to push forward in strength. These lacklustre assaults will bog us down, but they aren't a significant commitment. Every bolt we have could kill a trooper and we'll achieve nothing. It is Dorn's sons that are the spine of this defence. I need to make sure the Imperial Fists deploy in numbers against us.'

'So, what does that mean? What objective do we aim for?'

'Once we have cleared away this chaff, send out eight scouting forces. Ten legionaries each. I want even dispersal, vertically and horizontally, as far as they can go. Have each report levels of resistance every two hundred metres. In particular, keep an eye out for our cousins in yellow. Any contact with Imperial Fists must be signalled immediately.'

'Yes, triarch…' Gharal's uncertainty was betrayed by his wavering affirmative. 'What are they seeking?'

'Whichever force encounters the greatest increase in resistance is the one we shall follow.'

The armoured Imperial troopers pushed on again, using their surge to cover the arrival of a pair of tripod-mounted multi-lasers. Soon rapid-fire beams of blue burst along the eastern corridor, sparking from the armour of Forrix's warriors and leaving scorch marks along the pale yellow walls. Missiles and heavy bolters roared in reply, turning the heavy weapons and their crews to broken metal and flesh.

'I... Excuse my ignorance, triarch. Why would we knowingly advance into the hardest defence?'

'If you were defending the space port and you had enemy roaming at will, how would you organise your troops?'

'I would assign defenders based on a scale of significance and vulnerability. The greater the value of a potential objective, the better defence...' Gharal laughed as he reached his conclusion. 'The best defences will be arrayed around the targets that are worth the most to our enemy.'

'Exactly. It doesn't matter what we attack, only that the Imperial Fists prize it highly. The more they fight to defend it, the greater its value to them.'

'And when we have identified the target, triarch?'

'We move in full force, rapid spear point assault. We'll break the defence, seize whatever it is the sons of Dorn are trying to protect, and then prepare ourselves for the counter-attack. The greater their response, the better we're doing...'

Nagapor Territories, fifty-nine days before assault

The scale of the damage was hard to take in. As Zenobi looked along half a kilometre of twisted, burning metal it reminded her of the time when, as a child, she had seen a furnace implosion. Even that didn't really compare: a brief, violent episode that had slain hundreds but caused little permanent damage to the production line of the cradlespur.

At least seventeen carriages and gun cars had been derailed completely, including the one Zenobi had been in. Half a dozen more had skipped the tracks and were listing one way or the other, zigzagged together by the sudden slowing of the train. The frontmost four cars showed signs of hits but were otherwise intact, as were the last dozen or so.

It was not the sight that reminded her of the flashfire back in Addaba, it was the smell. Charring bodies and burning oil. It brought the memory back, stark and hot, her parents screaming for lost relatives.

It was calmer here. The immediate mayhem had subsided while she'd been trapped in the turret. Search teams picked through the wrecks that were not alight, pulling free the living and the dead. A steady stream of wounded, walking and stretchered, passed by to the rough medicae stations that had been set up away from the train.

With a shock that brought her aimless pacing to a halt, Zenobi remembered the aircraft. She looked up, scanning the smoke-smudged heavens. Dusk tinged the sky with purples and reds.

'They left.'

Zenobi turned at the sound of Seleen's voice. Menber was just behind her, a spare uniform in his arms.

'Put this on, it'll be getting colder,' he said, passing her the coverall.

She struggled into the bulky uniform, which was made for someone at least five centimetres taller. She folded up the cuffs and it bunched around her ankles out the top of her boots.

'I feel like a child,' she said, flopping her arms up and down.

'You're not, cousin,' said Menber.

'You a smart woman,' Seleen told her. 'Good thinking, using your uniform to put out that fire. That's a bright brain inside your skull.'

'Do we know who's dead yet?' Zenobi asked quietly, surveying the wreckage.

'Sergeant Alekzanda,' said Seleen, swallowing hard.

Zenobi choked back a sob and Menber held her arm as she swayed.

'Come on, sit down,' he said, leading her away from the burning train. She took several steps and then shook her head, pulling herself away.

'I can help,' she told him, wiping soot and tears from her face with the sleeve of her new clothes. 'I'm not hurt.'

'You took in a lot of smoke, Obi,' said Seleen. 'That's not good.'

'I'm not hurt,' insisted Zenobi, starting back towards the carriage behind the gunnery car. 'And the company banner is in there somewhere.'

She saw the two of them exchange a glance.

'It's important,' Zenobi insisted.

There were two piles of bodies, one at each end of the car a few metres from the doors. The whole carriage had tipped along with the gunnery carriage, but there was space between them to get to the entrances. Zenobi squeezed through easily enough, once again thankful for her small size.

It was strange to see everything at a right angle to its former position. She walked along the wall between the ends of the benches and the windows, trying to find where she had stowed the banner.

There were puddles and smears of blood on the painted metal, and a few hands and feet stuck out from under the mangled remains of benches that had come loose from their fastenings, too entangled to be removed. The roof was on her left, the hammocks still bundled where they had been before the attack.

Luckily there had been no fire here. Or perhaps it was something more than luck, she thought. She remembered what the Beta Platoon trooper had tried to tell her, about powers greater than her. Maybe there was a force that was protecting the standard, the physical proof of her loyalty and dedication to the cause.

She found the banner pole but it was stuck behind the webbing of the hammock. Looking around she found a bayonet that had slipped from a kitbag. She used it to saw through the straps, until she, the hammock and the banner pole fell backwards, tumbling over a bench.

'You okay?' Menber called from the door, his shock of curled hair silhouetted against the ruddy twilight.

'Fine, cousin.' Zenobi struggled to her feet, untangling the hammock from her boot. She picked her way back to the door, slipping twice on drying blood. Coming out into the open air made her realise how dark it had been inside the carriage, though day was rapidly giving way to night-time.

Flames added to the crimson illumination, and by its light she saw integrity officers moving through the gangs of labouring troopers. One of them approached the gathering members of Epsilon Platoon and other scattered company soldiers.

'Any vox-sets here?' she asked. One hand was on her holstered pistol, a slender disciplinary cane in the other.

'Yeah, I got the platoon set,' said Beley, pointing to a bulky transmitter box that was set on the dirt nearby. There were lasguns, power packs and a few rations boxes heaped next to it.

The integrity officer walker over to the vox-set, raised a booted foot and stamped hard on the communications equipment. The box was sturdy and hardly bent under the blow.

'What are you doing?' Beley took a few steps towards her amidst cries from the others, but a glare from the integrity officer stopped him mid-stride and silenced the rest.

She kicked the set over, exposing the speaker to her

descending heel. Again and again she drove her boot into the controls, until grille, dials and internal circuits were scattered about, sparks and crackles emitting from the dying voxcaster.

'What was that for?' asked Zenobi. She regretted the outburst, but was still unsettled from her recent trauma and couldn't stop the words coming out. 'We might need that.'

'There will be no unauthorised transmissions. Several vox-sets will be retained for corps command.' The integrity officer stepped closer, looking at each of them. 'Someone tried to contact the incoming aircraft prior to the attack.'

Zenobi drew in a breath, exchanging glances with the others nearby.

'What happened to them?' asked Kettai.

'Dead, in the attack,' replied the integrity officer, scowling. 'Unfortunate that she died before we could learn if there were any others that thought as she did.'

The integrity officer drew away from them, cane swishing in her hand.

'The closer we come to the battle, the greater the risk of treachery. There can be no complacency.'

'Yes, bana-madam,' said Kettai, snapping off a salute.

'Get down to the intact carriages. Work parties are separating the locomotive and functional cars. You'll be detailed your labours. There's no way we can move this mess,' a sweeping cane indicated the buckled remains of the train's middle cars, 'so we'll be walking the rest of the way to the Palace.'

Basilica Ventura, five days since assault

To Keeler the encampment of the Lightbearers was to the shanty shrines as the Sanctum Imperialis was to the shack of a toll keeper. In the ever-twilight of the besieged Imperial

Palace, gloom had become the norm, but the Lightbearers had decided to be literal with their name. By some means they had reactivated the energy grid around the Basilica Ventura, which was a gate keep that guarded the Via Oxidentus. The forbidding walls of the barbican were hung with brightly coloured lights and the rooftop avenue that led to it was lined with lamp posts gleaming with red and blue lumens.

Most of the Palace was in collapse nearby, having been struck by several orbital lance bursts during a failure of the aegis. Into the desolation a small sect of the Lectitio Divinitatus had ventured, Keeler had learned, led by a man called Olivier Muižnieks. There was little known about him from before his arrival a few weeks earlier, but already the Lightbearers numbered several hundred devotees. They were sending out messengers to other groups of the Lectitio Divinitatus, actively inviting members to come and join them.

This certainly was not a furtive prayer-meet in an abandoned tithe house. Keeler was surprised by the number of people that were gathering. It was late evening, though nothing could be seen of stars and moon through the storm above the Palace. Ranging from individuals to extended families, the faithful of the Lightbearers climbed up through the broken ruin of a scriptorum and onto the Via Oxidentus, which ran towards the western districts. The imposing towers and domes of the Capitol Imperator loomed above them, shadowed against the faint glimmer of void shields.

Keeler had come alone, wanting to see for herself the nature of the Lightbearers' rituals without the distraction of Amon's presence. The Custodian's desire to investigate had been placated by a promise that she would meet with him the next morning and report everything she witnessed. In addition, she wore a brooch shaped like a rose, into which had been secured a miniature pict recorder so that Amon could review the encounter himself.

The immense double doors of the basilica were open, more light spilling from inside, bathing the brickwork road in a yellow glow. Everything seemed clean compared to the shanties that held sway everywhere else, with barely a piece of grit to mar the swept pathway.

Half a dozen children stood at the doors handing out small lanterns made from the pierced casings of large bore cannons, with twisted wire for handles. She wasn't sure what had been used for the oil within, but assumed it had been salvaged from one of the hundreds of downed planes that had fallen around the Palace during the height of the aerial battle. Nobody gave Keeler a second glance as she took up one of the lamps and stepped within.

The basilica itself had been almost hollowed out by a blast that had pierced the roof. Floors and walkways of metal sheets and wooden planks covered the hole that burrowed half a kilometre down into the body of the Sanctum Imperialis' foundations, and parts of the upper levels remained like mezzanines, lined with more of the faithful. The glow of so many lanterns suffused everything with visual warmth, and Keeler could feel a spirit of welcome embracing her as she ascended a ramp to the nearest level.

She found a place between several families – there were all ages here, including a few attendees in their Imperial Army uniforms. Smiles greeted her but thankfully no questions.

About half an hour passed until the doors swung closed, leaving only the light of the lanterns that spiralled up the inside of the basilica. About halfway up, some forty metres above the doors, a curtain was pulled back from an archway and a youthful man stepped out, flanked by a pair of older women. They were dressed in identical robes of white and yellow, a glittering of metallic thread around collar, hem and cuff. All three had shaved heads, a sheen of perspiration on their hairless scalps. The two women each carried a large volume, bound in black leather or mock-leather, embossed with silver writing. Many scraps of paper jutted from between the pages, marking particular passages of what Keeler knew to be the *Book of Divinity*. Her hand moved to her far humbler copy beneath her dress, and saw others around her doing likewise, the book itself as much a totem as a reference work.

Olivier Muižnieks, for such it had to be, advanced a few paces further than his companions, his hands clasped to his belly. There was a softness about him, a little flesh on the jowls, a bit of a paunch at the waist. Unusual in such dire times, when so many ate only rarely. On further study, Keeler saw a looseness in the skin that suggested Olivier had been carrying a lot more weight until recently. He wasn't putting himself above the food shortages suffered by his congregation.

'Faithful!' he declared, raising his hands. He had a soft voice, smooth and assured, an accent that Keeler couldn't exactly place but which brought to mind the Europa hives. Despite his tempered demeanour, his words carried well in the confines of the makeshift temple. 'Raise up your lights so that we might feel the gaze of the Emperor in the darkness.'

The congregation lifted their lamps and Keeler copied them. Though each offered but a small yellow flicker, the combined effect of so many tallow-lights was a warm suffusing of the basilica's interior. As flames danced in the draughts, shapes moved in half-shadow on the walls.

'Feel the breath of the Emperor entering your lungs,' Olivier said, commanding but gentle.

Keeler took a breath. She tasted tallow smoke and sweat and… Impossibly, she thought she could smell blossom, the fragrance of nightrose that used to grow near her window when she was a child. Delicate gasps from others around her revealed that she was not alone in the experience. Her gaze drifted between Olivier and the near-invisible movement of the wall shadows. His voice continued, hypnotic and low.

'Feel the hands of the Emperor lift you up.'

The basilica faded as the shadow images grew clearer. Olivier's voice was a breeze in the swaying bushes that surrounded Keeler. There was long grass under her bare feet. All about her the wind stirred a beautiful garden – not an ornate, ordered plot but a natural flourishing of wildflowers and heathland, which stretched onto far hills broken by copses of golden-leafed trees.

Her eyes were open as she wandered, taking in the bucolic voice of the wind, the buzz of insects and creaking of bending tree trunks. She walked slowly, with purpose, gazing upon each flower as though it were a newly revealed wonder, the warmth of the sun always on her back no matter where she turned.

She tried to see the sun, to look upon its brightness, but the light was omnipresent, yet without source. Keeler told herself that it was not wise to look upon the font of this power. To gaze upon the soul of the Emperor was to see into the heart of divinity. The sons and daughters of the Navis Nobilite had been bred over generations that they might see the chink of the Emperor's spirit that was the Astronomican; to see it in full splendour would surely shred one's own soul from the body.

She was drawn across a babbling brook into a broad pasture, where she came upon the greatest tree she had ever seen. How she had not observed it before defied logic, but she knew this was a place of faith not reason and accepted it as such.

The tree stretched beyond the clouds, its sprawling limbs holding up the vault of the heavens themselves. The branches quivered with life, bending beneath their burden, and from this came a tremendous creaking. She listened awhile, trying to hear the voice of the Emperor in the sound of the tree.

Her transition back to reality was abrupt but not harsh, like waking naturally from a deep slumber, refreshed and clear of thought. She heard weeping, but those around her shed tears of joy not woe, clasping each other in their shared ecstasy. She took a moment to steady herself, unsure of her own body.

A man in late middle age approached her, a broad smile on his face, eyes alive with delight.

'Did you see the tree?' she asked, wanting to share the feeling that bubbled inside her breast.

'Tree?' He laughed. 'I followed the rose path. You saw a tree?'

'The lord of trees, the strength of the Emperor holding His shield above us,' Keeler confessed. 'It was incredible.'

The man's eyes widened further and he reached for her arm.

'Amazing! Come, come, you must tell Olivier of your journey.'

She allowed herself to be led around the rampway until she was brought before the head of the Lightbearers. His gaze turned to her as she approached, his eyes a startling green, reminding her of the verdant gardens.

'Olivier!'

'How can I help you, Vili?'

'This woman, she says she saw the Tree of Hope!'

Olivier's first reaction was a smile, no hint of suspicion or surprise.

'Indeed?' He held out a hand and Keeler shook it. 'That is a blessing that you have come to us and shared such a thing. Who are you, daughter of the Emperor?'

She hesitated, not sure if she wanted to reveal herself in this way.

'I understand,' Olivier continued. 'We all have pasts – and presents! – that perhaps are to be kept secret. We are united in our single purpose under the light of the God-Emperor, and that is all that matters.'

There was an openness about him that Keeler could not resist. She had been used to doubts and suspicion and questions, and here was a man who wore his faith like a light, accepting of her without reservation.

'Keeler. My name is Euphrati Keeler.'

Others nearby heard her reply and a small pool of silence spread around them. Eyes turned towards Keeler, faces displaying a mixture of fascination and delight.

'Euphrati Keeler?' It seemed impossible that Olivier's smile had widened even further. 'The Guide? The one that brought the Light of the Emperor back to Terra?'

'I…' She had accepted her role as a messenger for the Lectitio Divinitatus, but being confronted by the truth of what that meant caught her off guard. 'If that is your belief. I am Euphrati Keeler, and I would like to know more about the Lightbearers.'

TWENTY

Rann fights back
Solidarity
A deeper loyalty

Lion's Gate space port, stratophex core, six days since assault

Hour after hour the enemy continued to push towards the sky-bridges. Pressed on all sides, it took the best part of a day for Rann to muster a force capable of pushing back against the Iron Warriors' advance. As the traitors moved further down the Starspear they overran defence emplacements, reducing Rann's anti-air and anti-orbital fire. Cannons from lower regions were still capable of keeping back larger vessels but a stream of drop-ships had reinforced the initial enemy landing.

The technophage that had been introduced to the port's systems continued to plague everything from gun control to energy output, bringing rolling blackouts, environmental support shutdowns and weapons misfires. Every tech-priest was spared other duties to coordinate the response, but for the most part Rann had access only to crude hard-line communications between the strategium and his defence posts, and short-range personal vox between companies in the battle.

'Simple is best,' he told Haeger and the six Imperial Army colonels who'd travelled to Lion Primus to receive their briefing in person. All communications equipment in the chamber had been shut off, just in case the Dark Mechanicum had devised some means of reversing the transmitters to listen in on the council. Word of mouth was slow but hard to intercept. 'Our objective in the base is to slow the advance and contain it where possible. There's almost no leadership that I have seen, so redirect their attacks to non-vital areas. Let them rampage around the hab-blocks and loot what they can – the citizens will fight to keep them at bay as well. Haeger, what's your assessment of the infiltration attack in Sky City?'

'Problematic,' said the lieutenant-commander. He zoomed in the monochrome briefing slate to show several key port systems that were situated close to the Iron Warriors' attack. 'Plasma reactors, conveyor access and the bridges themselves are all within a few kilometres of the enemy insertion. We have no more information regarding how they arrived, so there could be further reinforcements on their way that we cannot detect.'

'Prioritise vulnerable sites by value and location. There are ten thousand Imperial Army veterans in Sky City. Deploy them and reinforce with a thousand legionaries.'

'And what are you going to do with the rest of your warriors, lord seneschal?' asked Colonel Maigraut. The Imperial Army chief of staff fidgeted with the brim of the officer's cap on the table in front of her. 'There is another Iron Warriors column approaching along Highway Four. It is possible that a sally from one of the minor gates could assault the enemy forces from the rear, catching them before they gain access to the outer defences.'

'We have to deal with the enemy already here,' said Rann. 'I'm taking ten thousand legionaries into the Starspear to meet the aerial assault head-on. It's the worst area in terms of our data, so I need to see for myself exactly what sort of trouble we're in.'

'But if we allow–'

'Your troopers cannot fight in the depressurised levels. If you wish to contact Lord Dorn and request an Imperial Army armoured reserve be despatched to counter the Iron Warriors, I will endorse the move. But I cannot ignore the army landed on the orbital docks.'

The colonel acquiesced with a nod of the head. She put her cap back on and stood up, straightening her uniform. The other officers also stood, looking to Maigraut for guidance.

'We will hold to the last trooper,' she assured Rann. 'I shall send request for an armoured thrust as you suggest. For the Emperor!'

She raised a hand to her cap in salute, copied by the other colonels. Rann banged a fist to his plastron.

'For the Emperor,' he replied.

He waited a few seconds as they filed into the strategium, and then followed, Haeger at his side.

'There is a Rhino outside ready to take you to the muster, commander. Your Huscarls are already waiting for you at the transfer ramps into the Starspear.' Haeger moved quickly to one of the scanning consoles and returned with a flexisheet showing the top third of the space port. It looked like a heat map, blurs of white over a complex wireframe model. 'Latest augur returns.'

'I'll study it on the way,' said Rann, taking the flexi. 'Remember, our mission is to slow them down. Give ground to preserve resistance, no unnecessary offensive action unless the opportunity is too good to pass up.'

'Defence first. I understand, commander.' Haeger thumped a fist to his plastron, the crash of ceramite momentarily louder than the grinding of cogitators and the murmuring of servitors.

Rann turned and left, knowing there were a hundred things he wanted to tell Haeger, and knowing equally well they were all redundant. The lieutenant-commander was a highly capable war leader. As he clambered through the Rhino's rear hatch, Rann knew that protocol really dictated that Haeger lead this attack while he, the senior officer, continued in the role of strategic command. He was grateful that Haeger hadn't even mentioned swapping places.

Son Basin, forty-one days before assault

The weather rapidly worsened, so that even the days were a frigid ordeal. The further north the Addaba Free Corps trudged, the colder they felt. As altitude increased, so did the chill wind. Eighteen days since the train had been attacked and the sun was a memory. Smoke choked the upper airs, spread far and wide from the continuing bombardment of the Imperial Palace. Even at midday it was as cool as an Addaba dusk.

Zenobi huddled close to the other squad members, swathed in a thick coat, the bulky gloves on her hands making it difficult to grip her lasgun and the banner pole. Despite the burden she was grateful for the clothing, supplied by the seamstations back at Addaba – for months they had known they were destined to fight at the Imperial Palace in the heights of the Himalazia. It had not mattered when they were deployed, the turn of seasons did little to change the climate of the high mountains. Every kitbag had contained a coat, gloves and a body stocking to be worn beneath the uniform coveralls. Though much had been lost in the wreckage, there were enough kitbags for everyone.

They followed the line of the solitary rail, the locomotive and four carriages chugging along with them. The officers rode on board, but most of the available space, those four cars not adorned with cannons, was packed full of weapons, power packs and such other supplies as could be fitted into every nook and gap. One wagon had been turned into a rolling hospital, where the seven surviving medicae did their best to ward off starvation, dehydration, frostbite and exhaustion, with diminishing success.

Zenobi's company had got off relatively lightly, with only a handful of walking wounded and perhaps a score of dead. Some platoons had suffered almost fifty per cent casualties, while the companies in the middle carriages had been all but wiped out. The survivors had been spread into the existing formations, so that two new arrivals had joined Zenobi's platoon.

One was the new squad sergeant, a gruff woman named Attah, who was as different to Alekzanda as the Himalazia were to the plains around Addaba. She barked her commands with a sneer, derided her squad's efforts and was generally unpleasant. It was also clear that she was as unhappy with her assignment as her subordinates and missed no opportunity to compare them unfavourably to her former squad. At night she muttered the names of her dead troopers, restless in her sleep. For this she was given more latitude than perhaps she was due, for nobody could imagine what it would be like to survive when everyone else around you had been killed.

The integrity officers carried out hourly inspections, hovering like vultures around the marching platoons, ears and eyes alert to any mischief. The influx of relative strangers into the surviving companies stirred up suspicions and there had been a flurry of accusations and counter-accusations.

Just as they were bedding down for the night, three integrity officers approached through the dark, their pistols in hand. Jawaahir arrived a few seconds later.

'Which of you is Seleen Mogowe?' she asked.

'That's me,' Seleen replied, standing up from her bedroll. There was frozen dirt on her coat and she brushed it off self-consciously. 'What do you want?'

Zenobi knew Seleen well, that no belligerence was intended, but she cringed at her friend's forthright manner in front of the integrity high officer.

'You submitted a message for return to Addaba this afternoon?'

'Yeah, that was to my niece. She's only six years old, I thought she'd like a letter from her auntie.'

'Come with me.' Jawaahir turned away, expecting compliance. Seleen did not give it.

'What's this about?' she demanded. 'What's the problem?'

Others in the platoon, Zenobi included, roused themselves from their sleeping sacks. The integrity officers twitched, but none of them raised a weapon. Jawaahir was calmer, regarding the minor insurrection with a calculating gaze, her eyes reflecting the orange gleam of the camp burner they had clustered around for warmth.

'I wish to clarify a statement you made in your letter,' said the integrity high officer.

'Then ask me here,' said Seleen. 'I got nothing to hide.'

Jawaahir looked at her for several seconds, unmoving. Her hand slowly dipped into a pocket and produced a folded piece of paper.

'Is that my letter?'

'You wrote, "I know this battle is inevitable, that it couldn't have ended any other way, but I wish that it didn't have to be fought by us."' Jawaahir folded the letter back along its creases and returned it to her pocket. 'Why are you reluctant to fight for Addaba? Does the future freedom of your niece mean nothing to you?'

'Come on, Seleen's as loyal as any of us,' said Tewedros from the ring of half-gloom beyond the immediate gathering of troopers. 'Which of us hasn't wished we didn't have to fight?'

There were a few murmurs of agreement but Zenobi remained silent, watching her companions carefully. She glanced to her right, grateful to see Menber standing a few metres away. His arms were folded and his brow creased in a scowl, but he kept his lips shut too.

'Would you have others die and fight in your place? Would you trust the future of Addaba to others?' growled Jawaahir, stalking further into the light, her anger flashing as she glanced at the group of troopers. 'Nothing – nothing! – less than total dedication will see us to victory! When your friend Seleen has her lasgun pointing at an enemy, do you want her to wonder for a moment if she has the right to kill them? Is your life worth her hesitation?'

'I wouldn't–'

'You already have,' snapped Jawaahir. 'Selfishness breeds cowardice, Trooper Mogowe.'

'What's going to happen to her?' Zenobi asked quietly, stepping towards her squadmate. 'What's the punishment?'

'Close observation,' Jawaahir replied. She looked at Seleen. 'Yours is not a grand transgression, but we must be sure of your integrity to the cause. You and others are being formed into a dedicated platoon under the direct command of an integrity officer.'

Seleen laughed, her relief evident.

'That's it? Redeployment to the naughty girls' company? A punishment shift… I thought…' She made a slashing motion across her throat.

'Lieutenant Okoye!' Jawaahir's voice cut across the whine of the wind, summoning the officer as if by magic, though Zenobi assumed he had already been warned regarding the arrest of Seleen.

'Yes, integrity high officer?'

'The solidarity of your platoon is admirable, but please remind them that they are not to question the authority of integrity officers.'

'Yes, integrity high officer,' growled the platoon commander. He raised his voice to address the assembled soldiers. 'You will all stand watch for the next two hours! Patrol by squads on the perimeter. Sergeants, take the names of any man or woman that complains.'

A chorus of yessirs echoed back, accompanied by a swell of suppressed sighs and grumbling.

'See you on the battle line,' said Seleen, lifting a hand to a salute that turned into a wave. She disappeared into the darkness with the integrity officers.

When they were gone, Kettai slipped out of the gloom, joining Zenobi and Menber.

'Punishment platoon?' he whispered. 'Do you really believe that?'

'Not a word of it,' said Zenobi. 'I'd be surprised if we ever see Seleen again.'

Zenobi slept fitfully, disturbed by the cold and a slew of disjointed dreams. She awoke as the engines of the train growled into life, fumes billowing from its stacks. Dawn tinged the horizon and she could see the silhouettes of the sentries atop the ridge to the east. Northwards the rising sun touched upon the snow-covered flanks of the mountains, but it was the continual shimmer of purple and blue from beyond them that caught the eye.

Menber rolled out of his blankets and came over, following her gaze.

'Do you think it'll still be going on when we get there?' she asked.

'I don't know if I want it to or not,' he replied, expression pensive. 'If it stops, that might mean we're too late.'

'But you don't want to be walking into that storm...' Zenobi finished for him.

He nodded and looked at her. 'I'd rather we had our chance to make a difference.'

Movement behind her caused both of them to turn. It was Kettai, rubbing sleep from his eyes.

'You think we will? Make a difference, I mean.' He crouched and started to roll up his blanket, breath steaming the air. 'Millions of soldiers. Titans. Legionaries. Starships. You really think the Addaba Free Corps makes a difference in all of that?'

'Why not?' replied Menber, fists balling. 'In a close battle, who knows what would swing it one way or the other?'

Kettai conceded the point with a nod and shrug, and started packing his belongings into his kitbag. Others were rousing, but the morning calls from the officers were still a few minutes away.

The first they knew of the gunship was an explosion that ripped through the camp of Second Company, a few hundred metres west of where Zenobi gathered her stuff.

The blast wave tossed bodies high into the air, tatters of burning bedrolls and shards of camp stoves hurled with them. The thud of the detonation rolled across the slumbering companies, a snarl of plasma jets growing louder in its wake.

'Get down!'

Kettai threw himself at Menber and Zenobi, tackling both of them hard into the frozen dirt. Zenobi felt something crack in her side as his weight landed on top of her. Past his sprawling body she saw the blunt-nosed gunship diving groundwards, cannons mounted atop the fuselage spitting shells. She could trace the impacts through the camp, those on their feet cut down while those still waking were tossed into the air like dolls by the barrage of explosions.

The bark of the train's guns joined the noise of the attack, blossoms of shrapnel detonating around the incoming aircraft. Smaller guns on its flanks opened fire, the flare of bolts raking more death through the fleeing and huddling soldiers of Addaba.

'This way,' said Menber as the gunship banked away, revealing a symbol Zenobi knew well – the Legion badge of the Luna Wolves, who had taken the name Sons of Horus just before the outbreak of the war.

'Where?' she asked, getting to her feet, Kettai and a handful of others joining them.

'Under the train?' someone suggested.

'It'll target the train next, I bet,' said Kettai.

'Split up.' Lieutenant Okoye arrived with two other squads, some of them wounded. With him was an integrity officer, his uniform torn down one side, left arm a bloody mess strapped across his chest with a belt.

The pitch of the gunship's engines changed and it looped over, turning to bring its main weapons to bear again.

'Spread out!' bellowed Okoye. 'Don't give the gunners an easy target.'

They broke like iron ants from a disrupted nest, running in all directions. Zenobi found herself heading in roughly the same direction as Kettai, the integrity officer and three others. They headed almost directly away from the roar of the attacking gunship. She almost covered her ears, wanting to block out the increasing snarl of its approach, wincing as she expected to feel a bolt in her back at any moment.

She thought about the banner, left among the packs and sleeping sacks. She slowed, thinking to go back for it.

Hesitation saved her life.

A rocket exploded about twenty metres in front of her. She saw an instant of brightness, Kettai lifted bodily by the blast, two others engulfed by flames. The wounded integrity officer, alongside Zenobi to her right, turned away but she was caught looking directly at the detonation.

A hot wind lifted her from her feet, carrying her several metres before she landed hard, her back catching against a jut of rock, gouging through coat and coverall into the flesh of her right side.

For several seconds she thought she was deaf and blind, her world nothing more than ringing and blackness. Through the sensory static emerged other sounds, her name being called. Her vision started to fuzz back into something recognisable – the face of Kettai.

Blinking hard, she pushed herself up, feeling pain slash through the side of her face as the skin stretched. She lifted a hand and blood came away on the fingertips of her glove.

'Just a gash,' said Kettai. 'You'll live.'

Part of his left ear was missing, crimson dribbling down the side of his neck. There was a burn mark on his coat near the left shoulder too.

'Look here.' One of the third squad troopers was standing over something a few metres away. He had his lasgun in his hands, pointing down at the integrity officer, who lay crumpled and unconscious at the man's feet.

Zenobi's eye caught a glint of metal in the light of the flames from the rocket. She stooped and pulled the wounded officer's pistol from the melting frost.

'This is the one that took Seleen,' the trooper said, his finger moving from the lasgun guard to the trigger. 'Nobody's going to miss this bastard.'

'What?' Zenobi took a step. 'What are you doing?'

'I'm done with this,' the trooper said. Zenobi remembered his name was Tewedros. 'These integrity officers will kill more of us than the enemy.'

Zenobi was aware of the weight of the pistol in her hand. She lifted it, aiming at Tewedros' right eye.

'Put down your lasgun,' she said.

'Why? You're not going to choose me over him. What've they ever done for you? This type would have been grinding you about slacking on the line. Bullies, nothing more.'

'There's too much at stake to fight among ourselves,' said Zenobi. 'Did you hear what happened about the voxcaster?'

'So what? So what if someone tri–'

'It's all or nothing! You're either for the cause or you're the enemy. Jawaahir is right. They're all right. Look at you, thinking to kill your own.'

'They're not our own! This one wouldn't give your body a second look. You don't know anything, barely old enough to work the line. We don't need them to know what we're fighting for.'

'I've worked the line,' said Zenobi. 'And my family worked it. I worked since Horus started this war, so don't tell me I don't know what we're fighting for. It's not so we can turn on each other. This is our chance to fight for our future.'

She saw the look in his eyes, the tightening of the skin as he grimaced, and knew he was going to pull the trigger.

She pulled hers first.

The las-bolt hit him in the cheek, searing through flesh and bone in an instant. He fell, folding in on himself like a worker exoskeleton suddenly powered down.

Her hand started to shake, until she felt strong fingers closing around her own, another hand gently lifting away the pistol. She turned her head, numb, and looked at Kettai.

'Your first one,' he said.

'First what?'

'First kill.'

She looked at Tewedros' body, a trickle of blood leaking from the neat hole in his face. The moisture in his eyes was already glistening with ice.

'Didn't think it would be one of our own,' she said quietly, lowering her hand.

'It wasn't,' Kettai told her.

She couldn't take her eyes off Tewedros. Who knew the enemy would look so much like her friends and family?

TWENTY-ONE

Give no ground
A tense ascent
The long walk

Lion's Gate space port, mesophex skin zone,
six days since assault

As though it were the fist of Dorn himself, Rann's counter-attack punched deep into the oncoming companies of Iron Warriors. Hall by hall, conveyor by conveyor, they drove back into the Starspear, while assault companies bounded from level to level, scaling the skin of the space port to fall upon the enemy from without.

While they waged a fresh offensive into the Starspear, the Imperial Army surged from Sky City into Low District.

Rann led from the front. The deployment of the First Assault Cadre on open ground had been something of an oddity, although highly effective. Their specialist equipment and tactics were intended for warship-to-warship boarding and defence, as well as combat in close urban environments. The confines of the Lion's Gate space port were perfect ground, with broad areas linked by narrow choke points he could easily defend, or tight channels and passages along which his troops could advance with near impunity behind their boarding shields. In their wake, several thousand more Space Marines consolidated their hold on the reclaimed territories, guarding against counter-attack and flanking forces.

Siegecraft was no mystery to the IV Legion traitors. Their specialist wall-breakers and assault companies had been landed en masse across the Starspear. Having swept away the remnants of the standing defence force, whose efforts had been much hampered by the lack of environmental protection, the Iron Warriors had secured several wide bridgeheads around the highest landing decks of Sky City and were bringing in squads by the dozen to reinforce any contested position. In a few more hours they would be able to meet up with the enemy force at large in the Sky City core, undercutting almost half of the Imperial Fists' offensive.

Rann was determined to retake at least one of the docks, cutting off the reinforcements at source and giving the Iron Warriors cause to think twice before sending another wave directly into Sky City. From across the nearby commands he pulled together the breach companies of the assault cadre. A steady slew of transports moving along the inner ringway brought in many, others arriving on foot from closer postings.

'It's just a matter of time before they have so many troops, we can't hold them back,' Rann explained to Sergeant Ortor.

'Attack is the best form of defence, lord?' the veteran laughed. 'Nothing to do with you not wanting to be sitting in the strategium looking at screens rather than running about with an axe in your hand?'

'I resent that implication,' the commander replied with a grin.

The four hundred-strong assault cadre gathered ten levels below the extent of the Iron Warriors' furthest advance. Pockets

of Space Marines from the IV Legion had established themselves across the upper tier, but seemed reluctant to advance
into Sky City, as though waiting for something despite the advantage gained by their rapid and unexpected advance.

'They should have pushed on for the bridges,' Rann continued, marching at a steady pace with his warriors. Three
hundred of them made their way to the great loading conveyors in the skin of the Starspear, while a hundred-strong force
under Lieutenant Koerner had been sent ahead to make a long
climb by stairwell. Koerner's force would arrive a few minutes
before the main attack, sowing some discord among the Iron
Warriors, who undoubtedly had strong cordons across the rapid
transit shafts and docking elevators.

Haeger's periodic updates painted a grim picture. The
technophagic invasion continued to intermittently play havoc
with the scanners, vox-network and transportation systems.
Even with the assumption that many of the augur readings
were false positives acting as a mask for the true location of
the enemy, there were several thousand Iron Warriors in the
Starspear while ten times that number were reinforcing the attack at the base. It was unimaginative, a simple pincer assault
on the vertical rather than horizontal, but the traitors did not
need to be sophisticated. They had orbital supremacy and the
advantage of numbers. Rann was only thankful that it seemed
the World Eaters and Emperor's Children were reluctant to join
the attack in force without their warp-twisted primarchs. If the
psychic shield failed and the Neverborn appeared, as they had
during the latter stages of the void war, there was likely nothing
short of the Emperor Himself that could hold the space port.

'It's time,' he told his companions, signalling Sergeant Ortor
towards the control panel between the two massive conveyor
gates. Ortor plugged in the device supplied by Magos Deveralax, which contained a cipher devised by the magos to override

any lingering technophage. It could only be introduced to systems locally and physically at the moment, but Haeger had assured Rann in the last update that a more widespread cure was being created.

'Hope this works,' said Ortor, pushing the call buttons. The clamour of arriving troops echoed around the loading bay.

'What is the worst that could happen?' joked one of the assault veterans.

'This doesn't work and the enemy override the emergency protocols so that we get dropped ten kilometres straight to the bottom of the shaft,' the sergeant replied gruffly, his usual humour stifled by the tension that was building among the legionaries.

'This will also mask our arrival,' Rann broadcast, seeking to find something more reassuring for his warriors to think about. 'Unless someone's stood looking down the shaft, they'll have about thirty seconds warning before we arrive.'

'We're treating this as a bridgehead engagement, even though technically we're defending,' said Ortor, reiterating the briefing Rann had given them all half an hour earlier. 'We break through the first defence line and then set up for hit-and-run raids across the neighbouring grid zones. We're the shield for the companies that are following. Ten thousand of our brothers are ready to counter-attack, but they'll get nowhere if we don't keep the enemy off the transitways and conveyor shafts.'

'Deployment is critical,' Rann told them over the vox. 'The conveyors are large enough to carry the whole force between them, but if we get stuck on the exit we can't bring numbers to bear. Lead squads will take hits but we need a fifty-metre zone of control within ten seconds of arrival. Use your shields, advance under cover fire. You've done this a thousand times.'

He almost said, *It's just another battle*, but chose not to at the last moment. This wasn't just another battle; his warriors knew it and would see such a speech for the platitude it was. Rann took a different approach.

'We're going to be in the battle of our lives in about three minutes. Lord Dorn and the Emperor are depending on us to hold this space port for as long as possible. No pointless heroics – we fight for as long as we can and make them pay for every pace they take on our world. They advance ten metres, we'll drive them back five. You look after your squad-brothers, keep tight and trust in one another.' He took a breath, and in the pause heard the rattle of the approaching conveyors. 'This is why we are here. This is what we were created for.'

With a squeal of metal and crunch of braking gears sliding into place, the two massive platforms arrived. The command overrides keeping their approach secret had shut down the motors for the doors, meaning they had to be manually cranked apart. Four legionaries apiece started on the lock wheels that flanked the gateways, like sailors of old on a capstan. Nearly thirty metres high, a metre thick, each sliding gate weighed several hundred tonnes. Step by step, boosted by their armour, the legionaries worked the wheels, the doors creaking apart a few centimetres at a time.

When the gap was wide enough for a Space Marine to pass through, the squads started to board, pushing on into the cavernous interiors, boots echoing as though in some grand hall.

'These are just the small service shafts,' Rann remarked to Ortor. 'You can fit tanks or Knight walkers in here, but it's the mega-conveyors in the core that we really need to hold. They're the Titan-lifters.'

'Couldn't we disable them, lord?'

'Lord Dorn has made it clear that the facilities for a strong counter-attack must be maintained.'

The doors were about ten metres apart and Rann joined the

cluster of warriors pressing through the gap, shield on one
arm, axe in the other hand. His bolter and second axe were
clamped to the inside of his boarding shield, which was as
big as a tank hatch. Ortor joined him, the magos' electronic
key-box in hand.

'We're going to use the door motors at the top, aren't we?'
the sergeant asked.

'Yes, sergeant, we are.'

When the last of the assault force were aboard, the door
gears were disengaged and counterweights rattled past the conveyor, pulling the gates shut. The crash of the closing portals
shuddered through the immense cage, echoing up the shaft.

'Just another bang,' Rann assured his warriors. 'There's about
ten megatonnes of ordnance hitting the port every second,
nobody's going to care about one more bang.'

The floor vibrated as the conveyor motors kicked in, juddering at first as the weight was taken up by immense chains
and gears, becoming smoother as the mechanism found its
pace. Rann ignored the urge to look up. He knew there was
no ceiling, just empty shaft above where chains swung and
clanked. Instead, he turned and focused on the doors. The rest
of the company followed suit, an about-turn that had them
all facing the way out when they arrived. Lead squads jostled
past those assigned support duties, bringing their shields to the
fore, while others readied their bolters. A few had more exotic
weapons – flamers, graviton guns, plasma guns.

Mentally counting off the levels as they passed, Rann calcu-
lated that they were forty seconds from arrival. In ten seconds
the noise of the conveyor would be too loud to miss. Thirty
seconds ago the stairwell force should have begun the attack.
Everything had to be timed; the technophage interruptions to
the vox meant anything but almost line-of-sight communication was likely to fail or, worse, be intercepted.

'Fifteen seconds!' he called out to his troops.

Ortor connected the key-box to the rune pad and the lead squads advanced several more strides, almost to the gates themselves. Shields crashed together, forming a wall inside the conveyor.

'Ten seconds!'

Every warrior had a visor chronometer but there was nothing like an insistent voice in the ear to concentrate the mind. Rann took a moment to push power through the auto-senses of his armour, blanking his vision whilst boosting the aural signal. Through the mess of machinery and detonations he thought he could pick out bolter fire nearby. If he was right, it meant the vanguard had arrived just at the right time.

'Five... Four... Three... Two... One...'

There was a pause, two more seconds, before the conveyor thudded to a halt, dipping ever so slightly so that the whole company tilted. Armour whined, compensating for the motion.

'Doors!'

Ortor activated the connection and the great portal groaned open, revealing an expansive chamber as large as the one they had left, lit by strip lumens and the flare of bolt shells. A waft of lubricant, bolt propellant and stale sweat flowed past Rann.

Rounds started clanging against the doors and zinging into the conveyor. Detonations sparked along the front line of legionaries' shields. Beyond them Rann could see the metal armour and yellow-and-white stripes of Iron Warriors squads, many of them turned to face a blur of yellow emerging from a distant stairway. Others had kept their weapons trained on the conveyors – Rann couldn't fault the enemy fire discipline.

'Advance!' he bellowed, lifting his axe.

The conveyor filled with thunder as a hundred and fifty legionaries pounded out through the doors, soon joined by the clamour of bolters and the snap of plasma. A roar emanated in unison from four hundred external address grilles.

'For Dorn and the Emperor!'

Varanzi approaches, thirty-five days before assault

It was hard to remember if this was the fifth or sixth day since the blizzard had begun. At least it spared them any more strafing runs from passing aircraft. The integrity officers had given up trying to marshal everybody into a single column; there were simply too many stragglers and they were losing their own in sudden flurries of snow or down unseen crevasses.

They'd been forced to leave the locomotive behind three days earlier. The track had simply stopped, running into a blasted plasma crater that shone like glass. It was impossible to know whether the hit had been deliberate or simply collateral damage from the ongoing bombardment of the Imperial Palace.

Now and then Zenobi thought she could see the towers among the half-seen mountain peaks, but Menber assured her it was impossible. Just more mountains, he said. The aurora of the defence screens still danced beyond the horizon, tinging the snowstorms with a blue-and-purple aura, flickered with the gold and silver of orbital attack. The rumble was constant, broken every few minutes by the higher-pitched whine of some other kind of projectile or the drawn-out, excoriating snarl of a plasma detonation. That they could hear anything over the strengthening winds was testament to the fury of the attack.

The cold reminded Zenobi of the first time she had been taken to the upper levels of Addaba by her aunties. The hive was nothing like the towering spires of some other cities, most of it spread a hundred and sixty kilometres outwards in the cradlespurs across the plains. Even so, its highest point was several kilometres above sea level, the air bitter.

She'd cried, only seven years old, her face stinging, glove-less hands bitten to the bone by the chill. She had wondered why her aunties had taken her there, but had been too upset to ask, thinking it was perhaps a punishment. She'd certainly appreciated the view, such as it was from freezing, scrunched eyes. And she'd been very fond of the heat of the forge line when she'd returned, reminding her that she belonged there.

Now she realised they'd just been showing her something different. They'd said nothing, faces wrapped in oil-stained rags as scarves, but she remembered now their look as they gazed far across the wastes of Afrik. It was a lesson that not everywhere was the same. Zenobi looked back and thought how different, how much bigger her world was now. They'd tried to show her a glimpse of what could be, of the lands beyond the walls of her home. Back then there might have been a chance she'd leave Addaba, either by herself or on a caravan, maybe meet someone she loved and travel to their home.

That had ended with the war. Nobody was allowed off the line without good reason. Dorn, and through him the Emperor, had needed Addaba to labour hard and unceasingly, dreams of distant cities and strange shores forgotten.

She almost stumbled over something at her feet. Zenobi thought it was a rock at first, dark beneath a thin layer of snow. Kettai stopped and pushed it with a foot, revealing it to be a coat-swathed corpse. It wasn't someone from Addaba: the skin was far too pale, the hair straight and brown, not curled and black. He wore a blue uniform, a long dress coat of black with silver braiding hiding most of it.

'Guess we're… not the only ones that… came this way,' said Menber, teeth chattering. His face was almost hidden between collar, improvised scarf and hood. He folded his hands under his armpits and stamped his feet.

Zenobi planted the banner pole in the snow and crouched beside the body. She reached out a hand covered with three layers of glove – the two larger pairs salvaged from companions that had succumbed to the elements. There was something on the man's chest, almost hidden by ice.

'Cut open,' she said, pointing to a horrendous wound that ran from shoulder to gut. The injury was a wide, ragged cut that had splayed his ribs and chewed through internal organs. 'What could do that?'

'Keep moving!' Okoye told them, emerging from the snow, his right side clad in white from the wind-blown ice. 'If you stop you might not start again.'

Nobody had strength enough to protest. Zenobi retrieved the banner and plodded on, following in the larger footprints made by Menber, her shorter legs making harder work of the snowdrifts.

They found other mounds in the snow, more corpses. All of them were dressed as Imperial Army conscripts. Advancing with lasguns at the ready, about half a kilometre later they came upon the broken wreckage of tanks and transports, thirty in all. The vehicles had tried to form a circle but were heavily damaged, some of them with their roofs blown out, others with shattered track guards, links scattered beneath the snow waiting to trip the unwary.

There were hundreds of bodies, most of them still inside. Everything was frozen solid like a pictograph.

General-Captain Egwu had stopped amid the carnage and was in conference with Jawaahir and several others. Zenobi caught snippets of their conversation through the wind as she and the others trudged past.

'...moved on by now. So many bolt impacts, it had to be

the Warmaster's legionaries,' Egwu said. 'We haven't any choice but to push on. There's a road about forty kilometres further along, we'll follow that towards the Palace proper.'

'And if we get attacked, captain?' countered one of the attending lieutenants.

'We fight, of course,' answered Jawaahir. 'We're not here to martyr ourselves. The Addaba Free Corps will fight for its people, in whatever way it has to.'

Hers was the final say and the cabal of officers moved to continue on their way.

'You!' Egwu called out through the blizzard. Zenobi stopped and looked around, trying to see who she was shouting for. The general-captain pointed directly at her and turned, forging through the snow.

'Trooper Adedeji!' Egwu's face was burnt down one side, the scar tissue twisting strangely as she grinned. 'Zenobi, isn't it?'

She nodded her reply, not sure what to say. Jawaahir loomed out of the snow beside the general-captain, brow furrowed.

'What's this?' Egwu asked, pointing to the pole across Zenobi's shoulders. 'You're still carrying the banner?'

'Of course, bana-madam. I'd never leave this behind!'

'See?' said Egwu, rounding on her officers, proving some point that Zenobi was not aware of. 'Trooper Adedeji has carried the company standard for two hundred and thirty kilometres already. Nothing's going to stop her getting to the battle.'

Zenobi saw an opportunity to ask a question that had been nagging at her and her companions for several days. There were quite a few of them nearby, having stopped to witness the conversation.

'How much further, bana-madam? How long until we reach the Imperial Palace?'

Jawaahir replied first, waving a hand to the north. There

were frozen droplets on her eyelashes, her cheeks even more sunken than before.

'Are you sure that's where you want to go, Adedeji?' she asked. 'The wrath of Horus falls with a thousand shells an hour. The Emperor's aegis weakens by the day. You know it is only a matter of time before it fails and the Palace will break under the Warmaster's anger.'

'Where else would we fight?' said Zenobi. She turned her gaze back to the general-captain. 'How far is it?'

Egwu glanced away and for a moment Zenobi thought she was not going to answer. Then she looked back at the trooper, her expression intent.

'Nearly a thousand kilometres, Zenobi. Over mountains and valleys, higher and higher, the air thinner and thinner, as winter grows colder.'

'Thank you.'

Zenobi shifted the weight of the company standard and turned to the other troopers. She met the gaze of a few, Menber included. Some looked worried, confronting the challenge ahead. Others matched her look of determination.

She said nothing else but started walking, concentrating on putting one foot in front of the next, for as long as she needed to.

TWENTY-TWO

Attrition
Iron within
Amon and the Neverborn

Lion's Gate space port, stratophex core, six days since assault

The darkness was split by the flare of bolts snarling back and forth across the lading hall. The vast space echoed with the discharge of weapons and the crack of impacts, cut through with the hiss of plasma bolts and high-pitched whine of melta weapons. Every flash threw stark light onto the rows of Iron Warriors that held the upper gantries and walkways, and across a black void a solid barrier of shields emblazoned with the device of the Imperial Fists. Half-seen chains and lifting rigs lurked in the shadows, the floor and mezzanines scattered with the broken remains of the IV Legion's last attempt to cross the open ground.

That assault had been ten hours earlier. Since then Forrix's Iron Warriors had been caught in an ever-tightening noose of Imperial Fists and Imperial Army auxiliaries. The latter were a lesser threat, the confines of the chambers and passages around the reactor relays a poor environment for massed platoons.

Unable to make their numbers count against their far superior opponents, the Emperor's soldiers were being used to slow down breakout attempts, selling their lives for just long enough to allow the Imperial Fists to bring more potent opposition to bear.

It was a callous tactic, and Forrix found himself admiring the commander that employed it, whoever that was. Perhaps Sigismund, the famed First Captain, though there had been no report of Dorn's Blade in any of the encounters so far. It might have even been the hand of Dorn himself that pulled the defenders' strings.

It didn't matter. Forrix had only two concerns as he stood on the line with his warriors, firing his bolter down at the shield-bearers below. Concerns he voiced when Captain Gharal voxed a request to withdraw several squads to the rearguard.

'If we weaken here, the Imperial Fists will push us into the anterior channels. They will be able to set up a secure picket across five levels of the transfer station, blocking all access to the reactor conduits.'

'If we continue to engage at this intensity, triarch, we will run into logistical issues within seven hours. Better to withdraw and temper the level of battle, and fight for longer. The lead companies of the aerial assault force are only two kilometres away.'

'Logistical issues? You mean ammunition supply?'

'Stimulant infusions are reaching unsafe levels. Armour recycling systems need flushing before they start passing toxic elements back into our bodies. Nobody has slept. At the ninety-six-hour mark mental fatigue starts to accelerate rapidly.'

'You want to rest?' Forrix poured all of his scorn into those words, then regretted the rebuke immediately. Gharal was leading the upper elements of the force, half a kilometre away. If he chose to make a breakout – not an unreasonable strategy – he would leave Forrix utterly bereft of support. He assumed a more accommodating tone. 'Your attention to the longer-term viability of our force is commendable. And yet, survival is only one of our two objectives, captain.'

'What do you mean, triarch?'

A lascannon pulse burned through the wall just above Forrix's head showering droplets of molten plasteel onto his armour. He shifted to his left, allowing Merrig and his reaper autocannon to take position and return fire. The pound of the twin-barrelled weapon shook the walkway for several seconds until the gunner stepped back, lifting his smoking weapon.

'Enemy heavy weapon eliminated, triarch,' he said with a hint of pleasure.

Forrix banged a fist against the warrior's shoulder guard, a mark of praise, and then pointed for him to move further along the walkway to find another target worth expending his precious ammunition upon.

'What was I saying? Survival. I don't plan to simply be the bone these dogs of Dorn chew on while Kroeger takes the bridges above. I aim to live long enough to see them all dead. To do that, odd as it seems, we have to make ourselves as much trouble as possible. We're not getting out of here alive by ourselves, Gharal. We need that relief column.'

'It's no good to us if we're all dead when it arrives,' said the captain, voice strained.

'The wave attacks through the lower levels ran out of momentum six hours ago. Thirty thousand of the Fourth that followed the lesser formations are engaged in brutal back-and-forth with Dorn's sons. Most of them are new recruits, barely worth the armour they wear. They are not coming. That leaves just the suborbital attack force. If they are going to reach us, we need to draw away as much opposition as possible. We have to remain a mobile and relevant threat.'

'I understand, triarch. If I relocate westwards by three hundred *metres there is a maintenance conveyor shaft. We'll be abandoning the upper perimeter but we can flank the defence of the plasma conduits.'*

'So commanded,' Forrix said without hesitation. 'I will pull back a company on my left as a feint, to draw more enemy inwards towards the central force. That will give you time to break off engagement and move.'

'Affirmative. Will commence manoeuvre in ten minutes.'

The vox crackled into inactivity, replaced by the cacophony of the battle that raged around Forrix. Once he'd ordered Lieutenant Sarpara to pull back on the flank, his mind's eye shifted from the wider area to his immediate locale. The warriors of the IV Legion needed to get across the open ground between the conjunctions of stairwells and walkways, but the Imperial Fists were content to defend the opposite side of the hall, ready to cut down anything that ventured out from cover.

'Lieutenant Dreik, have your Iron Havocs ready,' he voxed. 'Assemble on me for dedicated strike force. All other legionaries maintain fire discipline.'

He mustered together eight squads from his surroundings, moving them down several levels towards the floor of the lading hall while squads of Iron Havocs with lascannons, plasma cannons, multi-meltas, autocannons and other support weaponry made their way to him from across the force. At the ten-minute mark, as Sarpara and Gharal would both be making their moves, Forrix ordered the attack.

Targeting a narrow front of the Imperial Fists' line, about a hundred metres wide and five storeys high, the ad hoc Iron Havocs company unleashed a torrent of shells, las-bolts and plasma, while Forrix's squads burst down the remaining steps and loading ramps.

'Hold bolter fire!' he bellowed at his warriors. The fusillade above masked their energy signature and he didn't want anyone to give away their position in the darkness. 'Wait for my command.'

Plasma bolts smashed into shields and armour, slashing through both while salvos of reaper rounds and heavy bolter fire tore into the gaps carved by lascannon hits. Pounding across the ferrocrete floor, splashing through puddles of blood and oil, Forrix panted hard, hearts and lungs pushed to capacity.

The first sparks of bolter fire sliced down into his force, passing over him into the squads behind. There were several shouts from injured legionaries.

'Keep moving!' Forrix ordered, straining even harder, his armour carrying him forward in three-metre strides.

The heavy weapons flared hard for several more seconds, punishing those foes that had remained in the arc of fire. By light of lascannon bursts and detonating bolter rounds, Forrix saw yellow-armoured legionaries ripped apart, their plate no match for the power of the weapons levelled against them.

Through the flare of the Iron Warriors' heavy weapons poured more bolter fire from the Imperial Fists above – but not directly ahead. The brief but massed fire of the heavy weapons had done its job, carving a narrow but telling wound into the defence line. Forrix and the lead squads gained the stairwells opposite unhindered, crashing over the bodies of Dorn's sons.

'Split by combat squad and provide cover to gather weapons and ammunition,' Forrix ordered. Half of his warriors set upon the corpses of the Imperial Fists, ripping free bolters and magazines, tearing boarding shields and blades from their dead hands. The others pushed outwards as more squads piled into the breach, securing the level above.

'Lieutenant Uhaz, what are the enemy doing?' he voxed.

'Pulling back, triarch.'

'Not mustering for counter-attack?'

'No, triarch, they are moving away from your position.'

'Good. Cover fire and advance by company.'

'*Affirmative, triarch.*'

Forrix turned back to the open hall, almost tripping over the body of an Imperial Fists legionary. He looked down. The warrior's helm had been cracked open by an autocannon hit. Moving his gaze back to the hall, he counted his dead. Thirteen more. Not a bad price to pay for getting across the hall, but he'd expended a good amount of heavy weapons ammunition and powercells to do it.

All to get two hundred metres closer to an objective he wasn't even trying to destroy.

Exultant Wall zone, eight days since assault

Amon was known for his patience even among the Custodians, but he had not expected his investigations to be quite so lacking in progress. Gatherings of the Lectitio Divinitatus were scattered all across the Palace, and far beyond he suspected, yet he had seen nothing more threatening than glorified debating groups and book discussion. Whatever power the officers in the quarantine barracks had tapped into was so far absent elsewhere.

Keeler's information about the Lightbearers was the only solid lead they had, but Amon shared her opinion that such progress would be wasted if he made his involvement known. Consequently, the Custodian had agreed to allow her to return at the next gathering to see if there was a repeat of her previous experience. She had claimed it might have been her own, unique connection to the Emperor that had brought about the vision, although Amon was inclined to believe it was more a case of shared massed hallucination. Even without artificial induction, such shared manias were possible, and under the constant stress of the siege all kinds of psychological phenomena were bound to surface among the stifled populace.

Pessimism was no excuse for lack of thoroughness, and Amon was determined to continue to observe as many of the remaining sects as possible, in case the Lightbearers proved to be a false hope. His current self-assigned target was a gathering of Imperial Army recruits taking place in one of the makeshift medicae sprawls that had been set up a few kilometres from the fighting at the Exultant Wall, where many casualties were arriving from the offensive through the Lion's Gate space port.

His presence would be considered exceptional if not threatening, and so he went clad in nondescript cloak and robes. If anyone paid him attention it was likely they would take him for a warrior of the Legiones Astartes rather than a Custodian. He expected no trouble but carried a gladius-style blade favoured by the Imperial Fists concealed within his garb.

He caught the smell of blood and rot even before he came to the outskirts of the medicae encampment. Though ostensibly a field hospital, there was little more here than in the other slums, the only exception being that the inhabitants were wholly of the Imperial Army rather than from the dwindling non-combatant populace of the Palace. The hospital stretched for three kilometres and over several storeys of former Administratum hab-blocks, the cells and dorms well suited to wards and quarantine rooms. Infants carried ration packs and water flasks, while older children acted as stretcher-bearers, a constant stream of wounded coming in from the front lines. The grisly task of disposing of those that did not survive fell to them also, in almost equal numbers, bodies carried to funeral pyres in an old power plant building a few hundred metres west of the facility. The furnaces burned as constantly as they had done before the siege but now with a far more grotesque fuel.

Flies swarmed thick, drawn by gangrene. Every effort had

been made to provide sanitation but the stench of urine and faeces could not be masked. As Amon picked his way through the lines of miserable wretches, he encountered no few that were dead in their cots, their fluids seeping into the bedding. The more he observed the dismal scene, the greater his misgivings. Having witnessed the horrors of the quarantine zone, and the proximity of the first apparition to that degradation, it occurred to Amon that this great hoarding of the dead and dying might be some other part of the Death Guard's plague-scheme.

It took only a few minutes to locate the shrine that had been erected – the surrounding chambers were empty of patients, which made it instantly stand out among several city blocks of virtually wall-to-wall casualties. In what had once been a ranking clerk's offices, the wooden aquila that had served as a backdrop to the administrator's duties had been brought forth onto an altar of ammunition crates, draped with service medals and identity tags. Laspacks and bullets were placed at the foot of the altar, ankle-deep, as offerings to a far more belligerent form of deity than the one worshipped by the Lightbearers.

Watching the hundred or so wounded troopers, Amon observed the usual ritual forms – incantations, marching songs instead of hymns, and finally a shared moment of silence. The soldiers were instructed by their leader – a nondescript woman in the uniform of a corporal, the side of her head wrapped in bloodied bandage – to turn their thoughts to those still fighting, to ask the Emperor to lend them strength in the ongoing battle.

Amon was about to depart, seeing nothing amiss, when he caught a sweet-smelling breeze. The troopers were talking in unison, the words barely audible but clearly intoned.

'He is the Life Within Death. The Breath on your Lips. The Hope in your Heart.'

A ghost light played about the aquila on the makeshift table, like dappled sunlight reflected from water. A breeze stirred the pile of offered munitions, so that casings clinked against each other, settling into the pile.

The chanting grew louder, the same words over and over.

'He is the Life Within Death. The Breath on your Lips. The Hope in your Heart.'

The troopers, heads bowed, swayed to the tempo of their invocation, the corporal-priest standing before them with eyes closed, hands clasped to her chest. A line of glistening drool fell from the corner of her lip and dripped to her filthy shirt.

That was not all. Her eyes moved back and forth rapidly beneath their lids, like one in the throes of deep sleep. The veins in the back of her hand grew darker, as though black fluid ran through them.

Amon's fingers closed around the hilt of the gladius as he moved from beneath the shadow of a broken stair, boots crunching grit underfoot.

The woman's eyes snapped open, orbs of pure black, glistening with a sheen of mucus that dribbled down her cheeks. She turned towards Amon as he broke into a run, a screech rousing the hundred-strong congregation from their reverie. Opening their eyes, they cried out in disgust and alarm, even as the corporal threw a hand towards Amon, another shriek of command issuing from cracked lips.

A few responded, pulling at combat daggers and pistols, leaping forward to intercept the accelerating Custodian. They fell, gutted or headless, not even interrupting his stride. The Neverborn creature hissed and pounced like a hunting cat, fingernails that had become claws lancing towards Amon's face. He swerved and brought up the short sword, stabbing through the creature's chest as it passed, cutting from breastbone to pelvis.

Almost bisected, the remains flopped to the dusty floor,

where the monstrosity continued to flap and flail through a trail of filth and blood, turning back towards Amon. The rest of the gathering erupted into mayhem, some trying to flee, running into others immobile with terror or stepping forward to aid the Custodian.

He stepped around a lunging hand and brought the sword down hard, tip piercing skull and ferrocrete. He ripped it out and struck off the head to be sure. Even then the body quivered for several more seconds, claws raking at the dirt. When it finally flopped sideways, Amon saw that the clawing had not been random, but had etched a diabolic symbol into the floor, the shallow inscription filling with bodily fluid.

Amon was at a loss as to what to do next. Several of the congregation had already fled, others were starting to run. Were they tainted? Did he need to hunt each of them down? Others were clearly shocked, ignorant of their part in the manifestation.

He stepped quickly to the altar. The aquila shone with a coating of ice.

'Nobody leave!' he bellowed, drawing back his hood. 'I am Custodian Amon Tauromachian, and by the authority of the Emperor you are all under arrest.'

None of the remaining congregation tried to leave, awestruck by the presence of the Custodian revealed in their midst. Amon struck the aquila with the pommel of the gladius, knocking it from the altar, before striding back to the corpse. It had all but melted into a puddle, like an oil slick in the dust and grime. Even as he activated his vox to call for assistance, his thoughts turned to his companion in the investigation.

Keeler would not be able to argue away this event quite so easily.

TWENTY-THREE

The Keeler issue
Kroeger's plan
Phosphex

Exultant Wall zone, twelve days since assault

'How could you possibly not see the threat posed by this cult?' Amon rarely raised his voice outside of battle, but his words rang back to him from the vaulted roof of the hall, the last word echoing menacingly.

Keeler opened her mouth to answer but was quieted by the raised hand of Malcador.

'It is to that very point that this debate is turned, Custodian,' said the Regent.

They moved in brisk procession along an inner passage of the Ultimate Wall – Dorn's decree was that they speak only as he moved between other engagements that required his attention. The thunder of impacts and the counter-fire of the towers was a constant vibration in the walls and floor. The clank of magazine hoists pulling up shells to the macro cannons and the tramp of booted feet echoed from side corridors and bastion chambers.

Footfalls ahead betrayed the presence of four Imperial Fists squads clearing the path to the Praetorian's destination – a moving cordon of Templars from Sigismund's command. Their presence ensured the impromptu conclave went unheard.

As well as Malcador and Dorn, the gathering included First Captain Sigismund, and Constantin Valdor. These giants were forced to pace slowly so that Malcador could keep up, his staff tapping on the bare ferrocrete floor. Keeler was accompanied by Kyril Sindermann, who now spoke for the first time.

'To accept that is to concede that Lady Keeler herself poses a threat to the Emperor,' said the former iterator. He smoothed a crease in his robes with precise, delicate hands. 'And my own beliefs, though they are of substantially less importance at this juncture.'

'Captain-general, I know what occurred in the hospital,' said Amon. 'Coupled with the evidence from the quarantine barracks, it is obvious that there is a link between the rites of the Lectitio Divinitatus and daemonic activity.'

'And what do you propose?' said Malcador. He cleared his throat of the dust that drifted through the beams of lumen light. 'I am not certain a purge of the theists will be productive, even if possible. The siege is too finely poised to risk immense resentment among a significant swath of our soldiers.'

'This is not a discussion of prosecuting a law, but of guaranteeing the sanctuary of the Imperial Palace,' said Valdor. His armour hummed as he turned to look at the Regent. 'The battle rages on many levels, you know this.'

'I cannot spare any warriors,' Dorn said bluntly. He looked aggravated at being waylaid outside of the strategium, but his presence was essential. Amon had hoped the Praetorian would be a staunch ally, but he apparently needed some further persuasion. 'I cannot tell you how the spirit war fares, but the physical conflict stands upon the balance. The enemy are in control of half the base levels of the Lion's Gate space port, and nearly a similar amount of territory in the upper spire. A force of unknown size is targeting objectives in Sky City, but Commander Rann cannot spare the firepower to eradicate them without weakening the defence of the transport bridges. I have drawn together a reinforcement strike that Captain Sigismund will lead within the hour, but that leaves me with no reserves. *All* of the Legions are stretched thin.'

'Given your recent encounter with the daemon Samus aboard the *Phalanx*, let us recall that timely reminder of the perils posed by the Neverborn,' said Amon, moving his gaze to Keeler. 'Let us not also overlook that incident's connection to you, through the figure of Mersadie Oliton.'

'I know little of what happened,' replied Keeler, looking from Amon to Malcador. 'In any event, Mersadie and I parted company long ago.'

'I hear accusations but no solid proposals,' Malcador said again, shaking his head. 'Rogal is correct, we cannot spare warriors from the walls to patrol the Inner Palace. Such a diversion may be the only intent of these manifestations.'

'We must trust in the Emperor to protect us,' said Keeler. 'I witnessed His power, I swear. It is by His will that the Neverborn are kept at bay. The worship of the Lectitio Divinitatus will only strengthen that power.'

'That is true, to a point,' conceded Malcador. 'It is the tela-ethesic ward that shields us from daemonic intrusion. The Emperor is under constant assault, perhaps it is not surprising that the odd leak is now occurring.'

'Is the Emperor in danger?' demanded Valdor. 'What of the security of the Imperial Dungeon?'

'The Emperor is always in danger, Constantin. It is the nature of being the adversary of the Four Powers to live with their enmity. But is He physically threatened by this? I think not.'

'What of the Silent Sisterhood?' asked Keeler. 'Should they not have a representative here?'

'The Sisters of Silence are as stretched by these attacks as all of our other forces,' Dorn told her. 'Having been forced from their lunar facilities, they lack some of the support they would normally have to conduct widespread anti-psyker actions. They guard the walls against sorcery even as the Emperor guards Terra against the daemonic.'

'Perhaps it is simply the psychic that we should investigate,' suggested Valdor, looking meaningfully at Keeler. 'You profess powers that can only be described as coming from the warp.'

'From the Emperor,' she said, folding her arms. 'Not from the enemy.'

'A distinction only you seem to be able to make,' said Amon.

'You ignore several pertinent facts,' argued Sindermann, stepping protectively next to Keeler. 'Firstly, I myself have witnessed rites of abjuration using the holy text.'

'The supposed banishing of a daemon aboard the *Vengeful Spirit*?' Malcador scratched his chin. 'Was not that conjuration precipitated by your own hand?'

'In error,' Sindermann said hastily, 'through a cursed book. Regardless, it was the power of the Emperor that allowed Lady Keeler to dispel the Neverborn.'

'I felt real power with the Lightbearers,' said Keeler. 'Power we could harness. Why should the Emperor protect us at His expense without us giving back? Our prayers can be used as weapons against the unholy, just as surely as bolts and las-blasts are the foes of mortals.'

'Let us put that aside for a moment, lest we are sidetracked,' Malcador said quickly. He looked at Sindermann. 'You said "firstly", indicating you have other reasons why we should not suspect Keeler in this matter?'

'The first apparition took place when she was in confinement.

The second when she was elsewhere. The only manifestation we have when Lady Keeler was actually present seems to be entirely benign.'

'Is such a thing possible?' asked Sigismund, breaking his silence. The Templar followed a little apart from the group and Amon had almost forgotten him. 'Can it be possible to channel the essence of the Emperor in such a way?'

Amon noticed Dorn's deep frown, as though vexed at the First Captain's contribution.

'We will not be indulging in superstitious speculation,' the primarch growled.

'Is it superstition, when one has evidence of the supernatural?' said Sindermann, receiving a glare of admonishment from the towering commander. He absorbed the brunt of Dorn's displeasure with a visible flinch, even his long experience of the primarchs no surety against the intimidating presence of the Emperor's gene-sons. He continued in more subdued fashion. 'If the power of the Neverborn can be channelled by sorcery, cannot a person of faith act as focus for the Emperor's might?'

'I do not know if this is a discussion of theology or metaphysics, but neither is useful for our purpose,' Valdor said, cutting off a reply from Malcador. 'What is to be done about these cults? I accept the argument that for the time being a harmless worship of the Emperor may be good for morale, and perhaps keep minds looking for a greater power from wandering down paths left unexplored.'

'Harmless?' said Amon. 'Twice we have seen what these ceremonies can do, breaching the ward that protects Terra.'

'I did not say it was harmless, only that if it is so, it may have a use,' Valdor told his subordinate. He swung his gaze down to Keeler. 'There are hundreds of groups practising your faith around the Imperial Palace?'

'At least,' she replied. 'For longer than the siege has been in place.'

'So it seems to me there is more connection to the efforts of the Death Guard than the cults themselves.' Valdor stopped and the group halted with him at the junction of the main corridor and a side passage that led back towards the Inner Palace region. 'The quarantine zone and the hospital are the common denominator, more than the cult. Amon, concentrate your efforts on other such pits of misery, for any activity by the Lectitio Divinitatus in such places brings greater risk of corruption.'

'What of the Lightbearers?' asked Amon.

'Keeler will continue to attend and monitor their meetings,' said Malcador.

'I will report anything untoward as soon as it occurs,' Keeler said.

Amon shook his head. 'I find that little assurance, given the bar that has been set to judge what is untoward.'

'We shall need to trust each other a while longer,' Malcador intervened, stepping between the Custodian and Keeler. His unwavering gaze met Amon's. 'Will you take my assurance?'

Amon hesitated. There was only one being that he fully trusted, but in placing his trust in the Emperor he had to submit to his master's decision to appoint Malcador as His Regent, with the full authority that entailed. He glanced to Valdor and received a subtle nod in reply.

'Very well, Lord Regent.' Amon lifted a fist to his breastplate. 'I will investigate the plague aspect of the attack and leave the Lightbearers to your appointee.'

'My officers can provide you with data on field hospitals, plague zones, Death Guard assaults.' Dorn gestured along the side passage. 'I will signal Bhab Bastion to be ready to respond to your requests immediately.'

'Our thanks, Lord Praetorian,' said Valdor.

'I shall return to the Sanctum Imperialis with you,' said Malcador, stepping after the two Custodians. 'I am sure Lord Dorn would prefer to have no more distractions from his duties at the wall.'

Lion's Gate space port, mesophex mantlezone,
twelve days since assault

Workshops that had once resounded to the beat of hammers and hiss of forges now rang with the crack of bolters and snarl of plasma. Maintenance lines became bulwarks held by the Imperial Fists, their bright armour smeared with grease and soot, the flare of bolts bright pinpricks in the gloom of the massive halls. Lascannon beams and detonating missiles cast shadows of tractor skeletons and hauler carcasses.

The Sons of Horus pushed from one cavernous workshop to the next, thrusting deep into the territory reclaimed by the counter-offensive. At their head Abaddon and his Justaerin formed the point of the spear, as they had been in so many battles before. The First Captain urged his warriors on by example, plunging into each fresh firefight without relent. Bolter, sword and fist took their toll of the enemy, while at his side the sorceries of Layak split apart their armour and bewitched their weapons. Combi-bolters blazing, the Terminators followed, clearing aside any that survived the wrath of their leader.

The bulk of an auto lathe offered a few seconds' respite, giving Abaddon opportunity to assess the broader situation. Issuing orders to send a company to the upper levels of the refitting houses, he checked the sensorium of his war-plate. More enemies were arriving from a travel duct that ran along the far side of the installation, the heat plumes of five vehicles approaching at speed.

'Why do you pause now?' asked Layak, his blade slaves picking through the fallen enemy, plunging sword-limbs into each. 'You have the momentum.'

Abaddon regarded him for several seconds, undecided whether he would respond or not. It was no business of the sorcerer what he intended. He signalled for Haork to bring the auspex. The legionary dashed through a sudden flurry of Imperial Fists bolts as he broke from the cover of a half-dismantled cargo loader that looked like a giant, dissected beetle.

'Only days ago you lamented that the Iron Warriors risked failure by their inability to seize the bridgeways. Now you spend your warriors clearing out maintenance sheds and transit terminals.'

Checking the schematics, the First Captain saw that there was only one way to advance without being exposed – directly through the Imperial Fists' line. Whoever commanded the local forces had chosen the workshops as a choke point, easily supported from the internal ringway. If the Sons of Horus could break through, they would turn the flank of a five-kilometre-long defence line protecting the upper approaches of the skybridges.

'When it comes time to seize your prize, you cannot hesitate,' Layak continued, oblivious to Abaddon's apathy.

'I have had a change of heart,' Abaddon told him. His auto-senses picked up the rumble of the tanks. 'A longer view.'

He rounded the end of the auto lathe, sighting along his combibolter. Spying the flash of yellow behind a pile of gears and other spare parts, he opened fire. The volley sparked from the heap, filling the air with a cloud of shrapnel. Taking his lead, two squads of Justaerin poured fire into the same position, incendiary rounds mixed in with the regular bolts to set the metal pile ablaze.

'Perturabo wants to seize the space port to bring in Titans for Horus,' Abaddon explained as he advanced behind the curtain of fire, his own weapon adding half a dozen more rounds to the fusillade. 'It has not fallen quickly enough, so it is better to use this battle to draw in as many defenders as possible. Every Imperial Fist that dies here is one less to defend the wall.'

Layak appeared at his side, black energy leaping from his staff. The sorcerous lightning engulfed an enemy squad pulling back from the Terminator attack, leaping from one Space Marine to the next. They crashed to the ground in turn, bloody vapour coiling from shattered eye-lenses and ruptured armour joints.

'Time is our enemy, you know this.' The Word Bearer thrust his staff forward and his blade slaves stormed ahead, the detonations of enemy bolts across their half-armour skin no dissuasion. Vaulting the next line of work benches, they set upon the Imperial Fists beyond. Abaddon ran after them, exploiting the gap in the enemy fire created by the sudden assault.

'The threat of Guilliman may be overrated,' he growled back.

'The arrival of Guilliman, the Lion and Russ is not the only factor,' Layak warned. 'You have seen the toll paid by your master to channel the energy of the True Gods. Every day he must contain their power is a day closer to his ruin.'

Abaddon smashed a bench out of the way with his power fist, flipping it into the armoured warriors beyond. He followed up with a burst of fire that cut down two sons of Dorn.

The roar of vehicle engines shook the workshop, flakes of rust falling on both sides from the high rafters. Abaddon's focus was on the foes to his left and right as he clamped his bolter to his armour and drew his blade, parrying the chainsword of an Imperial Fists sergeant. His fist closed about the legionary's arm, crushing armour, flesh and bone to a pulp of blood and broken ceramite.

The thunder of heavy bolters and autocannons cut across the din of the escalating melee, followed by the crack of breaking war-plate. The vox was strangely silent for a few seconds.

Abaddon turned aside a boarding axe with his glove and cleaved his blade into the bearer, parting his foes for a glimpse at the armoured squadron pulling up beyond the main gateway.

He saw dark metal armour broken by stripes of red and black, their hulls festooned with scrawled dedications to Perturabo and Horus. Skulls and pieces of armour hung like bunting from exhaust stacks and weapon pintles.

Iron Warriors.

From a pair of Land Raiders emerged two squads of iron-clad legionaries, just as the transports and their escort of Predators opened fire again. Lascannon blasts and explosive shells raked into the surrounded Imperial Fists, tearing apart war-plate and genhanced bodies.

'Hold position!' Abaddon bellowed to his warriors, concerned that they would charge forward into the fire of their allies. 'Mark your targets.'

Bolters adding to the fury of the attack, the Iron Warriors advanced, more squads arriving behind them in a wave of Rhinos. In their midst strode an officer with old-style Cataphractii plate, armour coated with bloody handprints as grisly livery.

'Warsmith Kroeger,' said Layak. 'Come to welcome the right and left hands of Horus.'

A knot of several dozen Imperial Fists tried to break out, turning from the newly arrived legionaries to seek escape through the Sons of Horus. Abaddon despatched his Justaerin with a word and gesture, his focus turned to the Iron Warriors commander.

Kroeger used a crackling fist in great sweeps, breaking open helms and plastrons without any thought of defence. He advanced without pause, treading over the slain of both sides, rivet-studded boots cracking ceramite beneath his weight.

Abaddon sheathed his blade and took up his bolter once more, turning to fire the rest of the loaded magazine into the withdrawing Imperial Fists. He passed the weapon to one of his companions to reload as he came face to face with Kroeger. The Iron Warrior's shoulders heaved as though he were panting, something primal in his hunched stance. His blood-specked mask looked up at Abaddon, eyes hidden behind red lenses.

'Captain Abaddon,' Kroeger grunted, raising his fist in salute.

'Warsmith Kroeger.' Abaddon touched a finger to his brow in return. 'I was not expecting you.'

'Been looking for you. Came on a Dorn-scum flying column and wondered where they were going. Saw there was a fight going on where one of my companies were, so I took them out on the way and came here to see what the fuss was.' Kroeger took in a shuddering breath. 'Here you are. Haven't heard from your Legion command since you captured the upper sensoria.'

'I am the Sons of Horus command,' Abaddon said pointedly. 'I choose our objectives and the manner in which we will achieve them.'

'I'm not here to tell you otherwise,' said Kroeger. 'You're Ezekyle Abaddon, one of our greatest commanders! But if you find yourself wanting something to do, I think we can stop this counter-attack within the day.'

'How do you plan to do that?' asked Abaddon.

'An unstoppable force, Captain Abaddon. My Dodakathik Guard will take the brunt of the fighting. Hardened warriors, unshakeable. Dreadnoughts, automatons, mobile support weapons. Khârn and his Blooded are joining me.'

'A keen blade edge to cut through the morass,' said Layak, tone betraying his relish at the idea.

'You must be the Crimson Apostle, the Warmaster's daemon-caller.'

Abaddon felt a stab of amusement at the petty title, but Layak bridled.

'I am the spiritual aide of Horus Lupercal, prophet of the Dark Gods, Lord of Mysteries.'

'Have you broken the Emperor's psychic shield yet?'

'The process is ongoing. One does not pierce a–'

'Thought not,' said Kroeger, turning back to Abaddon. Horus' lieutenant was drawn to the warsmith's brusqueness, so at odds with the theatrics of Layak.

'I thought you were trying to link up with the force inside Sky City,' Abaddon said, noting that the blade slaves had closed in on Layak, perhaps in an attempt to intimidate Kroeger. 'What of the warsmith trapped behind the lines?'

'Plans change,' Kroeger said with a shrug. 'I've not heard from Forrix in days. Probably dead.'

'You would abandon one of the Trident?' said Layak. 'One despatched by your own orders?'

'Don't think Forrix would spare a second thought for me, warp-talker. He had a fighting chance, which is more than he'd give to those he wanted rid of.' Kroeger swung his gaze to Abaddon. 'Think about it. You, me, Khârn of the World Eaters… Just let them try and stop us.'

Abaddon was thinking about it, very carefully. In a war of gods and demigods, here was a chance for the Legions to prove their strength was undiminished. Even as his genefather drew ever greater strength from his immaterial patrons, it would be wise to remind him of the mortal power still at his command.

There was still much that could be done with a bolter and a blade, and a legionary behind them.

Lion's Gate space port, stratophex core,
twelve days since assault

'Phosphex!'

The call echoed down the passage and across the vox, just seconds before a junction thirty metres ahead of Forrix brightened with yellow light. He thought his engineered body was already pushed to the limits but that single word set his hearts racing, his armour pumping the last drops of stimulant into his body.

The squads nearest the attack had no chance. The air around them ignited, a cloud of fire crawling through nothing to engulf their armoured forms. Their shrieks – noises that no legionaries should ever produce – were thankfully brief. The silhouettes of diminishing figures danced in after-image as Forrix tried to blink away the glare of the phosphex, having been forced to discard his damaged helm the day before. Even at this distance, he felt the prickle of impossible heat in the first moments and was turning to run even as he bellowed the order to pull back.

Space Marines did not panic, but the retreat from the living flames was hurried and disorderly. Snaking tendrils of fire raced along the high ceiling, overtaking the slowest runners, droplets raining down on their helms and pauldrons. The phosphex made fuel of whatever it landed on, and it devoured with all the rapaciousness of a starved glutton. A fully armoured legionary was reduced to ashes in less than seven seconds, and once they started burning there was nothing that would stop it.

'Dorn's bastards!' swore Uhaz. 'Burning their own city!'

It was a terrible but effective tactic, and Forrix was grudgingly impressed that the commanders of the VII Legion had the stomach for such a move. Unless, and he voiced this thought to nobody, the phosphex had come from the Iron Warriors' own bombardment. It was possible that some of the barrage unleashed on the first day was still creeping around the space port like a burning mass murderer looking for fresh victims, even fourteen days later.

Three more legionaries thrashed their last as the phosphex speared after them, creeping up from their boots to swallowed them legs first, the rounds in their bolters snapping as they detonated, spraying flecks of metal that turned to mist in the heat of the flames.

Eleven days.

Forrix reached a stairwell and turned into it, throwing himself up the steps with the others. Distance was the only saviour.

Eleven days since they had mustered, expecting reinforcements after two days. They had certainly tested the defenders. The Imperial Fists had stopped sending their allies after eight days, perhaps baulking at the immense casualties inflicted by the warriors of the IV Legion. It was the ideal fight, in a way, for an Iron Warrior. Fighting stubbornly for its own merits. No broader strategy. No vague objectives or collateral concerns.

Engage.

Kill.

Survive.

Forrix continued past the next landing, seeing through a set of open doors that the level above was already flickering with eerie phosphex light.

'Regroup at seventy-five metres up,' he voxed to all in range. He transmitted to the command channel as he ran, gulping down breaths that tasted of his brothers' charred flesh and molten armour. Glancing down the stairwell he saw the phosphex creeping towards the steps. 'Gharal! What is your position relative to the eastern stairwell in designated sector six?'

There was no reply. He tried again, wondering if it was his vox malfunctioning, or a problem with Gharal's reception.

'*Engaged by Dreadnoughts and heavy gauge power armour. Cataphractii and other squads.*'

'There is phosphex creep from level eighty through eighty-three.'

'*Understood. Has it reached the maintenance bays we moved through last night?*'

'I don't think so. Seems to be moving vertically more than

horizontally, burning down through the plasteel decking around here.'

'I'll lead the heavy infantry towards it then. Let's see Dorn's filth run away from the stuff for a change.'

Gharal chuckled and the link cut off.

Forrix reached the summit of the spiralling stair and slumped against the wall. Every muscle burned with fatigue, even with the assistance of his war-plate. He waited while scores of Iron Warriors hurried past, most of them sporting broken and patched armour, wearing elements of yellow stolen from their foes, burned and scarred and riddled with craters from bolter impacts. Others bore heavier injuries, missing hands and arms, their skulls exposed or cheeks pierced by shot.

Those without helms met his gaze, and all he saw in them was determination. This was the iron in their blood, the metal of the spirit. The retreat slowed to a steadier pace, becoming a march. A chant started, the words issuing to the beat of armoured footfalls.

'From iron cometh strength. From strength cometh will. From will cometh faith. From faith cometh honour. From honour cometh iron.'

Never had Forrix seen his warriors so undaunted and formidable. The longer they were hammered upon the anvil of battle, the harder they became.

But it would not be enough. Forrix had been keeping track of their losses and movements, and they were being hemmed in, corralled by the Imperial Fists. Contained. That was not the act of a foe worrying about assault from further afield. Something disastrous must have happened to the main assault, leaving Forrix's force the only functioning Iron Warriors formation. And he was running out of room to fight. Once they were cornered it was over.

It was a testament to their character that they had lasted this long, but they could not prevail indefinitely. Perhaps two more days at most. That's all they had left.

He needed a better plan.

Himalazia, thirty days before assault

They heard engines long before they saw the tanks. The rumble of scores of vehicles reverberated along the valley, following the course of the road as it wound towards the highest peaks.

'Off the road! Off the road!' The bellow echoed from officers and integrity officers, sergeants and troopers alike.

With the rest of the platoon, Zenobi broke left, up the slope of the mountain. There was little enough cover – boulders and outcrops. There were no trees, but thousands of knee-high stumps, every square centimetre of forest having been stripped for materials to bolster the Imperial Palace. They hunkered down as best they could, plumes of white following them as they waded through the snow.

The growling grew louder and louder, until it rivalled the dull, constant noise of the production line. Gears clanked, metal creaked, adding mechanical voices to the continual background wail of the Himalazian winds.

Lying down in the snow made little difference to Zenobi. She had long since lost any real feeling in her legs. Her feet were a constant aching throb inside her boots, and her hands, even inside three gloves, barely flexed. She stripped off the gloves to use her fingertips to clear ice from the trigger guard of her lasgun.

She pushed the arming stud but nothing happened – no vibration of the energy cell activating, no indicator lights turning from red to amber to green.

'Powercells are frozen,' she whispered, turning her head to Sergeant Attah on her left.

In reply, the sergeant pulled out her own lasgun and repeatedly breathed on the main body of it. After a minute or so of this, a flickering light lit the sergeant's face from below.

Zenobi nodded and copied Attah, holding the lasgun close to her mouth to maximise the body heat that reached it. She tested the activation stud each time, and after the fourth misty exhalation the lights glimmered into jade life. Whether it would be enough to hold a charge after a shot was another matter.

'Not that they'll be much good against tanks,' muttered Kettai. Squad structure had been abandoned on the march; everyone moved at their own pace as best they could. Several dozen more troopers had been lost in the time since they'd come across the frozen battle – six days? Seven days? More?

She shifted, a root digging at her thigh. The sound of engines changed, growing louder but also more diffused as the source came closer. Rather than reverberating down the valley as a single noise, she thought she could pick up individual vehicles and the rumble of tracks on the road.

It sounded familiar.

Bulky shapes loomed through the flurries of snow, and the wind brought the distinctive tang of fuel exhaust. The steady clank-clank-clank grew louder still as they approached. The snarl of gears and squeal of a turret rotating on its ring punctuated the noise. There were dozens, perhaps scores of tanks driving slowly up the road, the back of the column lost in the distance and snow.

Accounting for the fact that they were in the open air rather than a cavernous testing chamber, the sound took her back to the times she'd crept into the arming hangar at the end of the line, where the fully assembled tanks were driven from the production facility. She wasn't the only one that thought so. There were exclamations around her.

'These are our tanks!' said Menber.

Green pennants flew from whip aerials, bent forward by the prevailing wind. Every few tanks there was one that bore the flag of a squadron commander. These were large, square standards decorated with the laurels of the Imperial Army encircling two crossing curved blades.

'I know that flag,' said Kettai, rising to his knees. 'That's from Bakk-Makkah, one of the cities we sent our tanks.'

All along the line troopers and officers were breaking from the banks of snow, their shouts almost lost in the cacophony of engines. They waved their hands to attract the attention of the crews.

Someone in command must have seen them. One by one the tanks ground to a halt, turrets and sponson guns bearing on the approaching infantry.

Menber helped Zenobi up, as she cradled her lasgun under her arm and pulled the standard pole from a white drift. Flanked by her cousin and Kettai, she waded back towards the road, using the banner like a staff to negotiate the parts that came almost to her waist.

There was a tank almost directly opposite their position – a gap of ten metres between it and its neighbours. A heavy bolter in the closest sponson was trained on them, as was the massive battle cannon in the turret. Steam billowed from the engine vents and grey slicked the blizzard from the exhaust stacks at the rear. Melting ice left streaks on the dirty hull, revealing a grey camouflage scheme that made Zenobi laugh.

'I might have painted that,' she said, her main labour having been with the spray brush just before the end of the line. Her family were – had been, she reminded herself – fitters and finishers by trade.

The hatch atop the turret creaked open and a young man – no more than twenty or twenty-one, Zenobi thought – rose cautiously from within. He had a laspistol in hand, his face hidden behind broad goggles over a tanker's cap. His mouth and nose were swathed in a scarf woven of bright red, emerald green and dark blue. What she could see of his skin was lighter than her own, though it might have also been caked in grime.

He pulled up the goggles, squinting against the wind.

'Stay where you are, do not approach.' The voxmitter of the tank didn't mask his clipped accent. He raised the laspistol as if the threat of the battle cannon and heavy bolter were not enough.

'We're from Addaba,' Kettai called out. 'We made your tanks!'

'Keep back,' the commander warned. They did as he said, stopping about twenty metres from the low wall that ran along the roadside. 'We *will* open fire if you come closer.'

The message was the same all along the column, so that the Addaba Free Corps formed a near-continuous line three and four deep. Platoon commanders wearily told their subordinates to remain in place and assured them that General-Captain Egwu was communicating with the leader of the armoured regiment.

'You from Bakk-Makkah?' Menber called out. 'How long have you been driving?'

'Fourteen days, including resupply stops,' the commander called back over the voxmitter. 'Where did you say you come from?'

'Addaba,' Menber told him.

The commander stiffened with surprised.

'You've walked five thousand kilometres?'

There were laughs from the Free Corps troopers.

'Feels like it, but no,' Menber explained. 'We had a train but it was attacked. Been walking the last five hundred kilometres or so. Do you know how far we've got left?'

The tank commander leaned forward, resting his arm on the turret roof, holding the laspistol more casually now.

'About another three hundred kilometres until we reach the Katabatic Plains.' He pointed eastwards, towards the roiling aurora of the continuing attack. 'The road goes pretty much straight from here, but that's at least another fifteen days on foot in these conditions.'

'And more,' said Menber. 'Everyone's exhausted.'

'Any chance of a ride?' Kettai called out.

'That's what I'm waiting to hear from General Mushezibti. I'd say yes, but it's not up to me.'

They fell silent as they awaited the verdict of the consultation between their commanders. A figure approached along the line, one arm in a sling. It was Tesfaye, the integrity officer assigned to the platoon, the one that Zenobi had stopped Tewedros murdering. Okoye and a few of the sergeants gravitated towards him, seeking news.

The integrity officer continued along the line, looking at the troopers. He pitched his voice to be heard above the wind, but not so much that it would carry over the idling engines of the tanks. He repeated himself every dozen steps, speaking to the troopers in clusters.

'Remember to keep your tongues still,' said Tesfaye as he came upon Zenobi and the others nearby. 'Any one of these Bakk-Makkahi might relate anything we say to those that would see us thwarted. They are temporary allies at best, do not become overly familiar.'

Tesfaye carried on, his words lost in the snowstorm, and soon so was he.

'I guess that means we'll be getting a ride,' said Kettai.

His guess was proven correct a few minutes later. Shouts moved along the line from the front, but before they reached the survivors of Epsilon Platoon the tank commander was on the voxmitter.

'Good news, my new friends. Climb aboard!'

One of the gunner hatches opened and a crewman exited, guiding them to where they could safely sit on the track skirts, avoiding the hot engine grille and exhausts.

Most of them were used to scrambling over the giant beasts of metal, and probably knew their way around better than those within, finding handholds and spaces amongst the baggage and spare track links already strapped along the flanks.

'If we come under attack, you get off instantly,' the commander continued as they pulled themselves and their gear up the tank's sides. 'You don't want to be aboard when we get into battle.'

Zenobi found herself helped up to the turret itself. She saw the commander looking at her with dark brown eyes, and wondered what he made of the dishevelled, coat-swathed shape in front of him. His appraising gaze made her smile, appreciation in his eyes as they lingered on her rimed face.

'Why are you looking at me like that?' she asked.

He pulled down the scarf to reveal thin lips smiling, beneath a generous moustache. Zenobi found the shape of them appealing, as she did the broad cheek bones and the rest of his features. Very appealing.

'I like what I see,' said the commander. He held out a hand and she clumsily shook it. 'I am Nasha and this,' he thumped a hand on the armoured turret, 'is *Breath of Wrath*.'

'Nice,' said Zenobi, stroking a hand along the welded plate. 'I hope you're taking care of her.'

'Her?'

'Everything we make in Addaba is a girl,' said Zenobi. She grinned, having not really thought about it before. 'We find they have a better temperament that way.'

'And you are?'

'Zenobi. Zenobi Adedeji.'

Their eyes met and she felt the frisson of attraction again.

It seemed ridiculous, to be flirting with this man she had just met, in the middle of a blizzard, on the way to her first and last battle. She couldn't help it; the chemistry was immediate, the feeling mutual.

'You're a small one, Zenobi Adedeji.' He leaned back in the turret hatch. 'I reckon I might be able to squeeze you in here. If you're willing and allowed, of course.'

Zenobi moved closer and he pulled himself out fully, offering her his hands to help her, strong around her waist.

She half-heard Menber saying something behind her and Kettai laughing. It didn't matter. To get away from the snow and the cold and the wind for a few minutes, Zenobi would have accepted even had Nasha been a toothless, ugly brute of a man.

It was just a bonus that he wasn't.

TWENTY-FOUR

Call for a champion
Complications
Plague of belief

Exultant Wall zone, twelve days since assault

Keeler watched the Custodians and Regent move away before she turned back to Dorn and Sigismund. She could feel the antipathy of the primarch like a physical force, as though waves of heat emanated from the immense warrior. He turned a belligerent stare down to her, a lip curled.

'We have nothing further to discuss.'

Keeler struggled to find her voice in the face of the primarch's disdain. Swallowing hard she remembered she was doing the Emperor's work and forced herself to look up at the glowering demigod.

'I would like to speak with Captain Sigismund.'

Dorn stepped closer, just half a pace, but in that small movement he changed from bulky to menacingly oppressive. Like a moon being eclipsed by its planet, Keeler's world shrank to the couple of metres between them, as though nothing else existed. Her hand moved to the book concealed in her breast pocket.

'Your lies have done enough damage. There will be no more.'

She trembled as she met his iron gaze, knowing that those eyes had looked upon the deaths of thousands, millions even, and shown not the slightest compassion. It was as if Dorn were made of the same unfeeling stone as the fortifications he built.

'I have not lied. Is it not true that had he travelled to Phall, Sigismund would now be among the thousands of dead?'

'He is no better than those that gave their lives. Now he thinks himself special. Weakened by *your* delusion, he took the coward's choice.'

Keeler stepped back, giving herself space to breathe. She felt the reassuring presence of Sindermann at her shoulder, his hand lightly touching her arm. Past Dorn she saw the First Captain a few metres away, head turned towards them. She addressed her next words to him directly.

'The Emperor has need of you, Sigismund.'

'No more!' Dorn clenched his fists. Keeler drew back with a gasp, though she did not think he would swing them with lethal intent. His shoulders flexed within his bulky armour, servos whining as he sought to control his temper. 'Is it not enough that you robbed me of one of my finest sons? Do not turn him further from his duty!'

'He is not your son, he is the Emperor's!' snarled Keeler. She recoiled, shocked by her own vehemence; her voice lowered and she looked at the warrior in yellow and black. 'The great enemies we face choose their champions and pour all of their spite and power into them. Horus is at the pinnacle, a vessel for all the hurt and tragedy and wrath that the warp-twisted body can hold.'

Her eyes moved back to Dorn.

'Your brothers, I hear they have become something else, have they not? The perverted gifts of their gods give them abilities beyond even those that the Emperor bestowed upon you. You have not the strength to face them without accepting the power of the Emperor into your soul.'

'Soul? Keep your nonsense to yourself.'

'Then what is it that stays their advance? A psychic shield? Or the soul of the Emperor, bright and hot to them, as the Astronomican is to the Navigators.' She made one more entreaty to Sigismund. 'Who will face those champions of the Dark Powers? The Emperor needs His own, and through me He has guided your step from disaster to stand here upon these walls to face them.'

'No more.' Dorn's voice was a growl as he loomed over Keeler. He thrust a finger towards Sigismund without looking in his direction. 'Go to the gate keep now, captain.'

Sigismund remained a moment, silently watching Keeler, before he turned and continued down the corridor.

'It is only the mantle of Malcador that keeps you from your deserved cell, Keeler,' Dorn told her, bending low so that they were almost eye to eye. 'Report to him. Work with the Custodians. If I learn that you have spoken to any of my warriors again, Malcador's protection will not keep you safe, and it will not be imprisonment that silences you.'

He straightened and composed himself for several seconds, eyes closed. When he opened them, he looked at Sindermann, silently appraising the old man. The primarch said nothing of his conclusions but pivoted on his heel and marched after Sigismund.

Keeler stood shaking, Sindermann's hand on her arm. Taking a deep breath, she stood upright, drawing her hand away from the book within her dress. Sigismund's ascension to the truth was but one of the tasks she had been set by the Emperor. The matter with the Lightbearers required her full focus.

* * *

Lion's Gate space port, mesophex approach,
fourteen days since assault

How many times had Sigismund sat like this, in a drop pod or gunship or boarding torpedo, hurtling towards battle, sat in quiet repose? His Templars knew him well and did not interrupt his silence, save for the periodic countdown to their landing. Three minutes.

It was therefore strange for Sigismund when the pilot, Kassar, contacted him on the command vox-channel.

'First Captain, apologies for the interruption, but there has been a development.'

'What sort of development?'

'Augur scans show a notable hole in the Iron Warriors' deployment. A landing apron behind their advance appears unprotected.'

'A trap?'

'Unlikely, First Captain. Energy signature suggests that a force landed there in drop pods but rather than securing the site they have pressed onwards in totality, leaving no rearguard.'

'Where?'

'Fourth Eastward quay-spur, First Captain. Large enough for the whole force to land.'

'Agreed. Send word to the rest of the expedition. Redirect attack to the Fourth Eastward quay-spur.'

'Affirmative.'

Sigismund felt the craft bank as it adjusted course, so that it would come around the space port and approach from the opposite direction. The captain of the Templars tried to regain his focus, drawing into himself once more. He brought his hands together, remembering the conversation with Lord Dorn and Euphrati Keeler. He had not thought to see her again and her presence was a source of some turbulence in his mind.

He could not afford to be distracted. The Iron Warriors and

World Eaters would break through Rann's defensive line within hours. It vexed Sigismund that he did not know whether Dorn had despatched him because of the urgency of the situation or because he had finally wanted to be rid of the First Captain.

Had he been sent to Lion's Gate space port to die?

Ninety seconds.

The Stormbird slowed. Gunners opened fire as defensive batteries overrun by the traitors targeted the incoming assault force. Flak shells exploded around the descending gunships, shrapnel rattling against the armoured hull.

Sigismund drove the sound away. This was his chance to prove himself. If he delivered the space port from the enemy it was proof that he had been right to return to Terra rather than join the ill-fated expedition to Phall. This was the battle for which he had been directed.

Keeler herself had said as much. Had Lord Dorn been convinced by her words? He had departed in anger, but perhaps cooler, wiser counsel could yet prevail.

Ten seconds.

Sigismund stood up, checking the chains that kept his sword locked to his armour. Bound by metal, bound by oath, bound by fate to his blade.

The Stormbird dropped almost vertically, plasma jets roaring. Assault ramps slammed down and Sigismund was first to the ferrocrete, eyes scanning the abandoned landing quay.

Nothing but empty drop pods. Not a trap.

It did not matter. There would be plenty of enemies to face.

Himalazia, thirty days before assault

The warmth inside the bivouac was deceptive. Outside, a gale howled and snow piled up against the tank which formed one wall of the tent. Zenobi shifted, feeling the heat from Nasha, cocooned in their shared bedroll. The hab-unit she'd lived in with her family had been cramped; the bivouac had been intended for a crew of five and now housed an extra fifteen troopers. She and Nasha had found intimacy in the simple act of closeness, but space and an opportunity for anything more amorous had so far been denied them.

'Two days,' he said, stroking fingers across the curls of her hair. His breath on her neck sent shivers through Zenobi. 'Only two more days.'

'Until the battle?'

'Not yet. That's when we arrive at our muster point. It's still another hundred kilometres to the Katabatic Plains.'

She said nothing but listened instead. Their companions' heavy breaths and snores. The whine of the tank battery lighting the small lantern hung on the pole that held up the centre of the bivouac. And thunder that wasn't thunder but the detonations of gigatonnes of ordnance crashing against the shields of the Imperial Palace. Every few minutes there would come a crack of a different timbre as some new projectile hit home or a void shield temporarily failed.

'We might not ever…' she whispered, stroking the back of her hand along his thigh. 'You know, might not have time to…'

'Be united?' he said with a smirk. 'I know. It's not that important.'

'Maybe not for you,' she said sadly.

'Oh.' He pulled her closer. 'We might not be moving from the muster point for a while.'

'I think we'll be carrying straight on.'

'Really? What were your orders?'

Zenobi felt a sudden pang of awareness. She couldn't let down her guard, even for a moment of pillow talk.

'I don't know, but we were all expecting to get straight into the battle.' She listened for a few more seconds. 'The attack's well underway.'

'The battle for Terra!' he said, eyes comically wide. 'Never thought I would be part of it. Never considered that the war would come here.'

'It's been here a while,' said Zenobi. 'The touch of it, I mean. I don't know anything about Bakk-Makkah, but Addaba was first affected seven years ago.'

'Changed, yes,' said Nasha. 'They flattened the old precincts to make a testing and training range. Three hundred square kilometres of city from before the Old Night. Ancient, really ancient buildings.'

He sighed and she laid her head on his arm.

'Don't be so sure about what's going to happen,' he told her. 'It'll take a day or two for your formation to receive fresh orders from high command. You're not even supposed to be here.'

'Glad that we are,' she said. She kissed his neck and their conversation ended.

Basilica Ventura, thirteen days since assault

'An impressive gathering.'

Sindermann was right. Through a window in the upper reaches of the Basilica Ventura, mostly frame with only a few shards of glass remaining, Keeler could see some distance down the Via Oxidentus. There was light everywhere, not just clustered at the gateway below but stretched out along the approaches to the improvised fane. People brought their own lamps as well as those that were handed out at the doors, their bobbing progress easy to follow in the evening gloom.

'Here because of you, holy one,' said Olivier. 'Word spreads that the emissary of the Emperor graces the Lightbearers with divine blessing.'

'Blessing is not mine to deliver,' Keeler warned him. 'Only the word of the Emperor.'

'Of course, but He has sent you to us as a sign of His favour,' Olivier said quickly. He gestured and his two attendants, Maryse and Essinam, came across the small chamber, holding the massive bound copies of the *Book of Divinity*. Keeler had meant to ask where they had come from but had not yet had the opportunity. 'It would honour me if you would lay your hands upon our texts.'

Keeler did so, putting a palm to the cover of each, feeling the embossed lettering under her fingertips. It was as though she could feel the words inside stretching to be read, eager to leave the page and set themselves free in her thoughts.

She pulled her hand back, a tingle of sensation running up her arms.

'Would you address the congregation tonight?' Olivier asked.

Keeler considered it and shook her head.

'Not yet. These are your people, this is your creed. I am the follower here and would not take that from you.'

'I simply heard the message that you whispered in our ears, holy one,' Olivier said, clasping his hands together. He looked pointedly at the tomes carried by his companions. 'And the words of truth as laid down in this book, of course.'

'Do not undersell yourself,' said Sindermann, clasping a hand to Olivier's shoulder, gently guiding him towards the door. 'The lights hang because of you, and the whisper travels because your voice has been added to it.'

Before he realised what was happening, Olivier had been coaxed to the curtained doorway, Essinam and Maryse diligently flanking him.

'I will join you shortly,' Keeler assured him.

He accepted this with a smile and left. Sindermann took a deep breath and crossed back to her, gaze moving to the scene outside the window. It was not only the light of lamps that broke the twilight. It seemed as though a patch of sky at the horizon were ablaze, but in truth it was the Starspear of Lion's Gate space port, lit with the fires of battle.

'The traitors are pushing hard to take the space port,' said Sindermann. 'It may be only a matter of hours or days before they are at the Lion's Gate itself.'

'A victory that would have been far swifter if not for the protections against the Neverborn,' Keeler replied.

'There have been more apparitions, lady.' Sindermann rubbed his hands slowly, as though wiping away something in his palms. 'I have heard rumours of visitations and received word from Custodian Amon that he has uncovered two more sites of what he claims to be daemonic activity, though the gatherings that caused them had dispersed before his arrival.'

'The blind guess at what they see, but those that have seen know the truth,' Keeler told him. 'If one expects the infernal, one sees it.'

'Amon would argue that if one expects the divine, one would also see it.'

'He would be wrong. I have touched the light of the Emperor. It cannot be feigned.'

'There have been other stories, that tell of warming lights, and of soldiers on the walls seeing gold-clad ghosts sallying forth into the murk. A group of staff officers that meets by the Pradeshi Way says that they shared a group dream of the Emperor, in which He came to them and commanded they defend the wall at a certain place. The following day the traitors launched themselves at that section and were barely repelled. Had they followed Dorn's deployment orders there is a chance the enemy would have gained a foothold.'

'It is too much for a pragmatist like Rogal Dorn to place his faith in forces he cannot comprehend,' said Keeler. 'Though I feel he is starting to appreciate more their magnitude in opposition with each passing day.'

She fell silent, lost in her thoughts. Sindermann withdrew across the chamber, moving to another window. A rumble of jet engines shook the basilica as a flight of bombers flew low over the stretch of the Palace, heading towards the outer wall.

Keeler took out her *Lectitio Divinitatus* and opened it to the first page.

Rejoice, for I bring glorious news. God walks among us.

She lost herself in the words, as she had done the first time the scripture had been shown to her. It described with certainty the divinity of the Emperor, rightly placing Him among the celestial spheres as a being to be venerated. She knew the opening chapters by heart but took strength from her own simple handwriting forming the words, as though her voice were given permanent form.

It was with some effort that she roused herself on hearing Sindermann speak her name.

'The congregation is ready,' he told her. 'Olivier will be waiting.'

She reluctantly closed the book and headed down to the broken stairwell that took her to the platform of the chief Lightbearer. Without ceremony she passed through the archway and came up behind him, not willing to place herself before him.

He turned and acknowledged her with a simple nod, and then began his sermon.

She did not listen to his words so much as the cadence of his voice. As before, she let the flowing shadow-pictures take shape in her thoughts, growing branches and leaves from flickering light, while the voice of Olivier took on the role of the gusting breeze once more.

And even more simply than the first time, she slipped into the garden. She was more intent on her purpose than previously and she barely spared a thought for the glorious flora that surrounded her. Greater than ever were the blooms that clustered close, petals and stems turning towards her as though drawn by her life, seeking her energy rather than that of the sun.

Keeler stepped quickly through the waving grass, ignoring the tickles at her legs as seed-heavy heads brushed at knee and calf, caressing her as though trying to entice her to remain.

She was dimly aware of others now, her fellow worshippers each picking their own path through the cultured wilderness. Like the shadows of cloud wisps far above, they drifted past, almost unseen, heading to their own destinations. Keeler paused to reflect that they seemed to be going the opposite way to her.

She considered following them for a moment, but pushed on instead, eager to lay eyes on the majesty of the arboreal Emperor once again.

She found it in a deep valley this time. As before, the immense arch of the upper leaves were a roof to the sky. But where before the lower limbs had also reached up, now a few were bound by golden chains that stretched to the ground, taut and unmoving.

Keeler's heart skipped a beat at the vision, both awed and concerned. She broke into a run, but no matter how far or fast she tried to approach, the tree remained as distant as ever, out of her reach.

She stopped, knowing that she could not come closer by physical effort. This was a place of faith, and through faith would she one day climb amongst those boughs and know the embrace of the heavenly leaves.

TWENTY-FIVE

Lord of the Huscarls
Breakout
A waiting army

*Lion's Gate space port, mesophex skin zone,
fifteen days since assault*

The corridor rang with crashing boots, the whine of servos an undercurrent to the pounding charge of Rann and his Huscarls. Flecks of ceramite splintered from bolt impacts but they did not slow even as the intensity of the fire greeting them increased to a storm.

Only when they were thirty metres from the Iron Warriors did they lower shields, slowing their pace. Ortor was slightly ahead on Rann's right and checked his stride so that the others came alongside.

Ahead, the sons of Perturabo drew chainblades while combat attachments on their bolters whirred and gleamed in anticipation of the charge.

'Ram breach!' Rann called, just ten metres from the gateway held by the enemy.

Seamlessly the Huscarls manoeuvred on the charge. Ortor

and Rann came together, shields angled to form a point. Their companions fell in beside and behind them, shields braced against their backpacks.

As a single blade of powered ceramite, the tip of the Imperial Fists company hit the Iron Warriors' line. With full power to his legs, Rann drove forward. His axe was in his hand but he held it back, shield locked to the sergeant's, the triangle of their edges slamming into the breastplate of a IV Legion warrior, splitting armour like the prow of an ancient galley holing a foe.

The wounded Iron Warrior was spun away by the impact, going down to one knee. The Imperial Fist behind Rann, to his left, leapt over the tumbled legionary. The Space Marine behind drove his blade into the enemy's throat, ripping the sword free as the mass of ochre-and-black plunged onwards.

Cut down or hurled back, the Iron Warriors broke apart, allowing the flying wedge to burst through the gateway and onto the broad landing apron beyond. A battle raged across the kilometre-wide span of ferrocrete, a blur of yellow and black on one side set against iron and red on the other.

In the wake of the Huscarls' attack, seven hundred more Imperial Fists pounded out into the freezing air, the moisture carried with them crystallising on their armour as they advanced, their bolter reports sounding stifled in the thin atmosphere. The fire of missiles and laser beams criss-crossed the sky above, from circling gunships and companies ranged across the outskirts of the storeys above.

Rann urged his warriors onward with raised axe. There was no time to lose. The reinforcements led by Sigismund had drawn much of the ire from the Iron Warriors and their allies, but if Rann's force did not break through to them they would be driven back from the space port, their mission failed, their losses sustained in vain.

'Over there, that's the one!' Ortor pointed with his sword

to the right, into the shadow of a jutting boarding quay that ran over the landing pad.

A knot of fighters in Iron Warriors livery hewed their way through a line of yellow. The legionary at their head was a brute of a fighter clad in old Terminator armour, using his fist like a gleaming hammer. Rann saw an Imperial Fist go down under a series of vicious headbutts, his mask mashed into the flesh and bone of his face, blood splashed across the Iron Warrior's grille.

'Secure the left flank,' bellowed Rann even as he altered direction towards the Iron Warriors champion, breaking the formation.

A dozen warriors came with him, Ortor included. The others peeled left, bolters and blades directed against a wave of blood-stained World Eaters pouring along the edge of the landing apron.

The Iron Warrior recognised the challenge inherent in Rann's charge and lifted a gore-spattered fist in reply, taunting the lord seneschal. The Imperial Fist could see the rank markings of a warsmith among the blood spatter and daubed graffiti of defiance.

'Stay close,' Rann warned his companions, remembering this was a battle, not a duelling cage. He had no desire to face the Cataphractii alone. 'Take down their leader.'

Far from waiting to receive the attack, the warsmith leapt forward to meet Rann's charge. Shoulder lowered, arm braced, the Iron Warrior met the boarding shield at speed. The impact lifted Rann off his feet and sent the warsmith spinning away.

Rann crashed to the floor a few metres away, watching his Huscarls slamming into the warsmith's guard. The warsmith advanced, fingers of his power fist flexing in anticipation.

So much for not being drawn into a duel.

His shield bent at almost a right angle, Rann tossed it away and drew his second axe, the heads of both weapons crackling with licks of power. Crouched, legs braced, the lord seneschal waited for his opponent to come to him.

The Iron Warrior obliged, rushing forward without any attempt to mask his attack nor to use his combi-bolter, fist swinging with sudden speed towards the seneschal's head. Rann brought up an axe, deflecting the blow to the left, and swung the other upwards, looking for the exposed armpit.

The blade caught on chestplate instead, a split second before the warsmith crashed into him, taking them both down with a thunder of breaking armour.

Rann rolled, using the last of the Iron Warrior's momentum to push the warsmith away before regaining his feet. The Iron Warrior was slower, but still raised his massively armoured gauntlet in time to meet Rann's next attack. Lightning flared and the glove burned red in contact, dimming the seneschal's auto-senses. Quicker than his bulk and armour should have allowed, the warsmith's fist thudded into Rann's gut.

It was an odd blow, a brawler's punch rather than a trained Space Marine's attack, but its power cracked abdominal armour and sent system warnings flaring across Rann's display. He was forced back a step and in the moment of regaining his balance realised that momentum had turned against him. The power fist swung for Rann's chest but caught him on the arm instead, the flare of energy sending splinters of ceramite slashing through the air.

There was not a hearts' beat of hesitation in the warsmith: he came on without pause, almost crushing Rann's head, clenched fist missing by millimetres to split his pauldron with an impossibly powerful blow. It was more than his Terminator plate that powered such blows, his strength unnaturally boosted.

Rann went down on one knee, vision swaying. On instinct he raised his axes, warding off two more blows to regain his feet.

Pride told him he could swing the fight back in his favour. Experience called pride a liar.

'To me!' Rann called. 'Huscarls, to me!'

His guards were too embroiled to come to his aid. Rann tried one last time to take the initiative, ducking beneath the blur of the fist, axe angled towards his opponent's thigh. Blade bit into riveted armour, slashed through into flesh.

Rann gave a triumphant shout as he dragged the weapon clear, expecting to see a fountain of arterial spurt. Instead the warsmith backhanded him across the face with his combi-bolter, a trickle of thick, black fluid leaking from the wound.

The power fist caught Rann square in the chest, shattering his plastron, pulverising the bones within. A sudden loss of breath told him he'd lost at least one lung. Armour warning sigils filled his vision with flashes of red.

The warsmith loomed over the seneschal, lightning-wreathed fist raised for the killing blow. It was impossible to see the warrior's face but Rann could imagine the gloating eyes, the homicidal grin of a foe that seemed more beast than man.

Something black arrived at speed, a gleaming blade flashing out to meet the descending strike. The sword deflected the fist to send it crashing into the ferrocrete just beside Rann's head. Then it spun, catching the side of the Iron Warrior's helm, though it glanced off the angled plate.

Blood flowed from a shattered eye-lens, bright against the tarnished silver armour.

Squinting through swirling pain, Rann saw the knightly helm of his saviour – a second before a wall of yellow crashed around him, the Huscarls responding to his call even as the Iron Warriors closed about their own leader. The black-armoured legionary took a step as though to continue the attack but a blaze of bolter fire from the Iron Warriors dissuaded pursuit.

Ortor appeared in front of Rann, asking if he was all right. Rann tried to answer but tasted blood bubbling in his mouth. Pain punched up through his ribcage as he tried to stand and he fell back, desperately trying to suck air into damaged lungs.

'Sergeant, get him to safety,' snarled Sigismund. 'The rest of you, hold ground here.'

Lion's Gate space port, tropophex core, fifteen days since assault

There had been three Apothecaries in Forrix's original force, of which only one had made it to the rendezvous – Oumar. Forrix had fought alongside him since the Unification Wars, both veterans of the Terran Legion. Battle cared little for history, but had perhaps a penchant for irony, and so Oumar had been one of the first casualties following the muster. A krak missile had opened up his skull as he had tended to one of his fellow legionaries.

So it was that Forrix patrolled the corridors that had become their home, Gharal at his side, looking at the wounded but with no specialist to treat them. Some were so still that it was only the beat of their armour's transponders that betrayed any sign of life. Others moaned and writhed without sedation. Pieces of broken battleplate were piled out of the way, removed to get access to las weals, plasma burns and bolter wounds.

Turning down a side passage Forrix came upon a bloody scene, arterial scrawl drying on the wall and ceiling. Two of his warriors were knelt next to a third, holding his plastron onto his chest. Blood foamed around its edges and dribbled from the legionary's mouth. His eyes roamed sightlessly, fixing on the faint lumen hanging from the ceiling. The two Iron Warriors turned to their superior, one of them delivering a simple prognosis with a shake of the head.

Forrix stepped over the blood spray, fingers flexing in agitation.

'How many?' he asked the captain.

'Left?' replied Gharal.

'Yes, left,' he snapped.

'Two hundred and four, including walking wounded.'

'Nearly eighty per cent casualty rate...' Forrix whispered. Judged against some of the Iron Warriors' past victories, that would count as acceptable. Had Perturabo tasked him with surviving in the midst of enemy territory for so many days with only a thousand legionaries and no armoured support he would have thought it impossible.

'Triarch!' one of the wounded legionaries called out, wheezing breaths breaking the flow every couple of seconds. 'Help me... up. I can still... fight.'

Forrix looked at the warrior, saw the plasma scarring on his left side.

'You've lost a lung, legionary.'

'That's why they... gave us... a third.' His bloody grin showed broken remnants of teeth.

Forrix offered a wrist and the legionary grabbed it, pulling himself up with a moan. Forrix heard air whistling out of the wound in the Space Marine's side. The warsmith stooped and picked up the warrior's bolter, pressing it into his grasp.

'It's Zorovar, isn't it?'

'Yes, triarch. Sergeant.'

'It will be lieutenant when we're reunited with the Legion.'

Zorovar nodded his thanks, a trembling fist raised to his chestplate in salute.

'See you... on... the assault line.' He winced with the effort, pain etched into every feature. 'Triarch.'

Forrix returned the salute and turned away. His pace quickened as resolve hardened in his gut.

'He'll not live out the day,' Gharal said, glancing back at the wounded sergeant.

'Of course not. If we stay here, none of us will.'

'I need you to be very clear, triarch. You want us to move from this position?'

'Only those that can fight,' Forrix said slowly, fists clenched. 'We're leaving–'

'Keep your voice down.'

'We're leaving the wounded, triarch?'

'Yes. We need to jettison the burden.' Forrix stopped and rounded on the captain, struggling to keep his voice low. 'We cannot save them, Gharal. Either we die with them or we give ourselves a chance to live.'

'And if the enemy take them alive?'

'Let them. What are they going to reveal? That we came in here without a specific objective? That we only have two hundred fighters left? None of this will be news to our enemies.' Forrix rubbed a knuckle across an itch on his forehead, smearing soot and blood over skin cracking from dehydration. 'There is a tiny chance that our foes might even treat them. There's not much honour left in this war, and I know the Fourth had little enough to begin with.'

'We could finish them ourselves,' Gharal suggested quietly, hand tapping the side of his bolter.

'We haven't got the ammunition,' Forrix told him with a frown. The warsmith stepped back and waved towards a pair of legionaries slumped against the wall nearby. 'And do you really want to take your blade to their throats?'

Gharal's helm turned as his gaze moved between the triarch and the injured. Back and forth, deliberating. Forrix would have told Gharal it was a command, that his opinion mattered nothing, but the warsmith was living off borrowed authority. If Gharal, or one of the two surviving lieutenants, decided to lead a mutiny, there was a good chance Forrix would get a bolt in the back of the head.

'I am thinking about those of us that have a chance,' said Forrix, grabbing the captain's arm. 'We need to break through to the outer levels. There's a monorail terminal one kilometre north of here. We'll move fast, head down the track to a skybridge.'

'*Towards* the Imperial Palace, triarch?'

'Better than deeper into the space port.' Forrix cocked his head and raised a finger, indicating for Gharal to listen. The distant pound of explosions had become nothing but background noise. 'The barrage continues. Lion's Gate space port is still contested. If we can get to the outer levels, we might be able to contact Legion command.'

'Fast. Precise. We can do this.' Gharal pulled free his arm and offered his hand for Forrix to grip. The warsmith did so, wrist to wrist in Olympian custom. 'We will live so that we can remember the fallen.'

Himalazia, undisclosed location, twenty-eight days before assault

The valley opened out, stretching a dozen kilometres from side to side. The mountainsides around it were artificially hewn, a semicircle of laser-cut cliffs that soared hundreds of metres above the mustering site.

Zenobi had a perfect view perched alongside the battle cannon of *Breath of Wrath*, able to see down the road as it dipped below two bastions built out from the slopes themselves. Gun turrets as big as the tank festooned each pillar tower, tracking the incoming column with macro cannons and immense laser batteries.

Overhead the sky was black and grey, swathed with smog

from the bombardment. Nothing could be seen of the fluctuating aegis of the Palace itself, a hundred kilometres beyond the far wall.

Even more incredible was the sea of machines and people that thronged the artificial caldera. Squadrons of walkers, batteries of self-propelled guns and artillery were spread out along a grid of roads stretching from the main highway, as well as companies of mechanised infantry with troop carriers.

'How…?' Zenobi looked up again, seeing just the faintest shimmer of an energy field distorting the dark clouds and streaming embers. A faint drizzle of rain misted the air. Debris was still falling from orbit weeks after the void battle had ended, streaking the fumes with false meteors.

'It's a special type of void shield, called a reflex shield,' said Nasha. He shrugged. 'They briefed us before we left, but I'm not sure how it works. All I remember is that it's keeping the muster base hidden from scans. Even light doesn't escape. One of the traitors' aircraft could be right overhead and they'd just see a haze of rock.'

'But there's so many troops here,' said Zenobi. 'Why aren't they fighting?'

'Some plan of Dorn's, I'd say. A reserve force.'

The column continued on. It was joined a few minutes later by a score of provosts on motorcycles, the flashing beacon lights of their steeds guiding the tanks to their allotted encampment. The roadway was raised here, giving them a view across the crater. Nasha pointed out various companies and regiments as they passed.

'Over there,' he said excitedly, pointing to a company of building-sized tanks in black-and-red livery, stark among the camouflage of the surrounding regiments. 'Anzakk Heavy Brigade. Those are the very same Baneblades that broke the Noose of Kabbala!'

'How do you know this?' Zenobi laughed to see him so en-thused, like a child allowed free rein with another's toys.

'We have our own claim to the Old Hundred. The Golden Hegera came from Bakk-Makkah. Well, the Old Precincts that were there before it. My ancestors have been fighting for the Emperor since the earliest days of the Unification Wars.'

'And now you're following that proud tradition,' she said.

'Maybe not *my* ancestors... I'm not from any of the heralded bloodlines. My family are algae farmers mostly. A few made it onto the local council, but that's it. If not for the Warmaster, I'd be slopping wet mush from vaporators instead of com-manding this magnificent metal creature.'

They came to a halt about two kilometres from the entrance, squadrons of tanks peeling to left and right. At shouts from their officers the Addaba Free Corps spilled from the backs of the parking vehicles, like a metal snake shedding its skin from nose to tail.

'I need to be g–'

Nasha grabbed her arm and pulled her close, his lips finding hers a heartbeat later. Tears welled up as she tasted him, won-dering if it would be the last time. Eventually they parted.

'Red border, gold braiding, green pennant,' he told her, nod-ding to the banner flying from a pole at the back of the turret. She gave him a quizzical look. 'There's a lot of tanks here, but only my one has that flag.'

'Red border, gold braiding, green pennant,' she repeated, fixing the sight of it in her memory. 'I don't know where we'll be...'

'If you don't find me, I'll find–'

'No, don't do that,' Zenobi said sharply, causing him to flinch. She softened, stroking fingers down the lapel of his tanker's jacket. 'We have... security officers that would punish us both if you were found.'

'So, this is it?'

'Maybe not. I'll find you if I can.'

She kissed him again, gently, lingering in the moment of connection.

It took more effort to drag herself away from his embrace than it had to forge through the blizzards. Zenobi mustered the strength to do so, turning away. She picked up her kitbag and tossed it down to where Menber was waiting beside the tank. She handed him the standard pole next and then followed, her lasgun slung over her back by its strap.

'Saying farewell, cousin?' he said, expression stern. Everybody else had moved away, leaving just the two of them. 'You know nothing can come of it.'

'Something already has,' she said with a smile.

'Say nothing to the integrity officers. If they think… If they question your loyalty for an instant…'

'I'll be careful, cousin. I promise.'

Lion's Gate space port, tropophex mantlezone,
sixteen days since assault

There were breakthroughs all across the boundary levels between the Starspear and Sky City. Sigismund did the best he could to shore up the weakening defence, but he leaned heavily on Lieutenant-Commander Haeger to see through the implementation. Remembering the words of Keeler, the Templar put himself in the forefront of every counter-attack, and for two solid days had fought as though he could single-handedly drive back the Iron Warriors and their twisted allies.

'First Captain, *new report from the core patrols.*' Haeger had timed his vox call to coincide with Sigismund's transit from one embattled area to the next, a window of a few minutes' relative peace. *'Captain Thudermann requests reinforcement or withdrawal orders. We are experiencing augury blackout on the orbital scans. Lord Dorn has sent instruction that we hold for another eighteen hours.'*

Boarding the Rhino that would take him across the level to the conveyor station around the besieged skybridges, Sigismund considered each of these in turn.

'Tell Thudermann to pull back to the second cordon. There is no gain in getting trapped between the two advancing forces. The augurs are in the purview of the tech-priests, we can do nothing except stand ready for the enemy to receive more troops from orbit. As for the third… I plan to hold as long as possible. Did Lord Dorn indicate what would happen after eighteen hours?'

'He said there would be further assistance but did not care to share the details.'

'Transmit to Legion command that we will hold the Lion's Gate space port for as long as the Lord Praetorian wills it so.' Sigismund spared a moment to check the Rhino's progress on the telemetric display. 'We shall be at Gate Stratos-Fourteen-Delta in two minutes. Have the companies on levels seven hundred and eight through seven hundred and thirteen push to my position for counter-attack.'

'Affirmative, First Captain.' There was a pause of several seconds but the link did not cut. *'I have heard that a new enemy strike force has been assembled and is cutting through our defences more swiftly than we can recover.'*

'Is that a report, Haeger?'

'More of a rumour, but there is scattered vox-traffic that claim sightings of Sons of Horus led by Ezekyle Abaddon himself. We are losing contact with anyone that they come upon.'

A shudder of apprehension and excitement coursed through Sigismund. This was the words of Keeler made clear, his purpose suddenly revealed.

'Where was this last rumour, Haeger?'

'If I extrapolate, I would say that the enemy strike force is heading for level nine oh two, somewhere near beta quadrant.'

'Redirect all commands in the bridge sector to my direct authority. Full assault preparation.'

'What of Lord Dorn's command to hold?'

'If we do not parry this strike before it lands, there will be no point holding.'

His fingers moved to the runes of the terminal, keying in commands to locate the shortest route to beta quadrant of Sky City. Visions flashed through Sigismund's thoughts, of himself with blade in hand standing against the lord of the Mournival. Surely if Abaddon fell beneath the blade of the Templar it would be a great victory for the servants of the Emperor.

TWENTY-SIX

Intrusions
The half-born
Dangerous relations

Europa Wall zone, sixteen days since assault

Some would have called it luck, others destiny. Amon suspected Keeler would attribute his timely arrival to the will of the Emperor. As far as he was concerned it was nothing of these, simply the inevitable result of diligence and logic coupled with a pre-emptive attitude.

He was swiftly becoming more absorbed in the nature of the Lectitio Divinitatus, day by day getting more acquainted with their customs, personnel and movements. What had seemed a disorganised clutter on the surface belied a sophisticated, organic communications network on par with the most complex espionage cell-systems he had encountered. But it was all the more remarkable because there was no nefarious puppet master at the centre, nor were the vast majority of those participating in the movement even aware of the greater part of the whole.

By ways and means originating in necessity, the faithful had discovered how to identify each other without direct contact, centring themselves around commonly regarded symbols, phrases and mannerisms without ever directly communicating them. It was like a virus, passed on by contact, embodied in the sermons that were delivered, the pamphlets handed out, the pages of the *Lectitio Divinitatus* itself.

The similarity to the spread of a disease was not lost on Amon, and he had coined a term for it: the plague of belief. It was, he was sure, as potentially threatening as any physical malaise, being a corruption of culture that undermined the tenets of the Emperor's vision for humanity.

As soon as he had considered the spread of faith as an epidemiological issue he had found tracing it from one place to another far more straightforward. Though he had begun with plague victims and medicae facilities, the premise had led him farther afield, beyond the Sanctum Imperialis to the Ultimate Wall itself.

And in doing so he had noticed a pattern, or rather a void in a pattern. Despite the clandestine support of a handful of higher-ranking Imperial Army officers, the worship of the Emperor was still forbidden among the ranks of the troopers. As such, soldiers were forced to gather off-duty or to make time and space within their duties when not directly engaged – opportunities for either were exceedingly rare with the enemy at the walls themselves.

A break in vox-chatter, uncovered by Amon, had piqued his interest. A patrol that had made excuses for a late return, whose sergeant had been absent or delayed on other occasions. He might have ignored it, but their proximity to the garrisoned quarantine zone where the matter had been brought to light demanded further investigation.

He came upon the bodies in a disused way station about a kilometre and a half inside the curtain wall, just within the perimeter of the Palatine Arc quarantine zone. The detritus scattered about the bare chamber had all the markings of an impromptu fane, including a bloodied copy of the *Lectitio Divinitatus*. It seemed likely that others from the garrison had performed a rite in this place.

The corpses had been torn open, ribcages splayed from the inside, skin and flesh hanging in tatters from broken bones. Amon had not seen the like; it was as though the killer had emptied the victims of their insides. Each had been hollowed out, the tattered edges of ribs and breastbones showing striations like gnaw marks.

How all ten of them had succumbed was another mystery, for each lay in close proximity and though their weapons were close at hand, not one of them had fingers on a gun or pistol grip.

Whatever had overcome them had done so with instant and brutal swiftness.

The floor was muddy, tracked by boot marks in and out, but among the blood spatter were other footprints. They appeared barefoot with long nails, some with three toes, others four or five. It was impossible to tell how many assailants, but at least four and quite likely more.

The stench was far worse than simple dead flesh and evacuated bowels. Amon knew the smell of death and this was edged with an acidic tang. In total contradiction he thought he also detected a floral scent, and on closer inspection of the corpses could not find any soap or other perfume that would explain its lingering presence.

He voxed the closest Legio Custodes outpost, on the outer barbican of the main Sanctum Imperialis almost ninety kilometres away.

'Argent Tower, this is Custodian Amon. I am pursuing a possible incursion force into the Palatine Arc, heading north-east through the quarantine zone. Urgent despatch of support required.'

His vox buzzed for several seconds. Before a reply was forthcoming a shadow on the wall warned him of movement behind. He was fully armoured, his guardian spear in hand – a lesson he had learned at the hospital. Amon was turning, the blade blurring with its energy field, even before he registered the nature of his attackers.

The tip scored a line across the chest of the first, bubbling ichor spilling forth in its wake. The creature that flopped back reminded him of the Neverborn he had seen in the webway, supposedly incarnations of the Plague power. The others, nine more, closed fast with clawed hands, their limbs famine-thin, bellies swollen like old corpses.

But there the similarity ended. These fiends looked more human in feature, with a pair of eyes rather than one, lank hair hanging from scalps and, on three of them, cheeks and chin. Their flesh was a mottle of pinkish-white and dark brown, and their eyes were startlingly human.

As he slashed his spear tip through the throat of another, his thoughts sprang back to the mutilated bodies of the patrol and the origins of these half-daemon hybrids became obvious. The thought sickened him, even though he had seen sights that would have driven lesser warriors to madness – that somehow these creatures had emerged or incubated themselves within the bodies of the troopers.

He did not pause in his assault, not allowing his enemies any advantage from their ambush. His spear's bolter roared, hard and bright in the confines of the chamber, the salvo cutting down two more of the daemonkin.

One thing was for certain, these were no ghostly manifestations, drawn of warp power and nothing more. They died as easily as mortals, perhaps shorn of true daemonic resilience by their hybrid birth and the shield of the Emperor.

Some tried to flee, which was also a first for Amon. In his

experience the Neverborn were near mindless in their assaults, uncaring of personal danger or tactical disadvantage. They survived only by the whim of the power that created them. But these half-born knew fear. He saw dread in their eyes as he cut them down, his armour bathed in sickly gore.

Four eluded his immediate ire, disappearing into the adjoining hallway. He gave chase, guardian spear roaring more bolts after them. Another fell, legs blown away by the detonations.

'This is Argent Tower control, we have received your message,' the vox buzzed. Amon realised it had been only a few seconds since he had made his transmission. His altered physiology had made it seem far longer.

'Standby for update, copy broadcast to personal channel of the captain-general,' he told the operative on the other end of the vox-link.

Three swift strides took him to the junction at the end of the corridor. Blood and mud trailed left and right, two tracks leading in the first direction, one in the other. The half-born were faster than humans, already out of sight as he turned the corner. They were heading into the quarantine zone, which had become a shifting maze of shanty and open plague pit.

He pursued as fast as he could, coming upon the two abominations about a hundred metres further along the domestic palace. The third survivor would be half a kilometre away by now.

'Rapid pursuit teams required at my position,' he voxed. 'I need airborne support and search inbound immediately.'

Hissing, hearing the thud of the Custodian's boots coming upon them, the creatures turned on him. One held up its hands as though to plead for its life; the other had ripped a support bar from the rubble and swung it like a ferrocrete-headed club. The blow bounced from Amon's auramite war-plate without leaving a scratch, the creature that wielded it almost spinning from its feet as it was unbalanced by its own blow.

Amon's weapon punched forward, slicing off a warding hand before entering the chest directly through the heart. The half-born gave a screech of pain – a chillingly human sound from such an otherworldly apparition – and slipped backwards from the vapour-wreathed blade.

The second tried again to strike the Custodian, heaving up its improvised club. He smashed the butt of the guardian spear into its forehead, crushing the skull and snapping its neck with one blow. Grey fluid splashed from the wound as it fell.

Sparing a second to ensure both were truly dead, Amon turned on his heel and set off after the other, though he knew it was likely too late to find it by himself. Lost among the walking dead of Poxville, there was no knowing what further damage it might do, nor what others of its kind might yet appear.

Himalazia, undisclosed location, day of the assault

It should have been a month of tedium and misery, but for Zenobi the time spent at the mustering was one of the best experiences of her life. Compared to the harrowing train journey and nightmarish march that followed, spending four weeks cooped up with rations, shelter and the company of her fellow troopers was almost bliss. It was better than life in Addaba.

And then there was Nasha.

The illicit nature of their relationship only heightened the excitement. Illicit insofar as the integrity officers warned against spending excessive time with the other regiments being held at the hidden base. A month was a long time to avoid any contact whatsoever, though, and the needs of simple decorum and logistics had required that the Addaba Free Corps acquaint themselves with their new neighbours. The local commanders had agreed to attach the Free Corps as infantry support to the reserve force, pending confirmation from high command that seemed to have been lost somewhere in the reports.

Zenobi almost stopped thinking about the battle that was being waged just a hundred kilometres away. The noise of bombardment, the flights of aircraft overhead were constant reminders, but just as the reflex shields kept the reserve base undetected, so its inhabitants were isolated from the ongoing bloodshed.

'What if we never get called up to the fight?' she asked Nasha after one of their midnight couplings. It was still cold, their hot breath fogging the air, sweaty bodies layered in coveralls and coats that had doubled as bedding a few minutes earlier.

They lay in the dark underneath an empty supply transport, not far from the lot of *Breath of Wrath*. Everything was in blackout to help maintain the cover of the reflex shield – the less energy it had to absorb the greater its effectiveness, she had learned. What was good for remaining undiscovered on the larger scale applied equally well to the small scale, affording her ample cover to make her clandestine rendezvous.

'Would that be so bad?' he replied, lying with his hand behind his head, his chest making a pillow for her.

'You don't want to be part of the fighting?'

'I don't want to die, if that's what you mean.'

'No, I mean do you want to fight for what you believe in, or let others do it for you?'

'That sounds like an accusation.'

'It's not.' She stroked his face. 'I just… Our futures are being decided and we're just sitting here, not involved at all. I joined… I don't want to be on the losing side just because someone forgot we were here.'

'There's a plan. Dorn commissioned this secret muster personally. He'll deploy us when we're needed. If we're needed.'

'When will that be though?' It wasn't the first time she had asked the question and she knew she was sounding increasingly petulant each time. 'I'm not in a hurry to leave. Not leave you. But I want to do my part.'

'Do you think you can make a difference?'

'Why do people keep asking that?'

'There's less than six thousand of you left in the Free Corps. There must be as many tanks, transports and armoured walkers in here as you have people. And we're the tiniest fraction of the Imperial Army's might in the Himalazia.'

'I work on the line. Everything has a place. Everything is balanced and timed and has a rhythm. A small disruption, the least amount of change can cause catastrophe. It's not just about how many of us are still alive, it's about where we are, when we fight. We'll die trying, anyway. Better that, if you ask me.'

'You think you'll die?'

She shifted as he sat up.

'It's a certainty. Like you said, there's not many of us. Enough to swing a battle, but only if every last one of us is ready to lay down our life.' She sighed and swivelled to sit next to him, her hand on his thigh. 'I never expected to have this long.'

'Don't you... Don't you have something you'd like to live for? Maybe someone?'

She grinned and punched him lightly on the arm.

'If it was different, then of course I'd want to live. But I wouldn't trade the future of Addaba for this happiness. Not even for you, my beautiful man.'

He looked at her for some time, perhaps memorising her features, perhaps just trying to think of something to say. She let the silence stay, relishing the quiet she knew could not last much longer.

A couple of hours later she parted from Nasha with a last kiss and made her way back towards the camp of the Free Corps. Though it was almost as dark as an underspur sewer she made her way unerringly through the maze of tanks, tents and roads. She crossed a berm separating the Addaba companies from several platoons of the Nor Alba Steelwatch and turned left to avoid the checkpoint at the junction a hundred metres ahead.

She froze as a voice issued from the darkness.

'Nice stroll?'

Zenobi said nothing, weighing up her options. She could bolt and hope that she hadn't been recognised. She could see nothing of the other person and it was likely only her foot-steps had betrayed her presence.

'Have you been to see Nasha, Zenobi?'

She swore as she recognised the voice of Kettai. Zenobi swung towards the sound, a snarl building in her throat.

'Breaking curfew is serious. Socialising with outsiders, even more serious.'

'What do you care? It's not like you haven't broken a few rules in your time. Turn me in to the integrity officers and maybe I'll let them in on a few of your secrets.'

His laugh was low, almost a hint of menace in his humour.

'What's so funny, Kettai?'

'You really don't know?' His next laugh was more fulsome. She heard footsteps. A shuttered lantern flickered into life to her right, revealing his flat face but little else. Flecks of snow and ash fell through the yellow glow. 'You must be the only one left in the platoon that hasn't figured it out.'

'Figured out what?'

'I'm with the integrity officers!' He grinned. 'Hidden in plain sight, I hear is the expression. A spy. There's an old phrase for it, an agent provocateur. Testing from within, offering the temp-tation before it becomes vital.'

'So, everything you've been saying was a trick? Trying to lure me into giving myself away?'

'Not you particularly, yeye. Everyone. You're a remarkable soldier, nothing swerved you from the cause.'

'Nothing until now, you mean?'

He stepped closer, just a few paces away.

'Nasha is rather handsome. Obviously, he's not inclined in my direction, so I'll never know anything more than that, but I can see why you would want to have a little fun before the killing and dying starts.'

'Are you going to report me? For… socialising. I've told him nothing.'

'You don't know anything to tell him.'

'That's a good point. But, please, it's not done any harm, has it?'

'Some might say the disobedience itself was the harm.'

Zenobi didn't say anything. As when she'd seen Jawaahir the first time, she knew that any further conversation just opened the way for more possible recriminations. He had already decided; any resistance would just make matters worse.

'You seem calm,' he said.

'What else should I be? It's up to you what happens next. What am I going to do? Kill you, like Tewedros tried? Run away to…?' She waved a hand vaguely behind her. 'To where? To do what?'

Kettai smiled and shook his head, a sort of impressed disbelief.

'Egwu chose you well. You've got a spine of titanium in that little body of yours, and a heart that burns like forgefire. You know that you could have your throat slit for this, and you just face up to it, no worries at all?'

'I'm worried,' she admitted. 'I'm worried I'll die before I get a chance to make a difference for Addaba. But the death itself, that's not anything to be scared of.'

'Well, you'll not have to worry any longer.' He took a step back and half turned, raising the lantern to light her way between two privy blocks. She hesitated. 'On your way, yeye. I trust you to fight for the cause more than I trust myself.'

'But I'll have to stop seeing Nasha?'

He shrugged.

'Why? You've got a good thing, why spoil it? Just remember that in an hour, a day or a week we could get the command, and from that moment on, it's Addaba first and nothing else. *Nothing*.'

'I know that.'

'Of course you do. Get going.'

She gave him a long look as she walked past, searching for deceit in his face, but saw none. When she was concealed by darkness again, relief crested through her feelings and erupted as a broad grin.

TWENTY-SEVEN

Desperate times
The power of faith
No stragglers

Palatine Arc quarantine zone, eighteen days since assault

Katsuhiro wept as he fired. He had thought himself sapped of all emotion by his experiences but the sight before him plumbed a depth of self-loathing he had not known before. The orders given to him and the hundreds of other troopers that lined the quarantine walls were brutally simple: destroy all targets.

That had been his life for the past two and a half days. Sixty hours of near-continuous duty as the living and the dead tried to break out of Poxville, time spared only to catch naps and meal breaks on the wall. It wasn't as though everything had happened all at once. The malaise had spread slowly: first they had come in ones and twos, then larger groups. Two hours ago there had been a surge, hundreds of vacant-eyed corpses juddering towards the walls, a few living amongst them, screaming for help, trying to dash free of the nightmare gripping the quarantine ghetto.

Nothing was to reach the wall, whether warp-tainted or

human. It was impossible to tell, the officers had said, who was carrying the seed of corruption within them. So they came on in their hundreds, the plague victims and the refugees, the medicae that had volunteered to help them and the self-appointed carers and families who had chosen isolation with their loved ones, fleeing the abominations in their midst.

He pulled the trigger and the las-blast hit a young woman in the chest, knocking her back into a pile of corpses. Katsuhiro fancied there might be a smudge of a rash on her face, seeking the smallest justification not to hate himself every time his finger twitched.

He had become quite a marksman, he realised, almost throwing up at the thought.

His next target was definitely warp-infected. A limping gait and the spattering of mucus from the lolling mouth had to be evidence of taint. He swallowed hard and fired again, shooting the old man in the forehead.

The fusillade had ebbed and flowed, sometimes near constant for half a minute at a time then dying down to sporadic shots for an hour. Now there was just a steady rhythm to it, flashes of red and blue a few times every minute.

His lasgun whined mechanically about its empty powercell and he pulled the pack free, discarding it with the other three at his feet. Each was good for a hundred shots... He slapped one of his two remaining packs into the weapon, charged it and lifted the stock to his shoulder again.

His aim trembled and he took a deep breath, steadying his hands.

'Just stop,' he whispered, choking on the words. 'Please stop.'

A commotion behind him caused him to turn, others of the squad doing the same. A striking woman in a flowing blue dress had mounted the rampart, a man in light-coloured robes behind her, followed by two women bearing large books. With them came a host of people in civilian clothing, and among them a few in uniforms from different defence regiments. They each carried a lamp, even though it was midday – as far as such a time existed in the siege-gloom.

The defence officers crowded close but seemed to be greeting the new arrivals rather than challenging their presence. They pointed to the ferrocrete battlement and the newcomers continued on, spreading out along the stretch of wall. The woman that led them came close to Katsuhiro. She looked at him and smiled, and the sight soothed away the anguish. She held a lantern made out of an artillery shell casing, but the light seemed to emanate from her pale skin as much as the lamp.

'Let us slay the unworthy and protect the innocent,' she said, her words carrying some distance along the firing line. The thought came to Katsuhiro to step back and he did so, shouldering his lasgun. Others also made way for the woman's silent acolytes, until the firing step was populated by them.

'Who are you, lady of light?' Katsuhiro asked.

An older man came forward, interposing himself between Katsuhiro and the pale figure that looked out into the devastation of Poxville.

'She is the Holy Messenger, trooper. Blessed of the Emperor.'

Looking at her radiance against the darkness of the broken palaces Katsuhiro could easily believe it.

'Is this safe?' Olivier asked, voice trembling. His gaze kept straying from Keeler to the dead and dying heaped upon the road about seventy metres from the wall. Shambling figures moved among them, some crawling over the charnel piles, others trying to pick routes through the rubble around them.

'Of course not,' she told him. 'I told you we would confront the enemies of the Emperor. They do not dwell in safe places, not in these times.'

The truth seemed to reassure him more than any platitude, and he visibly calmed.

'Your strength is an inspiration,' he said.

'It is the Emperor's strength, not mine. My faith connects me to Him. It will connect us all to Him.'

Olivier looked along the curve of the wall and nodded. Here and there the spark of a las-bolt spat out into the ruins but far fewer than when they had arrived.

'I think we are ready.'

'Then raise up your voices in prayer and let us banish this evil.'

Olivier raised his voice, beginning one of his invocations. Keeler listened to her heart beating in her chest, a little faster than usual. She stared at the flame inside her shell-lamp, watching the dance of light on the blackening metal. Olivier's voice became an undercurrent of her thoughts as it had at the bastion. It was joined by the rest of the Lightbearers that had come with them, nearly four hundred souls.

Each of them was a light, a patch of brightness in the darkness of Horus' shadow. Keeler could feel that oppressive shade laid upon the Palace as much as the twilight of ash and smoke that obscured sun and stars alike.

She felt also the soul of the Emperor again, though rather than a tree it felt more like a dome, the skies themselves. But all was not well. The dome was assailed from without, its surface blackening like the interior of the lamp, the daemonic accretion growing thicker, in places enough to stifle the light from within.

Keeler felt her breath coming in short gasps, panic threatening her. Almost unnoticed a hand slipped into hers, gripping the fingers. She felt the closeness of Sindermann and relaxed.

The light. She turned her thoughts to it again, taking the illumination of the Emperor and casting it as a flame in her thoughts. She let the heat build, becoming an inferno of ecstasy. She knew nothing else, not of the wall beneath her feet, the men at her side, the hundreds of souls along the wall and within the ruins. But she did see the blots, the stains on the fabric of the Emperor's vision.

To these she directed the flames, her lips moving as words came unbidden to her.

'With the Emperor I am righteous. With His light the darkness is broken. With the fire of purity I purge the unholy.'

'Look!' grunted Olivier.

Keeler opened her eyes. From the ruins of the Palatine Arc dozens of figures staggered into view. Each was human-like, but obviously twisted or infected in some way. Fire burned in their skin, consuming them from inside as they flailed into the walls and fled over the rubble, bodies crumbling like ash as they fell.

'Praise the Emperor!' Keeler shouted, feeling the power flowing through her.

The call was echoed, weakly at first, and then again with greater vehemence.

'Praise the Emperor!'

The keening cries of the dying Neverborn were drowned out by the third triumphant shout, the words coming from the lips of the soldiers as well as the Lightbearers.

'Praise the Emperor!'

The sudden uplift of faith swept through Keeler like a hurricane, so that it felt as though her soul ascended on a hot wind. She was borne away by it, losing the sense of her body, and in that moment she found herself flying over the gardens of faith.

The great Emperor-tree spread its branches against a falling twilight, more sombre than before. Darkening clouds gathered about the treetop, flecked with malevolent lightning.

Keeler raced closer, no longer walking, but with wings like the aquila, feathered with pure faith.

For a few heartbeats she thought she might actually reach the branches that she desired so strongly, but even as she neared them her wings began to fade. She did not fall, but descended lightly to the ground, clawing at the air with her hands as though she might climb through the space between her and the Emperor.

Through tears she saw that the chains binding the branches to the ground had grown thicker, and more numerous. Each was like a great docking cable, broader than her shoulders, and she thought she could make out writing etched into every link.

She fell back into her body before she could read the words.

It took some time before she reacquainted herself with her physical form, though it must have been only moments since her departure. She sat down, back against the battlement, Sindermann bent over her with concern. She gave him a smile of assurance but could not speak, robbed of words by her experience.

The former iterator deterred others that tried to crowd closer, Olivier among them. One of the troopers approached from the other side, the slight-looking man that had spoken to her before.

'Was that…?' He stared back over the wall. 'How did that happen?'

Keeler held out her hand and the man helped her to her feet.

'The Emperor protects,' she told him, handing him the shell-lamp. She raised her voice, addressing Olivier and the others nearby. 'There will be other times we are needed, when the evil of Horus and his allies takes form. Our faith will be the light that banishes them back to the abyss that spawns them.'

Lion's Gate space port, tropophex core,
nineteen days since assault

Pushing forward into the brightly lit monorail terminal in the company of his warriors, Forrix saw the tunnel at the end of the light. Three lines ran across his advance, separated by broad platforms broken by rows of pillars. A flurry of bolter rounds greeted the arrival of the Iron Warriors, shattering the tiles on the wall and the entrance gate, slamming into armour already much-punished. Yellow-armoured foes lurked behind many of the columns and along the sunken trackbeds. The crack of bolt-guns and crunch of armoured boots on shattered tiles echoed back and forth across the open station.

The warriors of the IV Legion split, breaking left towards the tunnels and directly ahead to the nearest foes. The noise of their bolters sounded wrong in Forrix's ear, like coughs instead of barks, as close to the point of failing as those that carried them. Likewise, their armour whined and creaked and moaned with every movement, hissing and snarling from battle damage and lack of maintenance.

Forrix's own armour had seized at the left ankle, giving him an awkward limp. For the past four hundred metres of the advance he had adopted an almost crabwise gait, bolter pulled tight to his left pauldron, sighting by naked eye along its length.

'If you fall behind, you're left behind.' It wasn't the most inspirational speech Forrix had ever delivered, but it conveyed everything his weary legionaries needed to know. 'Keep pushing forward.'

He reached a square pillar and almost fell into it, turning at the last moment to lean his backpack against the blue-and-white tiles. A glance up showed a roof vaulted with broad arcs of plas-teel, the rockcrete between cracked and showering trickles of dust. The bombardment was distant, targeting another part of the space port, but its effects were still obvious.

'Triarch! I'm reading multiple power armour signals in the vicinity,' Allax reported from the next pillar along, about thirty metres closer to the track.

'Yes. The occupants are shooting at us!' Forrix bellowed back.

'No, there's even more.' Allax gestured with his free hand towards the tunnels and upwards. 'Hard to pinpoint, but scores, maybe hundreds of signals.'

'From the tunnels? Are you sure?' Forrix asked, heart sinking. There was no other way out.

Allax's reply was cut short by a beam of red energy that punched through the pillar and out of his chest.

'Lascannon!' The warning was shouted from behind Forrix, too late for Allax. The legionary's armour collapsed to its knees and then toppled forward. The auspex was still clasped in one hand, the green glow of its screen flickering on the tiles.

'Cover fire!' commanded Forrix. He rounded the pillar and let loose three rounds, aiming towards the closest blurs of yellow. A fusillade of fire erupted around him and he broke cover, limping as fast as he could to Allax's body. A bolt-round detonated on his backpack, spraying the back of his head with hot shards. As he ducked beneath the hole left by the lascannon blast, he felt blood trickling down his neck.

He ignored it and prised the auspex from Allax's fingers. First glance confirmed that there were readings in the direction of the tunnels and on the same plane as the Iron Warriors. Forrix slid down to a crouch, the auspex falling from his fingers.

It had all been a ridiculous gamble.

If he had really examined the plan, rather than just accepting it as Perturabo had instructed, he would have seen that it required a great many factors to come together to succeed. Too many, it had turned out.

He checked his ammunition. Seven bolt-rounds in his weapon, another magazine of twenty mag-locked to his thigh. He corrected himself, pulling the magazine from Allax's discarded bolter and fixing it to his spare. Another six bolts.

It was hopeless. The only reasonable objective left was to kill as many foes as possible. Trying to escape would make that harder. Forrix was about to order his remaining warriors to hold fast and die fighting when an orange blur on the screen of the auspex at his feet drew his attention.

'That's weapons discharge…' he muttered to himself, leaning forward to retrieve the scanning device. He panned it back towards the tunnels. The energy signatures grew stronger.

As though in confirmation, his vox buzzed into life, chiming three times to indicate a long-range command channel broadcast. He subvocalised the acceptance.

'This is Captain Rannock, subordinate command of the Third Spear. Nobody is supposed to be in this warzone. Who is this?'

'Triarch Forrix. Were you expecting someone else?'

'Triarch… We thought you were all dead!'

'We're not. We're in the monorail terminal. Heavily engaged. What is your situation?'

'We've been positioned to stall a counter-attack across this axis. There's a significant force of Imperial Fists and auxiliaries heading right past your position. Arrival time in less than five minutes.'

'Can you come to us?'

'Not my orders, triarch. If you command it, we'll try…'

'No. No point risking your mission. We'll come to you.'

'I'll send forward five squads to link up.'

'Good. We'll have company when we arrive. Forrix out.'

Forrix stood up, avoiding the hole in the pillar, and attached the auspex to a belt clamp. He tuned his vox to general address.

'All legionaries make speed for the tunnels. Cover and advance by threes. If you haven't got a three, make pairs. Suppressive fire maximal. We have two minutes to get off this station.'

Fire from the Iron Warriors intensified immediately. Forrix looked around, finding his closest companions were Gharal and a legionary called Dexalaro.

'On me,' he called to them, moving to fire a burst through the lascannon hole. 'Dexalaro, move on.'

They covered the next hundred metres in that fashion, two covering the third from cover to cover. Around them the rest of the force did likewise, though the return fire of the Imperial Fists grew in response, converging on those closest to the tunnels.

'Onto the rail and then run!' bellowed Forrix. A score of Space Marines broke cover with him, covering the twenty metres to the edge of the platform while bolts screamed both ways around them. Forrix almost fell into the gap, landing heavily against one of the other legionaries. As Iron Warriors threw themselves against the far platform edge to renew their fire, the next wave pounded across the platform.

Forrix heard a cry and turned to see Gharal down on one knee, thigh armour shattered, blood streaming. He tried to rise but the Imperial Fists were merciless, their fire tracking towards him like a pack of wolves scenting wounded prey. Another round caught Gharal square in the chest, a moment before a third bolt exploded against his shoulder. Three more successive eruptions slammed him backwards, his bolter flying from his grip.

Forrix saw him roll to his belly, clawing through his own blood. Through a shattered lens, the captain looked at the triarch.

'Fall behind…' wheezed Gharal. He stopped crawling, reaching out to retrieve his weapon. 'Left behind.'

Swearing, Forrix looked away and broke into a run, limping along the rail amongst his warriors. He heard the snap of Gharal's bolter as he resumed firing.

It felt like an eternity before the darkness of the tunnel swallowed him, footfalls loud in the sudden confines. A gleam ahead, suit lamps another couple of hundred metres away, dragged him onwards.

He didn't look back.

TWENTY-EIGHT

Ultimate sanction
Dorn's hidden army
A banner unfurled

Galleria Formidus, Senatorum Imperialis,
twenty days since assault

It was not often that Amon felt the need to demonstrate obeisance to his superiors, but he did not resist his urge to kneel before the captain-general.

'I have failed you.'

His confession felt small and worthless, lost in the expanse of the Galleria Formidus, which arched a hundred metres over their heads and stretched three kilometres from end to end. Once a busy thoroughfare between the chambers of the Senatorum Imperialis and the Tower Auris of the Custodians, it was now deserted but for the pair.

'Failed?' Valdor gestured for Amon to stand but he ignored it, determined to make plain the depth of his contrition.

'The daemonic peril continues. Escalates, in point of fact. Faith in the notion of the God-Emperor is spreading more quickly than ever. Keeler and her Lightbearers number almost a thousand devotees now and more sects are making themselves publicly known, no longer fearing admonishment.'

'Stand up.' The two words were issued with such vehemence that Amon had to comply. The commander of the Legio Custodes clenched his jaw, and Amon prepared himself for his chastisement. 'This self-flagellation is unbecoming of a Custodian.'

Valdor turned and gestured for Amon to continue alongside him, towards the halls of the senate where he had been heading when Amon had caught up with him. His expression remained stern.

'I tasked you with investigating a single incident of untoward behaviour. You may have taken it upon yourself to launch a single-handed crusade against the rise of faith and a daemonic invasion, but that was never my command.'

Amon accepted this in silence.

'I am on my way to speak with Malcador, I am happy for you to join me.'

'I do not think that would be the wisest course of action. The Regent clearly has his own agenda in this matter, whether he shares it or not.'

Valdor looked at him sharply.

'You think he works against the will of the Emperor?'

Amon did not reply immediately, careful of his words. When they had advanced a few more strides, footfalls echoing along the great marble-and-gold transitway, he gave his answer.

'I do not believe any of us know the will of the Emperor, not on any specific topic.' Amon controlled his tone, trying to avoid implication of accusation or complaint. 'We have only the past and our own counsel to guide us. Unless you have some hidden contact?'

'No, you are right,' Valdor conceded with a sigh. 'I have not been in communion with the Emperor for some time. We can only forward guesses on how He would view the current situation, and in that we must rely on the wisdom of Malcador as much as our own.'

'On other matters, I would not hesitate to agree. But this is a direct threat against the Emperor, and also a flaunting of one of His most emphatic decrees. I was at–'

'Yes, Monarchia. However, I was at Nikaea and yet I see even Rogal Dorn makes use of his Librarius again. The Emperor has not issued forth to chastise us for what you must agree would be perceived an even greater crime.'

'It all revolves around the same tenet of the Imperial Truth, does it not? Faith and psykers. Intricately linked.'

'The Sisters of Silence had Keeler for many months. They detected no psychic talent within her.'

Amon checked the arguments that came to mind. Instead he focused on practicalities.

'Keeler is amassing too much power. If she continues it will become harder to remove her.'

'Remove her?' Valdor frowned. 'I thought she had some success in banishing these incursions?'

'The incursions continue to grow in frequency and magnitude, so I would not make any claims to their efficacy. In fact, the greater the influence of the Lightbearers, the more daemonic activity has increased.'

'I understand that we have not yet seen anything more potent than these warp-flesh hybrids. Is that true?'

'For the time being. As Malcador speculated, it seems some physical focus is required. The Emperor's ward continues to keep at bay any pure manifestation of the Neverborn. Even so, it can only be a matter of time before the corrupted primarchs will be able to breach the barrier. We should proceed on the assumption that Angron, Mortarion and the others will soon directly attack the walls.'

'I will pass that on to Rogal Dorn. Malcador informed me that Keeler believes there may be some central figure or group responsible for the occurrences.'

'She has shared that theory with me.'

'You disregard it?'

'No, but speculation is unproductive. The connection to the Death Guard and the power they now serve is plain. Whether they have operatives, sympathisers or unwitting allies within the Palace does not change matters.'

'This fascination with the Lightbearers seems to be personal. It is a distraction from the task of combating the daemons.'

'The two are linked. Faith is growing in correlation to daemonic presence. I have yet to determine if there is causality, and in which direction. I do not deny my personal distaste for the misguided belief in the Emperor as a deity, but we cannot ignore the evidence.'

Amon took a breath, readying himself for what had to come next.

'I believe that even if she is not directly responsible for the daemonic attack, Keeler's spreading influence is a threat. It is too late to simply incarcerate her again, and as we saw with Sindermann, she has associates that will find ways to aid her and promulgate her creed.'

'You propose to kill her?' Valdor asked the question without sign of surprise or judgement. 'To be clear.'

'Yes, captain-general. If she is the source of the daemonic breaches, they will end. If not, we have still curtailed the rise of a dangerous anti-Imperial demagogue.'

They continued on in silence for several minutes. Amon knew not to prompt his superior for a reply but instead reviewed his own plan for the execution should Valdor ask for it. They were almost at the gate into the halls of the Senatorum Imperialis when Valdor spoke.

'No. Keeler is not to be harmed.'

It was not in Amon's nature to question the judgement of his superiors, but he could not hold back his question.

'What good do we achieve by letting her live?'

'The enemy of my enemy...' Valdor stopped, about fifty metres short of the steps leading down to the sealed gates. Two Custodians stood guard at the portal, their auric armour partly concealed behind surcoats of white that indicated they had been assigned as bodyguard to Malcador.

'Horus sent an assassin after Keeler,' Valdor continued. 'Until she presents a provable threat to the immediate safety of the Emperor, I take guidance from that fact. If the renegades desire Keeler dead, I suggest to you that it is in our interest to keep her alive. It may well be for the very acts we see now that her assassination was ordered.'

'I had not considered that,' admitted Amon.

'I will take command of the wider fight against the daemons, in concert with the Silent Sisterhood.' He raised a finger to stall Amon's next words. 'This is not admonishment, simply practicality. I need you to focus on the cause. The threat has expanded far beyond the original intent of your investigation, so I am commanding you to focus on that first purpose. Examine Keeler and the Lightbearers, and determine *with certainty* whether there is a connection between them and the Neverborn attacks. If there is, we will deal with it appropriately. If not, we can make use of them and spare ourselves the distraction.'

Amon knelt again, this time out of gratitude for a renewed sense of purpose.

'As you will it, so I obey.'

* * *

Himalazia, undisclosed location, twenty days since assault

Excitement rippled through the mustering base, moving from one camp to the next like a virus.

The order to attack had arrived.

For the Addaba Free Corps the next twelve hours were spent waiting for their companion regiments to get ready. There was little enough for Zenobi and her companions to do other than pack their kitbags and make sure they were ready to march. Their lost heavy weapons had been replaced by donations from other regiments, along with other supplies such as the rations they'd been eating while awaiting their new mission. The muster point had been well victualled – evidently Dorn had expected his reserves here, and perhaps in other places around the Himalazia, to be waiting for some time.

Unlike with the looting of their first transport train, this time the troopers from Addaba didn't load themselves down with unnecessary supplies. They took only power packs, grenades and anything else that could be used for fighting. For them the war was almost over, the day of glory upon them.

'Aren't you off to see your lover?' asked Menber, when he and Zenobi were left washing the squad pans after breakfast.

'No. We've said goodbye every night as though it was the last time. There's no need to make this difficult.'

'You mean more difficult?'

'No. This is what we've been waiting for. I'm happy it's here.'

Egwu brought them together to address the entire corps. A couple of armoured command transports had been liberated from one of the other formations and it was from atop one of these that the general-captain spoke, voice amplified by the voxmitters below.

'Now is the day of our first and last test. Rogal Dorn has sent word for the reserve force to advance on the Lion's Gate space port. It is sorely contested, the strength of the Imperial Fists and their allies matched against the might of the Iron Warriors and their supporters.'

She paced along the roof of the vehicle, baton in hand.

'The timing of the attack will be crucial, I have been told. This force, this mechanised column, will arrive along an axis that will turn the flank of the Warmaster's forces. A counter-attack from within the Palace will be mounted as the blow from this army falls, catching the Iron Warriors unawares.'

She stopped her walking and took the baton in both hands, staring down at the ranked squads of her companies.

'Lord Dorn has impressed upon the command staff the necessity of this attack. It is the engagement for which he has been waiting, one to which we have been delivered by fate to witness. The position of the Emperor's forces will be untenable if this attack fails. I do not need to tell you how happy that makes me! This is the battle that our cause has needed. This is the opportunity to prove ourselves that we have wanted for seven years. Some of you will be detailed with special operational preparations. The remainder of the Free Corps will stand ready for my commands.'

She bowed her head and her voice was barely audible even over the voxmitters.

'Soon the effort and sacrifice and blood we have shed will be made worthy.'

The companies were dismissed and a tense quiet descended on their encampment, pregnant with expectation. These last hours were the worst for Zenobi, far more excruciating than the weeks and months that had come before. To be so close and yet not quite at their goal made every minute tick past with torturous slowness.

By midday, the reserve force was almost ready to move out. A few scouting companies had been despatched already to provide reconnaissance on the route to the Imperial Palace. The Free Corps made their way to the main highway, bringing their new lascannons, heavy bolters, mortars and other weapons with them. Running the length of the enclosed base, a viaduct gave them a vantage point that looked out across the regiments both historic and newly raised.

Zenobi and first squad received the call to attend to Egwu. She started shaking as they marched along the road for the head of their column. Memories flocked for attention, of family and friends, time spent on the line and the experiences she'd had since leaving Addaba. All of it crammed into her thoughts, bringing her to that time and place.

So much labour, so much loss, all in the name of the Emperor. It was this thought she held on to as she clambered to the top of the command vehicle, assisted by Menber and Kettai.

Egwu waited there, Jawaahir alongside. The integrity high officer spared a brief smile for the standard bearer and with a flick of a finger directed her to place herself next to the general-captain.

The smog of hundreds of engines blackened the sky, adding to the gloom of the filth-choked heavens. The thunder of tanks and transports, some the size of city blocks, created a deafening wave of sound that reverberated from the mountainsides, an assault on ears already numbed by the winds of the high Himalazia.

The growl of machine voices all but drowned out human shouts, even those amplified by voxmitters. Electronic clarions howled into the whirl of noise, sounding the advance or stand-to, their modulated calls overlapping.

Everything was sudden movement, dust billowing from treads and boots alike.

'This is it.' General-Captain Egwu did not raise her voice, but her words were carried by the tongues of those under her command. 'Everyone stand ready.'

Beside her, Zenobi Adedeji fidgeted with the cover of the banner she carried, eyes flicking between her company commander and the scene of organised bedlam being enacted around the troopers from Addaba Hive.

'Everything we have done, the oaths we have sworn, the hardships we have endured, has led to this moment.' Now Egwu shouted, not simply to be heard, but filled with passion. Her remaining eye stared wide amongst the burn scars that covered most of her face, fresh tissue pink against her dark skin. 'Now is the time we strike at the enemy! Our families laboured and died to deliver us to this place. Our courage and determination has carried us this far. We may not live beyond this day, but our deeds will!'

'Now?' asked Zenobi, her voice quavering with emotion, a shaking hand reaching towards the cover of the standard.

'Yes,' said the general-captain. 'Now.'

The cover fluttered from Zenobi's grasp and the banner unfurled as she waved the pole, greeted by a roar from the troopers arrayed along the roadway. The voxmitter picked up her cry as the cloth straightened to reveal a red flag, a black stylised eye embroidered upon it, the names of thousands of Addaba families stitched in long lines beneath.

'For freedom! For Addaba!' she shouted as las-fire ripped into life around her. A series of sharp detonations echoed across the base, plumes of yellow fire erupting within the tank columns and artillery batteries from demolition charges concealed that morning. 'For the Warmaster!'

TWENTY-NINE

Dorn capitulates
Shattered iron
A terrible revelation

Bhab Bastion, twenty-one days since assault

Standing on the central platform of the Grand Borealis Strategium, Dorn turned his head one way and then the other, sensing a change in the atmosphere. It had been the first time in a week since he had been able to return, forced to lend his physical presence to the most pressing battles for the wall. His brothers did likewise, each of them needed in more places than they could reinforce, moving from one battlezone to the next without pause. Only the necessity of retaining his overview of the siege had brought him back.

There was muttering. Not the quiet conversation of reports being made, communications being passed along. Murmurs of disquiet. He saw Imperial Army adjutants hurrying from one display to another, exchanging concerned looks. The few remaining Imperial Fists officers – those with fresh wounds or older injuries that prevented them from fighting – gathered in conspiratorial clusters.

One of them, Captain Vorst, broke away and limped across

the strategium as fast as his augmetic leg allowed. Dorn regarded him without comment as he ascended the steps to the command platform. The captain's hand rose to his plastron and fell quickly in a hurried salute.

'Lord Dorn, all contact has been lost with the Lion's Gate space port.'

The agitated manner of the equerry was at odds with the normally calm demeanour that made him so suited for his position. Even with such momentous news, Dorn could not allow any laxity in discipline.

'Steady yourself, captain.' Dorn's gaze took in the great sweep of the strategium. 'Others are looking to you for example.'

'Apologies, Lord Dorn.' Vorst straightened as best he could with a crude hunk of metal for a leg, banging his fist to his chest in sharper salute.

'When was the last communication?' Dorn asked.

'Thirty minutes ago. Lieutenant-Commander Haeger reported that the enemy were within five kilometres of the skybridges, my lord. Captain Sigismund had drawn down all remaining forces from the Starspear to contain the threat.'

'And what are the enemy dispositions now?'

'Unknown, my lord.' Vorst glanced up at the long line of sensor terminals on the level above. 'All comms and scanners are being jammed.'

'How? We have the most powerful, most sophisticated surveyor arrays in the Palace.' The scale of such an event explained his equerry's discomfort.

'It seems that the space port's own scan and docking systems have been corrupted, my lord. Inverted, so that they are blocking every conceivable spectrum analysis and communications frequency. It's silenced and blacked out every link we have with the forces inside.'

Dorn swallowed back his immediate reaction, which was to

demand how such a thing was possible. If there were an explanation it would have been offered, even if highly speculative.
Another recent loss of communication came back to mind.

'Any further report on the relief force at Station Ultima?'

'Scattered vox-chatter. As previously reported, it seems there
was a rogue element introduced into the relief camp, my lord.
Nobody is sure how. They attacked the camp from within. It
will be another eighteen hours before they are in any state to
mount an offensive.'

Dorn ground his teeth, fists clenched. The timing was disastrous.
Though he had other reserves, of much less strength, the Ultima
force had been ideally positioned to strike behind the siege lines
at just such a moment. It seemed more than coincidence that
traitors should attack from within just as his need was greatest.

Similar stories had been trickling in from across the Palace.
Imperial Army units not responding to orders. Others disappearing entirely. Turncoats, from a few dozen individuals to
whole regiments, were turning on their companions, gunning
down former comrades, bringing their tanks and artillery to
bear upon loyalist positions. A few incidents had become a
much deadlier phenomenon over the last twelve hours.

All was building to a long-anticipated crescendo.

'This is it,' said the primarch. 'He will be coming now.'

'It is what, my lord? Who is coming?'

'Perturabo. The Lord of Iron. This is his masterstroke, he
thinks. Blinded, cut off, our forces are ripe to be swept away
by his arrival. A self-indulgent finale to his victory.'

'Why now?'

'Sigismund has been too focused on the bridges. He has forgotten he needed to defend the Starspear as well.' Dorn let his
pent-up anger free, slamming a fist into the palm of his other
hand. Vorst withdrew a step, aghast at this unusual display from
his lord. 'This has always been a battle for the docks, not the

bridges. With the upper guns overrun or blinded, my traitor brother can bring in as many ships as he wants. He can bring in whatever strength he needs to overrun the space port terminals.'

'Titan transports,' said Vorst, hushed by the notion.

'Or a battle-barge,' snarled Dorn. He turned his gaze upwards, as though looking into orbit, imagining his brother on the bridge of the *Iron Blood*. Would he be brooding or exultant? His first victory on Terra was close at hand. How did it feel, taking that step closer to the Inner Palace?

'Orders, Lord Dorn?'

The primarch realised it was the second time of asking.

'Alert all forces at the Lion's Gate. Prepare supporting fire and sally attacks to cover the withdrawal at the space port. Keep trying to signal Sigismund. He is to order full, strategic retreat to the bridges and then to the Lion's Gate.'

'Retreat?'

'The space port has fallen, Vorst. It is just a matter of time, and how many of our warriors we can extricate from under the enemy guns. Every soldier saved today will stand to fight tomorrow.'

He strode towards the steps, reaching for the helmet that hung on a stand at the back of the platform.

'You are leaving, Lord Dorn?' Vorst hurried after him.

'Yes. Prepare my gunship and my Huscarls.'

He had matched wit and will with Perturabo across star systems, siege lines and palace walls. Now it was time to face his brother in person.

Lion's Gate space port, tropophex exterior,
twenty-one days since assault

Sigismund's sword sheared through the bolter of the Iron Warrior that faced him. The blade detonated the round in the

breech so that his sword was aflame as it cut deep into the
legionary's helm. The warrior of the IV Legion stumbled back,
blood flying. Sigismund followed, relentless, driving the point
into his target's throat.

Around him bolter and blade made a cacophony of war,
but he fought as though in a bubble of silence. The battle
had sprawled out into the concourses and galleries around
the skybridges, so that gunships and anti-air cannons roared
and thundered above while gun batteries upon the skin of the
space port tracked fire across the melee, seeking foes of opportunity. Loyalist and traitor were too embroiled with each other
to mark friend and foe apart, like two combatants with blades
in each other's guts and hands clamped to each other's throats.

Striding past the falling corpse of his enemy, Sigismund
looked not at the next Iron Warrior but beyond him to the great
conflagration that had erupted around the monorail terminals
and the immense archways that led to the outer platforms.
Dreadnoughts and tanks duelled along the kilometres-wide
station front, while in the further distance thousands of others ebbed and flowed like a tide of power armour, as the last
of both forces committed to this final battle.

Far below, where mortals could breathe the polluted air, hundreds of thousands of Imperial Army troopers toiled against
the horde of turncoats, beasts and mutants, but their war was
without victory even if the cost continued to rise – the fate of
the space port would be decided in the next hours at the gates
of the skybridges.

Ducking beneath a chainsword, Sigismund fired his bolt
pistol into the faceplate of a legionary, following the bolts with
the edge of his blade. He let another snarl-toothed weapon
ricochet from his angled pauldron, the blow deflected away
from his head, exposing the wielder's neck to a downward cut.

'Where is Abaddon?' he cried, letting his frustration free

through his external address. There had been no sign of the Sons of Horus at the point of the enemy attack.

His vox crackled, but not in reply to his challenge. The voice that came through the static was that of Lieutenant-Commander Haeger.

'Captain, I have an incoming transmission from Lord Dorn.'

Sigismund paused in his assault, taken aback by the news. There had been no communication in or out of the space port for more than an hour.

'I stand ready to receive.'

The static crackle increased as the link was established. Lord Dorn's voice was tinny and distant. The surrounding clatter of small-arms and crash of weapons on power armour swelled around the Templar.

'Order immediate withdrawal from the Lion's Gate space port.'

Shocked, Sigismund almost missed an axe swinging from the melee towards his chest. He parried at the last moment, stepping back to allow Gaurand and Elgeray to pass him on the left and right, taking the brunt of the fight from him.

'This is their last effort, my lord. We can hold.'

'The cost is too high. This is not our last battle to fight, it is only the first wall.'

'Abaddon is here, my lord. And other commanders of the foe.'

'It is of no consequence.' Bitterness entered the primarch's voice. *'Do not let the lies of Keeler lead you astray a second time.'*

Sigismund choked back his argument, knowing that he had nothing more to say to his genefather than had been said already. Dorn must have taken his silence as objection; his tone was fierce when he next spoke.

'These warriors' lives are not to spend for your superstition, Sigismund. Nor are they currency for your personal glory. You want to hurl yourself at Abaddon? You have my leave. Discharge your last efforts as you wish, but do not call it honour, do not call it duty.'

Darkness fell upon Sigismund, but it was not a product of his genefather's words but a literal shadow. He sensed the fighting diminish around him, a pause as though both armies took a breath together.

He looked up and saw a silhouette against the purple dusk-lit clouds. An immense starship descended from orbit, its prow aflame with friction heat, energy discharge crackling across its dark hull.

Not a single cannon fired in defiance of its landing, the orbital batteries seized, blinded or destroyed.

'My lord, we have been fools,' Sigismund told Dorn, voice breaking, recognising the warship as plumes of fire carried to the upper docks. 'This was never to seize the bridges – all was a ploy to clear the defences of the high dock.'

'*Too late the truth comes to you,*' said the Emperor's Praetorian, censure dripping from every word. '*It is the* Iron Blood. *Perturabo's flagship.*'

Sigismund looked up again at the shadow passing across the heavens, its plasma engines leaving wakes of azure. At full magnification he could see launch bays opening, gunships pouring forth like wasps from a nest. There would be other ships coming, bringing overwhelming force to bear directly from orbit.

Would Rann have allowed it to happen?

Sigismund would not accept that this was failure. The space port could never hold forever; it was always his lord's intent to slow the enemy and then withdraw. He brought up his sword, touching its hilt to his brow as he closed his eyes, trying to find the peace he sought.

Instead he saw the face of Keeler. He heard her voice, telling him he was the Emperor's chosen.

The port would fall but there would be other battlefields. It was up to him to make sure the greatest of the enemy did not survive to see them.

'What is your command, my lord?' he asked, opening his eyes.

'*Unchanged. The flow of time bleeds the foe greater than any wound. Hold the bridges just long enough for the withdrawal.*'

A great shout burst across the battle, bellowed from thousands of voxmitters and external address systems. Accompanied by the crashing of fists and the thrum of revving engines, the Iron Warriors gave voice to welcome their arriving primarch.

'Iron within! Iron without!'

With their battle cry rebounding from the walls, echoing from the broken plascrete and burning wrecks, the Iron Warriors surged again.

Lion's Gate space port, tropophex skin zone,
twenty-one days since assault

Forrix had spent weeks at a time aboard ship during the Great Crusade and the subsequent war against the Emperor, and had never thought anything of his confinement. Emerging into the open air of the Lion's Gate space port's primary skybridge terminal made him realise how closed-in he had been for the previous twenty days – days spent in constant fighting, just one mistake from death.

Fighting continued below, about twenty storeys down and a kilometre away. It seemed that not a balcony, bridge or mezzanine was not home to an iron-clad warrior or ochre-armoured foe. Armoured vehicles slashed through the periphery while cannonades from support battalions rained fire onto the bridges themselves. Among the metal of his brothers he spied a thrust of red aimed at the heart of the Imperial Fists' line, a smudge of grey next to it.

It seemed impossible that for all the time he had fought inside the port, only now were the bridges being seized.

He cared nothing for it, wearied beyond imagining in body and spirit. He longed to suck in lungfuls of air but he was still eleven kilometres up; unsealing his armour would be a mistake, a salvaged Imperial Fists helm adjoined to his plate. He wanted to spit the dryness from his mouth and wipe the congealed sweat from his face. Instead he let himself slump to his knees, bolter in one hand, blood-caked knife in the other. His suit sighed with him, fluctuating power readings scrolling across his visor.

Like everyone else, his eye was drawn to the massive starship descending to the uppermost tower of the Starspear, wreathed in flame, accompanied by a shower of shooting stars as orbital debris fell with it. The pyrotechnics of its approach were greater than any celebratory display. Sparks of blue betrayed the presence of descending attack craft, a swarm of fireflies falling from a flame-wreathed behemoth.

The *Iron Blood*, seat of Perturabo – the primarch now come to claim his prize on the backs of his warriors' efforts.

The urge to spit returned, this time out of disgust. Kroeger's whole plan had been a simplistic disaster waiting to happen, and only the bloody-mindedness of the Iron Warriors – fighters like Gharal – had wrested any kind of victory from the mess. Now the conquering Lord of Iron would arrive and finish the job his sons had started. After so many years of other Legions using the IV as their battering ram, it sickened Forrix to think of his own genefather doing the same.

Telemetric transponders warned him of the approach of more Iron Warriors, alighting from an industrial conveyor a few dozen metres away. Six squads emerged, battle-damaged and wary. Forrix recognised their leader immediately and pushed himself to his feet to raise a hand in greeting.

'Stonewrought, I didn't think I'd see you so far from your guns!'

Soltarn Vull Bronn signalled to his warriors to take positions at the wall overlooking the platforms below, before breaking away to approach the triarch.

'Thought you were dead,' said Bronn.

'Should be, by any sane calculation,' Forrix replied with a shake of the head. 'If I suspected Kroeger of any intelligence, I would say he intended to have me trapped and slain in that murderzone. But, he's too stupid for that kind of politics.'

'He seems to have your measure. Who else has come this close to seeing you dead?'

Forrix just grunted, not willing to concede anything in favour of Kroeger. Had it not been for Perturabo's injunction, Forrix would have not been forced into a suicidal infiltration.

'Stupid, but standing on the brink of victory,' the Stone-wrought continued. He pointed across the skybridges where, level with the terminal of the space port, the Lion's Gate itself stood tall and undaunted. 'This is just the first wall to cross. The gate itself is the prize.'

'Prize? There is no prize left.' Forrix looked past the bastions of the Lion's Gate to the flare of the last shields of the aegis above the Sanctum Imperialis. 'Not for us mortals. You've seen the tides of this war, the things that have changed. We're lubricant in a war machine built for gods, as expendable as bolts and powercells.'

The Stonewrought said nothing, offered no argument, so Forrix continued.

'My brothers… Maybe some of them would still fight for me, but most have their eyes turned up, seeking a higher glory, wanting to elevate themselves. This Legion isn't worth my blood any more. Perturabo? He is as much a danger to us as the enemy. His temper will be the ending of us yet, and we'll follow him into the abyss despite it. Horus?' Forrix laughed bitterly, tasting the acid in his mouth. 'He and his gods see only the Emperor. We are ants under their boots as they fight, thinking to sway the course of the galaxy with a bolter and a blade. A stone in the Ultimate Wall will have more influence over the end of this war than you or I.'

'You're not coming with me?' said the Stonewrought, pointing to a set of steps that ran down from the overlook to the main terminal. 'I've been ordered to flank the Imperial Fists position while Kroeger, Khârn, Abaddon and Layak lead the final assault.'

Forrix looked back up at the *Iron Blood* and then to his warriors, such as remained, standing in the darkness of the terminal archway. The battle continued to rage below, the reports of bolters as sharp then as they were the first time Forrix had been in battle. The flare of laser and shell lit the fog below, winds carving glimpses of firefights and melees ranging across the rampways and rails of the kilometres-long skybridges. The battle might be concluded before Perturabo arrived – that at least would give Forrix some satisfaction.

'Form on me!' he called to his warriors. They responded wearily but without complaint, falling in to rough squads around their commander.

'You've found something to fight for?' said the Stonewrought.

'No,' Forrix told him as he started towards the stair, Bronn falling into step beside him. 'But I would rather win a battle fighting for nothing than lose one.'

Basilica Ventura, western processional,
twenty-one days since assault

It was with a mixture of disdain and foreboding that Amon watched the 'faithful' gathering on the processional just to the south of the Basilica Ventura. More than ten thousand disciples, each of them carrying some form of home-made lamp, a sea of flickering lights that stretched along the walled transitway.

From a ledge-walk around the outside of a former assayer hub, Amon had an unblocked view of the three-kilometre-long processional, from the ruins of the Basilica Ventura all the way to the Westmost Gate. It was a commonly used route for those approaching the Senatorum Imperialis for petition, though of late much of its length had been populated with refugee families and scavengers. It was very public, which was the reason Keeler had given for the choice of venue for this unprecedented gathering. Convinced that the Lightbearers were innocent of any connection to the daemonic attacks, she saw the expansion of their numbers as the only defence against the Neverborn.

It reminded him too much of Monarchia. How long before they erected their first monument to the Emperor? Statuary abounded within the Palace, of philosophers and warlords aplenty, but none of the Emperor Himself. A city had been levelled because it had been constructed in praise of the Master of Mankind's divinity. The Imperial Palace wore the mantle of fortress of late, after so many guises, but what of those days after the defeat of Horus and the lifting of the siege? Would the Emperor be forced to walk among cathedrals raised to His false godhood, or would He have to break apart every stone of His own greatest work to be rid of the taint?

Amon had secured a copy of the *Lectitio Divinitatus*, studying it in the hopes of learning more about the cult that took its name. It was a mixture of truth and wishful thinking, with many passages expanding upon the original doctrines that took it into the realm of pure speculation – that it was the work of multiple authors was clear to see in the various sections, each seemingly trying to outdo the last in pomposity and self-reflection.

Despite his deepest misgivings he was powerless. This phenomenon had to be allowed to run its course, barring direct intervention from the Emperor, so that the folly of religion would be made plain to all once again.

Already Keeler had passed on information about a faction within the Lightbearers that was demanding she and Olivier were vocal in denouncing other cults around the Imperial Palace. Infighting would inevitably follow, and internecine debate could well become another civil war.

He corrected himself. Not entirely powerless. Twelve Custodians and a detachment from the Silent Sisterhood stood by to assist should his suspicions of the sect and its parade prove correct. Never before had so many gathered together in singular purpose, and it seemed to Amon that if anything was amiss among the rituals of the Lightbearers it would become clear today. He would have preferred more support, but ongoing regular unrest as well as more immaterial incidents kept the much-diminished force of the Legio Custodes spread thin across the Imperial Palace. The very real threat of the daemon primarchs gaining ingress to the Palace occupied the thoughts of Valdor and the Silent Sisterhood.

He could see Keeler upon a platform erected on the far side of the processional, flanked by address systems to carry her voice to the growing mass around her. She had not confided in him the nature of her sermon. The Custodian also noted several dozen uniformed troopers near the base of the platform, weapons in hand. How they were at the procession and not at the walls did not concern him, but their presence was a further complication.

A click behind Amon drew his attention to the concealed doorway through which he had passed to come to his observation post – one of many secret routes the Legio Custodes maintained throughout the Imperial Palace. He turned, expecting another Custodian, and was surprised to see Malcador framed in the doorway. A flash of gold and white in the vestibule behind betrayed the presence of at least one guard, though the Custodian remained within the building when the door swung shut behind the Regent.

'Bracing weather,' said Malcador, robe and thin hair tousled by the strong wind. He stayed close to the door, unwilling to approach the wall-less edge.

'Is this what the Emperor desires?' Amon asked, gesturing with his spear towards the converging masses.

'There is power here.' The Regent closed his eyes, head tilted back. His lips barely moved as he spoke. 'A great pressure from without pushes upon the telaethesic ward. Daemons beyond counting expend their existence to break through. Sorcery abounds in the camps of the Dark Mechanicum, the Death Guard and the Word Bearers. Magnus is finally committing his psychic might to the assault.'

Malcador opened his eyes, a last glimmer of gold in the irises as he looked straight at Amon.

'The Emperor has greater concerns than a few hymns and prayers.'

'The Neverborn are drawn to power.'

'Yes, but it can also keep them at bay. If I could be definitive, I would tell you for certain that this gathering of faith was good or bad. In such matters there is no certainty, only intent.'

'And you trust the intent of these people?'

'I trust Keeler, as I told you before.'

Amon returned his attention to the woman at the front of the platform. She had started to address the crowd, the words audible to his enhanced senses, though he paid them little mind.

'The webway was only one means for protecting mankind from the lure of Chaos,' said Malcador, taking a step forward, eyeing the drop with some concern. 'The Emperor thought that the best means to break the Dark Powers was to starve them of energy at the source.'

'Mastering the secrets of the webway would have allowed humanity to traverse the stars without the warp. No warp, no Navigators, no psykers.'

'Yet psykers are still born among us.' Malcador tapped the side of his head, reminding Amon that he spoke to one with such abilities. His next words materialised directly inside the Custodian's thoughts. It was not pleasant, something he had only experienced from the Emperor previously. +What would we do with all of those psykers?+

'The Astronomican is power…' Amon realised the meaning of Malcador's question. 'With the webway there is no need for the Emperor to project the light of the heavens. The void would fall dark.'

Malcador edged closer, fingers tight around his staff as he peered down to the processional far below, people still making their way to the gathering.

'What if that psychic power was used by the Emperor rather than projected?' Malcador shrugged. 'If our base emotions feed the Dark Powers, what of our common humanity?'

'The webway project failed, this is idle speculation.'

'Not so. Not for me. Dorn wrestles with the logistics of waging war across a continent-sized fortress-city, I contend with the implications of a battle that rages over the boundless realms of the immaterial.' Leaning on his staff, he sighed, gaze turning towards the distant speaker. 'If we cannot stifle the gods' power in the warp, then what better means to defeat them than to channel it away? Or perhaps given sufficient psychic energy, could the Emperor weaponise the Astronomican? Rather than light the warp, could He purge it?'

'This discussion is a distraction. I do not understand why you came here.'

'To see it for myself. To see faith growing, in the flesh even as I feel it in my thoughts.' Malcador smiled but there was no humour in his eyes. 'You see, everyone is a psyker. Everyone has a tiny connection to the warp, even you. Except the Silent Sisters, of course, and a relative handful of others. Instinct, empathy, sympathy… They are products of the soul, communicating in infinitesimally small ways with the souls of others. What if a force bound not just the powerful psykers together, but every soul in humanity?'

'That force is faith, you think?' Amon was not sure he could deal with the nuances of Malcador's suggestion. It was as outside his expertise as algae harvesting or Martian theologika poetry. 'You want to see if faith has power? Is that why you have let this folly grow so wildly?'

'Let us call it weapons research,' said the Regent.

'The Emperor forbade His own worship.'

'And the moment He makes known His will to end this, I will order the extermination of every last member of the Light-bearers and any other cult.' Malcador drew up straighter. 'Until that time, I am the Regent and I allow it to continue.'

Amon realised the speaker had changed – Olivier had now taken centre stage and was pontificating to his followers. Something he had said had pricked Amon's suspicion.

'Is something wrong, Custodian?'

'Yes.' Amon reviewed the last few seconds of his unconscious memory. 'Olivier just said to give praise to the Emperor, the creator is hope in the heart of every person.'

'So?'

'I heard the same, the first time I encountered one of the half-born. The corporal said, "He is the Life Within Death. The Breath on your Lips. The Hope in your Heart." And I heard him call the Emperor the Life within Death earlier, but it did not trigger the memory.'

'Titles from the holy book, perhaps?'

'No, I have read three different copies and not one of them

contained those specific phrases.' Amon started towards the doorway. 'You are about to find out just how dangerous faith can be, Lord Regent.'

Lion's Gate space port, interstitial bridges,
twenty-one days since assault

It was foolish to think that a single battle would change the course of a war already seven years progressed, but as he advanced along a boulevard filled with the wrecks of Imperial Fists, Iron Warriors and Imperial Army tanks of both sides, Abaddon felt a sense of shifting momentum. The void war, the suppression of the Lunar defences, even the slaughter of millions around the walls was simply preface to the assault on the Imperial Palace.

An assault that would commence within days if the sky-bridges of the Lion's Gate could be captured. The *Iron Blood* was no longer in view, docking with the orbital pilaster, but it was only a matter of time before the Lord of Iron joined his warriors.

'Enjoy your victory,' Layak told him, the six eye-lenses of his helm gleaming with their unnatural light as twilight rapidly fell on the smoke-shrouded terminal.

'It is not mine,' Abaddon replied.

'When you are dedicated to the powers, all victories are shared, for the ascension of one is the ascension of all. Rejoice in the knowledge that we step closer to Lord Horus' final confrontation with the Emperor. We are delivering the Warmaster to his fate.'

Abaddon was not so sure he knew what that meant, but the arrival of ochre-clad warriors ahead of the vanguard pushed aside all other considerations. Bolts speared out to meet the oncoming warriors, while fire from heavy weapons sited further down the bridges flared past. With his knot of Sons of Horus around him, Layak and the two blade slaves at his left shoulder, Abaddon strode forward with purpose.

Wordless cries drew his attention to the left. From among the silver-clad companies of the Iron Warriors burst forth a stream of red – legionaries of the World Eaters racing ahead of their companions. At their head pounded Khârn, the teeth of *Gorechild* flashing in the flare of bolt propellant, his armour encased in dried gore.

'There goes a champion who is at one with himself,' said Layak. 'Khârn embraces the gifts of Khorne and is freed the indignities of doubt and self-concern. See how he charges right at his enemies, no longer afraid, no longer wondering at his purpose. He is fulfilled and through him so Khorne's power grows, a mutual glory.'

'He becomes more mindless, unable to focus, losing what he was,' replied Abaddon. 'And Typhon – Typhus – what has he turned into? What of the lodge-brother I once swore oaths alongside? We have travelled a long road, and I am not sure it leads to the destination we wanted when we set out.'

'The destination has always been written. Destiny, you see?' said Layak with a short laugh. 'Perhaps you were blind to it. Erebus thought that guile was needed on occasion, but I have hidden nothing from you. All power comes at a price.'

The captain of the World Eaters was almost at the line of Imperial Fists, running ahead of his brothers by twenty metres, uncaring of the bolter fire that turned towards him. Thirty Imperial Fists converged on him, shields coming together like a thunderclap. Five metres from them, Khârn leapt, turning salmon-like in mid-air as he passed over them, *Gorechild* taking the heads from two before he landed. The champion of the Blood God did not stop to attack the shield wall from behind, leaving his followers to crash against it in a welter of chain weapons and blazing power axes. Instead he pushed on, heading for the next line of Imperial Fists, where Abaddon saw a large banner flying, carrying the crests of the Legion and their First Captain, Sigismund.

'He'll be surrounded and cut down, no matter how much the forces of the warp grant him power,' said Abaddon.

'What do you care?' crowed Layak. 'It is the will of the gods!'

Abaddon gave no reply, but the sorcerer's words spurred him. He owed Layak no explanation and doubted the Word Bearer would understand anything of fraternity, of the bond between battle-brothers stronger than loyalty to distant gods and nebulous powers.

He broke into a run. His warriors followed without hesitation.

Khârn thought himself powerful but in fact all he was offering up was his own life. Abaddon would fight to save him that sacrifice, if only for another day. To allow otherwise, to stand by while the gods turned a great warrior of the Legions into their puppet, was to start along a winding path that led back to the Warmaster, and raised questions Abaddon was not yet willing to ask of himself.

THIRTY

The Custodians attack
Faith sustains
Sigismund's test

Unknown

It was impossible to tell where the leaves ended and the storm began. The crown of the tree was a blend of fire and lightning, the flicker of its conflict reflected in the thick chains that wrapped about its great trunk, golden vines biting into valley-sized ridges in the bark.

Keeler felt impotent, blown about on hurricane gusts that emanated from the battle in the heavens. She yearned to spear upwards into the roiling blackness of the Chaos cloud, to become a bright thunderbolt of the Emperor's wrath.

The memory of burning the half-born brought back the intoxicating sense of power that possessed her when she became a vessel of the Emperor. She trembled at the recollection, aquiver at the thought of the Emperor's spirit passing through her again.

For all she tried to channel that power, it remained as elusive as the lightning bolts that rained down on the upper limbs of the god-tree.

Circling as close as she could, blinded at times by the ferocity of the sky war, Keeler tried to latch on to the faith of the Lightbearers around her mortal body. She could hear the sermon of Olivier, and beyond his words the distant, slow pulsing of souls from ten thousand witnesses.

It was as though she tried to grasp fog. The faith bubbled and flowed through her spiritual grip, refusing to be ignited by her passion. It whirled from touch like a magnet presented with its opposite pole, always just out of reach.

The mist in her thoughts manifested about the arcing roots of the tree, seeping up from cracks in the arid ground. Keeler had not noticed before how parched the landscape had become. Nothing was left of the fecund wilderness, the earth drained of its vitality.

Where the fog touched the tree it left smears of colour, patches of brightly sprouting fungus. They matured rapidly, filling the air with spores, and the spores became flies, buzzing about the cracks in the bole, eager to lay eggs into the sap of the god-tree.

Screaming tore Keeler from her reverie. Her thoughts flooded back to the real world, her senses confronted with panicked shouts, the roar of plasma jets and buzz of rotary cannons.

To the west a golden gun-cutter soared over the tall arch that denoted the end of the processional, wing cannons spitting tracer rounds into the packed column of pilgrims. Keeler retched as she saw a line of Lightbearers gunned down, their bodies turned to tatters by the hail of bullets.

From the east a black gunship of the Silent Sisterhood appeared, the sky about it churning with strange energy, flickering with black and purple. To look upon it made Keeler sick, her vision swimming dizzyingly as she tried to watch the approaching craft.

'Custodians!' gasped Sindermann, who was at her shoulder,

his hand tight on her arm to pull her away. She refused, standing her ground.

'Wait!' she called to Olivier as he turned to run. The single word stopped him and he turned. 'This is a test of faith.'

He took another half-step, conflicted. Keeler held out a hand. 'Trust me,' she said. 'Trust in the Emperor.'

Olivier glanced over his shoulder at the gold-armoured figures advancing on the crowd from several directions. Keeler could guess his thoughts – that the officers of the Emperor should turn their guns upon them.

'Share your faith with me,' she urged him, extending her hand again. 'Show your followers the path of righteousness.'

He seized hold of her hand, grip almost painfully tight. The contact was like a shock of electricity, jolting up her arm.

Sindermann slipped his hand into her other, and she felt another surge of power. When others on the platform joined her, Keeler felt the pulse of their faith pushing outwards.

Some in the crowd, which was surging back and forth between panic and anger, saw the unity of their leaders and copied them, joining hands. Though separated by several hundred metres, it was as if they were next to Keeler, adding their prayers to hers. She felt light-headed, as though the ground dropped away.

The further she reached out with her faith, the greater the strength that flowed back to her. Her calmness multiplied, propagated through the crowd by a ripple of awed silence as worshipper after worshipper turned away from the attacks and towards the fulcrum of their belief.

It was then that Keeler saw the light of the Emperor shining from the congregation, spreading like a dawn from person to person. As it stretched further down the processional, she saw bolt-rounds sparking from the gleam, as though a power field had been switched on. The holy ambiance pushed further, forcing the gunship high, its rocket salvos exploding prematurely in thin air.

'Have faith, brothers and sisters!' she called, her voice echoing like thunder.

They were joined as one; she was the tree and her faith was the roots. As the water and sun nourished the tree, so the prayers and souls of the faithful gave her strength.

Keeler felt a small pinprick of cold in her consciousness and turned to see a golden warrior ascending the stairs to the platform. He strode with purpose but without undue haste, guardian spear in one hand rather than at the ready in both. Though he wore his helm, she knew it had to be Amon.

Amon advanced through the swarm of flies around the platform as though passing through a black curtain. They crawled over his armour and visor, almost obscuring the handful of figures beyond. A glance down to the processional confirmed that the cloud that had enveloped the congregation was thickening still, blotched with patches of darkness that seemed to assume humanoid shape before flowing back into formlessness. He heard the reports of the Custodians, their weapons still unable to penetrate the miasma that shrouded the Lightbearers, while the processional itself was like a mire, immobilising any warrior that tried to set foot upon it. Even the Sisters of Silence were unable to penetrate the fog bank, warning that it was not wholly psychic in nature, something they had not encountered before.

'Keeler!' he called out. She had a strange half-smile as she turned fully to him, still holding hands with Olivier and Sindermann. 'You have to end this madness.'

'Madness? I see only the faithful protecting themselves.'

Amon knew better than to argue. The daemonic presence had cloaked itself in a garb of righteousness before. Whatever

Keeler and the other Lightbearers witnessed was not the reality he observed. As much as he had vowed to execute Keeler if she had proven to be the font of the incursions, now that he confronted her he saw that he would need to find another way. Energy crackled across the platform, the flies coating everything with furred black bodies, the buzzing drone enough to drive a listener insane. He was not sure if killing her would release the full power of the Neverborn or end it, or even if he would be able to land a fatal blow within the miasma that protected the 'faithful'.

'Why do you turn on your own, Custodian?' Keeler demanded, her smile turning to a frown. Black lightning crawled across her skin but she seemed oblivious to it. 'Why do you murder the faithful?'

'It is a lie,' he told her. 'Your faith has been perverted. The Life within Death is not the Emperor. The Breath on your Lips is not the Emperor. The Hope in your Heart is not the Emperor.'

'What would you know of it?'

'Listen to me. I have stood at the Emperor's side for a lifetime. I have fought His wars and nearly died a score of times in His service. You are being corrupted, just like the soldiers in the hospital.'

'We are the righteous!'

Amon glanced into the miasma below. The shadow within moved like a shark through water, gliding between the immobile faithful, solidifying for a few seconds before dissipating. Each time it darkened it seemed to do so for longer. Its power was growing.

'Will you kill us all?' she asked. As she spoke, black vapour issued from her mouth, falling like smoke from parting lips.

If I could, Amon thought.

'You must see the truth for what it is.' He took a few paces closer, beetle shells crunching underfoot, flies batting against his armour with each step. 'If you believe the Emperor is a god, then pray to Him to let you see what is truly happening.'

'You do not believe.' Keeler shook her head, but he could see uncertainty creeping into her expression. 'Your words mock my faith.'

'You are right, it is not my faith. It is yours. Claim it. Confront it.' He dropped his voice low. 'Look with your faith, Euphrati.'

Unknown

Hearing her name spoken by the golden giant sent an eddy of chillness through Keeler, like the draught from a window briefly opened. The golden giant was almost invisible among the haze of the faithful, a looming shade in the brightness. His voice seemed like the boom of distant waves on a shore, powerful and incessant, but it was only her name that she really heard.

The words that had preceded it filtered through the throbbing of her blood, a command to look with her faith.

Not a command. A… plea? A prayer, almost, from the lips of a Custodian.

Faith.

What was her faith?

That the Emperor was a god?

It was more than that. The *Lectitio Divinitatus* had shaped that belief, but it was not the foundation of her faith. In being confronted by the immortal nature of the true enemy she had looked upon a universe as removed from humanity as the void was separated from the depths of the oceans. And she had turned to the Emperor.

With the faith that whatever He was, the Emperor was the Master of Mankind; not just humanity's ruler but also its guide.

That same Will had shaped the Custodians, and now Euphrati Keeler heard her name uttered by one of them, asking her to look with faith.

He could not know what she meant when she talked of faith – such devotion to an abstract was written out of his personality. Instead he had appealed to *her* sense of faith.

The tree.

The instant her mind turned to it, she closed her eyes, seeking to look upon its shining boughs as she had the first time she had walked into the garden of the Emperor.

The garden was there again, the parched plains replaced with a sprawling, verdant landscape. But this was not the garden she had wandered in with such pleasure. The sky was dark, the ground a mire underfoot, where thorny tendrils clasped at her feet and ankles. Gases bubbled from the marsh, and flies buzzed over flowers that stank of corpse-rot.

In desperation she looked for her tree, scratching arms and legs as she burst through bushes of black roses and scrambled down bramble-choked dells.

She saw the faintest glimmer of gold beyond the ridgeline ahead, the hill crowned with forbidding forests.

It was not to run that she had come here, but to fly. With a last effort she propelled herself into the skies, as pustule-like growths erupted from the mulch and belched forth clouds of hideous wasps behind her.

They pursued Keeler but the swiftness of her faith was greater, taking her high into the air where the clouds felt like cold oil on her flesh, the wind knotting her hair like briar tangles.

Below she saw the Lightbearers. Each was no longer a shining lamp but a marsh-flame, burning the decay of centuries that burbled from the underbelly of the world. Ghostly eels prowled amongst them, pale-flanked bodies moving in sinuous waves between the small hillocks of bone and flesh.

Sickened, she turned her gaze back to the tree, seeing weeping sores upon the bark, streams of black-threaded sap pouring from burrow holes.

As before she longed to ascend to the branches, where dark clouds hung like creepers among the dying leaves. Instinct told her to look down, right to the base of the great tree where the roots pushed hard into the earth. That was where she had felt the faith lifting her, feeding her from the roots, and that was the strength of the Emperor too.

She dived, heedless of the wet ground rushing up to meet her. Mouth closed, she plunged into the murky waters that drowned the tree's roots, feeling coldness on her skin, thick ooze pushing into ears and nostrils, eyes closed tight.

Keeler thrashed into the sucking mud, trying to force herself deeper and deeper, feeling her heart hammering as her breath grew short.

She forced her eyes open, straining in the filth, hands groping in front of her, following the root trails deep into the ground, far from light and air.

Faith.

Faith exists to be tested.

She recalled the line from the *Book of Divinity*.

Faith sustains when all else is lost.

Keeler grasped the root tendril ahead of her and used it like a rope, pulling herself further and further from salvation, letting its roughness between her fingers guide her when all other senses were blinded and numb.

Her hand came upon something slick, her fingers sinking into a slug-like growth. Her questing revealed it to be one appendage of a much greater entity coiled deep in the mud, sucking the life from the tree.

Here was the source of the rot.

She could not fight it here, but seized the rubbery limb in

both hands, turning to ascend through the murk. Something far below, something ancient and vast, bucked and resisted, but she gritted her teeth, the rancid muck dribbling into her mouth, threatening to choke her.

With all her strength she started to pull, dragging the creature away from the tree roots, kicking her way back towards the light.

Lion's Gate space port, interstitial bridges,
twenty-two days since assault

Sigismund watched the crimson-armoured figure arc above the shield wall of his brethren, incredulous that such a jump could be made. His belief was stretched further as he watched Khârn running straight at him.

'Shall we gun him down, captain?' asked Eghrlich, lifting his plasma gun.

'No, save your fire for them,' replied Sigismund, raising his sword towards the Sons of Horus and Iron Warriors that swept forward in the wake of the World Eaters' headlong charge. He saw the bulk of a Terminator suit among the Warmaster's gene-sons and recognised the markings of Ezekyle Abaddon. 'When I am done with Khârn I will cut off the right hand of Horus.'

The World Eater did not slow in his approach but swept up the dragon-toothed axe over his shoulder. A crude, slow move that Sigismund would easily counter as he moved forward to meet Khârn's charge.

Spinning teeth smashed against the edge of the Templar's sword with a force he had not reckoned for. The strength of the blow jarred Dorn's son mid-stride, knocking him off balance. Taken aback, Sigismund spun, dodging the next blow while he assessed his options. Khârn gave him no time at all, rushing like a bull with a wordless bellow.

Khârn's axe rang against the sword, swept away and lashed back again. He was breathing hard, a fog jetting from the vents of his helm, swathing them both in a ruddy mist as dusk light pushed through the cloud cover below them. Sigismund took one step backwards, deflecting each blow as it came. Khârn pulled away, growled, and hammered in again.

Now expecting the greater strength of his foe, Sigismund parried with a looser grip, turning aside with timing rather than meeting force with force.

'I have your measure, as always,' he told the traitor. 'This time there is no cage.'

He swerved away from the next strike, letting the tip of his blade lash out towards Khârn's chest. It carved a furrow through the dried blood and ceramite, leaving steaming, ruddy swirls in its wake.

'Still… Hnnh. Still chained to your duty, I see,' Khârn snorted, shoulders heaving with effort as he stepped back. *Gorechild*'s head weaved a figure of eight, as though moving with a life of its own while Khârn stepped to the left, seeking an opening.

'Better duty than the emptiness of self-service.' Sigismund stepped and thrust hard, but *Gorechild* flashed down to meet the attack with stunning speed and impact, sending the Templar staggering away.

'You are weak. Duty isn't purpose, Sigismund.' Khârn flexed his fingers on the haft of his chainaxe, moving from side to side on the balls of his feet. 'Your lord is empty. He cares nothing for your blood.'

Sigismund attacked again, lancing his sword towards Khârn's groin. The haft of *Gorechild* met it, but Sigismund had been relying on the parry, having seen Khârn employ it many times before in the World Eaters' duelling cage.

'Enough talk,' he spat as he turned, swinging the sword in a wide arc, the blade crashing against the World Eater's pauldron. He rained down another blow against his foe's chest, seeking to keep him off balance.

Khârn pushed into the attack rather than retreating, so that the blade edge struck his helm a glancing blow. *Gorechild* screamed as it slashed into Sigismund's arm and juddered down his vambrace to shatter the chain binding the Templar's sword to his wrist.

'Jubal was right. Hnnh. You are better without them.'

It was a fool's move, a gesture that left Khârn open to a deadly attack. Sigismund cared nothing for ceremony, hacking doublehanded towards his enemy's gut. The blade bit deep, searing into armour and flesh. Blood spilled as he ripped it free.

He swung again, blade meeting axe overhead. Sigismund braced, trying to turn aside his enemy's weapon. With a deafening bellow, Khârn flexed, thrusting Sigismund back with raw strength.

Stumbling, almost falling to one knee, Sigismund saw the seams of Khârn's armour parting, splitting where plate met plate. Slabs of muscle bulged beneath, unnaturally swollen even for a Space Marine, veins as thick as power cables taut beneath thick skin.

'I serve a power greater than yours,' Khârn roared, lifting up *Gorechild*, sunlight sparkling from its mica-dragon tooth blades. Flecks of the Templar's blood showered down upon him. 'You are hollow, Sigismund. Hnnh. You'll never beat me again.'

Sigismund dived aside, too late to fully avoid the blow. Dragon's teeth caught his left thigh, ripping chunks from power armour and genhanced muscle.

In that moment Sigismund understood Keeler's words and knew that he was beaten. As legionaries there were none among the traitors that could match him. The Legions' greatest had always been his inferiors. Corswain of the Dark Angels. Jubal of the White Scars. Khârn of the World Eaters. Sevatar of the Night Lords. Lucius of the Emperor's Children. Abaddon of the Luna Wolves.

But as he looked at the warped figure that had once been his sword-companion, he knew that he no longer fought legionaries. He had to be more too, something pure to match their vileness. To draw strength from a power beyond himself.

The Emperor.

If only he had heeded the lesson earlier, learned its full meaning.

A shadow covered them both for an instant before a flare of weapons and plasma jets lit the fog. Missiles scythed down while lascannons spat sparkling beams of death. Khârn looked up and the Templar spared a glance to recognise the shape of *Aetos Dias*, the personal gunship of the Praetorian.

The nose opened and from the assault ramp appeared a large armoured figure. It fell through the smoke, glinting gold, and slammed into the ferrocrete a few metres from Sigismund and Khârn. A giant clad in the same auric-adamant of the Emperor Himself, bearing a two-handed chainsword as tall as a legionary. In the flash of gunfire Sigismund looked upon the face of his genefather, nostrils flaring, teeth bared. Dorn's eyes were not on him, but fixed upon the wider battle.

Bellowing, Khârn hurled himself at the primarch. Dorn swung *Storm's Teeth* to meet the captain, the force of the blow throwing Khârn a dozen metres through the air. Dorn spared not a second glance as warriors clad in Terminator armour materialised around him, sent from the teleportaria deep within the bastion of the Lion's Gate.

At the same moment, the Imperial Fists' shield wall broke, a spearhead of Sons of Horus and Iron Warriors crashing through amid bolter volleys and gleaming powerblades. Sigismund tried to stand but his wounded leg gave way, cut to the bone.

Dorn's gunship landed and more Imperial Fists swept forward around their lord, the white of an Apothecary among them heading for the Templar. He lost sight of Khârn beyond the erupting melee, an instant before hands grabbed his pauldrons and dragged him towards the Thunderhawk.

Sigismund's thigh was agony, but it was nothing compared to the pain of his shame.

THIRTY-ONE

Keeler confronts the taint
Manifestations of false hope
Layak's destiny

Unknown

Gaining speed, Keeler focused her thoughts on the branches of the great tree, imagined them in the bright sun as she clambered up through the labyrinth of roots. The parasitic worm thrashed in her grip, mewling and shrieking, occasionally falling silent when promises of everlasting life and eternal hope whispered in her thoughts.

She realised that in her haste she had lost herself amidst the tangle, suffocating and blinded by the putrescent mulch that ebbed around the roots. She had no sense of up and down, only the tug of the creature away from her offering any feeling of direction at all.

She continued on until another passage from the *Lectitio Divinitatus* came to mind.

Faith should not be blind. Faith is not ignorance, but acceptance. Faith should always be measured, and directed, and serve the purpose of the Emperor not the faithful.

How was she to find direction in the lightless morass? If faith alone could not buoy her up, how was she to ascend to the light again? She fought back a surge of panic, during which the creature's whispering grew in vehemence, offering her a lifetime of certainty and purpose if only she followed it back into the depths.

Rather than succumb to despair, she forged on, but stopped shortly after, second-guessing herself. She had been fooled once by the Hope in her Heart; was it possible that it was trying to mislead her now? What if it was pulling towards the surface, trying to trick her into plunging deeper into the darkness?

Doubt assailed her, bringing weakness to her grip, so that she almost let go of the slick tendril in her fist. It had been so long since she had taken a breath but she dared not open her mouth. The thought of the malignant ooze around her slipping into her throat, infecting her lungs, caused a flurry of terror. Sensing her weakness, the worm-creature thrashed hard, forcing her to reach out a hand to seize a root to brace herself.

Her fingers closed not around the rough texture of wood, but something smooth, and cool.

Metal.

Gold.

She could not see it but she sensed it. Her exploring fingers identified the link, slender here, but as she pulled herself up a short way the chain grew stronger and thicker.

Chains of faith.

Keeler was confused. She had thought the chains were some kind of prison, an artifice of the enemy ensnaring the Emperor. Yet her faith had brought her to them, and through them she climbed, growing in courage again. One arm wrapped about the squirming entity, she heaved with the other.

After an eternity, her head broke through a layer of rotted leaves and broken carcasses. She opened her mouth and took in a long draught of air. It was tainted by decay but tasted as sweet as nectar after her confinement in the bog.

Grunting, giving vent to her frustration and effort, she pulled an arm free, clinging to one of the massive chains that stretched up into the branches. Finally, she saw the letters inscribed on the chain and she let out a short laugh.

Kyril Sindermann.

It was his faith that had saved her.

Though it was a mighty limb, the bough from which the chain hung bent under her weight, the tree swaying ever so slightly as she used the links to pull herself out to her waist.

She realised that each time she pulled herself up, she also dragged down part of the tree.

Basilica Ventura, western processional,
twenty-two days since assault

The fly swarm had thinned around Amon, though hundreds of the loathsome insects clustered around Keeler, encasing her in a writhing coat of darkness. She seemed oblivious and immobile, though one hand dropped away from Olivier's, the other still clung tightly to Sindermann, who stared vacantly ahead. In the periphery of his vision Amon also saw the miasma dissipating, seeping into the thousands of worshippers gathered around the platform. Their skin greyed and their eyes rolled up as the cursed fog entered them, jaws lolling open, trails of saliva falling from slack lips.

More than a century of warfare had honed Amon's instincts to the sharpest edge. So it was that he brought his guardian spear to readiness a fraction of a second before Olivier leapt at him. The Lightbearer's eyes had also rolled back, black tears falling from the ducts to coat his cheeks in oily grime. He had no weapon, his lunge met by the tip of the guardian spear, which split his shoulder open, his left arm flopping to the metal decking of the stage even as Amon sidestepped to let his attacker flail past.

The blood that gushed from the injury bubbled with something unnatural, so that it hissed and spat as it hit the platform. Olivier stumbled and turned, not the least afflicted by the wound.

Amon fired, three bolts direct to the tainted man's face, tearing apart the skull and brain. The body toppled, lifeless.

The two book-bearers came next, gurgling through mouths filled with sickly yellow mucus, the same black tears dripping from their eyes, pustules erupting around their nostrils and on the backs of their hands.

His guardian spear whipped out, beheading the first. Amon stepped close, ramming his fingers into the throat of the other, snapping the neck. The woman slapped her hands against his armour, sustained beyond the breaking of her spine. Amon tore the head completely free and kicked the twisting body away.

He ran to the edge of the platform. Many of the crowd were surging up the steps towards him. The chatter of bolter fire announced that the protective field had failed – or been withdrawn – and that his companions were assailed in a similar manner. The snarl of rotary cannons split the background din of the bombardment, joined by the noise of plasma engines as the Custodian cutter renewed its attack run down the processional. The Sisters of Silence had disembarked from their gunship at the far end of the route. Muzzle flare marked their slow progress into the horde of aimless worshippers.

The stage was flanked by two sets of steps, each three flights high. Amon could not defend both: to stand at the top of one would be to expose his back to the other.

He looked at Keeler. She was still entombed within a

sarcophagus of flies, only her hand where it held Sindermann's visible among the welter of buzzing wings and furred bodies.

He could not abandon her, either.

Amon levelled his guardian spear and took up a wide stance just in front of Keeler. The metal steps creaked as scores of tainted Lightbearers raced up them, pants and moans growing louder as they ascended.

The first group appeared to his left. He leapt across the distance between to meet them with his spear, three slashes taking down the first handful. Spinning, he fired across to the other steps, stitching explosions across the bodies of four more. He cut down another half a dozen before breaking away, dashing past Keeler to bring the tip of his spear down through the skull of another.

He fired, emptying the spear's remaining ammunition in a series of controlled bursts, aiming high into the crowd pouring up the left-hand steps.

There was no attendant to reload for him, but he managed to swap out the magazine with a second to spare before they came upon him from the right. The bolter attachment roared, turning the head of the closest half-born to a bloody mess.

Nineteen more shots, and then he would be down to his blade alone.

Lion's Gate space port, interstitial bridges,
twenty-two days since assault

Abaddon's experiences of late had somewhat inured him to the presence of primarchs, but he still felt a primal shiver of response to the sight of Rogal Dorn carving his way through the Warmaster's forces like a golden blade. Bolts and blades struck his armour without effect while great sweeps of his chainsword dismembered and decapitated legionary after legionary, leaving a trail of bloodied armour plates and broken corpses in the primarch's wake.

What had been a victorious final charge to drive the Imperial Fists from the space port faltered in the face of the Emperor's son. Across the bridges, companies slowed in the advance, baulked by the prospect of facing Dorn's wrath, waylaid by the reinforcements that he had brought with him.

Abaddon slowed, his remaining warriors taking station around him, weapons raised towards the incoming giant. He had expected he would have to face one of the Emperor's greatest sons before the war was over, but the prospect was far from thrilling.

'It is not your time.' Layak continued onwards, his blade slaves flanking him, a halo of power writhing about the tip of his staff. 'I see now that this moment was ordained for me long ago. Remember that the gods always demand a price, but if you are willing to pay, their power is yours to command.'

The urge that had drawn Abaddon to push forwards in support of Khârn did not surface for Zardu Layak. The lord of the Mournival watched with detached interest as the priest conjured a gleaming hemisphere of power about himself and advanced several dozen metres to take up position between the oncoming primarch and the Warmaster's First Captain.

He felt no brotherhood with the creature Layak had become, any more than he did the Neverborn that wore Grael Noctua's skin or cloaked itself in the guise of the Word Bearers' *vakrah jal*. Not that Layak was no longer human, but his motives had long since departed any mortal concern. He was wholly a creature of Chaos, and as such served only the gods' ends, not those of any other around him.

Layak's blade slaves dashed forward to confront Rogal Dorn, whose unstoppable advance had carried him a hundred metres ahead of his gene-sons. It was clear his intent was not to support the legionaries, but to pursue a more personal mission.

Wickedly serrated blades lashed at the arms and legs of the primarch as the two blade slaves attacked in unison, dodging the churning blades of *Storm's Teeth*. The air about the sorcerer churned with power, but Abaddon could see the faint shimmer of Neverborn struggling to manifest. The Emperor's shield was still protecting the port; no daemon could answer the Word Bearer's summons.

Loosening the grip of one hand, Dorn swung a hammer-like fist, crushing the skull of a blade slave. It fought on for several more seconds, jerky and weak, until it fell backwards and thrashed upon the floor for a few heartbeats more. The second drew back, putting itself between the primarch and its master.

Abaddon could feel a hot wind rushing over him, emanating from the sorcerer. It was strange, a sensation felt through his Terminator plate, not of the physical realm. His skin prickled at the sensation and his gut crawled at its touch, even as he saw the shapes of the Neverborn growing more substantial.

Had Layak known this? Could he sense the thinning of the Emperor's protection?

Abaddon's armour snarled as he took a step forward. He checked himself. To be cut down by Dorn was pointless. Perturabo was on his way, a primarch to counter a primarch.

Dorn drew a bolter, chased with gold and styled with the Imperial aquila, like a pistol in his hand. He fired at Layak even as his chainsword sought the blade slave, bolts exploding against the warp shield of the sorcerer, *Storm's Teeth* carving a furrow through ferrocrete where the blade slave had been half a second before.

Then Dorn was upon the priest, ignoring the blade slave to crash his weapon thrice against the dome of power that guarded Layak. The sorcerer responded, wrapping himself in scarlet lightning before unleashing it from the tip of his staff, the bolt sending Dorn back three steps.

Snakes of dissipating energy crawled over the primarch, flicking between armour and the blades of the slave creature as it leapt to the attack once more, sleeve-swords aimed for Dorn's midriff.

The primarch drove the hilt of his chainblade down, slamming the pommel into the neck and shoulder of the slave. Spine snapped, the Neverborn-infused carcass flopped like a netted fish, spasming across the ferrocrete ahead of a trail of blood and dark ichor.

If Abaddon was to strike it had to be now. Dorn would be upon Layak in moments.

The vox crackled and Layak's voice hissed into his ear.

'I give up my life not for you, mortal soul, but for the glory of Chaos that you will come to serve.'

Gathering more Chaos power, Layak let his shield collapse, the energy of the dome whirling into his staff head, becoming a burning black flame. He swung with sword and staff together, both trailing sorcerous fire to crash against the golden armour of the Emperor's Praetorian. A storm of power exploded from the contact, once more forcing the primarch back, arm raised across his face as sable flames engulfed him.

Again Layak attacked, this time to strike the ground at Dorn's feet. His voice rose in unintelligible supplication, a screeched prayer to the gods of the warp. Ferrocrete exploded upwards, becoming claws that snatched at the primarch's limbs. Dorn fended them off with swings of his chainsword, spinning teeth chewing through the animated surface in a shower of sparks and stone.

Still the air about the sorcerer writhed faster, Neverborn flitting into and out of existence, half-glimpsed by Abaddon as his gaze moved between the duel with Dorn and the wider battle.

Dorn's arrival had bolstered the defence, but he had not brought sufficient reinforcements with him to retake the terminals. Khârn had resumed his rampage further along the main bridge while Iron Warriors companies led by Kroeger, seeing Dorn engaged, forged ahead across flanking viaducts and monorail tracks. Dreadnoughts crashed like battering rams into the last ranks of the Imperial Fists, met by cannonades from tanks arrayed along the approaches to the main bastion.

Higher burned the immortal flames that wreathed Layak, so dark they swallowed light yet edged with a power that was blinding in its intensity. A third sorcerous detonation rocked the primarch, but Abaddon could see that such conjurations were not given freely. Layak's armour was peeling away like skin flaking from charred flesh, carried away on the thermals of warp energy that he channelled through his body. Revealed skin was ancient like wrinkled parchment, yellowing and thin, devoid of the muscle one expected of a warrior from the Legiones Astartes, little more than withered bone.

There was another form around the sorcerer, far larger but less distinct: a winged mind-shadow that matched Dorn in height, but far broader of shoulder, and possessed of arms like writhing tentacles.

Abaddon wondered if this was the true form of Layak or some Neverborn brought to his summoning. Whichever, the daemon struggled to manifest as did any other, sometimes seemingly whole and flesh, other times nothing more than a sketch of vaporous movement.

Dorn advanced with purpose, hanging his bolter upon his belt to take up his chainblade in both hands once more. Layak was almost unmoving before him, flares of warp power spitting from his amorphous, shifting silhouette. The Praetorian ignored the sparks as they scythed across his armour, bringing back *Storm's Teeth* for a blow.

'Remember this moment, Abaddon. I give my life so that you will take my place upon the path to glory.'

The chainsword fell, cleaving through apparition and physical body alike. Flames and blood were as one, showering from the churning teeth as they slashed down through horned head and armour.

What was left of Layak detonated with a burst of multicoloured light. Abaddon had never seen a primarch tossed aside like a child's toy before, and felt the psychic shock wave wash over him like a hurricane across his nerves.

Abaddon's vision blurred and for an instant he thought he saw a great tree, its leafless branches ablaze with dark flames. The fires crawled down its trunk, burning down to the roots.

The crash of heavy war-plate drew him back. Dorn had landed a score of metres away and lay unmoving, coils of oily smoke drifting from the joints of his armour. Dozens of Imperial Fists sprinted towards him, voices raised in despair.

Of Layak all that remained was a rune-marked crater in the ferrocrete, its metres-deep sides glowing with power from sigils burnt into the material.

From the ripples of flame left in the bottom of the hole, a clawed hand appeared, red-scaled and taloned. An arm followed as a Neverborn pulled itself through the breach, struggling like an obscene chick from an egg, dripping with the life fluid of the sorcerer. It was not much larger than a human, spindly of limb and possessed of a long, bulbous head with dead white eyes and curling horns. A belt of skulls hung about its waist and a triangular-bladed sword of dark grey gleamed in its fist.

It pulled itself out fully and stood upon the stone of the Imperial Palace, the first true daemon to set foot upon Terra.

Beyond, Dorn rose to one knee amid a creaking of armour, hand still gripping the hilt of his chainsword.

A second daemon emerged from the ruin of Layak, baring needle-teeth, forked tongue tasting the sweet air of this forbidden world.

Yet it was not the daemons that drew the eye of Dorn: his head was tilted back, looking up to the darkening skies. Abaddon turned slightly to follow his gaze and saw the blue plasma jets of a gunship falling through the murk, dark against the continuing muzzle flare of cannons higher up the flanks of the space port.

As it approached, Abaddon saw the colours of the Iron Warriors, with the IV Legion's symbol embossed in gold upon its prow. Legionaries scattered as it landed behind the Warmaster's captain, front ramp whining open even before the landing gear touched down.

From the ruddy interior advanced six automatons, striding in perfect unison, weapons trained outwards as they formed a half-ring around the front of the gunship.

With thunderous tread on the metal ramp, the Lord of Iron followed, his immense hammer in hand.

THIRTY-TWO

Cor'bax Utterblight
Faith prevails
Two brothers meet

Basilica Ventura, western processional,
twenty-two days since assault

More than forty half-born had fallen to Amon's blade yet they thronged around the platform in even greater number. The pile of corpses acted as a barrier of sorts, forcing them to come at him in ones and twos as they pushed past the mounds or crawled over the dead. Keeler stood behind him with Sindermann, neither of them moving.

His guardian spear was slicked with blood and other fluids, affecting his grip. He could fight for hours more if needed, but soon the whole platform would be choked with the dead. His footing would be uncertain, and he would have no room to swing his blade properly. Long before he tired in mind or body he would be overwhelmed by the sheer weight of his foes.

He signalled the Zenith gunship.

'Raptorae Sextus, I need support run on my position.'

'*Unable to locate you, Amon. Too dangerous to fire in your vicinity. Set transponder to maximum broadcast.*'

'I am at maximum!' Amon chopped the head from a tainted woman and calmed himself. 'Attack runs on the platform steps. Cut off the flow to my position.'

'*Understood, Amon. Inbound in thirty seconds.*'

Amon sensed movement behind him, coming from Keeler. He took a narrow grip on his spear haft and swung wide, slashing its tip across a handful of foes in a single arc. In the precious seconds between their bodies tumbling and fresh foes replacing them, he glanced back.

The fly swarm that had surrounded Keeler was breaking apart, becoming individual insects that drifted up like motes on the thermals of a fire. The spread of their disintegration rapidly increased, becoming a whirling vortex streaming upwards and revealing Keeler beneath. Her head was tilted back, mouth agape, and from it issued a dark smoke that followed the swarm, adding to the unnatural maelstrom that twisted higher and higher.

The half-born foundered, tumbling into each other, tripping on bodies. Like sleepers waking from long slumber they blinked and gazed numbly at their surroundings. Some slipped in the viscera spilled on the platform, crying out in horror.

The fly-funnel merged with the smoke, forming the body of an immense wormlike creature with a yawning maw at one end, arching over the platform. It passed a few metres above Amon's head, bending down towards the processional.

Keeler gasped and fell to her knees, pulling Sindermann down with her. Moans and grunts from those that had moments before been tainted by the Neverborn presence betrayed that they were free of its grasp. Amon saw intelligence in their eyes – fear and shock as they gazed at the golden warrior in their midst.

The tail of the smoke worm detached from Keeler and it

flopped to the ground, becoming more solid as it did so. Flies churned in the interior, becoming pulsing muscle, while the smoke rippled like grey-green skin over the forming mass.

Amon realised that the Zenith was still on its attack run.

'Raptorae Sextus, abo–'

The ripple of rotary cannons cut off his transmission as the golden attack ship swept over at cruising speed, wing cannons chewing furrows through the people milling on the steps.

'Abort! Abort!' Amon transmitted. 'Target the creature!'

The worm-beast reared up, a tendril-ringed mouth lunging towards the gunship. Glinting teeth sank into a wing, and the daemon-thing wrestled against the thrust of the engines. The gunship's structural integrity gave way before either beast or jet, the wing tearing away. The gunship spun crazily for several seconds, spiralling down until it crashed into the crowd on the processional.

The worm-beast continued to change, becoming smaller and obesely humanoid. Its mouth widened and limbs sprawled from its sides, while horns like shattered tree limbs extruded from its mucus-sheathed flesh. Its gut billowed in folds like a cloud, wart-ridden skin turning to patchy green and grey.

Amon raced to the edge of the platform as it started to feed, massive jaws engulfing two or three people at a time. Its body rippled as it gulped them down, swelling with power as it devoured them. Many were still in numb shock, easy prey for the bloated monstrosity, mindless of the ravening daemon. Its hands became jaws, snapping up even more victims, shovelling their mangled corpses into its distended gullet.

Three Custodians emerged from the downed cutter, spears cracking bolts at the abomination. They detonated harmlessly across skin thick with scabs and patches of lichen-like growths. A fang-limb swept out, picking up one of the Custodians, auramite shrieking as impossibly strong jaws crushed his armour. His companions set about the arm with their spears, hacking hunks of flesh away, ichor spilling from the wound. Where it fell, the fluid of the daemon formed into small, rotund creatures that cackled and pointed at the futile attempts of the Custodians.

Amon was about to leap down when he heard footfalls behind him. Keeler approached, leaning heavily on Sindermann. She looked down at the monstrosity without saying anything, her chest heaving as though from great effort.

The daemon had grown again, the size of a gunship now. It plunged forward, trampling another of the Custodians beneath its bulk. The worshippers were still recovering from their mass possession, and screams echoed back from the high buildings. Panic spread outwards like a ripple, terrified Lightbearers stampeding over each other as they fled.

Amon's auto-senses activated as a blinding flash filled the broad roadway. Through the filter of his helm, the Custodian saw a figure emerge from one of the doorways opposite. Light as bright as a star almost obscured the person completely, an indistinct silhouette at the heart of the blaze.

His auto-senses adjusted, Amon saw a man swathed in a voluminous robe, a staff in hand.

Malcador.

The Regent swept out his staff and the nimbus of light became a flurry of burning bolts, siphoned through the staff's head to fly across the processional. Each impact sent the daemon reeling, slipping and squirming across the ferrocrete, a trail of slime left in its wake. Eyes bubbled up from the frothy trail, tentacles stretching out of the murk. Blue flame leapt from where the bolts struck home, igniting immaterial flesh, feeding on its corrupted nature.

The monster flexed, partially turned itself inside out, its incorporeal body extinguishing the flames within fleshy folds.

A new fang-ringed mouth puckered open, widening to its previous immensity. Malcador raised his staff once more, but before he could let loose with another blaze of psychic power, the Neverborn abomination retched out a tide of body parts and filth. Heaving, it projected already rotting carcasses at the Regent, the noisome deluge spraying from a hastily conjured shield of silver energy.

Where the daemon vomit slid to rest, a gang of the smaller creatures gambolled from the bodily ruin, pelting Malcador with handfuls of dripping offal and faeces, forcing him back towards the doorway as disgusting projectiles smeared across his immaterial ward.

'Wait!'

Keeler's injunction came just as Amon tensed to jump down to the processional. She held out her hands towards the daemon, eyes closing. Amon saw nothing physical linking her to the monster but a moment later it reared up as though struck, gurgling madly, tongue lolling as if it were being choked. Keeler pulled her hands and the worm-beast writhed as though on reins, flopping backwards over itself. The daemon slithered back to its two stubby legs, turning a nest of milky eyes up towards its tormentor.

Its guts started rippling in preparation for a fresh torrent of filth.

Beyond, Malcador swept away his diminutive tormentors with a sheet of white fire. Their cackles became shrieks, the popping of their bodies like wet wood in a bonfire, a greasy smoke rising from their demise.

'Wait...' Keeler gritted her teeth, eyes screwed shut, and wrenched her hands again. The huge Neverborn yelped, a startlingly high-pitched noise for its girth, and fell sideways again. Malcador unleashed a flurry of psychic bolts into its thrashing maw, setting fire to its pustule-crusted tongue and gums, teeth melting like iron in a foundry fire.

'Now!'

Amon leapt, guardian spear in both hands.

He fell onto the exposed gut of the creature, the tip of his spear cutting deep through immortal skin and blubber. With all his weight behind it, the spear pushed deep into the daemon's innards and he followed, plunging into a coagulating mass of blood and greenish ichor.

The monster heaved around him, but Amon reversed his grip and thrust upwards from inside the beast's belly, piercing what would have been the brain in any corporeal animal.

He waded through bile, the guardian spear torn from his grasp as the monster bucked, trying to eject him out of its burning mouth. Amon grabbed hold of slime-covered flesh, gauntleted fingertips tearing chunks from its insides.

With a last scream, the daemon exploded, becoming a fountain of gore and mucus that rained down over a hundred metres of the processional, splashing over the buildings in a final tide of filth.

Amon lay among the ruin of its body, slicked from head to toe in viscera and gelatinous waste. Feet slipping on bodily debris, he retrieved his spear, wary lest the daemon reformed in some manner. A few blobs of flesh quivered here and there, but cleansing fire from Malcador's staff turned the remains into a pyre, forcing the Custodians to retreat along the processional.

In the distance the craft of the Silent Sisterhood took off, jets screaming as it accelerated away to the south while gold-and-white armoured figures intercepted the fleeing worshippers.

'There is your faith,' Amon told the Regent.

'We might never know where faith ends and corruption begins,' replied Malcador, leaning heavily on his staff, wisps of fire dancing about his fingertips.

He turned his gaze upwards and Amon followed it. Keeler

stood at the front of the platform, and for several seconds it seemed as though she were bathed in a golden corona of power.

A trick of the light, Amon told himself.

Lion's Gate space port, interstitial bridges,
twenty-two days since assault

A hundred metres of bloodied ferrocrete separated two demi-gods. Created as brothers by the same bio-alchemy yet raised so disparate in temperament. One lauded as the builder, the other as a destroyer, but in skill and aptitude identical. Dorn, the Praetorian of the Emperor, the bastion upon which the Imperium had been built. The Hammer of Olympia, Perturabo, doom of a thousand fortresses.

The Lord of Iron stood *Forgebreaker*'s pommel on the broken stone of the ground, leaning forwards to rest his arms on its wide head.

'Brother.'

All of Perturabo's scorn poured into that one word. His external address carried his voice easily across the distance, while vox-transmit broadcast it across an open channel for all to hear. He had nothing to keep from friend or foe today.

Dorn did not reply.

'Do you wish to discuss terms?'

At this, the Praetorian stiffened, hands moving on the grip of the two-handed chainsword.

'You think me beaten?' The reply drifted back, derision in the tone.

Perturabo cast his gaze about the terminal. His forces were on the advance everywhere he looked. A small cluster of the Blood God's Neverborn had emerged from Layak's remains, ashen swords flashing as they fought with a ring of Imperial Fists Terminators. Red tendrils of power snaked around the crater, forming into more creatures. The daemons appeared unable to venture too far from the portal, but only for the moment. It was a matter of time before more powerful entities manifested and the Neverborn would walk abroad on Terra.

The Emperor's lackeys were in full retreat.

Except here, on the main skybridge, where Dorn had launched his counter-attack.

'I think you are a good enough commander to know when you are outmatched.' Perturabo chuckled at a thought. 'Were you expecting some assistance, perhaps? Some hidden reserves?'

'You have turned lies into a weapon and guile into your shield,' Dorn said. 'Cultists, traitors, warp abominations… These are your allies now. To win with such powers is no victory at all.'

The denial snagged at Perturabo's pride and he straightened, the Iron Circle clattering into attack formation around him.

'No victory? Am I not allowed my alliances, brother? Send away the Khan and the Angel. Will the Custodians and the Silent Sisters stand aside to let us settle this equitably? If I bring a weapon it is only to break a defence you have erected. If you are truly superior, it is time you stepped out of the protective shadow of our father.'

'Is that what you wish?' Dorn brandished his chainsword. 'You and I, blade against hammer?'

The temptation was almost overwhelming. For long years Perturabo had thought of this moment. He had pictured in exquisite detail how he would humble his brother and prove himself the greatest commander in the galaxy.

The vox buzzed, distracting him from the daydream.

'Lord of Iron, the defenders are withdrawing in good order while we delay the pursuit.' With some surprise he recognised the voice

of Forrix, whom he had thought dead in the midst of the space port. *'Dorn is playing for time.'*

'You would like that, wouldn't you, brother?' Perturabo declared, not deigning to respond to his triarch. 'To take the petty road rather than settle this as generals. A brawl in the dirt may suit you, but it is not enough for me.'

'You may brawl, but I am an expert swordsman.'

The barb tugged again, but Perturabo would not be drawn by his brother's insults. He pictured again the vision that had sustained him.

'I will crush you, Dorn. *Forgebreaker* shall shatter your armour and break your bones before we are done. But that proves nothing save my physical superiority. Before I end you, I will lay low everything you have raised. I will topple your towers and shatter your walls. I will deliver the Warmaster to our father, and you will watch everything you have trusted be torn apart.

'When you have nothing left but the rubble of your ambition, and I stand triumphant amid the folly of your inferiority... When all the world's weeping will not save you and all you have is regret for bricks and despair for mortar... When you look at me and know that you were bested by the Lord of Iron and accept the truth of your hubris... *Only then* will my victory be complete and I will end your suffering.'

'Bold words from a man that sent his minions to do his fighting for him.' Dorn stretched out a hand, gesturing to the space port and its surrounds. 'A million souls it has cost you for a few kilometres of ground. You always were wasteful, Perturabo. Lacking finesse.'

'When Terra burns and the Emperor's corpse is ash, we will see the value of finesse!'

'Lord, Imperial Army forces are pulling out too. If we do not secure the skybridges soon, we'll be facing them all again at the Lion's Gate.'

Perturabo cut the link to Forrix with a snarl.

'This is just the first wall,' Dorn called out.

The golden-armoured giant turned away and strode back along the bridge to his waiting gunship. The vox crackled with various commanders informing the Lord of Iron that they had targeting solutions on the Thunderhawk. He ignored them all and watched the gunship lift away on azure plumes.

It did not matter how many escaped to the next battle, it would never be enough. Brick by brick he would pull down the Palace. The space port had taken too long, but soon the Warmaster would have his Titans and then Perturabo would show Dorn the meaning of siegecraft.

Perturabo sent one final broadcast.

'See you on the next wall, brother.'

THIRTY-THREE

The next wall
Harsh counsel
A strange arrival

*Lion's Gate space port, interstitial bridges,
twenty-four days since assault*

The Iron Warriors took little time to establish their new front,
throwing up immense siegeworks around the docks and bridge
terminals of the fallen space port. Some of them even erected
a bunker around the site of Layak's last act and hung trophies
from their fallen foes upon the walls within. The portal had
closed but the crater remained, dark shapes burned into the
ferrocrete. A shrine of sorts, Abaddon realised, to a martyrdom
he would never accept.

He had been given a command post, erected among the
gun pits and communications towers. Standing in front, just
a few strides from the forward edge of a monorail terminal
and a ten-kilometre drop, Abaddon could see the entirety of
the Lion's Gate and the massive wall that stretched from its
impossibly vast towers. His post was dwarfed by a far larger

structure about a kilometre to the west, the headquarters of Perturabo, already dubbed the Citadel of Iron.

Abaddon did not intend to stay long; he felt the need to return to the *Vengeful Spirit* so that he could see his lord again. Layak's words troubled him, especially his ambivalence regarding the outcome of this war. Were Horus' patrons as uncaring of the result, and did that explain why the Warmaster refused to join the battle in person? Abaddon needed to see for himself what could be done to stir his lord to action.

News from across the Palace was mixed, and gave him little optimism. Khârn and the bulk of his World Eaters had moved on from the Lion's Gate, travelling south along the Eternity Wall to reunite with their primarch. Though he had no confirmation, there was rumour that Magnus had been sighted among his Legion, taking to the field of battle for the first time. Mortarion had drawn back to the outer lines while his fractured Legion regrouped from their month-long assaults. Fulgrim and his Emperor's Children had headed away from the Palace to the south. They had tens of thousands of prisoners and refused to respond to any broadcast from the First Captain or Perturabo. Perhaps Horus would bring them to heel.

Strong winds had dispersed cloud and toxin, so that from the promontories of Sky City it was possible to see the ground far below. From this altitude it seemed as though the surface of Terra writhed with a carpet of colour, broken by blotches of metal in places, bruises of darker hue in others. In reality it was a horde of daemons uncountable in its vastness, their great generals and princes leading the attack against the massive walls of the Palace.

The spirit war had merged with the physical war, but Horus had rebuffed Abaddon's calls for him to join his warriors on the surface. He still awaited some anointed hour it seemed, much to Abaddon's chagrin. Looking at the tide of Neverborn, the First Captain curled a lip.

A deafening noise drew his attention back to his surroundings and the terminal behind him. Turning he saw the immense conveyor doors opening, a dozen lights streaming from within to cut beams across the twilight.

From the shadow stepped a Warlord Titan, greater than fifteen times Abaddon's height, festooned with kill banners. Its armour shone like the shell of a beetle, broad flame-stripes decorating the amber carapace, greaves and abdominal plates. A horned, grotesquely feline face leered from under the superstructure where the princeps' control station would have been. Multi-launchers jutted from its back, crusted in bony growths, its left arm a cannon that gleamed with unearthly pale light, its right a bone-sheathed claw that opened and closed in slow anticipation.

Taking another step that sent dust billowing along the bridgehead, the Chaos god-engine opened its mouth and bellowed its challenge to the defenders, its call echoed by the war sirens of two others emerging behind.

The Legio Fureans, first of the Warmaster's Titans, had arrived.

Sanctuary of Satya, Sanctum Imperialis,
twenty-four days since assault

Amon looked out across the besieged city from the window of the Sanctuary of Satya, to the distant siege lines battering at the walls, and to the roiling storm above. He could see the fires in the summit of the Lion's Gate space port, and the jets of gunships strafing back and forth along the Ultimate Wall to the south-east.

'The damage has been done.' Dorn made this pessimistic proclamation. 'Daemons – pure Neverborn – are taking over the Starspear atop the Lion's Gate space port. Reports from the observatoria say that manifestations in impossible numbers are appearing before the walls. Angron is leading his World Eaters south, towards the Eternity Wall. The sorcery of our foes has breached the wards on Terra and we shall face Neverborn without limit.'

'This was not a victory for our enemies, but a concession to necessity,' said Malcador. He turned, looking at the others in the hall: Amon, Valdor, Sanguinius and the Khan. 'The telaethesic ward was not breached, it has shrunk. The Emperor cannot protect all of Terra forever. The shield of His protection has been withdrawn to the Inner Palace.'

'And then?' said Valdor. 'When it cannot protect the walls? The Sanctum Imperialis? The Dungeon?'

'It does not matter,' Dorn said curtly. 'It has always been a question of how long we can hold, not of defeating Horus with the troops we have to hand. Guilliman, the Lion and Russ are on their way. We held the port at the Lion's Gate far longer than I had hoped, certainly longer than Horus desired.'

'I am not content to sit back while the enemy makes ground,' said the Khan. He laid a hand on the pommel of his sword and stroked his chin with the other. 'If you have no argument, brother, I will stand at the defence of the Lion's Gate, where the next great blow will fall.'

'Why so?' asked Sanguinius. 'You have not been quiet in your distaste for standing behind walls.'

'I do not intend to remain behind them for too long,' the Khan assured them with a slight smile. 'But the wall is the best place to prepare for the next attack, not the depths of the Palace.'

'We will need to secure the space port again,' said Dorn.

'Should I need to call the *Phalanx* to remove the Emperor from Terra, it is the best way to reach it. On the other hand, should Guilliman arrive he will face the same issues as the traitors – how to get into orbit and down to the surface with sufficient forces to win the battle.'

'So, you agree?' said the Khan.

'Of course,' Dorn replied. He held up a finger to emphasise his next point. 'Yet I would appreciate that you consult with us before you launch a counter-attack.'

'The least courtesy I could do,' the Khan said with a grin.

They said nothing for several seconds until Amon broke the silence.

'What is to be done with Keeler?'

'She has returned herself to my custody,' said Malcador. 'And offered parole that she will not try to grow or influence the Lectitio Divinitatus whilst the siege remains in place.'

'Is that wise?' Amon waved a hand to the window, indicating the ongoing war. 'Daemons now join the fray because of the actions of these cultists.'

'Yet daemons were also kept at bay and banished by them,' the Regent replied sharply, his eyes moving from Amon to Valdor. 'We must be vigilant but there can be no persecution of the Lectitio Divinitatus for the time being, for reasons we have discussed before. If the Emperor chooses to outlaw the cult, we will wage that war when this one is concluded.'

'The threat to the Emperor cannot be underestimated,' said the captain-general. 'You recently said, Lord Dorn, that the business of protecting the Palace is for the Legions. I find myself forced to agree now. The Legio Custodes must concentrate on our primary purpose, to safeguard the Emperor. We surrender the outskirts to you, the Legiones Astartes, and will maintain a strict cordon within the Sanctum Imperialis. No citizens, no troopers, no Space Marines will pass within unless given specific licence by me.'

'I would keep watch on these "faithful", if I may, captain-general,' said Amon. 'My task is not yet complete.'

'As you deem right.'

'I approve,' said Malcador.

'You do?' said Amon, surprised.

'It is fitting that someone watches the Lectitio Divinitatus. You have performed your duties with diligence and honour. Captain-general, might I suggest the awarding of a name to Amon?'

'You may,' said Valdor.

'In one of mankind's oldest traditions there was an item known as the spear of destiny. Perhaps you would take the name of its supposed bearer, as a symbol of your duty to guard against the unholy and the holy alike?'

Amon nodded.

'What name would that be?'

'Longinus.' Malcador pulled up his hood and turned away, his staff thudding on the floor. He stopped at the doors to address them all. 'We have suffered setbacks, but we are not defeated. Come, we each have our parts yet to play.

'There is still a war to be won.'

Khertoumi Wastes, date unknown

A hot wind blew dust clouds across the desert basin. In the distance the twilit sky was illuminated in red as flames devoured a hive city. Here the sky was still clear save for the fume of the inferno, so that the heavens shone with stars – the starships that had levelled the city had moved on to new targets.

One dust cloud in particular stopped in place for several seconds, spinning faster and faster, as though trapped in itself.

The air around it crackled with nascent power, sparks

springing from the motes of dust, whirling away to form a vague outline of a man.

A blue spark appeared in the air, falling to leave a jagged trail of colour. A crack opened in nothing, parting to allow waves of blue and purple light to spill forth.

From this aperture stepped a man, ostensibly of middle age. He had short, dark hair and his chin and cheeks were covered with recent hair growth, patches of silver in the black. His eyes were sunken with fatigue, his cheeks hollow, and he licked dry lips as the aperture closed behind him, leaving him alone in the desert.

A cough caused him to turn.

Sat on a rock was an old woman, wrapped in pale scarves and a dark red coat. Her eyes were wide with shock, white orbs against dark skin. Tattoos the colour of ashes marked her face, painting flames on cheeks and brow. Her eyes narrowed in suspicion as she watched the man, who was dressed in a worker's coverall, a tattered backpack over one shoulder, a belt hung with many pouches about his waist.

'Hello,' he said before a bout of coughing wracked him.

The woman pulled a flask from her coat.

'Drink?'

'What is it?' the man asked.

'Just water.' She frowned. 'You speak Khert?'

'I speak anything,' the man replied with a smile, reaching for the flask. 'Where am I?'

The nomad raised a wrinkled finger towards the burning hive.

'That was Addaba,' she told him.

'Oh.' The man slumped, took a drink and then straightened his shoulders. He nodded to the north-east. 'The Imperial Palace is that way?'

'Yes. A long, long way.'

'You don't seem scared.' He gestured to himself. 'My arrival.'

'Should I be?' She raised an eyebrow. 'I seen a lot these last weeks. My family taken by the Emperor. The sky burning. Addaba broken by light from the stars. So... A man that steps from the air? Not so dangerous.'

'No,' he laughed. 'I suppose not.'

The man handed back the flask and started to walk away, heading in the direction she had pointed.

'Who are you?' the woman called after. 'Are you with the Warmaster? The Emperor?'

'No, I'm not one of Horus' servants.' The man carried on walking, almost swallowed by the dust and night. His voice drifted back on the wind. 'My name is John, and I'm on my own side.'

A heartbeat later, he was gone.

ABOUT THE AUTHOR

Gav Thorpe is the author of the Horus Heresy novels *The First Wall*, *Deliverance Lost*, *Angels of Caliban* and *Corax*, as well as the novella *The Lion*, which formed part of the *New York Times* bestselling collection *The Primarchs*, and several audio dramas. He has written many novels for Warhammer 40,000, including the Dawn of Fire novel *The Wolftime*, *Indomitus*, *Ashes of Prospero*, *Imperator: Wrath of the Omnissiah* and the Last Chancers series. He also wrote the *Rise of the Ynnari* novels, the *Path of the Eldar* and *Legacy of Caliban* trilogies, and two volumes in The Beast Arises series. For Warhammer, Gav has penned the End Times novel *The Curse of Khaine*, the Warhammer Chronicles omnibus *The Sundering*, and, for Age of Sigmar, *The Red Feast*. In 2017, Gav won the David Gemmell Legend Award for his novel *Warbeast*. He lives and works in Nottingham.

YOUR
NEXT READ

SATURNINE
by Dan Abnett

Horus' traitors tighten their grip on Terra, and the forces
of the Imperium are hard-pressed. Rogal Dorn needs victory –
but any such triumph will require sacrifice. Who will give up
their lives for the Imperium's future?

An extract from
Saturnine
by Dan Abnett

There's a bond stronger than steel to be found in the calamity of combat.

Willem Kordy (33rd Pan-Pac Lift Mobile) and Joseph Baako Monday (18th Regiment, Nordafrik Resistance Army) had found that out in the span of about a hundred days. They had met on the sixth of Secundus, in the crowds swarming off the Excertus Imperialis troop ships at the Lion's Gate. Everyone tired and confused, lugging kit, gaping at the monumental vista of the Palace, which most had never seen before, except in picts. Officers shouting, frustrated, trying to wrangle troops into line; assembly squares outlined in chalk on the concourse deck, marked with abbreviated unit numbers; adjutants hurrying along the lines, punch-tagging paper labels to collars – code marker, serial, dispersal point – as if they were processing freight.

'I swear I have never seen so many people in one place,' Joseph had remarked.

'Nor me,' Willem had replied, because he'd been standing next to him.

Just that simple. A hand offered, shaken. Names exchanged. Willem Kordy (33rd Pan-Pac Lift Mobile) and Joseph Baako Monday (18th Regiment, Nordafrik Resistance Army). The brackets were always there, with everybody. Your name became a sentence, an extension of identity.

'Ennie Carnet (Fourth Australis Mechanised).'

'Seezar Filipay (Hiveguard Ischia).'

'Willem Kordy (Thirty-Third Pan-Pac Lift Mobile). This is Joseph Baako Monday (Eighteenth Regiment, Nordafrik Resistance Army).'

No one stopped doing it. It was too confusing otherwise. No one came from here, no one knew the place, or anybody except the rest of their unit. They brought their birthplaces, regions and affiliations with them, in brackets, like baggage trains after their names. Like comforting mementos. It became second nature. On the eleventh, Kordy found himself saying, as he reported to his own brigade commander, 'Willem Kordy (Thirty-Third Pan-Pac Lift Mobile), sir.'

'Colonel Bastian Carlo, Thirty-Third Pan-Pac Lift Mo– What the shit is wrong with you, soldier?'

They lugged their brackets into the war with them, along with their packs and munition bags and their service weapons, like a little extra load. Then they had to cling to them, because once the fighting started, everything quickly lost definition and the brackets were all they had. Faces and hands got covered in mud and blood, unit badges got caked in dirt. By the twenty-fifth, the long red coats of the 77th Europa Max (Ceremonial) were as thick with filth as the green mail of the Planalto Dracos 6-18 and the silver breastplates of the Nord-Am First Lancers. Everyone became indistinguishable, alive or dead.

Especially after the gate fell.

Lion's Gate space port fell to the enemy on the eleventh of

Quintus. It was a long way from where they were, hundreds of kilometres west. Everything was a long way from everything else, because the Imperial Palace was so immense. But the effects were felt everywhere, like a convulsion, like the Palace had taken a headshot.

They were on the 14th Line by then, out in the north reach of the Greater Palace. The 14th Line was an arbitrary designation, a tactical formation of twenty thousand mixed Excertus and Auxilia units holding positions to guard the western approaches to the Eternity Wall space port. When the Lion's Gate fell, cohesion just went, right across the 14th Line, right across everywhere. A series of heavy voids had failed, soiling the air in the surrounding zone with a lingering sting of raw static and overpressure. The aegis protecting the Palace had ruptured in a cascade, spreading east from the Lion's Gate, and the electro-mag blink of that collapse took down vox and noospheric links with it. No one knew what to do.

Commands from Bhab and the Palatine Tower were not updating. There was a mad scramble, a fall-back, evacuating dugouts and leaving the dead behind. Parts of the Lion's Gate space port were on fire, visible from leagues away. Traitor armies were shoving in from the south-east, emboldened by the news that the port had fallen. They were driving up the Gangetic Way unchecked, piling in across Xigaze Earthworks and the Haldwani Traverse bastions, swarming the enclosures at the Saratine and Karnali Hubs and the agrarian districts west of the Dawn Road. The units of the 14th Line could hear the rumble of approaching armour as they ran, like a metal tide rolling up a beach. The sky was a mass of low smoke, scored through by the ground-attack aircraft making runs on the port-side habitations.

No one could believe that the gate had fallen. It was where they had all arrived, almost a hundred days before, and it had felt so huge and permanent. Joseph Baako Monday (18th Regiment, Nordafrik Resistance Army) had never seen a structure so magnificent. A vertical city that soared into the clouds, even on a clear day. Lion's Gate. One of the principal space ports serving the Imperial Palace.

And the enemy had taken it.

That meant the enemy had surface access inside the Eternity Wall, inside the Anterior Barbican. It had the critical operational capacity to start landing principal assault forces from the orbital fleet: heavy units, mass units, to reinforce the Terran traitor hosts that had begun the outer assaults.

'No,' Willem Kordy (33rd Pan-Pac Lift Mobile) told his friend. 'Not reinforce. Supplant. The first door of the Palace has opened.' An orbital artery had begun to pump. Until then, they'd faced men and machines. Through the yawning hole of the Lion's Gate, other things could now arrive, the way cleared for their advance.

Traitor Astartes. Titan engines. And worse, perhaps.

'How could there be worse?' asked Joseph Baako Monday (18th Regiment, Nordafrik Resistance Army).

They tried to make their way from Southern Freight Quadrant to Angevin Bastion, approaching the top end of the Gangetic Way where it crossed Tancred and the Pons Montagne, in the hope of skirting the traitor armour that was reducing Gold Fane Bastion to rubble. Captain Mads Tantane (16th Arctic Hort) had nominal command, but they didn't need a leader. It was move as one, in support of each other, or die.

Some fled, discipline lost. They were cut down inside two hundred metres, or overtaken by the viral clouds. Others gave up. That was the worst thing to see. Anonymous troopers, their identities lost under a film of grease and mud, no longer able to say their brackets, sitting in doorways, beside broken walls, in the stinking shadows of underpass revetments. A few put pistols in their mouths, or tugged the pins of their last grenades. But most just sat, ruined by despair and sleep deprivation, and refused to get up. They had to be left behind. They sat until death found them, and it never took long.

The rest, the still living, they tried to move. Vox and noospheric links remained dead. The constant flow of updating directives and deployment instructions had been choked off. They had to switch to Emergency and Contingency Orders, which had been issued on paper flimsies to all field officers. They were basic, spartan. For them, the units of the 14th Line, a curt general order written on a curl of paper, like a motto from a fortune cracker: 'In the event of breach or failure at 14th, withdraw to Angevin.'

Angevin Bastion and its six-kilometre line of casemates. Get behind that. That was the hope. A new line. Captain Mads Tantane (16th Arctic Hort) had about seven hundred infantry with him in a long, straggling column that kept breaking into clumps. His seven hundred was just a small part of the eighty-six thousand loyalist Army personnel in retreat from Line 14, Line 15 and Line 18. Packs kept stumbling into each other as they struggled through the ruins, yelling names and brackets frantically to prevent mistaken engagement. Enemy fire was at least only coming from one direction: behind them.

Then it began to come from the flank too. From the north. Close by and heavy, pricking through the colonnades and the gutted buildings, stippling rockcrete, raising puffs of powder-dust from rubble slopes.

And killing people.

Their line, their ragged column, began to crumple. Some scattered and broke for cover, others turned, bewildered. Some fell, as though they were tired of standing up. They dropped heavily, like sacks of meal, and tilted at ungainly angles, their legs bent under them, poses only death could accomplish. Captain Mads Tantane (16th Arctic Hort) started yelling above the chatter of weapons fire, urging them on to Angevin, and a few of the troopers obeyed.

'He's a fool,' said Joseph Baako Monday (18th Regiment, Nordafrik Resistance Army). 'My friend Willem, don't go that way! Look, would you? Look!'

The enemy had emerged. A wide, rolling line of traitor ground troops surged through the ruined fringes of Gold Fane, spilling through broken archways, and across streets, and down spoil heaps, flowing like water through every gap they could find. They were chanting. Willem Kordy (33rd Pan-Pac Lift Mobile) couldn't make out what. There was too much noise. But it was all one thing, voices lifted as one, a sound as ugly as the icons on the banners that wobbled and flapped over their ranks.

The kill-rate increased. Friends were dropping all around them. Willem Kordy (33rd Pan-Pac Lift Mobile) couldn't tell who. A body twisted. Was that Jurgan Thoroff (77th Kanzeer Light) or Uzman Finch (Slovak 14th)? Just a figure caked in mud, identity lost, no longer able to utter its brackets, no face left to wipe clean so that features could be discerned.

Smoke everywhere. Dust. Vaporised blood. Filthy rain. The chanting. The constant crack and rasp of weapons firing. The slap and scorch of impacts on stone and rubble. The hollow thump of impacts on meat. You knew when a body had been hit. A muffled punch came with an exhaled gasp as air was squeezed out of lungs. It came with the sharp stink of burned cloth and exit steam, the burned and atomised innards splitting skin to escape.

You learned the sound fast if you didn't already know it, because it repeated a dozen times a minute.

Willem Kordy grabbed his friend's sleeve and they ran

together. Others ran too. There was no cover. They scrambled up a bank of rubble, rounds slapping the tangled debris around them. Joseph Baako Monday made the mistake of looking back. He saw–

He saw that Captain Tantane had definitely gone the wrong way, and taken two hundred or more people with him. The traitor multitude had boxed them. He saw–

He saw taller figures pushing through the marching traitor files. Beast-giants armoured in black. He knew they were Astartes. War-horns bellowed through the smoke-fog. More now, more giants. He saw–

He saw these Astartes wore armour of dirty white, like spoiled cream. Their pauldrons were black. Some had great horns. Some had cloth tied around their armour like smocks or aprons. He saw–

He saw the dirt was caked blood. He saw the aprons were human hides. The Astartes in black slowed their advance. They let the Astartes in white rush ahead. They surged like dogs, charged like bulls. They weren't men, or even like men. The Astartes in black were upright, like handlers. The Astartes in white galloped, almost on all fours. They shrieked in berserk pain. They swung chainblades and war-axes that Joseph Baako Monday knew he could not have lifted. He saw–

He saw them reach Captain Tantane's group. He saw Tantane and those around him screaming and firing to hold them at bay. And failing. The Astartes in white ploughed into the mass of them, through them, running them down like trains hitting livestock. Slaughter. Butchery. A huge cloud of blood-vapour billowed up the slope, coating stones like tar. The Astartes in black stood and watched, as if entertained. He saw–

A hand on his arm.

'Come on!' Willem yelled into his face. 'Just come on!'

Up the slope, sixty, seventy of them, scrabbling up the

rubble incline, sixty or seventy that had not made the mistake of following Captain Tantane. Up the slope, dragging each other when feet slipped, up the slope and onto what had once been the roofs of habitats. The horror below them. The war-horns booming. The grinding squeal of chainblades. Billowing clouds of clotting fog.

The roofs ran out. A huge structure had collapsed, leaving nothing but its frame of girders and spars rising from a sea of shattered masonry. A twenty-metre drop. They started to clamber out along the girders, the sixty or seventy of them, single file, walking or crawling along girders half a metre wide. Men slipped and fell, or were knocked off by shots from below. Some took others with them as they clawed to stay on. They had all passed through fear. Fear was redundant and forgotten. So was humanity. They were deaf from the noise and numb from the constant shock. They had entered a state of feral humiliation, of degradation, mobbing like animals, wide-eyed and mindless, trying to escape a forest fire.

Willem nearly fell, but Joseph clung to him and got him to the far side, the roof of an artisan hall. They were among the first to make it. They looked back at their friends, men and women clinging like swarming ants to the narrow girders. They reached out, grabbed hands, brought a few to safety. Jen Koder (22nd Kantium Hort), Bailee Grosser (Third Helvet), Pasha Cavaner (11th Heavy Janissar)...

War-horns boomed. Bigger horns. Deeper, howling sounds that shook the breastbone. Two dozen streets away, true giants loomed out of the haze. Titan engines, glimpsed between the soaring towers as they strode along, demolishing walls and whole buildings, black, gold, copper, crimson, infernal banners displayed on the masts of their backs. Each was like a walking city, too big to properly comprehend. Their vast limb-weapons pulsed and fired: flashes that scorched the retina, static shock that lifted the hair, heat-wash that seared the skin like sunburn even from two dozen streets away.

And the noise. The noise so loud, each shot so loud, it felt as though the noise alone could kill. At each discharge, everything shivered.

We will die now, thought Joseph, and then laughed out loud at his own arrogance. The giant engines weren't coming for him. They didn't know he even existed. They were striding west, parallel to him, driving through the harrowed streets to find something they could kill or destroy that was worth their titanic effort.

The sixty or seventy of them had become thirty or forty. They slithered down slopes of scree and broken glass. No one had a clue where they were going. No one knew if there was anywhere left that could be gone to. Buildings around them were burning or blown out, the streets buried in a blanket of debris.

'We should fight,' said Joseph.

'What?' asked Willem.

'Fight,' Joseph repeated. 'Turn around, and fight.'

'We'll die.'

'Isn't this already death?' asked Joseph. 'What else are we going to do? There's nowhere to go.'

Willem Kordy wiped his mouth and spat out dirt and bone dust.

'But what good can we do?' asked Bailee Grosser. 'We saw what–'

'We did see,' said Joseph. 'I saw.'

'We won't measure it,' said Willem.

'Measure what?' asked Jen Koder. Her helmet was so badly dented, she couldn't take it off. Under the crumpled rim, blood ran down her neck.

'Whatever we are able to do,' said Willem. 'We'll die. We won't know. Whatever we do, however little, we won't know. That doesn't matter.'

'Yes,' said Joseph. He looked at their faces. 'It doesn't matter. We came here to fight. Fight for Him, in His name. Fight for this place. You saw how many people came. At the space port, when we arrived. So many people. Did anyone actually think they would do something significant? In person?'

Willem nodded. 'Collective effort. That's the point. If I break, or you break, then everyone will break, one by one. If I stand, and you stand, we die, but we are standing. We don't have to know what we do, or how little it is. That's why we came here. That's what He needs from us.'

No one said anything. One by one they got up, picked up their weapons, and followed Joseph and Willem down the street, picking their way over rubble, heading back the way they had come.

The Space Marine was in their path, hazed by a draw of thick smoke. Scarred siege shield propped in one hand, longsword resting across a huge shoulder guard. Plate dented and scored, even the ornate laurels on the breast. Eyes, slits of amber throbbing in the mauled visor.

Their weapons came up.

'Where are you going?' it asked.

'Back. To fight,' said Joseph.

'Correct,' it said. 'That's what He needs from us.'

'You… heard me?'

'Of course. I can hear a heart beating at a thousand metres. Follow me.'

The legionary turned. Its armour and siege shield were yellow.

'I am Joseph Baako Monday (Eighteenth Regiment, Nordafrik Resistance Army),' Joseph called out.

'I don't need to know,' the legionary replied, without glancing back. 'And show some damn noise discipline.'

'I need you to know,' said Joseph.

The legionary halted, and looked back. 'That doesn't matter–'

'It matters to me,' said Joseph. 'It's all we have. I am Joseph Baako Monday (Eighteenth Regiment, Nordafrik Resistance Army).'

'I am Willem Kordy (Thirty-Third Pan-Pac Lift Mobile),' said Willem.

'Adele Gercault (Fifty-Fifth Midlantik).'

'Jen Koder (Twenty-Second Kantium Hort).'

The Space Marine let them all speak. Then it nodded.

'I am Camba Diaz (Imperial Fists). Follow me.'

'Wait,' said Archamus, seeing them approach, but not looking up, one finger raised for patience.

Niborran, Brohn and Icaro waited. They watched the master of Dorn's Huscarls work at his station, carefully reviewing the data-feed. His eyes didn't blink. They waited. The constant motion and noise of the Grand Borealis encircled them. It was the first time any of them had not spoken in over a day. Waiting seemed wrong. High Primary Solar General Saul Niborran, Militant Colonel Auxilia Clement Brohn, Second Mistress Tacticae Terrestria Sandrine Icaro of the War Courts... They were people you did not keep waiting, not at this time, not in this extremity.

Unless you were in command of the warzone, running it from Bhab Bastion in the Sanctum Imperialis, the chosen proxy of the Lord Praetorian, and thus carrying, temporarily, the ultimate authority of Dorn.

Archamus, Imperial Fists, Master of the Huscarls, Second Of That Name, finished his review and sat back slightly. He looked at them. They were the senior duty officers of the Day Hundred rotation.

'Begin,' he invited.

'Where is Dorn?' asked Niborran immediately.

Archamus' eyes narrowed very slightly. At a nearby station, Captain Vorst looked up with a frown. Archamus saw the look, dismissed it with a small gesture. *Keep your seat.*

Niborran breathed deeply. He was tired.

'Your forgiveness, sir,' he said. 'Let me amend. Where is the Lord Praetorian?'

'Occupied elsewhere,' said Archamus. 'Begin.'

Niborran winced. He rubbed his augmetic eyes quickly with a knuckle. The silver socket frames gleamed against his dark skin, but the eyes within seemed dull. He took out his slate.

'We have run analysis of–'

'How is he occupied?' asked Brohn.

'What?' asked Archamus.

'Leave it, Clem,' Niborran murmured.

'I won't. How is he occupied? Right now? One hundred and more days of this, and the deepest shit yet, drowning in our own blood, and he's *occupied*?'

Archamus' face was expressionless. 'Consider your tone please, colonel,' he suggested.

'Screw my bastard tone, lord.'

Archamus rose. Vorst had risen too, heaving his yellow-plated bulk out of his seat. Again, Archamus signalled him to return to work with a brief gesture.

'We are all very tired,' said Niborran quickly. 'Very tired. Tempers fray and–'

'You don't look tired,' Brohn said to Archamus. 'Not at all.'

'Bred that way,' said Archamus. In the first hundred days he'd stood three tours on the lines. The grazes and dents on his yellow plate hadn't been finished out and were there for all to see. But no, he didn't look tired. He looked Astartes, the way he always did. Unmoving, as solid as a statue. He didn't look tired the way these three humans did, with their hollow eyes and drawn cheeks and shaking hands.

'I will allow you some latitude, colonel,' he said. 'The circumstances–'

'The circumstances are shit, and getting shittier by the second, and Dorn is absent. He is supposed to be running this. He's supposed to be the bastard genius–'

'That is now enough,' said Archamus.

'The Praetorian's absence is concerning,' said Niborran. 'Brohn is out of line, but his sentiment is–'

'We're screwed,' snapped Brohn. 'His plan is splitting at the seams. Lion's Gate is done. They're in. Inside Anterior. The aegis is blown in eight places. They've got engines on the ground and they're walking. Our plan is on fire. It's gone to shit–'

'Get out.'

The words were a whisper, a hiss, but they cut like acid through metal. Everyone in the Bhab strategium fell silent. No voices, just the chatter and babble of cogitators and the crackle of vox monitor stations. Eyes averted.

Jaghatai Khan stepped up onto the central platform. How anyone or anything so big could have entered the Grand Borealis without being heard, or could have walked silently from the chamber arch across the plasteel deck, in full, fur-draped armour plate...

He towered over them. There was blood on his cheek, beard, gorget, left pauldron, breastplate. It matted his cinched-back mane, freckled his ermyet furs, and ran down his left thigh-guard. It wasn't his. His left hip was scorched back to bare metal from a melta burn.

'Get out,' he repeated, looking down at Brohn.

'Colonel Brohn is tired, lord, and spoke poorly,' Niborran began.

'I don't give a shit,' said the Great Khan.

'My lord,' Niborran pressed. 'Colonel Brohn is a senior and decorated Army officer, and an essential part of the–'

'Not a single shit,' said the Great Khan.

Niborran glanced at the deck. He sighed.

'His question was insolently framed,' said Niborran flatly, 'but his point was valid.'

He looked the primarch in the eyes. He did not waver.

'My lord,' he added.

'You too,' said the Great Khan. 'Get out.'

Brohn glanced at Niborran. Niborran shook his head. He tossed his slate onto the desk, turned and walked out. Brohn followed.

The Great Khan didn't even watch them leave.